Praise for R. A. Salvatore's *Demon Wars* series!

THE DEMON APOSTLE

"Unforgettable . . . Another rousing and masterful *Demon Wars* adventure . . . A must-read for all fans of Salvatore's work."

—*Realms of Fantasy*

THE DEMON SPIRIT

"Absorbing . . . This is one of the finest books yet in Salvatore's prolific career."

—*Publishers Weekly*

"A gripping story . . . some of [his] best work."

—*Booklist*

THE DEMON AWAKENS

"Salvatore's best work since the *Dark Elf* series . . . An enthralling epic adventure story, it introduces memorable characters and an intricate scheme of magic the readers won't soon forget. I am anxious for the next."

—Terry Brooks

Books by R. A. Salvatore:

The Demonwars Saga
THE DEMON AWAKENS
THE DEMON SPIRIT
THE DEMON APOSTLE
MORTALIS
ASCENDANCE
TRANSCENDENCE
IMMORTALIS

The Chronicles of Ynis Aielle
ECHOES OF THE FOURTH MAGIC
THE WITCH'S DAUGHTER
BASTION OF DARKNESS

STAR WARS: THE NEW JEDI ORDER: VECTOR PRIME
STAR WARS: EPISODE II: ATTACK OF THE CLONES

Published by Del Rey Books

that. Belexus caught the sword in his left hand, though, before it had fallen far, as he was stepping ahead, and a quick turn of his wrist changed the angle and stabbed the weapon's point right into Mitchell's face. Belexus turned and slashed the holding arm next, then scrambled out of the tangle as the mace whipped in a flurry, black flakes filling the air. For all his speed and agility, though, the ranger didn't quite make it out; several of the flakes caught him on the back and hip, and he rushed away, grimacing against the burning pain.

The pair squared off once more. Mitchell was hurt, clearly so, with white lines creasing his chest and arm, a blotch of white marring his gray face, and another on his back. But Belexus was hurt, too, with several blistering burns on his back.

Mitchell narrowed his flaming eyes; he had no more taunts for the ranger, no more games. Just hatred, and a bit of respect.

For Belexus, there was only hatred.

They circled and stalked for a long while, each showing caution now.

A catapult shot broke the tension, a ball of pitch slamming into a boulder tumble not so far away, followed by the screams of burning talons.

"They're getting closer, Mitchell," the ranger said. "King Benador and Lord Arien. Yer army's to fall this day, along with their dead leader."

Mitchell glanced far and wide from the high rock. In the minutes he and Belexus had been fighting, battle had begun in full all about the rocky arm. He heard the twang of bows, the rush of horses, the swoosh of catapults, the cries of man and talon. This was the moment Mitchell had craved, the moment of his glory, and he was stuck up here with the ranger, fighting a personal battle.

Anger welled within him and drove him to the attack once more.

Belexus, understanding the wraith's urgency, understanding the frustration this delay would bring to Mitchell, was more than ready. Deceivingly, he stared at the spot where the catapult shot had struck, his smile wide as he watched one talon, engulfed in flames, thrashing about futilely. But it was all a ruse, and the ranger really watched the wraith's approach, and as the mace went high for a strike, Belexus exploded into motion, diving ahead and down, passing right by the surprised Mitchell and coming up a full stride away, but close enough so that he could hit home with a mighty backhand slash.

The wraith howled in pain and frustration and was quick to pursue.

The specter of Morgan Thalasi, that bone-skinny, hollowed creature, stole Bryan's breath. Rhiannon had faced him before, though, in magical combat, and she was not deterred.

"How dare you?" the Black Warlock cried.

A lightning bolt slammed him in response, throwing him back against the wall of his throne room. It hadn't really hurt him, but it gave Bryan's wits the time to recover. Rhiannon began her charge immediately, thinking it wise to get the Black Warlock in close, that she might disrupt his powerful magics, yet Bryan, so quick of foot, beat her to the spot, his sword slashing hard at the Black Warlock's arm, trying to cut loose the mighty staff.

Thalasi accepted the blow with hardly a flinch, and his backhand slap sent poor Bryan flying head over heels across the room. He landed hard, groaning, dazed, and by the time he looked up again, Rhiannon and the Black

Warlock were in a desperate clinch, sparks of power arcing all about their mortal forms.

The young witch howled in pain as she grabbed hard at the staff, for merely touching the perverted weapon wounded her to her soul. Grab it she did, though, and she held it with all her strength and stubbornness even as Thalasi began raining powerful blows all about her. Then they were wrestling, each holding tight the staff, all energy, magical and physical, bursting out about their twined forms, the cloud of Thalasi's blackness matching the white shine of Rhiannon's diamond wizard mark.

Bryan understood that the young witch could not win, not while the Black Warlock held that terrible staff. He forced himself to his feet, forced the dizziness from his head. And then he charged, headlong, hurling himself through the air to crash hard against Thalasi, twisting and pushing so that he was in between the Black Warlock and Rhiannon, facing Thalasi and with the staff behind him. Desperately, Bryan pulled the amulet from his neck and hooked it over Rhiannon's arm, and then he twisted and turned again, trying to find leverage to weaken Thalasi's grasp on the staff.

Rhiannon pulled it from Thalasi's hands.

Bryan tried to hold on a bit longer, to delay the Black Warlock's pursuit, but Thalasi slapped him aside once more, as easily as if he were some young child, and this time, crumpled against the wall, he could not muster the strength to regain his feet.

Lying twisted on the floor, he watched Rhiannon flee the room, the Black Warlock close behind. He saw the ghost of Rhiannon's father stand to block Thalasi, but the Black Warlock ran right through the apparition, apparently too consumed in his chase with Rhiannon even to notice Del.

BASTION OF DARKNESS

Book Three in *The Chronicles of Ynis Aielle*

R. A. Salvatore

A Del Rey® Book
BALLANTINE BOOKS • NEW YORK

A Del Rey® Book
Published by The Random House Publishing Group

Published in the United States by Del Rey Books, an imprint of The Random House Publishing Group, a division of Random House, Inc., New York, and simultaneously in Canada by Random House of Canada Limited, Toronto.

www.delreybooks.com

ISBN-13: 978-0-345-42193-7

Manufactured in the United States of America

First Edition: August 2000

OPM 10

Chapter 1

The Swordsman and the Witch

HE LOOKED AT her perplexed, an expression of confusion that caught the young woman off her guard, and, with an ambush set so close at hand, surely unnerved her.

"What do ye know?" Rhiannon asked, brushing her raven black hair from her face, her crystal blue eyes shining, flashing, to match the diamond that was set in her forehead—the mark of magic that identified her as a witch.

"The day," young Bryan of Corning replied absently, a wistful smile brightening his face. "This day."

"Ayuh," Rhiannon prompted, glancing about nervously. "Are we not to fight them then?"

"My birthday," Bryan explained with a wry smile.

Rhiannon's face lit up, as much with relief that the lad had not seen any dangerous flaw with their ambush plan as with her sincere joy at the news of Bryan's birthday.

"Sixteen," Bryan announced proudly. "Today I am sixteen years."

Rhiannon's smile only widened, but behind it came an honest surprise. *Sixteen?* she echoed in her mind, over and over, incredulously. With his delicate features and shining hair and eyes, the same brilliant gray orbs of his elven father, Meriwindle, Bryan did indeed have the appearance of youth. But his heritage was half elven, and even Arien Silverleaf, who was eldar of the elves and had lived through centuries, appeared youthful. Rhiannon had spent three months beside Bryan, fighting talons along the southwestern fields of Calva and in the Baerendil Mountains, and never would she have guessed that this cunning warrior, this hero to so many of the folk who had been trapped on this side of the great River Ne'er Ending after the war, this strong young man who had slain so very many evil talons, could possibly be so young! Rhiannon herself had just passed her twenty-first birthday, and she had thought Bryan—so wise, so composed—to be at least her own age.

"A birthday kiss?" the young man asked slyly.

"Yer thoughts should be to the fight," Rhiannon replied dryly.

"A kiss for luck, then?"

"A kiss for victory, when the day is won."

Bryan seemed satisfied with that. He gave a quick salute, then hoisted his shield, emblazoned with the crescent moon symbol of Illuma, the enchanted valley of his elven father's people, and the bow that Rhiannon had created for him, and ran off to his appointed place.

Rhiannon watched him go with mixed feelings, both for him and for her promise. She had indeed grown to love Bryan, to admire and respect him fully. And he had saved her life, she understood, for without his companionship, without him holding her hand and calling out to her, bringing her back from the depths of the darkest and strongest magic the young witch had ever known, she never would have survived the great battle with the Black Warlock, Morgan Thalasi. In that battle, young Rhiannon had come fully into her magical power, though that power and all the magic remaining in all the world paled beside the glory the four wizards of Ynis Aielle had known only a few short months before—before the power-hungry Thalasi had reached too far, had torn the very fabric of universal strength, had torn out the heart of the wizards' secret domain.

After that magical fight, Rhiannon and Bryan had run together, for they were on the western bank of the River Ne'er Ending, while their comrades remained on the eastern side. Neither was afraid, and each had come to trust and understand the other, and for Bryan, certainly, and even for Rhiannon, that had evolved into something deeper and more special.

But for all the young witch's love of Bryan, Rhiannon could not forget another, Andovar, the proud ranger of Avalon, her friend and her love who had been slain on the northern fields. Grief prevented the young witch from giving her heart to Bryan, and so soon after Andovar's demise, Rhiannon wasn't sure that the wound to her heart and soul would ever, ever heal.

So she watched Bryan go, and then let her promise fly away, replaced by thoughts of the more pressing situation fast approaching. The great river had been flooded by the magic of Rhiannon's mother, Brielle, the Emerald Witch of Avalon, and of Istaahl, the White Mage of Pallendara. That watery deluge, the swollen river rushing down north from Brielle's land and the sea itself sweeping in at Istaahl's call from the south, had, in effect, ended the battle, stranding Morgan Thalasi and the bulk of his remaining talons on the western banks, while the combined armies of elven Illuma and the human kingdom of Calva had made short work of those unfortunate talons caught on the eastern side. The stalemate had continued as fall turned to winter, but though the eastern fields of Calva, the forest of Avalon, and the mountain valley home of the elves known as Lochsilinilume were safe now, many monsters dominated the western fields and mountains.

That was where Rhiannon and Bryan fit in, combining

their talents—his with sword, hers with magic—to hinder and destroy many of the rogue monster bands, to nip at what remained of the Black Warlock's army, playing their part in driving the beasts ever farther to the west, back to the swamp and the dark passes of the dreaded Kored-dul Mountains.

Rhiannon brushed a finger over her lips and nodded, accepting this fate, her expression turning grim as she, too, moved into position. Once set, behind a large stone overlooking the pass, the witch sent her thoughts out to her friends.

She and Bryan would not fight alone this day.

Strong and handsome Benador, with fair hair and dark eyes, the king of Calva, trotted his stallion up and down the riverbank, taking care not to move too close to the steep embankment, which was slippery with snow. To those who had known him before the battle, Benador looked haggard now, but even so, he did not appear as old as his forty years. He had grown straight and strong in Avalon, secretly and under the protection of Bellerian, lord of rangers. He had been trained in the fighting arts by Bellerian's son, the famed hero Belexus, perhaps the greatest warrior in all the world. But now King Benador had seen his first real battle, the most vicious conflict Ynis Aielle had ever known, and the images of the aftermath of that brutal struggle, the thousands of dead, the fields soaked with blood, and the fall of these four bridges, marvelous and magical constructions of Aielle's greatest age, weighed heavily upon him.

More than anything else, it was the bridges, he decided. The blood would wash away, and men die in their time, but the Four Bridges of Calva, each construction a gift of one of the four original wizards, had been meant as everlasting. A spur still stood on the western side of the river where the northernmost bridge had stood. That had been Thalasi's bridge, taken down not by the floodwaters of Brielle and Istaahl, but by the thunderstroke of the fourth wizard, the Silver Mage Ardaz, who had stood tall and fearless against the horrid wraith that had served as Thalasi's general.

King Benador looked long and hard at that spur, as he often did when taking his morning ride, remembering the fateful day when all the world had been turned upside-down. He hoped the spur would hold fast through the ages, a battered reminder of what had once been, and of what must never be again. Then the king turned his stallion about and passed to the south, toward the foundations of the southernmost bridge, the one the Calvans were now painstakingly reconstructing. The finest masons, architects, engineers, and craftsmen of Benador's realm had come to aid in the work, but the king held no illusions that their combined efforts, however wondrous, would even come close to the majesty that had been the bridge of Istaahl the White.

No matter, King Benador told himself. The new bridge would be functional, would get him and his army across the river that they might finish off the remnants of the Black Warlock's army and pay Morgan Thalasi back dearly for the horrors he had brought upon them.

Benador prayed for that chance.

Bryan crouched low behind the ridge of a snowdrift, eagerly watching the approaching talon band, biting back the disgust and revulsion he always felt when looking upon the hideous creatures. They had mottled green skin and scraggly, uneven clumps of dirty hair, and their faces were purely horrible, with sloping foreheads and large, flat noses and pointy yellow teeth—yellow to match the sickliness that showed in their eyes—that seemed too numerous and too long to fit under their lips.

He rubbed his hands together often and blew in his cupped palms to keep his fingers nimble. The difficulties of the last months had hardened him to battle and to the weather, but the tips of his fingers had not yet grown accustomed, had not yet grown callused, to the use of a bow. Still, the young man had quickly become a fine archer—and how could he not be with such a bow as the one the witch's daughter had presented him! He looked to the wood now with the highest admiration, awed by the beauty of the weapon's delicately curving lines, the weave of its dark and light contours, all of it so perfectly smooth. This was no sculpted piece, but rather a created piece, a living piece, as though a tree had presented its child to the daughter of Avalon that she might train it in the ways of archery. The bow showed no marks of axe or knife, no scrapings at all, just a delicately curving piece of supple wood, polished by the light touch of magical Rhiannon.

Bryan's gaze drifted lower, to the sword hanging on his hip. He hadn't found much use of that weapon of late; no talon ever seemed to get close enough to him for melee combat. Truly the young warrior missed the dance of swordplay, but he agreed with Rhiannon's assessment. This war they waged, this mission to aid any human survivors trapped on this side of the swollen river, was too important for them to take foolish chances. Their duty was to kill talons as quickly and efficiently as possible with the least chance of getting themselves wounded.

Bryan patted his sword hilt, as if to reassure the weapon that he had not forgotten it, then fitted an arrow to his bowstring and peeked over the ridge again.

A sleek white form, barely visible against the snowy background, darted by on silent, padded feet.

Baerendil cougar, Bryan knew: a hundred and fifty pounds of fighting frenzy. Despite its proximity, the young man was not afraid, was not even uncomfortable. He knew that the cougar was guided by Rhiannon, and woe to the talon enemies.

The witch's daughter remained far back from the expected scene of the approaching battle, but Bryan knew that she would indeed play a vital role, directing her feline charges through a telepathic link. Her work in the matter would be limited really, simply to point out the enemy and beg the aid of her animal friends. As far as tactics went, no human, not even a wizard or witch, could hope to match the cunning of Baerendil cougars.

The talon band, just under a score in number, noted the cat's movement shortly thereafter, but paid it little heed. These talons had lived long in the Baerendils, and they knew that the cougars were usually solitary creatures, coming together only to mate or to battle over territory. While a lone talon might fall easy prey to such a beast, a group usually had little to fear.

Of course, though the talons could not know it, this particular cougar was not acting alone. It had come to the call of Rhiannon, as had the dozen other cats even then moving silently into position behind the distracted monsters.

Bryan eased his bowstring to rest and marveled at it all. The lone cougar darted from snowbank to snowbank, paralleling the movements of the talon band, demanding their attention. Finally the creatures decided to drive the pestering cat away, and threw a couple of spears in its general direction, hooting and hollering, kicking up snow and making a general ruckus. That only made the attack from behind even more of a surprise, as the dozen cougars, the hunting pride, leaped in at the talons as a wall of claws and fangs. Before the talons had even figured out what had hit them, half of them were dead or incapacitated, and those remaining were in no defensive position or formation. Some attempted feeble swings with spears that had been aimed the wrong way, but the cats were too close and too quick, springing past such tactics to bear their newest prey to the ground, where death found the talons, swift and sure.

The remaining talons wisely ran off, sprinting every which way.

But then Bryan of Corning went to work. Up came his bow, the half-elf taking a bead on one talon that was coming straight at him. The arrow hit the beast with such force as to knock it back two steps, where the dazed and mortally wounded creature was summarily buried by a cougar that had come in pursuit.

Bryan dismissed the creature with hardly a thought, already turning his sights upon the next target quickly, this talon running across his field of vision to the left. The young warrior pulled back his bowstring, holding the powerful draw perfectly steady and level, the arrow tip turning smoothly to follow the fleeing creature. Bryan noted the distance and the creature's speed, then shifted his aim just ahead of it and let fly.

Right through the lung, and the talon skidded down in a heap.

Bryan sighed as he turned his attention back to regard the area of main fighting, to see that the battle was already over. Before him lay a scene of utter carnage, a massacre so complete that no cougar had even been slightly wounded. The young half-elf shook his head and patted his sword once more, a warrior's lament. Somehow, with Rhiannon and her animal friends beside him, this was getting too easy. First the witch would speak with birds to learn the exact number and location of their enemies. Then she conferred with other animals—

otters and raccoons, wolves and bears and cougars—to determine the best area in the region for their strike, then bade the deadliest of her friends to join in the attack.

This was the third such rout in two weeks.

Bryan shook his head again and gave a respectful glance at the closest cougar, lying flat on its belly, heavy tail twitching excitedly as it fed upon the talon Bryan had shot down in front of it.

Then the half-elf turned to leave, and realized that he had gotten careless, that he had abandoned his own warrior instincts in the belief that they would not be needed.

The talon standing right behind him brought its axe overhead and down hard, chopping at Bryan's head. All the nimble half-elf could do was lift up Rhiannon's bow in both hands over his head, hoping to slow the wicked weapon's descent.

To Bryan's amazement, to the talon's amazement, the bow stopped the axe blade cold, blocked it as surely as if it had hit a stone wall.

Bryan didn't pause to consider the implications. He put his right foot under him and came forward a rushing step, punching out with his left hand and pulling in with his right to turn the bow and the axe out wide. A final heave sent the axe flying wide, and Bryan pulled the bow in close, then jabbed out with its tapered tip, poking the talon hard in the face, sending it stumbling backward. The half-elf could have quickly finished the task then, by leaping forward and beating the creature senseless, but he hesitated and dropped the bow, drawing forth his sword instead and quickly pulling his shield over his forearm.

It took the talon some time to gather its wits, but Bryan, wanting this fight more than he cared to admit—and more than he would ever admit to Rhiannon!—patiently waited. The half-elf preferred always to let his adversary make the first move, but he recognized that this talon's heart for the fight, especially with such a scene of carnage before it, had long flown, and it was thinking more of fleeing than of attacking. So, as soon as the creature had steadied itself, ahead came Bryan, his magnificent sword, his father's elven-crafted sword, flashing in the sunny, snowy brightness. The talon lumbered awkwardly, but somehow managed a parry with its heavy axe, and even tried to bring its weapon about for a fast counter.

Bryan let it complete the maneuver, let the axe turn about and come swishing in. He was down on one knee before it ever got close, though, and as it swished overhead, the half-elf poked his sword straight out, scoring a wicked hit on the talon's breast.

The creature tried to recover, but the momentum of the wide-flying axe forced it off balance, and that, combined with the prodding sword, confused the talon. Trying to counter, trying to retreat, it got its feet all tangled up and went down on its back.

Bryan moved forward for the kill, but changed his mind and veered far out to the side when he heard a low growl behind him.

The cougar leaped atop the talon in a flash of white lightning, its powerful maw clamping firmly on the unfortunate creature's skinny neck.

Bryan sheathed his sword and went to retrieve the bow, hoping the scar upon its beautiful wood would not be too evident. He was not surprised, whatever logic told him, to find that there was not a mark at all on the enchanted bow, to find that the heavy axe and its undeniably sharp blade had not even scratched the polished wood.

"Too easy," Bryan lamented, and he gathered up his belongings and set off in search of the young witch.

He found her resting in a hollow, her back against a tree, her eyes closed. She hadn't used much of her magic, certainly nowhere near the amount Bryan had previously witnessed, when Rhiannon had gathered the very strength of the earth itself and hurled it skyward to battle the gloom of Morgan Thalasi's thunderclouds. But lately, Bryan noted, even the simplest of enchantments seemed to tire Rhiannon, and he shuddered to think of what might happen if the young witch was ever forced to utilize her powers to their greatest limit again. Rhiannon had nearly died on that occasion when she had battled Thalasi, and not from any attack from the Black Warlock, but rather from her own sheer exhaustion, as if she had thrown a substantial amount of her own life force into that magical response.

Bryan remembered that day vividly, remembered cradling beautiful, unconscious Rhiannon in his arms, remembered how pale and fragile she had seemed, a flower dying in the cold wind. He had feared that he would lose her then, and he had realized that if she did indeed go away, a huge part of his own heart would forever die beside her.

He let her sleep now, just sat facing her, watching her, admiring the soft curve of her, the way her lips slightly parted, the beauty of her lithe form, a dancer's body with strong but smooth muscles. He was in love with her, only her, with all his heart and all his soul.

He couldn't deny it; he didn't want to deny it.

He wanted to shout it out to all the world.

Chapter 2

The Wraith

HE WAITED FOR the dark of a moonless night, his time, the time of lurking nightmares. His substance a shadow blacker than the darkest hole, the wraith of Hollis Mitchell glided along the riverbank. A creature half of this world, half of the realm of death, he made no weighted impression in the snow, but every so often he absently flicked his hollow-headed mace, his scepter, and loosed a small shower of black flakes that burned the white powder, that melted deeper, right through the watery stuff to stain the very ground beneath it.

All the while, the wraith's red-glowing eyes held their focus across the river, to the hundreds of burning fires showing the campsites of Pallendara's army. Only a few short months ago, those fires had been more than matched by the glorious blaze of Morgan Thalasi's army, which Hollis Mitchell had commanded, but the talons were gone now, all fled into the fields and mountains, many back to their swampy homes miles and miles away. They had scattered when they saw Mitchell, their general, drop from the blasted bridge, and when they saw their highest master, the Black Warlock himself, hurled to the ground by the great bolt of the witch's daughter, and when they saw the river itself rise up before them, defeating their charge and sweeping thousands of them away to a watery death.

This western bank of the River Ne'er Ending had remained dark since then, every night, an empty plain of blackness.

Until this night. The wraith had seen it; a single campfire, burning low on the plain less than a half mile from the river. Perhaps it had been set by talons, though the ugly beasts didn't normally set fires this close to potential enemies. Perhaps, the hungry wraith hoped, it had been set by human refugees trying to make their way to King Benador's side, or even better, by scouts from the Pallendara army. In truth, so full of venom was the wraith, that he knew it really didn't matter. Mitchell had pulled himself from the river far to the south and had gradually worked his way back to this spot, pausing only when he found talons or humans to slaughter. Those kills had proven few and far between, however, and hardly satisfying to this creature of death, this unnatural perversion whose very sustenance was the horror of others, the life force of others.

Mitchell had not killed in more than two weeks; he veered to the northwest, away from the river.

"Cold again," one of the men remarked, a tall and lean fellow of forty winters. His beard gave testament to his observations, for icy crystals glittered among the curly gray-and-brown whiskers in the firelight.

"Cold every night," a second man said. He was similar in build and features to the other—indeed, was his brother—except that he sported only a bushy mustache. "I'm wishing that the war had gone through the winter, leaving us to our duties in the warmer spring!"

"But how many might've died for your comfort, then?" the third and last of the group asked as he walked back in toward the fire, a huge black-and-tan dog at his side. He was the oldest of the party by at least ten years, his hair and beard silvery gray. But his eyes still held the sharp, twinkling blue hue of his youth.

"Very nice, Clouster," the first said. "So good of you to put things in such a comforting light."

"Comfort?" Clouster replied, spitting heavily on the ground, that simple action drawing a growl from the nervous, dangerous canine. "Comfort's not for the likes of us. I told you I'd teach you, so you best learn well and fast; a scout's life is a thankless, dirty one, and if you cannot get your satisfaction in knowing a well-done job, then, by the Colonnae, you're in the wrong line of work, I say!"

"Benador needs us," the second brother agreed. "All of Pallendara needs us."

"When they finish the bridge and come rushing across, they'll be better served if they know the positioning of the talon forces," Clouster added.

"What few remain," the first brother grumbled.

"Few?" Clouster barked. "Few! Why, ten thousand got away, and there's probably another fifty thousand still out there, waiting to come in. And don't you forget the Black Warlock. He was thrown down to be sure—I saw that with my own eyes, and a beautiful sight it was indeed!—but often's been the times we've thought him dead, only to see his ugly face arise once more!

"No, my friends, this war's not yet won. Not yet. Not until we chase the damned talons all the way back to Mysmal Swamp, all the way to Talas-dun and pull the damned place down around them."

The mere mention of Talas-dun, the black fortress, the heart of Morgan Thalasi, sent a shudder coursing down the spines of the brothers. They glanced at each other nervously, silently agreeing that poor old Clouster had lost his wits. Truly the men loved their king, good Benador of the line of Ben-Rin, restored to the throne after the fall of Ungden the Usurper at the Battle of Mountaingate. Truly Benador had given all of Calva back its pride and hope for the future, had secured an alliance with the rangers of Avalon and even with the Moon Dancers, the elves of Illuma. Yes, they each loved Benador, and would gladly take an arrow aimed for the king's breast, but neither entertained any notion of following the king to Talas-dun. Not that.

Not ever.

"You've gone daft, poor Clouster," the first brother, the older of the pair, said. "We'll win back the western fields, to Corning and beyond, perhaps even to the eastern edge of Mysmal, but no further: not to the coast, and certainly not to the Kored-dul! I've no desire to ever see the likes of black Talas-dun."

"Ah, but it does seem a wondrous place," an unfamiliar voice said from the side of their small camp, just on the edge of the firelight. At that moment, the dog raised his hackle and growled, white teeth gleaming in the firelight. "A place to seem as the fitting throne-seat of all the world," the deep resonating voice continued.

The brothers gained their feet quickly, swords drawn, standing beside Clouster, who held a throwing dagger in each hand. Of the group, Clouster was the most concerned, for he couldn't understand why his dog, Yostrol, a trusted companion for several years, hadn't noted the approach long before the man, or whatever it might be lurking in the shadows, got so close. The three couldn't get a good view of the speaker from this vantage point, but they knew, at least, that he was no talon. He was too large, much too large, for that, and his voice did not have the guttural croak of the wicked race, but sounded human, though perhaps more resonant than usual, a deep and commanding baritone.

Yostrol trembled then, growling and whining all at

once, a reaction Clouster had never before witnessed. Clearly the dog was afraid, terrified, yet Clouster had seen this brave companion go at a thousand-pound bear with hardly a thought, and had watched the dog rip up talon after talon in the fight for the river three months before.

"State your name and business," the older brother demanded.

The speaker held his distance and chuckled softly, an unnerving sound indeed.

"We can kill without fear of retribution," the younger brother remarked. "On word of the king—"

"Not my king," said the intruder.

"Benador is king to all!" the youngest man cried defiantly.

"Not my king," the intruder said again.

Clouster let go the leash, a movement that eager Yostrol would usually take as a signal to attack. Amazingly, though, the dog held his ground, even shifted a bit backward, behind his master.

"Who is your king then, if not Benador?" Clouster asked, hoping to clarify things in a proper light, but fearing, given the intruder's cryptic attitude and the reactions of his dog, that this meeting would end in a bad way. "Arien Silverleaf of Illuma, perhaps? Or Bellerian, lord of rangers?"

"Who is my king?" the intruder echoed, ending with a snort. "A fine question, and one that I must consider." As he spoke, he moved into the firelight, and all three men gasped in unison at the specter of the wraith of Hollis Mitchell. He was huge and barrel-chested, as Mitchell had been in life, but he was also obviously dead, his skin gray and bloated, blotched by rot, his eyes red dots of flame.

Clouster reached around and grabbed Yostrol and

yanked the dog in front, and the animal, spurred beyond reason, barked and charged.

Hardly considering the action, the wraith flicked his unholy scepter, and the air before it, the air in the dog's path, filled with black flakes. How Yostrol yelped when he entered that zone, when the flakes of the deadly weapon fell over him, burning his hide, boring through his hide. The dog whined pitifully, turning tight circles, biting at his own burning skin.

Clouster had both his daggers away, and both sailed right into the wraith—and both simply disappeared, as if they had passed right through the monster, or had been somehow absorbed within its blackness.

"Yes, my king," Mitchell went on, obviously taking no overt notice of the attacks. "Why, I believe that I shall be my own king! Yes, that will do fine." He looked at the three terrified men and advanced a long step.

"I am King Mitchell," he declared, then slyly added, "Tell me again, who is your king?"

Clouster never blinked, staring defiantly at the man, looking down only once to see that the poor dog was lying on the ground, panting his last breaths. The two brothers looked to each other desperately, not knowing how to respond.

Clouster spoke for them, though they weren't sure that he gave the right answer.

"My king is Benador of Pallendara," the man stated flatly, moving out toward the fire, standing across from the pallid specter. "The true and rightful king, and if you mean to call yourself a king within the borders of lawful Calva, then know that King Benador will surely destroy you."

Mitchell roared with laughter.

Clouster dove down and grabbed up a burning stick, then thrust it hard at the wraith.

The fire stung, but more than that, Mitchell was wounded by the sheer impudence, the sheer lack of respect. He grabbed the end of the burning brand, clasping it right about the fire, which immediately began to glow a weird, blackish hue.

Clouster cried out and let go of the brand, meaning to flee, but the wraith moved more quickly, striding right through the fire—and it, too, turned that eerie, blackish hue—and grabbing the horrified man by the hand.

How cold was that touch! Clouster cried out in fear and pain and wrenched wildly to break free. Then he saw his doom and shielded himself from the expected shower of burning flakes as Mitchell raised the scepter up high. But now the weapon served Mitchell as a conventional mace, an extension of Mitchell's wrath, and he brought the weapon down hard on Clouster's head, shattering the man's skull into a thousand pieces.

Back a few paces, the two brothers gasped and flinched, showered with flecks of their mentor's brains. "Run on!" the older cried. "And apart!"

And so they did flee, one running into the darkness to the left, the other straight back, and then to the right. It was the second, the younger of the two, that Mitchell first followed, gaining easily, for while the man stumbled in the darkness, the wraith, a creature of the night, surely did not. And then he was upon the frightened man, who turned and thrust his sword at Mitchell.

And then the man was dead.

With that kill completed, Mitchell tuned his senses to the night around him. He felt the eyes of night animals upon him, creatures huddling in deep holes, their hearts beating furiously as this undead monster passed by. In a few moments, Mitchell sensed a stronger life force, and a greater fear, the fear of a rational creature. Easily tuning in to that sensation, knowing it to be the remaining man, the wraith took up the pursuit.

Mitchell caught him near to the riverbank, and the horrifying shrieks of those last terrible moments echoed across the way, to the ears of the gathered Calvans, to the ears of King Benador, unnerving them, shaking them to the marrow of their bones. They knew not who or what had made the cries, be it human or talon or some other beast, and they knew not what manner of creature had brought about such terror.

Few on the eastern side of the river slept well that night.

Nor did the wraith, friend of the night, creature of the darkness, sleep. Hollis Mitchell stood quiet on the riverbank, looking across the way at the campfires, barely able to contain the hunger that burned within his bloated form, despite the recent feasting. It was never sated, this hateful desire to destroy and devour. It itched constantly, burning at Mitchell's belly, tugging at his will.

He controlled it this night, with all those inviting campfires so very close, only by reminding himself of who he was, of who he had been. He had come from the sea, drifting in on a life raft from the destroyed submarine, the *Unicorn*, along with six other men, survivors from another age. Two whose names were long lost to the perverted memory of the evil wraith had died quickly, before ever the party had reached the halls of the angelic Colonnae, before they had discovered the truth of this world, their world, burned in flames and reborn. A third man—the wraith could not remember his name, either—had died in Blackemara, the tangled swamp north of Avalon, the place where Mitchell, too, had died, and where his spirit, a score of years later, had been pulled from the realm of Death and brought back to this world.

The death of the third man had left only four survivors

of the *Unicorn*, and of the two who had sided with the elves in the Battle of Mountaingate, Billy Shank and Jeffrey DelGiudice, Mitchell now knew little. Of the last, Martin Reinheiser, once Mitchell's friend, then Mitchell's betrayer, the wraith knew much. Somehow, through some incomprehensible act of magic, Reinheiser had joined in body to become one with Morgan Thalasi, the Black Warlock. The result of that joining, that curious dual being, Reinheiser and Thalasi, had then brought the wraith to the world, to serve as commander of their talon army. And now the Black Warlock was gone from this place, slithering, Mitchell suspected, back to his dark hole at Talas-dun. Mitchell would go there and meet again with this creature, this betrayer, this salvation, this bringer of death and undeath.

And then what? the wraith wondered. Would he do battle with the Black Warlock? Like all otherworldly beings, creatures living half in the world and half in the realm of Death, surviving only through magic, Mitchell suspected that something was amiss within the realm of the wizard, suspected that the Black Warlock, and the other wizards and the witch of Avalon, as well, if they still lived, were weaker now. Might he then destroy the Black Warlock and take Talas-dun as his own?

The thought surely intrigued him—perhaps he would indeed name himself as a king. Again Mitchell found his focus in the distant memories. He recalled his feelings on the day the survivors of the *Unicorn* had set out from the halls of the Colonnae, across the brown stretches of the desolate land of Brogg. Mitchell had vowed then that he would someday soon rule this world.

Perhaps . . .

But it was a fantasy for another day, the wraith realized, for those campfires across the way tugged at the wraith's incessant hunger, promised him warm blood and flesh.

So there it was, settled in his mind. He meant to rule the world, but now, he understood, was not the time to reveal himself, especially on the other side of the river, where, perhaps, two wizards and a witch worked their magic.

No, not now. That night by the river, the wraith of Hollis Mitchell gained perspective and purpose. And direction. He would go west, not east, to the Kored-dul and the castle Talas-dun. He would confront the Black Warlock—as servant if Thalasi were still the more powerful, as master if not—and from that place of dark strength he would gather his powers and his minions.

The Calvans and their brave King Benador had won the day at the Four Bridges, and the magically swollen river was indeed an impressive barrier, but the war was not over, the wraith decided then and there.

Not at all.

He found a dark hole before the sun came up; he was on the road west soon after it had set.

Chapter 3

Reflecting Pool

"ONLY SIX," THE warrior muttered quietly as he stalked down the forested hillside on the western borders of Avalon. "Only six." He wasn't speaking to bolster his confidence as he approached the half dozen talons butchering the deer they had just slain. While lesser warriors might have needed such soothing words, or might have simply turned about and run away from half a dozen talons, this one's words sounded as an honest lament that there were merely six of the creatures to stand against him.

"Six, six." He spat, and then he called in an even louder voice, so that the talons surely heard him. "Where are all yer stinking friends?"

The creatures came up from the deer carcass, dancing all about, falling all over each other. They should have fanned out, forming a semicircle about this lone figure stalking them through the morning mist; they should have formed a defensive alignment, seeking any other humans that might be about; they should have set a line based on the strength of each, and which sidekicks best complement. They should have done many things, but talons were neither very bright nor very brave, and each glanced nervously at another, as if hoping to use its companion as a shield should the need arise to flee.

The warrior, Belexus Backavar, waded into them with

hardly a hesitation, his heavy broadsword swinging easily at the end of one arm. He was taller than the talons, and much stockier, with corded bulging muscles and broad shoulders that had not even begun to slacken with the passage of fifty winters. His hair, too, held the luster of youth, tousled and raven black, such a stark contrast to his sparkling blue eyes.

Those eyes burned with angry fires now, simmering and then explosive as the man neared the hideous talons.

"Alone?" the closest talon asked skeptically, and its lips curled into a smile at that notion, for indeed, there seemed to be no other humans in the immediate area. "Alone," it said again, not a statement and not a question, a remark that showed it thought the man foolish.

In response, Belexus leaped ahead in a wild rush, his sweeping blade leading the way. The talon put up a staff to deflect the obvious attack, but it couldn't properly gauge the strength of mighty Belexus, the strength of a giant, and even greater now for the rage that burned hot in his blood. The sword swept the staff aside, and Belexus thundered ahead, rushing past the talon and reversing his grip so quickly that there was no parry and no dodge for his vicious backhand swipe, the blade spilling talon guts.

The other talons whooped and charged, but Belexus skipped ahead another stride and launched a fast thrust at the nearest, beating the parry and skewering the beast in the chest. A roar and a heave brought the dying creature flying about with the blade, and then tumbling at the feet of the next two, tripping them up.

Belexus kicked one in the face, drove the butt of his sword hilt onto the back of the other's head, then leaped over them, growling like an animal. The blood lust had taken hold of him fully now, had brought a red blur into his eyes. The last two talons wanted no part of this monstrous human, and off they ran.

Belexus, swift and graceful, caught up to one as it turned about a tree. The creature made a deft move then, cutting left, then back to the right, actually putting itself in solid position to the warrior's left flank. With a shriek, thinking the prize grand indeed, the talon pivoted and sliced with its sword, but Belexus flipped his sword from right hand to left and swung, too, a powerful backhand, aiming for the descending weapon. By far the stronger, the warrior drove the talon's blade from its hands, sent the inferior sword flying far through the air.

The talon staggered and straightened, trying to catch its balance, trying to run away.

Belexus spun and came in fast, pinning its outstretched right arm with his sword, and clamped his free hand over the thing's face.

With hardly an effort, with a bellow that sent all creatures scurrying in fear, the powerful man lifted the talon from the ground and shook it violently.

The pitiful creature whimpered and clawed, thrashed desperately with both hands, and kicked futilely with dangling feet.

One long stride put the warrior in line and he drove the talon's head hard against the unyielding trunk of a wide oak, the resulting splatter bringing to Belexus' thoughts a distant time when his old friend Andovar had dropped a melon twenty feet to a flat stone.

The thought of Andovar sobered the mighty warrior. He tossed the talon aside and took many long and steadying breaths, then stalked back to the original scene, to the deer carcass and the four talons.

One, the one the warrior had kicked, was back up by then, trying to rouse its dying friend. The talon abandoned that course when it noted the approach of the dangerous man. Waving its sword defensively out in front, it steadily backed as Belexus calmly came on.

Blades met several times in quick, darting movements; hope came into the talon's sickly eyes as it parried thrust after thrust.

Belexus calmly continued, playing the fencer now, maneuvering, working his opponent's blade left, then right, then a bit farther left, then a bit less right. And so on, until he had the talon turned awkwardly. Then came a sudden, violent two-stroke, both hits aimed for the talon's sword, the first nearly knocking the creature all the way about, the second deftly weaving over and around the blade as the talon tried to turn back to face the man squarely.

A flick of Belexus' wrist sent the talon's sword skipping to the ground out to the right.

The creature whined and stumbled back, the warrior easily pacing. Both glanced to their surroundings, but only briefly, neither truly breaking the stare.

The talon noted a tree, Belexus knew, and he came forward in a slight rush, forcing the creature's hand. Predictably, the talon darted behind the tree, rushing past it, putting it in the way of the human.

"Andovar!" the warrior cried suddenly, brutally, throwing out all of his rage in one cut, taking up his sword in both hands and sweeping it mightily across, sweeping it through the two-inch diameter trunk of the young tree, and through the waist of the surprised talon behind it.

The top half of the tree fell to the side of the trunk, planted in the ground for just a moment, then fell away. The talon was already on the ground, its upper body lying awkwardly across its lower, mouth gasping in horror, gulping air uselessly.

Belexus spat on it and walked away.

In a clearing not so far from the spot, Calamus, the

winged lord of horses, awaited the warrior's return. Without a word, Belexus climbed onto the mount's strong back and the pegasus took to the air, flying low and steady to the northwest, the direction in which the last talon had fled. Belexus soon spotted the miserable creature, running, stumbling, out of the wood, along a grassy slope, cutting a straight line to the west. The warrior urged Calamus ahead.

But then a song came into his ears, causing him to hesitate, a voice sweet and pure, the soothing voice of Brielle, the Emerald Witch of Avalon. "Greater will be yer reputation, greater their fear of ye, if ye let some live to tell the tale," the witch coaxed.

Her words, or more particularly, the gentle way in which they were carried to the warrior's ears, almost made Belexus turn Calamus about, almost allowed him to let this last talon run off.

But then came that all-too-familiar image, the haunting memory of Andovar being bent in half backward by the horrid wraith of Hollis Mitchell, the image of the proud ranger, Belexus Backavar's dearest friend, then being tossed carelessly into the great River Ne'er Ending.

Calamus, charmed by the intonations of the witch, had indeed slowed and begun a long, easy turn.

"Onward!" the warrior demanded, grabbing the long white mane, forcing the pegasus back on course for the fleeing talon.

Calamus owed no man, could not be so commanded, but there was indeed a bond between this magnificent horse and Belexus, son of Bellerian, who was lord of the rangers of Avalon, and so the pegasus relented, dismissed the song of the witch, and flew on with all speed, angling for the scrambling talon, diving fast and straight.

The talon saw the terrible shadow, stretching long

from the east and the rising sun, and shrieked, diving into a roll.

Calamus swooped by, and Belexus leaped from the mount's back, scrambling as he landed, with amazing dexterity, and somehow holding his footing. A firmly planted, booted foot promptly stopped the rolling talon, and then a second clamped on its other side, holding it fast. The creature tried to turn about onto its back, to face and defend, and managed it easily enough, for Belexus wanted the talon to see him clearly, to see his rage, to know its doom.

As the talon turned, the warrior grabbed its spiked club with one hand and tore it free of the talon's grasp, throwing it far aside. The talon lifted its arms above its face, then moved them in confusion and gave an incredulous stare when the warrior tossed his own sword to the ground.

Any hope that surprising action might have inspired soon flew from the talon, though, as Belexus reached down and grabbed it by the head, one hand clamped to its chin, the other grabbing fast to a scraggly clump of hair on the back of its head. With a grunt, the powerful ranger lifted the talon to its feet, lifted it right from the ground so that it was looking straight into his piercing blue eyes.

The creature clawed at the warrior's cheek. Ignoring the claws, keeping firm his grasp, Belexus drove one hand out and yanked the other in, turning the talon's head right about on its shoulders. Then he tossed the thing aside and gathered his sword, calling for Calamus.

He spent a long while waiting, and thought of Andovar. Even the blood of six talons had done little to diminish the pain.

Finally the winged horse lighted on the field, and Belexus was swift to Calamus' back, urging him up into the air and then flying straight off for the deeper boughs of Avalon.

He was not surprised to find Brielle waiting for him, was not surprised that her look was clearly one of disapproval. Even so, even with a pout upon her face, and even with Belexus in so foul a mood, he could not deny her beauty. Her golden hair hung far down her delicate back, a wild and untamed mane, and her eyes shone greener than the emerald wizard's mark set in her forehead. Brielle was the shining day to her daughter Rhiannon's alluring night, and either of them could fell a man with a look, tearing his heart so completely that he would spend a long time retrieving his strength.

"And yet again, ye let the rage take ye," the witch said, her voice calm and even, and not overtly accusatory.

Belexus understood that tone completely, knew that Brielle was not really judging him, but was, rather, subtly forcing him to judge himself. That trial, both of them knew well, would prove far worse to the proud ranger's reckoning.

"I slay talons," he replied firmly after a moment of thought and a deep sigh. "That is me lot in life."

"Ayuh, and a good one it might be," Brielle answered. "It's the way ye do it that's got me so worried."

"I'm not for denying me pleasure at me tasks," the ranger said, and turned away. "With each talon that falls dead to the ground, the world, by me own estimation, is a bit better a place."

"Ayuh," the witch honestly agreed. "And so ye should be cutting the beasties down. But if ye let the rage take ye, if ye're thinking about what was, and not what is, then ye're losing yerself, me friend, and worse, ye're liken to make a mistake that'll cost ye yer own neck."

"Not to a talon," the ranger spat sarcastically. Brielle's words had stung Belexus profoundly, particularly her reference to "what was"—her reference, Belexus understood, to Andovar. She knew Belexus so well, too well—knew even his thoughts. Was he that transparent, he wondered, or was Brielle just so damned perceptive?

"There be darker things than talons walking the ways of Aielle," Brielle said quietly, but grimly, and her tone told Belexus of whom she was speaking. Again, that only added to the ranger's frustration. He wanted to destroy the wraith of Hollis Mitchell more than he wanted anything in the world, even more than he wanted the love of Brielle. Mitchell had shattered Belexus' world, had utterly destroyed his dearest friend, and through it all, the ranger had only been able to look on in horror. Nothing he could have done would have made a difference, would have bothered the wraith in any way, for his weapon, so solid and deadly to most of Aielle's monsters, could not even scratch the undead wraith.

Nor had the river brought any harm to Mitchell, Brielle had informed Belexus, and had told her brother, Rudy Glendower, the Silver Mage of Illuma, who was known by the name of Ardaz. For the fair witch of Avalon, with her senses so attuned to the natural world, had sensed the return, the sheer perversion, of the undead thing. She had sent out her eyes to search for her daughter, and had found instead the horrid wraith, staining the very ground with its every step.

"Might that the beast will come to Avalon," Brielle said after a long and uncomfortable silence. "I canno' go out and destroy the thing, for to leave would be to leave behind the power I'm needing against it, but if it comes near to me wood . . ."

She let the ominous threat hang there, but Belexus would not seize the thought and revel in it. He didn't doubt her claim, but neither did he want to see that battle. "The wraith is mine to slay," he announced coldly and determinedly.

"Ye canno'," the witch said calmly.

"Then, by the Colonnae, I'll die in trying!" the ranger growled, spinning back on her, his blue eyes flashing with fury.

Brielle took a good measure of the man, this man, this prince of rangers. Always, Belexus had been the cool and calm leader of men, the warrior who had single-handedly rallied the Calvans to hold the Four Bridges against Thalasi's assaults until reinforcements could arrive, the man who had saved the elves on the field of Mountaingate when he had put aside his own desires and used his body and that of his pegasus mount to clear the way for Arien Silverleaf, that the elf lord, fittingly, might be the one to slay wicked Ungden the Usurper, who had led his army north to destroy all of Arien's people. Always, Belexus had been unselfish, purely giving, and unquestioning of the code of rangers, a pledge to a set of tenets and principles that worked for the betterment of the world, and not of the rangers.

But now . . . now that Brielle had informed the man that the wraith was still about, that the wraith, with the weakening of magic in the last desperate battle, might well stand as the most powerful creature in all Aielle, Belexus had changed. Now his thoughts festered on poor dead Andovar, his rage becoming singular and all-consuming. His only smiles of late were ones of cruel glee, a grin that more resembled a grimace and that only appeared when he cut another talon down.

Brielle, so gentle and wise, remained patient with him. In his anger, he had taken a vow that superseded all others, she realized; a vow that he would avenge the death of Andovar. With that seeming an impossibility, the ranger's frustration continued to grow. Perhaps it would pass as the darkness further retreated toward the Kored-dul, as time itself replaced those last bitter images of Andovar's life with the memories of better times Belexus and Andovar had shared throughout the decades.

Belexus gave a nod then, a curt bow, and walked away into the forest, preferring to be alone, and Brielle was left to wonder if this frustration would ever pass, if Belexus would ever truly recover from his inability to fulfill his vow.

"He's gone ugly," the beautiful witch said to Calamus, and the pegasus, a creature far more intelligent than its equine frame would indicate, gave a snort and pawed the ground.

The truth of her words assaulted her, and made her determine then and there that she had to do something to help the man, for though he would not admit it, he needed her now.

At sunset, the emerald witch began her preparations upon a still pool of water, melted snow that had collected in the broken stump of an ancient oak, a tree that had been battered to death in the magical battle the witch had waged against Morgan Thalasi. There was still some resonance of power in that tree, Brielle knew, in its deepest roots and in the inner rings that had seen the dawn and death of centuries. And so it was here that Brielle began her enchanting, pouring oils into the water, singing and dancing about the tree, offering a bit of her own blood, and offering all of her thoughts and, more important, her wishes, to the mix. She focused those thoughts on the wraith, and soon the image of the blackness that was the zombielike Mitchell came into focus within the depths of the pool.

Brielle had found him with her divining, crawling out of a small cave—his daytime shelter, it seemed—stepping out into the night. The mere fact that she had so easily located the wraith, how easily her enchantment had sensed his presence though he was obviously far, far away, hinted to her just how powerful Mitchell had become. Now the witch called to the deepest knowledge of the tree, to the understanding of the earth itself, begging it to give her a sign, a hint, of how such a perversion as the wraith could be destroyed, of what magic, or magical weapon, perhaps, might at least hurt the thing.

The water clouded over, swirling, then a small spot appeared at the center of the pool. And in that spot, under the water, the witch saw a craft, a barge poled by a gaunt, robed figure, drifting upward, upward, closer and closer.

Then it was gone, and so was the fog, and all that remained in the bowl was the clear water and the reflection of the evening's first stars.

Brielle gave a long sigh; perhaps no such weapon existed. Perhaps Thalasi's meddling in places where no mortal belonged had loosed upon Ynis Aielle a horror that would endure for eternity.

"Not so," came a low, coarse voice behind Brielle. She froze in place, purely amazed that any person, that anything at all could so sneak up on her here in Avalon, stunned that her many forest friends had not alerted her to the presence—a presence that she felt so clearly now, so cold and deadly. She turned about slowly, thinking that she would face the wraith, thinking that Mitchell had somehow come through her divining instrument to strike at her.

Her fair face blanched even more when she saw and recognized the speaker. Not the wraith and not Thalasi, but one darker and more mysterious by far.

Death itself had come to Avalon.

It took the distracted Belexus a long while to realize that the wintry forest had gone strangely quiet around him, that the nightbirds were not singing, not even the snowy owl that always seemed to be about. But it was more than the absence of animals, the ranger somehow sensed; it was as if all the forest had suddenly hushed: the wind, the trees, the eternal music of Avalon.

The ranger spotted Calamus, flying in low, landing in a small clearing not so far ahead and pawing the ground frantically, as agitated as Belexus had ever seen the creature.

"What do ye know?" the ranger asked, and the pegasus snorted, though the sound seemed unnaturally muffled, as if it had come from far, far away, as if the air itself were heavy with dread. This was too wicked, the ranger realized, as if the very heart of Avalon—

"Brielle?" the ranger asked in a hush, hardly able to draw breath.

Again Calamus snorted, and stamped his front hoof hard on the ground.

Belexus sprinted across the small clearing and verily leaped atop the winged horse's powerful back, and Calamus sped away, running to the far end of the clearing and cutting a sharp turn, then galloping back—one stride, two—and leaping high into the air, wings beating furiously to get the pair up above the trees. A sheer sense of wrongness guided horse and rider, a perversion of the natural order, a darkness to the area where stood the emerald witch.

"Arawn," Brielle said quietly, respectfully, her name for this ultimate of specters, and truly she was surprised and confused, for though she knew that Thalasi's meddling with the universal powers had wounded her and all the magic users of Aielle, she had thought herself strong still, and in the best of health. "Has me time so passed by, then, that I did not even expect ye?"

"I came not for Brielle," the embodiment of death informed her.

"For whom then?" Brielle dared to ask, though she knew that death was a personal event, one in which she need not be informed. "For Bellerian, who is old?"

There came no answer, the specter standing impassively, leaning heavily on its long sickle.

"For Belexus, then?" the witch prompted fearfully, and she knew as soon as she heard the words leave her mouth that, if that was the case, she truly didn't want to know!

The specter tilted its hooded head, regarding her curiously.

"If ye mean to take Belexus, then know ye'll be fighting meself!" Brielle declared, though she understood her claim to be a foolish and impossible boast, for she could no more battle Death than she could burn down Avalon. They were the same, this specter and her forest, both embodiments of the natural order of the universe, and Brielle drew her power completely from that very order. She could not fight Death; she, above all others, who served the First Magic, the school of Nature, could not hope to battle that most elemental of all beings.

"Yer pardon," she said, and she respectfully lowered her gaze.

"I have come not for Belexus," Arawn replied somberly—the only tone Death ever used, Brielle thought. "You should fear, though, if you care for him, that perhaps he comes for me!"

The witch looked up curiously, not understanding—until she looked past Death to see the ranger swooping in on Calamus, flying straight for the specter's back. Belexus had no sword drawn, though, and seemed to be looking only at the witch, his expression as much of curiosity and relief as anything else.

"He canno' see ye," Brielle remarked, and of course, it made sense. Only the wizards had such insight, and no mere human or even elf could see Death until that final moment, the time of passage.

"And fortunate that is for him," Arawn remarked. "I am of no mood to tolerate the foolishness of lessers."

Brielle sent her thoughts out then, on sudden impulse, flooding the mind of Calamus, letting the winged horse know that she was not afraid, and more important, that this was not his place, and certainly not the place for Belexus. The ranger was just preparing to slip his leg over the mount and drop to the ground running when Calamus angled his powerful wings and broke the swoop, rising steeply into the night sky.

Brielle heard the ranger's protesting calls, calls fast diminishing as the wise pegasus, heeding her telepathic commands, carried him far away.

"Then who?" the witch asked of Death when that crisis was passed. "If I might be knowing. And if not, then why have ye taked the time to stop and visit?"

"Visit?" the specter echoed, a hint of incredulity slipping into the edges of its grave tone. "No, Jennifer Glendower," it said, using Brielle's older name, the name she had been given by her mother and father those centuries before—before *e-Belvin Fehte*, the killing fires, before the dawn of Ynis Aielle. "I have not come for any—in these dark times, they easily enough come to me." A rasping sound—a sarcastic chuckle?—emanated from the specter, sending the hairs on the back of Brielle's neck dancing. Death was the most serious and somber being in all the universe, the one Colonnae who could not, or certainly should not, laugh.

"And your ranger friend has kept me busy, lo, these last weeks," the surprising specter went on. "I dare say!"

"Then why have you come?" an unnerved Brielle

bluntly pressed, too fearful and too intrigued to allow this most unusual conversation to be sidetracked.

Death did not answer, and in the course of that uncomfortable pause, the wise witch solved the riddle. "Ye're angered at Thalasi," she reasoned. "He took something from ye."

"And still he takes," Death confirmed.

Brielle breathed a lot easier then, as she came to understand the truth. Thalasi had torn Mitchell from the grasp of Death, and that, above all else, the somber Colonnae specter could not tolerate. "Then ye hate the black thing as much as do we all," the witch said quietly. "And can ye destroy it?"

"Thomas Morgan, Martin Reinheiser, the two who have become one, has defeated even me," the specter explained.

Brielle was caught off guard, both by the revelation that Death, who, by the very definition of his name, could never be beaten, apparently had been, and also by the use of Morgan Thalasi's birth name, Thomas Morgan, a name the witch had not heard in many, many years. Also, the reference to both Thomas Morgan and Martin Reinheiser, used in the singular, was indeed telling. The two had become one, as Brielle had suspected and as Death had just confirmed. Yet another perversion, Brielle reasoned. Another insult against the natural order to add to Thalasi's growing list.

"Thalasi is not so strong now," Brielle explained, hoping that Death would whisk off right then and there and destroy the wretched Thalasi, and Mitchell, in one fell swoop. "He's bent the fabric—"

"Our score was settled," the specter interrupted before she could gain any real momentum.

"Then what do ye want?" Brielle asked impatiently—and nervously, once again.

"What is rightfully mine," Death matter-of-factly replied.

"Hollis Mitchell."

"May he rest in peace."

"Then show me how to deliver him to ye!" the witch growled. "Ye cannot take him back yerself, it'd seem, or ye'd have done so and been done with it, so show me how I might deliver him to ye!"

"That is what you asked at the pool," Death said calmly. "And that is why I have come." And with that, the specter lifted one bony arm, its skeletal finger pointing past the witch to the broken tree stump.

Brielle followed the line and moved to the side of the pool, and in its dark waters, as the image of the many stars now overhead faded away, she saw clearly a vision of a sword.

And such a sword! Shining metal edged in diamonds, and glowing of its own inner light. She stared at it for a long, long while, saw into it and through it, glanced at its vast surroundings only for a few moments—enough time to see a treasure hoard beyond anything she had ever imagined; enough time to see the scaly guardian, its wings folded about it as it slept comfortably.

Hardly drawing breath, the witch turned about, but Death, Arawn, was gone. She looked back to the pool, to see only the reflection of stars.

"Brielle!" came a desperate cry, the voice of Belexus, huffing and puffing as he ran and stumbled through the trees. He burst into the clearing, brandishing his sword—a sword that had always seemed so magnificent to the witch, though she cared little for instruments of war, but that now, considering the vision she had just witnessed in the pool, seemed rather ordinary indeed.

Chapter 4

An Evil He Couldn't Know

THE YOUNG WITCH stared long and hard at the reflecting pool, which she had created just as her mother had taught her, but the image would not come to her. She knew that there were talons in the area—the birds had whispered as much—but for some reason she couldn't understand, Rhiannon's magical eye was blind to them.

Behind her, Bryan paced anxiously, fingering the hilt of his sword. A hungry lion, he seemed, impatient for the kill, and with prey close by.

That image of Bryan's distress spurred Rhiannon on, urging her to try more forcefully. She sent her heart and soul into that pool of dark water, pricked her finger and gave to it a piece of herself, a bit of her own life blood, though as soon as she let the drop of red liquid fall to the pool, she realized to her horror that she would never get it back. Somehow, throwing herself into the magic had taken that bit away from her forevermore.

She knew that beyond doubt, and suddenly the young witch found her breathing hard to come by. For all that she had learned in Avalon, the use of magic was not supposed to be like this. Her mother had practiced witchery for centuries, and had only grown, and surely had not diminished, by the summoning of universal powers. And yet, after only a few short months of truly coming into her power, Rhiannon felt weakened, felt as if the magic constantly took from her, as if it would eventually absorb her completely. She thought of her father, then, the mortal human, and no wizard. Perhaps her magic wasn't pure, she feared, for, unlike the four older wizards of Ynis Aielle, Rhiannon had not been taken away by the Colonnae to learn and experience the mysteries of the universe, that she might comprehend the universal powers she found at her fingertips.

The young witch could not know, of course, that all the magic was tainted now, that her mother and Ardaz, Istaahl, and Thalasi, too, suffered a personal loss with each expenditure of magical energy. True to her suspicions, though, the cost was more profound for Rhiannon than for the others. So young and inexperienced, Rhiannon did not recognize the barriers that she had to cross with each spellcasting, and did not fully understand the cost until it had been exacted upon her increasingly frail frame.

Desperate thoughts drifted away as the image in the divining pool at last came distinct. "Five o' them," the young witch said to Bryan, working hard to keep her voice sounding calm and steady. "Putting their camp on the rocky spur just south o' Bendwillow Pass. We'll find them easy enough, for they're setting a big fire to ward off the chill."

Bryan instinctively looked to the northeast, the direction Rhiannon had indicated, as if expecting to see a campfire spring up against the darkening background. The spur Rhiannon had spoken of was well sheltered, though, and the young man knew logically that he would see nothing from this perspective, especially not now, with the sky still light from the last rays of the cold day.

"Tonight," he said quietly.

Rhiannon tossed her black hair back from her face so that she could better view Bryan, for she knew that tone of his, the voice that Bryan held for occasions of planned mayhem.

"Tomorrow," Rhiannon replied against the young half-elf's cold resolve.

Bryan looked at her skeptically.

"I'm needing me rest," the young witch explained.

Bryan nodded, and tried hard to look away from Rhiannon, not wanting his stare to seem accusatory. "Tomorrow," he agreed, so obviously unhappy, but so obviously conciliatory to this woman. "When you are ready."

Bryan eyed Rhiannon often that evening, studying her whenever he thought her eyes focused on something else.

Rhiannon knew. She felt his stares keenly, a gaze complete with silent sighs, the looks of an impatient lover. She knew them and understood well, because her own looks at young Bryan were not so different, she had to admit—to herself at least.

They were not lovers, not yet, and neither had made any overt gesture of passion at all. Rhiannon, the older of the pair, wondered about that, wondered if Bryan felt the same stirring as she, and wondered if she should take the lead in their romance.

But she could not, she realized, closing her eyes and seeking the solace of sleep. She could not even afford to think about it. Not out here, and not now.

Bryan watched her through it all, stealing glimpses and holding them fast within his heart and soul. He wanted to go over and kiss her, and hold her, wanted it more than anything in the world.

And yet, Bryan, so mature for his sixteen years, so sympathetic and empathetic, and so pragmatic, Bryan who had been forced to grow up by tragedy and catastrophe, could accept the obvious hold in their relationship. He understood that there was something holding

Rhiannon back, something deep and powerful. But he knew that she cared for him, more deeply with each passing day, a budding love that he had to trust she would soon enough admit.

His looks this night were different than the simple gazes of a lovesick youth, though—they were of concern and very real fear. Bryan had seen the cost of the divining enchantment, had seen Rhiannon's shoulders slump when she had dropped a bit of blood into the pool. He knew that the magic was taking from her, was killing her, and yet he knew, too, that Rhiannon, so selfless, so giving to all the goodliness of the world, would not stop, would press on until her shoulders slumped to the ground, until her last breath drifted from her body.

That image shook Bryan of Corning more than anything in all the world, more than the thoughts of his father, who had died bravely defending his city, more than any thoughts of his own possible death.

He waited until Rhiannon was asleep, and that was not so long, and then he set out alone into the cold, cold night. It was time for him to take some of the tremendous pressure off the fair young witch.

Rhiannon, thinking that her dear companion was watching over her, and so weary from her divining, drifted to sleep.

Bryan felt the brutal bite of the north wind gnawing at his flesh even through the thick cloak he had confiscated from an abandoned farmhouse. Winter was not so punishing on the southern plains of Calva, but this high in the Baerendils, it came on early and held fast for a long time. Thus, the young man was not surprised when he did at last spot the light of a blazing fire on the jut of stone that Rhiannon had indicated.

He took a circuitous route, moving behind and above the talon campsite, to a second, higher plateau in the stone, overlooking the talon camp from a height of about fifteen feet. He carefully worked his way out to the very edge; the wind had cleared all snow from the stone, but traces of dangerous ice remained. A slip might send him plummeting over the edge, bouncing down a thousand-foot mountain slide, or even if he did not go over, his fumbling would surely alert the talons that they were not alone and leave him in a desperate position.

All that in mind, and with all due caution, he managed to get to the lip of the stone. Peering over, he was hardly surprised to find that the scene was exactly as Rhiannon had predicted, with five of the ugly talon wretches gathered about a central fire that was piled high with logs. At least a couple of the brutes were asleep, clucking and snoring, and only one was standing, pacing slowly in tight circles about the fire.

Bryan huddled against the wind, trying to keep his eyes from tearing. Logical battle tactics told him to wait until the camp had settled down even more, until all of the talons had fallen asleep, or at least until all but the sentry had taken up the chorus of snoring. But practicality told the young man that he could not wait for long. Already, his fingers tingled with hints of numbness, and such a chill had come into his body that he feared it might slow his blade. Worst of all, crouching here, so close to his enemies, he could not even move about to generate some body heat.

Bryan pictured Rhiannon's expression, one of shock and outrage, one of contempt for his foolishness, if she came in search of him in the morning and found him frozen to death against the stone, killed before he had ever even lifted his sword against the oblivious talons.

That sparked him to motion—a single, fluid movement that turned him about and brought his legs over the lip of the rocky jut, then had him sliding, sliding, to the end of his balance and dropping fast to the stone, drawing his sword as he descended, and landing lightly right beside the sentry.

The talon gasped, then gasped again as Bryan's sword plunged through its chest.

The young warrior spun about, slashing as he went, gashing hard and deep across the sloped forehead of the second as it tried to rise. He leaped to the side, stabbing hard and repeatedly on the third, until movement from the stubborn second forced his attention once more.

The talon, blood pouring over its face, was up in a crouch, bringing its spiked club to a ready, defensive position.

Bryan thrust high, thrust low, then launched his sword into a series of graceful, tantalizing sweeps, left to right, right to left, and back again, and again. Once or twice, the club got in the way to parry, but only a slight deflection that hardly disrupted the graceful dance of Bryan of Corning. He came ahead suddenly, breaking his momentum and altering the angle in midswing, stabbing wickedly, but the talon, no novice to battle, turned and blocked with the club. On came Bryan, and away backed the talon, matching him stride for stride.

"Yous will find no holes, human," the wretch taunted, as an evil yellow smile, one of pointed, broken teeth, widened on its face. "Garink's friends wake."

Bryan leaped forward, then stopped, then came on again, sword jabbing hard. That talon, Garink, was too far from Bryan for the thrust to score a hit, but Bryan understood that well, and understood, too—though the talon apparently did not—that the backing creature had retreated just a bit too far. The talon countered the first thrust by skipping back, smile widening, even offering a taunting laugh.

"Garink's friends wake," it said again, laughing

louder and then skipping back again, Bryan's second thrust falling harmlessly short.

Or not. For the talon's continuing laugh shifted suddenly to a scream of the sheerest horror as the creature slipped off the edge of the outcropping and plummeted and tumbled away into the darkness.

Bryan rushed back to the fire to meet the fourth of the group as it groggily staggered to its feet.

"Duh?" it asked when it wiped the sleep from its eyes and noted that this was no talon but a human standing before it.

Bryan grabbed the creature by its scraggly hair, yanked its head back, lifting the chin, presenting a target that his sword tip was fast to find. He retracted the blade quickly, its work complete, then quick-stepped across the flat stone, dying talon in tow, and with a powerful twist of his slender frame—a movement strengthened by the recollection of Rhiannon's slumping shoulders—heaved it from the ledge.

That left only one, and Bryan shook his head as he regarded it, sleeping soundly, undisturbed though its four companions were all dead about it. He killed it with a single stroke, then rolled it, and the remaining two, from the ledge. Then he sat down at the fire to chase the nighttime chill from his bones. As he rocked quietly, basking in the heat, letting it sink into cold skin and chilled bones, the thought occurred to him that he shouldn't have so quickly disposed of the bodies, that he should have taken something, their ears perhaps, to prove to Rhiannon that the task had been completed.

"Rhiannon," the young man whispered into the dancing flames, picturing her asleep where he had left her, so soft and so beautiful.

He fell asleep with that not-unpleasant image in his mind.

"Bryan."

The word came from far away, from the depths of his dream, he believed. The whisper of his lover—not a call to him, but rather, just the reciting of his name, the acknowledgment of him as the other half of a love that completed them both.

"Bryan," Rhiannon said again, more insistently, giving the grinning half-elf a nudge.

Bryan opened a sleepy eye. His blurry vision gradually sharpened, focusing at first on the image of the blackened logs, patches of orange, smoldering glow evident here and there. His smile slowly faded as he came to realize where he was, the talon camp, and that the morning had found him there, and that Rhiannon, standing before him, had found him there, and that they had not spent the night in each other's arms. That was just a dream, just a dream.

Just a dream.

"Bryan?"

"I am here," he replied groggily, rolling to the side a bit to shift his weight, and stretching his sore back.

"Are ye hurt then?" the witch asked.

He spent a moment considering that possibility, replayed the events of the previous night—the actual events and not his fantasies—and shook his head. "No. Not hurt. I haven't a scratch."

Her reaction caught him off guard, for she moved beside him, crouched low, and punched him hard in the gut. "Ye fool," she scolded, and her anger was not feigned. "How dare ye take me vision from me and put it to yer own stupid use?"

"I did . . . What do you mean?" Bryan stammered, balling up defensively as Rhiannon punched at him again.

"Who's telling ye to go off alone then?" the fiery

young witch went on. "Who said to ye that this was yer own fight? Yer own fight alone?"

"You were worried about me," Bryan responded, that boyish smile flashing bright, its undeniable charm stealing some of Rhiannon's ire.

"Of course I . . ." the witch began, but she stopped, caught by surprise as to where this conversation might be leading.

"Ha!" Bryan laughed into the morning light, clapping his hands together and leaping nimbly to his feet. "And so you care, daughter of Brielle," he accused poking a finger at her. "You care, and there will be no denying it!"

"Ye're me friend," the witch replied seriously, calmly. "I'd not deny that."

Bryan's eyes focused on her intently. "Just a friend?" he asked with a snicker.

Rhiannon's cold look stole the mirth from the young man, and told him without a doubt that he had pushed her too far too quickly.

"Ye're me friend," she said again. "And we been fighting together, a powerful team, and for ye to go off without a word o' explaining, for ye to take such a chance without even giving me the option o' telling ye ye're right or ye're wrong . . ." Her voice trailed off and she looked away, chewing her bottom lip, her blue eyes growing suddenly misty.

"I did not mean it like that," Bryan began, rushing over and dropping to a crouch beside her. He draped an arm across her shoulders. "This fight was not for you," he tried to explain.

"That choice is me own to make," the witch said firmly, avoiding his gaze.

"No," Bryan disagreed, and the bluntness of his tone did draw her gaze, a look of both curiosity and budding anger. "You have no choice. You would have joined me in this fight, however weak, however weary you might have been. You would have joined me because you see that as your duty. You would have aided me with your magic, despite the obvious price, because you feel you have to, though this fight was not so difficult a task for my sword alone."

The young witch started to look away again, but Bryan caught her chin in hand and turned with her, forcing her to look at him.

"You would have sought to protect me, as I would protect you, but that exertion, that call to magic, would have wounded you more than these pitiful talons could ever wound me." He let go and brushed his fingers gently across her cheek, and Rhiannon made no further move to turn away.

"Do you not understand, my Rhiannon," he said quietly past the lump welling in his throat. "By preventing you from protecting me, I protected you."

She stared at him hard.

"Would you not have done the same?" he asked gently.

"This is not about me, Bryan of Corning," the witch said suddenly, fiercely. "And not about yerself. We fight because all the world needs us to fight. Suren it's a bigger thing than me or yerself, or anything ye think we two might have between us." She pulled away then and rose, stepping quickly out of arms' reach.

"Then think of all the world," Bryan snapped after her, and he too straightened. "Then think of how little good a bone-weary Rhiannon can do for the world compared to what rested Rhiannon did only a few short months ago. How many did you heal then, at the great battle? And how many talons did you slay with your magics? And all of that before you battled the Black Warlock! Before you, Rhiannon of Avalon, flattened the

Black Warlock to the ground and sent him slithering back to his dark hole!"

"It was not me alone," the witch answered softly, her anger subdued by the painful memories of that horrible battle. She looked away, out over the lip of the plateau, out to the wide world spreading before her.

"But how much could you do now?" Bryan pressed. "If a hundred wickedly wounded soldiers lay waiting for you, how many now would survive?"

Rhiannon looked back to him and said nothing; she had run out of answers.

"So rest, my Rhiannon," Bryan implored her. "Rest and recover your strength, and be ready for that inevitable time when I truly need you, when all the world truly needs you. Do what divining tricks you might to point my sword in the right direction, but then let me take care of the rogue bands. In the end, they are little enough trouble."

"The day's to snow," Rhiannon said quietly, and started away, but not before she offered a conciliatory nod to the young warrior. "It'd not do for us to get caught up so high."

They made their way down the mountain, to a low and sheltered vale, and encountered no more talons that day, nor trouble of any kind. True to Rhiannon's prediction, a snow did begin to fall, but it was gentle down in the valley, not wind-whipped and stinging, as up on the higher plateaus. Often Bryan tried to broach again the subject of the talons, of his and Rhiannon's respective roles in their alliance. By Bryan's estimation, Rhiannon had done more good than any could have imagined, and she should rest now, let her powers be in case they would be needed again in more desperate times. "Whenever your animal friends speak of enemies in the region, pass the word to me," Bryan said with all confidence, "then take your rest and await my return."

Rhiannon was too weary to argue with the eager warrior. She understood that Bryan's words were as much boast—and a boast aimed at her, and how that set her back on her heels!—as reason. The young warrior wanted to puff himself up—as Rhiannon's mother used to describe it—in Rhiannon's eyes. Given the honesty of their relationship, where they saw each other so clearly and truly, she could hardly understand any need he might have to boast.

Still, given the efficient manner in which Bryan had disposed of the last talon band, and the fact that he had long survived without her help, without anyone's help, striking at talon encampment after talon encampment, freeing refugees and ushering them to safety across the river, Rhiannon had to admit that there was more than a little basis for his bravado. So the young witch—who had been sheltered in her mother's forest for so much of her life, but was at last beginning to sort out the wide ways of the wide world—took Bryan's boasting, his need to protect her and to impress her, as a compliment, and lay down by their fire that night thinking that she might find her first truly restful sleep in a long while.

Since before this power had awakened within her.

It was Bryan, supposedly keeping watch, but surely exhausted from the long hike and his escapades of the night before, who first began to snore. Rhiannon lay awake, smiling outwardly at the sound, but her inner turmoil roiled. She had not been properly schooled in the ways and the sources of magic, but she, too, like the other wizards of Aielle, knew that something was terribly amiss. At first she had thought the sudden magical weakness to be her own, but now she was coming to understand that it was the source of power that had been weakened, that those energies to which she might reach out were no longer pure and strong.

That notion brought other disturbing questions to mind. Her home, beloved Avalon, was a creation of magic, and was sustained by magic. If the source had been weakened, had the colors of Avalon, so pure and so rich, begun to fade? "Me mum," the young witch whispered affectionately into the wind, and indeed, at that moment, Rhiannon would have given anything to be wrapped in Brielle's warm embrace. She glanced over at Bryan, her would-be hero, leaning against a rock wall, his eyes closed, his snores as loud as ever, and she thought that she should take him there, to Avalon, to meet Brielle. This young man, barely more than a boy, had known only grief and war for so long, for months on end. Perhaps she might show him the quieter and more beautiful side of life, for if Avalon could not heal the emotional scars of war, then no place in all the world ever could.

She would take him there, she decided, and remind him of the goodness of life, to remind him of the beautiful things, to remind him of his own inner beauty.

Rhiannon paused in her musing and just stared at Bryan, and did not doubt that inner beauty for an instant.

She let those thoughts go at that, thoughts she had not held for any man save Andovar. *Not yet,* she silently told herself, and she lay back down, remembering her fine ranger, his easy yet emotional way with stories, his fine silhouette as he sat tall upon his horse, the graceful way the muscles of his legs held his seat as the animal galloped across the fields, leaping fallen trees with ease.

A darkness engulfed her, fell over her mental vision through the curtain of night; at first she thought it to be the emotions of the loss, the death of Andovar replayed in her imagination. But then Rhiannon recognized it as something tangible, not remembered or imagined, as some true darkness, and not so far away. The witch was up quickly, pacing about the encampment, wondering if she should try divining with a reflecting pool, or if she might simply concentrate and sense the presence more clearly. She reflected on it long and hard, and came to believe that whatever it was—and she feared it might be Morgan Thalasi—it was moving east to west, some distance north of her present position, out of the Baerendils and across the Calvan plain.

Indeed it was a darkness, a perversion, a hideous insult to Nature. That recognition angered the young witch, for indeed she was more like her mother than she could ever know, and her instincts to protect the natural world had her gathering together her things before she even realized the action. If she had sensed the darkness, then it would likewise recognize her, she suspected. Better that she go out and meet it on the open fields; better to be the huntress than the hunted.

But what of her companion? she wondered, glancing over at the sleeping young warrior. Should she wake Bryan and tell him her designs? Should she allow him to accompany her, as surely he would demand?

"No," the witch whispered. Not this time. This was not a battle of swords, if a battle it would be at all. This was a matter for magic, and in that, Bryan of Corning could play no role. This perversion was an evil that the young half-elf simply could not know. Still, Rhiannon hated to leave him behind, and so she resolved to go out with all speed, better scrutinize the source of darkness, and then return to Bryan's side, hopefully before the end of the next day.

She left Bryan with a gentle kiss on the cheek and floated out easily across the broken ground of the mountain trail, her black gossamer gown, the dress of her heritage, trailing behind her, shrouding her form in mystery.

Chapter 5

His Place and Hers

THE MORNING DAWNED soft and gentle, a growing hint of spring in the air, though the snow lay thick about Avalon. The warmer air brought up a wispy fog from that snow, veiling the dark trees, dulling the cold starkness from their leafless branches, and giving all the forest a surreal and dreamy quality.

Belexus stood perfectly still for a long, long while, collecting his thoughts one at a time, translating them into some tangible image—a block of stone—and then dismissing each of them into emptiness, throwing them away, falling deep into a meditative trance. Then slowly he began to reach for the morning sky, like the great oak, higher and higher, spreading wide the great limbs of his arms, stiffening them, grasping a firm hold on nothingness, the cords of his bulging muscles stretching taut. Then gradually he softened, became fluid, like the willow, that most deceptive of trees, the tree that successfully battled the greatest of winds through apparent submission. Side to side he went, always to his limits, always reaching. The ranger had seen fifty winters, but with the graceful stretching routines Brielle had shown to his father Bellerian, and that Bellerian had in turn taught to Belexus and to all the rangers of Avalon, his body remained supple and flexible, more the frame of a twenty-year-old.

It went on for many minutes, and then Belexus pressed his palms together and pushed with all his strength, working muscle against muscle, his forearms and biceps balling from the exertion. He came out of the isometric press with a violent leap, catching the lowest branch of a nearby tree and quickly inverting himself, wrapping his legs about the limb and hooking his ankles. Then he let go with his hands, hanging flat out, stretching toward the ground, again lengthening his back. Slowly he lowered himself, leg muscles tight so that his feet held strong as he gradually loosened his wrap on the branch. Then he let go with his legs altogether, dropping, outstretched arms first, to the ground, where he caught himself, holding the perfectly steady handstand for a calm and slow ten-count.

With a deep, relaxing breath, Belexus bent his arms, ever so slowly, until his face was low enough to kiss the sacred ground, and then he pushed back up to the handstand. He repeated the motion fifty times, until he felt the warmth of coursing blood flushing his huge shoulders.

The ranger sprang to his feet gracefully out of that last push-up. He repeated the beginning of the routine, giving a few final stretches, then gathered up his huge sword and belted it about his waist. Before he had gone five steps, he drew out the sword, held it across his open palms, and paused long to consider that trusted weapon, studying its workmanship, remembering the many battles it had served him, the talons slain, the whip-dragons skewered.

Ultimately, the ranger had to remember the one time the magnificent weapon had failed him, the one enemy against whom it had no power.

The ranger's gaze drifted up from the sword, staring into the fog, into nothing at all. He conjured to mind an image of the sword Brielle had shown to him in the reflecting pool the night before, a weapon superior to anything Belexus had ever seen, a mightier weapon even than Fahwayn, the enchanted sword wielded by Arien Silverleaf. He imagined the fine cutting edge of the displayed weapon, could almost feel its sharpness against his finger, the blade lined in diamond and edged in a white, inner light that promised power against even the wraith of Hollis Mitchell.

Yes, he could fight Mitchell with that sword, Brielle had assured him, could avenge the death of Andovar and put to rest the battle-lust demons that threatened more than his life, that threatened his very soul.

"I'm knowing yer thoughts," came a soft voice behind him, soft like the warm fog, like the essence of Avalon itself.

Belexus blinked his eyes and turned about to view the Emerald Witch, splendid, as always, in her white gossamer gown, her green eyes sparkling, golden hair shining, even in the dull light. "Might be that ye know too much sometimes, me lady," he replied with a grin.

"Sword in hand, sword in mind," the witch reasoned.

"Ayuh," the ranger confirmed. "And more in mind, and more in heart, is the task that sword ye showed me will bring to me."

Brielle's fair face clouded over. "One task at a time," she said in all seriousness.

Belexus understood her fear. When she had shown to him the sword, she had told him, too, of the guardian she suspected, for only one creature in Ynis Aielle could likely hold such a vast treasure hoard; only one creature could keep for itself a sword such as that, unused through decades untold.

Belexus had fought a true dragon once, and though it was but a hatchling, the creature had nearly sizzled the ranger's blood, and after Belexus had dealt it a mortal blow, in its wild death throes, its claws had torn deep ridges in the solid stone. What might a true adult dragon do, then, and how could Belexus ever hope to defeat it? For one brief instant, a cloud of doubt and weakness passed over his face. But it could not hold, for the memory of his dragon battle incited another thought, one of Andovar, for his companion had so often told the tale of Belexus and the dragon, to any who would hear, even if they had listened a hundred times before. And of course, coming from Andovar's mouth, the tale of Belexus' exploits had always sounded much grander, much more heroic.

"I have to go for the sword," the ranger said resolutely, those memories of Andovar steeling his gaze and his jaw.

Brielle said nothing for a few, long moments. "When winter lets go of the Crystals," she reasoned, but the stoic ranger was shaking his head before she ever finished the thought.

"This day," he said. "I'll not find the comfort of true sleep until Andovar's avenged, and each day lets the rage burn me heart more deeply, and takes me strength. This moment's not soon enough, I say, to start on the road that'll put the wraith back in the dark domain." He studied Brielle's face for a long time, her posture, too, to try to find some hint of her feelings concerning his declaration. And in trying to see things through the witch's eyes, the ranger recognized his words as a rash proclamation. Winter in the great Crystal Mountains could prove a more formidable foe than any ancient dragon! But, even with that discomforting thought so clear in mind, the ranger saw no choice before him, and he put up a firm, unyielding visage against the wave of reasonable protests he suspected Brielle would soon send his way.

"I know ye mean to go this day," was what she said, and quietly, both her words and tone surprising Belexus. "I'm only wishing that I might be going with ye."

He studied her some more, saw the pain in her green eyes, a resignation that showed she did not like the choice, but understood the necessity of it.

"But I canno' go," Brielle went on. "Me home's not safe from Morgan Thalasi, not yet, and I'm fearing, too, that I'd be of little help to ye, to anyone, outside me domain."

The way in which the words came forth, a great and rushed release, torn by truth from Brielle's very heart, showed Belexus that she dearly wanted to join him, desperately wanted to remain by his side, friends and allies, but that she could not. He understood that she had thought long and hard on the dilemma, probably had lain awake throughout the night in search of some solution.

But there was none, Brielle knew, and the ranger knew, as well. Brielle could not go off into the Crystal Mountains now, with the dark shadow of Morgan Thalasi still lurking about, with the deep wound to the domain of magic and hordes of talons running wild in the west. Brielle's place was Avalon, and no other, and only her heart and hopes could go out with the ranger. She would not try to dissuade him, though, he realized with some surprise.

"I'll say not a thin' to me Father, nor to any other rangers," Belexus explained, trying to offer some comfort, at least. "Nor will Arien Silverleaf know o' me going. The task is for meself, and for none other."

"Seeming a bit foolish to me for ye to be off on such a quest without a one to help ye," Brielle said dryly. "Ye might trip in a hole and lay out with yer leg broken until the cold steals yer life."

Belexus smiled at her concern, and understood that it was not without basis. Yet there was only one whom he could have trusted to go with him, only one who had been close enough to him to stand beside him through such a dangerous quest, and that one, Andovar, was dead. "I'll not trip," he said with a casual chuckle, but it was obviously a strained laugh.

Brielle nodded and moved closer. "Arien would go beside ye," she said. "The eldar of Lochsilinilume would see the quest as a way he could help in these times dark, a way he might be mending his own heart for the death o' Sylvia."

The words almost convinced the usually stubborn Belexus to run off and ask Arien. He had seen Arien's face, seen the grief, as profound as his own, when the elf lord had learned that his dearest daughter, Sylvia, his only child, had been killed and taken by the flood of the great river, had followed the same cold trail as Andovar. If the quest for the sword would bring to Arien the same hope of inner peace that it promised to Belexus, then how could he deny the elf lord that chance?

He had to deny it, he reminded himself, because if Arien went along, then so too would many elves, refusing to allow their eldar to walk off into such extreme danger without them. Then so, too, would Ryell, Arien's closest friend. And if the dragon wakened in all its terrible wrath, could all the elves of Lochsilinilume, could all the rangers of Avalon, could all the army of Calva, hope to contain its power? How many then would be devoured, and likely in a futile quest? If that chilling scenario ever came to pass, Belexus hoped that he would be among the first to die, for surely, if he lived to see the fall of those who accompanied him on this quest that he viewed as his own, his grief would multiply a hundred times over, and his life, and death, would forever be without hope.

"I go alone, because I must," he said quietly into the witch's face, for Brielle had moved very close to him, was standing right before him, her warm breath tickling his neck.

Her reply was a kiss, a long and sweet kiss, a passionate kiss, for luck and farewell.

It surprised Belexus, but only for a moment, and then he let his sword fall to the ground and wrapped his powerful arms about Brielle's lithe form, hugging her close, kissing her all the while, not letting go, wanting to never, ever let her go. They made love that morning for the first—and, they both feared, for the last—time, a joining that had been long anticipated by Belexus, and long feared by Brielle. When Belexus had come to her after the battle with the wraith, with Andovar dead and his own grievous wounds threatening to take him, Brielle had saved him with sympathetic magical healing—as intimate a bond as this lovemaking. She had gone into Belexus' soul to find his emotional hurts and take them from him, to restore to him hope that he could better fight against his physical wounds. She had gone in there, to that private place, and had seen clearly his feelings for her.

She had been surprised, though she had truly suspected all along that the prince of rangers loved her. But the depth of that love was amazing to her, for he loved her as deeply as Jeffrey DelGiudice had loved her. And what had surprised her even more was her own private response. Yes, she did love Belexus, but that realization carried with it more than a little guilt, for though Jeffrey DelGiudice had been gone from her for a score of years, she had given to him her heart, and he had given to Brielle her only child, Rhiannon, the lasting love.

But when Brielle made love to Belexus that soft and quiet Avalon morning, she was able to put aside any feelings of guilt. It was too sweet, too pure, and too real to be denied. She loved Belexus and hated the thought that he would go from her now, but if he went out from Avalon and never returned without this one lovemaking, without the two of them revealing the truth of their feelings for each other, without the dropping of defenses, the ultimate joining . . . That, the witch could not bear.

Later that morning, she walked Belexus to the edge of the forest, the narrow trail that led onto the field of Mountaingate, gateway to the Crystals. And there she kissed him again, softly, and then spun away, twirling in the soft light of morning, her gossamer gown blurring her graceful form, undefining the lines of Brielle until she blended fully into the fog and was gone.

Gone from sight, but Belexus surely took the scent of Brielle, the taste of Brielle, the burning image of Brielle with him as he exited Avalon and started his long journey into the great and towering range.

He was far up the mountain trail, having crossed the narrow field of Mountaingate and passed under the bended telvensil trees, their silvery bark lined with streaks of white, clinging snow, before he was able to clear his thoughts of the witch enough that he might consider the path before him. His travels could well take a month and more, just to get to the lair wherein lay the mighty sword. When Brielle had shown him the image of the glittering sword, her divining had also given him an outward clue of where it might be found: a peculiar outcropping of stone which, when viewed from a particular angle, resembled the profile of an old man. If Belexus could find that ridge of stone, he would be in the vicinity of the dragon's cave.

The Crystals were huge, though, with towering peaks,

many inaccessible, and luck would have to be with him. Perhaps, he feared, the dragon's cave had long been sealed; perhaps he would wind up standing atop it, oblivious and with no way to enter.

The ranger growled the negative thoughts away. He had to try. He owed that, at least, to Andovar, and was certainly duty-bound to attempt it for the sake of all the world. Indeed the task appeared daunting, even overwhelming, but the prize, a weapon that might rid the world of the wraith of Hollis Mitchell, was worth the try.

He was looking for speed and mobility, and thus Belexus had chosen to travel light, carrying only his sword, a pair of daggers and his bow, a pack with extra clothing, a warm blanket, and a waterskin strung about his neck and shoulder. His food, he would catch along the way, as he would build shelters from whatever material Nature offered to him. He was a ranger of Avalon, a prince among rangers, and if he had been dropped naked into the middle of the wintry Crystals, Belexus was confident that he could survive. Belexus believed that, with all his heart, and that was his greatest advantage.

So his progress that first day was remarkable indeed, ascending the southern face of the first mountain in line, passing by the entrance to the secret tunnels that snaked to the hidden valley, the Silver City of the elves known as Lochsilinilume, or in the more common tongue, Illuma. And then higher, the ranger went, seeking his first vantage point of mountain majesty, that he might lay his initial course more clearly.

He came upon a plateau on the northeastern face of the peak shortly before sunset, with the mountain range spread wide before him, mica rivers and fields of ice that gave the Crystals their name glittering in the slanting late-day rays. Belexus put down the wood he had collected on his travels, but he did not immediately start a fire, suffering the cold winds for the sake of the splendid view. He hadn't been up in the mountains often, just a handful of times over the course of the years between the Battle of Mountaingate—wherein an open alliance and friendship had formed between the humans and the elves—and the larger war with Thalasi's talon minions. On those occasions, he had hunted with Arien Silverleaf and his daughter Sylvia, and with Andovar. This was the ranger's first high view of these peaks since the war with Thalasi, and now it left a bittersweet taste in his mouth, full of fond memories, but with regrets in the clear knowledge that two of his companions on those previous occasions had been lost to him forever.

The ranger leaned back against the mountain wall, eyes locked on the view, seeing the present majesty as he was imagining the past. He found peace there, a serenity against which he had to guard closely, lest he fall asleep before he set his fire, in this open exposure where the mountain night winds would not ever let him wake.

With a great sigh nearly an hour later, Belexus forced himself up and went to the wood. The wind had begun to swirl, but not too strong, and the wall of the plateau was neither flat nor even, affording some protection. Just as the ranger put flint to steel, something distant caught his eye, a soaring form crossing an open expanse in the not-quite-dark sky, a black silhouette that quickly disappeared against the dark face of yet another mountain.

Belexus straightened, then went into a cautious crouch, slipping to the edge of the flat stone, then falling flat to his belly. He peered intently out from the ridge as he slowly readied his bow. Likely it had only been a bird, a large one to be sure, but with thoughts of a dragon cave fresh in his mind, the ranger was certainly more than a bit wary!

He continued his scan for several minutes, as the sky

continued to darken. Belexus blew a deep sigh; soon it would be so dark that even if the flying creature came out from behind a mountain background, it would remain invisible to him. A few minutes later, with the sky turned to blackness, he found himself faced with another decision: to retreat back down the mountain or to risk his current position, for though he would not see a flying creature's approach, it would certainly spot the glow of his fire.

"A bird," Belexus decided, and so he went to the kindling and struck his flint to steel, and soon had a warm fire blazing. He wrapped his blanket about him and put his back to the mountain wall, thinking to get some much-needed sleep, but he also placed his trusted sword, unsheathed, across his lap, and had his strung bow, arrow resting across string and wood, right beside him.

He sensed the approach soon after, his eyelids just beginning to droop, and all sleepiness flew from him in a rush of adrenaline. He forced himself to hold steady, though, slumped against the wall, and kept his eyes half closed, feigning sleep, with one hand clenched tightly about his sword hilt.

Up Belexus sprang as the creature glided in, his signature cry of "Oi Avalon!" issuing forth, his mighty sword flashing in the firelight.

And then Belexus nearly toppled in surprise, as Calamus, winged lord of horses, lighted easily on the plateau, stomping his hooves with delight at the sight of his ranger friend.

Belexus blinked many times as he viewed the unexpected, and not unappreciated, sight, as he noted the bulging saddlebags draped across the magnificent steed's back, right behind the saddle in which Belexus had sat so many times. He went to the pegasus at once, stroked the muscled neck and flank, then moved to the saddlebags and was not surprised at their contents of wrapped foodstuffs and warm clothes.

"Brielle," Belexus reasoned, for someone had saddled the pegasus, and no one in all the world held a closer bond to Calamus than the Emerald Witch. "Brielle sent ye."

Calamus snorted and stomped a hoof.

The ranger smiled warmly, glad for the company this cold night—but company he meant to keep only for this night. He had considered asking Calamus to accompany him—of course he had!—before he had ever left Avalon, but like his decision not to ask any of the rangers or the elves, Belexus had determined that he could not accept such a responsibility. Surely the pegasus would make his journey far easier—though he doubted he could fly very high for any stretch of time in the cold mountain air—but if anything ill befell the pegasus, Belexus would never be able to forgive himself. And dragons were known to prize horseflesh!

"I'll take yer bags," the ranger said. "And glad I am for the help. But in the morning light ye're to go back to Avalon, me friend, back home where ye belong."

The pegasus snorted defiantly, and the stomp of hooves came more insistent now, and surely not in agreement with the ranger's plan.

Belexus let it go at that, an argument to be resolved in the light of morning. He tended the fire, then went back to the wall and slept soundly, confident of his companion's diligence.

Calamus proved no more agreeable in the morning, and was not about to leave, even when Belexus tried to push the winged horse from the ledge. After nearly an hour of the futile dispute, the ranger finally relented. It would be foolhardy to take a horse into the rough mountain terrain, but a pegasus could go almost anywhere. And in thinking about it without the blinding influence of his stubborn pride, Belexus had to admit again that Calamus might certainly prove valuable on this expedition, the pegasus taking him faster and higher than he could ever hope to climb. How much easier might his search be from the vantage point of the flying horse's back?

"So ye win," he admitted to the pegasus, though he was really speaking to distant Brielle. He loaded up the saddlebags, climbed into the saddle, and urged the pegasus away, soaring high through the cold mountain air.

Unbeknownst to steed and rider, a third creature, a large raven, watched their departure with more than a passing interest.

Chapter 6

The Black Warlock

HE STOOD IN the driving rain on the narrow walkway overlooking the muddy courtyard. This was his home, his bastion, Talas-dun, that he, with powerful magics, had pulled up from the very stone of these mountains, bending and shaping it to the designs of his mighty will. Talas-dun had stood for centuries, since the time Morgan Thalasi had led the wicked talons, the first mutation of mankind, out of Pallendara, ostensibly so that they could cause no more mischief, but in reality, to breed them and train them and bend them, as he had shaped the stone of Talas-dun to the designs of his will. How like a god Morgan Thalasi had felt then! To bring an entire race under his absolute control! The talons were his pawns: sentient, reasoning creatures that he had transformed into mere extensions of his will. They would not disobey him, even if he told them to leap from a cliff to jagged stones, preferring certain and horrible death above facing the wrath of Morgan Thalasi, the anger of their god.

Because they feared him, feared the Black Warlock, more than they feared Death itself.

There were many of the ugly talons milling about the courtyard now, wandering aimlessly and without the strict discipline that had always been the norm of Talas-dun.

No, not always, the Black Warlock recalled; there had

been one notable lull in discipline before this latest one. When first Thalasi had come back to this place after the disaster at Mountaingate, after Jeffrey DelGiudice had brought forth that terrible weapon from the ancient times and shot him through the heart, he had been a weakened creature indeed. He had stolen the body of Martin Reinheiser, but with that feeble mortal coil came the stubborn and powerful spirit of the dispossessed man. The resultant dual being, Thalasi and Reinheiser in one physical form, so uncomfortable, so out of control of even its simplest bodily movements, had found little power over the talons those first years, those twenty agonizing years. But during all of that troubled period, even after a new generation of talons, one that did not remember Thalasi as he had been, had arisen as Talasdun's primary guard, the creatures had shown the Black Warlock fear, had shown him respect.

A movement along the walkway stirred Thalasi from his recollections. He turned to see a pair of talons walking his way, conversing in their guttural tongue and laughing, looking at each other mostly, and apparently oblivious to the presence of their master.

"Close enough!" the Black Warlock bellowed, and the talons skidded to an abrupt halt and looked up, their eyes wide with surprise.

Thalasi liked that look.

"How dare you disturb me?" The Black Warlock fumed. "I did not summon you."

The larger of the pair held up its arms helplessly, apparently having no excuses. It was obvious to Thalasi that the pair had come upon him quite by accident, that they had no idea he was up here, else they would have chosen a different route.

"Enough!" he cried, though neither talon had uttered a sound. "I care not for excuses. You," he said, indicating the larger, "throw your companion from the wall as penalty for your insolence!"

The larger talon's face screwed up curiously. It looked from Thalasi to its companion, who stood tense, eying it and the Black Warlock nervously. The big brute grunted and whispered something, then the pair, with a unified shrug, simply turned around and walked back the way they had come.

Thalasi tried to call out after them, but he was too stunned, too stupefied, to even get a meaningful word out of his mouth. He clutched the banister, his bony knuckles whitening even more than their normal, pallid hue, and trembled violently. How he trembled, explosive rage building within him!

But it was an empty threat of explosion, he knew, a firecracker's pop where once such anger might have leveled a mountain. Thalasi, perhaps more than any of the other wizards of Aielle, had been wounded in the war, had been struck hard in that special place wherein wizards found and fostered their power. Across the lands, Brielle used her pool for divining, Rhiannon spoke often with the birds, Istaahl worked with masons and magic to construct a new tower, and Ardaz often assumed the forms of various animals, that he might get about his mountainous home more easily. But all of those spells, even the simplest, were beyond Morgan Thalasi at that time. He could see only with his physical eyes, could speak only with creatures that used the same language as he, could build nothing, save what his feeble hands could place together, and could take no form other than this one: a battered, frail body, appearing more skeletal than human, face hollowed and eyes sunken so deeply that they appeared as black holes in a gray skull.

Yes, it was a pitiful thing that he had become, a weakling. And worst of all for the Black Warlock, the talons were apparently beginning to catch on to the truth of it. And unlike the last time Thalasi had been wounded, the talons now held a particular, seething grudge. Many thousands of them had been slain in the fight at the Four Bridges, the failed invasion of Calva.

The fight that Morgan Thalasi had demanded and commanded.

The Black Warlock looked back along the walkway where the pair of talons had disappeared. Now they were showing outright disrespect; before long, he realized, their lack of respect would become open hostility, and their outrage would find its sharp focus on the being who had led them to disaster.

The unseasonable rain poured down in wind-blown sheets, drenching Thalasi's red robes, weighing them heavily on the bowed shoulders of the Black Warlock.

The wizard Ardaz, the famed Silver Mage of Lochsilinilume, sat with the lord of Illuma, Arien Silverleaf, on a high ledge overlooking the enchanted valley of the elves. The chill wind whipped the wizard's voluminous blue robes about him and took his great pointed cap from his head again and again, and only the quick reactions of the elf lord, sitting downwind from Ardaz, prevented the great cap from spinning out from the ledge and soaring high and far on wild breezes.

"Benador continues the fight at the river," Arien said, snapping his arms up to catch the hat for the fourth time in as many minutes. He handed it over to Ardaz, and sighed when the sometimes-foolish wizard plopped it right back on his bushy head, where it was sure to be soon blown off once more. "Work will be completed on the bridge soon enough, and Benador will be swift across to the western fields at the head of his mighty cavalry."

"Well, he is king, you know," Ardaz replied dryly. "That is his job, of course, ha ha!"

Arien put a sidelong glance over the wizard, then slapped his hand on Ardaz' head as another gust threatened the cap.

"Wouldn't be much of a king, after all, if he let talons run wild all over his farmlands!" the wizard went on, apparently oblivious to the elf lord's hand. "Oh, I daresay, that would not do at all. Not at all, no, no."

"I, too, am a king," Arien replied somberly, drawing the wizard's gaze.

Ardaz screwed up his face as he looked over the stoic elf, Arien's long and raven black hair blowing in the breeze, his eyes staring below, to Illuma perhaps, but more likely to nothing at all. The wizard briskly rubbed his bushy beard, gray and flecked with white so that it had an overall silvery appearance. For all his outward foolishness, Ardaz was a wise and sympathetic friend. He understood Arien's dilemma here, the fact that the eldar of Lochsilinilume and his followers were back in the safety of their mountain home, though the wider world outside the elven valley was far from secured. The elves had suffered terribly in the battle with the Black Warlock; more than half of those who had gone to the Four Bridges to battle beside King Benador did not make the trip home, but though the swollen river had ceased the heavy fighting, and though the wizards had battered Thalasi and sent him scrambling to the west, the war, as Arien had said, was not yet won. Arien, torn by grief for his daughter, and on advice from Ardaz and Ryell, his closest elven advisor, had led the remainder of his battered people home, but even though that course seemed prudent—it made sense that Thalasi might strike out in smaller groups while he tried to reorganize his main host, and that some of those raiding bands might find their way to Illuma Vale—it hurt the proud and angry elf profoundly to be sitting here idly while the battle raged, while other swords sought vengeance for his lost daughter.

"Yes, yes," the wizard spouted on sudden impulse. "You are a king. But, hah, you have no western fields to reclaim! Or to defend, for that matter, ha ha."

The remark didn't have the impact Ardaz had hoped for. Arien seemed not relieved, but even more wounded.

"Well, you don't," Ardaz said more quietly. "You have your borders, and they are secured now, and that is your duty, of course it is. Oh, I daresay, Arien, play your part and let Benador and the far more numerous—and more prolific—Calvans, play theirs. The Calvans could not have asked for such a helping hand as your people gave to them, could not have asked for such a sacrifice, for any sacrifice, from a people they had persecuted for years, after all! Oh, I daresay, your guilt is not so well placed. Oh no, not at all!"

"It pains me," the elf said wearily, looking back over the small valley, the one little piece of Ynis Aielle that truly belonged to the Illumans. The valley was full of wide-limbed telvensil trees, shining silver against the white snow though their leaves had long ago drifted away. Most of the great trees supported crafted and decorated houses, all with sweeping balconies and many-pointed rooftops. Grander still were the stone houses on the ground, and Arien's was the grandest of all, shining with gemstones, edged by intricate, crafted gutterwork, gargoyles of young elves at play and the like, and with a roof with too many angles to count, and dozens of chimneys, all puffing out lazily drifting smoke and the promise of a warm hearth. A white carpet of snow now covered the thick grass of the valley, but that did little to slow the elves in their perpetual dance, a dance that continued even though so many of them were gone. A hundred elves at least were out and about now, though the day was cold, enjoying the company of their neighbors, enjoying the simple pleasure of being alive.

"Of course it pains you," Ardaz replied after a long silence, his voice quieter now, calmer and more in control. "Thalasi's force is scattered now, and in many ways, more dangerous. More unpredictable. We do not know now where they will strike, and if Illuma Vale is to be a target—and surely Thalasi hates no place more than Illuma Vale!—then Arien Silverleaf must be here with his people. Send a minor force back to Benador, if that is your will, as a symbol of Lochsilinilume's support, but you, as eldar, must remain here with your people, steadfast in your protection of your home, and of the Crystals."

The wind gusted again, sending the wizard's great hat flying away, and Arien, with typical agility, snatched it in midflight. "You are wise, my old friend," he said, rising. "And if I am to respect my elders, you are one of only four who qualify for that title."

Ardaz glanced up at Arien, surprised by that statement, and found the elf lord smiling at his own joke.

"So I must stay," Arien continued, the mirth passed. "I must remain in this, my home, though Fahwayn surely thirsts for talon blood, though Sylvia's spirit calls out to me for vengeance."

"No, Arien," Ardaz interrupted. "No, no, I say! Your daughter died content; her spirit is not restless. Content, my friend, that her role was well played, that the defense held and that wicked Thalasi was beaten back. That was Sylvia's choice, as it would have been Arien's choice if he had been in Sylvia's place."

"Would that Arien had been in Sylvia's place," the elf lord remarked, and to Ardaz he seemed very old and very weary indeed at that moment. He nodded and handed back the hat, then began the long and slow descent down the invisible stairway that would take him back to the valley floor.

Ardaz watched him go, knowing well that the light would never shine quite the same way as before in Arien Silverleaf's eyes.

With a deep sigh, a profound regret for all that was gone, Ardaz put his hat back on his head, and when the wind took it immediately, the wizard just getting his hands up to catch hold of it before it sailed miles away, he decided it was time to go in. He moved through an angled slot in the wall, cunningly concealed so that from below it appeared as no more than a crack, into a snow-filled lea. At the back end of the small clearing, which seemed smaller because of the towering sheer walls that encompassed it, stood Brisen-ballas, the wizard's tower, carved right into the side of the mountain, its darkened windows seeming as eyes and a nose, its great door as a mouth.

Ardaz paused as he headed for that door, hearing the imperative cry of a raven. He looked up as the bird descended swiftly, coming to light on the wizard's shoulder. The creature was purring even as the transformation commenced, a most curious thing for a raven to do, but then it was not a raven, but a cat, a shining black cat, wrapping herself comfortably about the wizard's neck and shoulders.

"Oh, Desdemona," the wizard complained. "Out causing trouble again, no doubt, you nasty little puss. Can I expect a hawk to come swooping in here on your tail?"

What passed between them then was more telepathy than speech, though the cat uttered a few "meows," mostly for effect.

"How very odd," Ardaz remarked as he considered the news, scratching at his bushy hair and beard. "How very odd." And with that, he pulled the complaining cat from his shoulders and threw her high into the air. With a shriek, Desdemona became a bird again, and so did Ardaz, a great and strong eagle, bidding his little raven companion to show him the way.

Thalasi sat in his throne room late that night, the storm raging outside, heavy rains and bright flashes of crackling lightning. His throne seemed too large for him somehow—both figuratively and literally—as if his corporeal form had shriveled as his powers had become less substantial. He had no talon guards stationed outside the room, as had always been the norm; the Black Warlock wouldn't risk putting any talons near to him at this time, when he was so vulnerable, when any of the wretched, warlike creatures could strike him down like the feeble old man he had become.

Thalasi's hand strummed absently on the throne, then he reached out to brush his fingers against the smooth wood of his staff, the Staff of Death, taken from the most ancient tree in Blackemara, the very heart of the swamp. With this staff, Thalasi had brought back the wraith of Hollis Mitchell, had battled and defeated Charon himself for the control of the dead man's spirit. If that feat alone wasn't amazing enough, Thalasi had then animated simple zombies, further extensions of his dominating will, further proof of his power over Death itself. He could feel the power within the staff still, brimming, tingling to his sensitive touch.

He had thought of using it again—he felt that he could safely do that, since the power would come not from him, but from the staff—but he feared the potential results. Surely another wraith such as Mitchell would laugh in his face if he tried to command it, would tear him and grab him and bring him down to the realm of Death, where Charon waited eagerly to pay back Thalasi for that past defeat. Even minor zombies, the Black Warlock feared, would be above his control, would devour him and mindlessly wander the world.

Still, despite the potentially dire consequences, the Black Warlock was thinking again of using the staff. His situation worsened by the day, he knew; talons were whispering about replacing him, and if they tried, he would have no counter, not even a bluff, to deter them.

Thalasi looked out the throne room's small window, to the storm, and viewed the storm, then, not as an unseasonable but natural event, but as a signal to him, a sign that the time had come. He took up the staff and gathered his robes and heavy cloak, then went out from the throne room and out from Talas-dun altogether, trying hard not to be seen—not so great a feat considering that the talons were all busy at their nightly orgies.

He made his shaky way along the rain-slickened stone paths, buffeted by the winds, his black cloak whipping about the red robes. Soon he came to a place out of sight of the black fortress, a place where the talons of Talas-dun buried their dead—when the talons even bothered to bury their dead.

Thalasi glanced around nervously at the many broken markers, at the mounds of raw, wet earth that showed newer grave sites. It was to one of these that he went, reasoning that a more recently dead talon would be easier to raise. He clutched the staff tightly, brought his lips to it, and tried to look inside of its power, to see if he was playing the fool. He almost left the cemetery, more than once, but the one image that kept coming to mind was the pair of talons on the walkway that afternoon, the pair that had disregarded him, had ignored him. No, he was no longer truly the master of Talas-dun; he was the buffoon, the sideshow for the benefit of the talon audience. And when that merciless audience grew bored . . .

Thalasi stamped the staff upon the earthen mound, released a bit of its energy, crackling like small arcs of black lightning into the dirt. "*Benak raffin si,*" he called softly, taking care not to look at the marker of the grave, not even to think of the talon's name, fearing that the sentient spirit of the thing might come forth with the body. He called again, and he could feel the magical enhancement of his voice, the power of the staff joining with his mortal coil.

And how grand it felt! That energy, that power, bathing him, strengthening him, though it was still a mere shadow of the glories Morgan Thalasi had once known.

Then he was done, and for a long while there was only the wind and the rain.

And then, finally, the mound of wet dirt stirred. Thalasi backed from it gingerly, then fell back yet another step when a gray hand, flesh holed by rot and filled with maggots, reached up through the ground and clawed at the empty air. Another hand came forth, and the pair found a hold upon the ground and pushed up the head and shoulders. And then the creature stood, shrugging away the dirt, barely a yard from the Black Warlock, who was poised to strike at it, and to take flight if that failed.

A long moment passed; even the storm seemed to hold quiet then, awaiting the rush, the charge of the undead predator.

It did not come. The zombie stood impassively, staring at the Black Warlock, the holder of the staff, through one dull eye and one empty socket.

Staring at its master.

When Thalasi discovered the truth, he could hardly contain his joy. With the staff, he had again found power—true, controllable power—and the zombie obeyed his every word without the slightest hesitation. Confidence mounting, the Black Warlock moved to another mound and brought forth a second zombie, then to an older grave, where a skeleton arose to his will.

Before the next dawn, he made his way back to Talasdun, an army of undead at his heels. As fortune would have it, he encountered a talon just inside the castle's open gate, the same talon that had been on the walkway the previous afternoon. Thalasi took particular delight, for it was the larger of the pair, the one who had disregarded a direct command. The horrified creature backed against a wall, hands waving, eyes bulging, and its voice surely caught deep in its throat.

With a thought and a shrug, Thalasi set the nearest zombies upon it, and when it was dead, the Black Warlock took up his unholy staff and, just for effect, raised that talon, too, into an undead state. "One way or another, you will obey me," he chuckled into the dead thing's blank stare.

Yes, he meant to teach the living talons, his pets, a few new tricks this day.

Chapter 7

The Witch and the Wraith

HIS SLEEPY EYES opened wide when the young half-elf awoke and realized that he was alone in the encampment; he should have known better, he believed, should have realized the depth of his companion's despair. And in these dangerous times, Bryan knew, such black despair often translated to foolishness.

Rhiannon had gone off alone, much as he had the previous night. To face danger, no doubt, probably to prove something that didn't need proving.

Bryan cursed himself repeatedly as he straightened his clothes and gathered up his other belongings. It was his fault, he believed, for he had stung Rhiannon profoundly with his words about the diminishing power of magic.

Now, if anything happened to her, he knew that he would never be able to forgive himself.

The young warrior found the witch's trail easily enough in the fresh covering of light snow. She was moving north—not surprisingly—out of the Baerendils, to the wider fields where talons were still thick for the fighting.

Bryan made fine progress that morning, running as often as walking, for there were few options along the rocky and broken terrain. Rhiannon was obviously traveling north, to the foothills, at least, and there were no more than a handful of trails she might follow that way, and the light snow, so revealing of even the young witch's light step, kept Bryan running fast and true. Still, he knew that he was not appreciably gaining on her, and that fact worried him greatly. For as they came to the lower foothills, and to the fields beyond that, Rhiannon's direction options would widen, and as they moved from the rock walls sheltering the lower mountain trails, the wind would erase the footprints. By the end of that day, Bryan was out of the mountains, following the one main road crossing this region to the west, the direction indicated by the last signs he had seen of Rhiannon. He trotted along, glancing side to side often and hoping that if the witch did leave the road, she would not be so far away that he could not see her, or that she could not see him.

The sun was setting in his face, and silhouetted against the pink background, the half-elf spotted a wagon, rolling along slowly. Bryan ducked low in a crouch but continued on, settling his shield comfortably on his arm and drawing forth his sword. These dark days, any wagons in the western fields meant talons, and only talons. Bryan wondered if Rhiannon had passed this band, or if, perhaps, she was off to the side of the road even then, scrutinizing the passing monsters, devising plans to destroy them.

Or, perhaps, on a darker note, if she had already encountered them, if she had met a foe beyond her diminished capabilities . . .

Spurred by that last thought, the half-elf put his head down and charged off in a dead run. Fortunately for the desperate Bryan, the two talons outside the wagon were experiencing more than a little difficulty with their burdened beasts, for a pair of great and huge lizards, and not horses or oxen, pulled the wagon, a task for which the reptiles were obviously not overly fond.

The wagon was covered, its back open, so Bryan, not

too concerned that either of the obviously busy drivers would turn about to regard him, veered out to the side instead of approaching from directly behind. Quiet as death, the stealthy Bryan slipped up to the back corner, took a deep and steadying breath, then leaped to the footboard on the wagon's tail and, in the same fluid motion, hauled himself in.

He tumbled into the midst of three very surprised talons.

Bryan's sword flashed out to the right, slashing one talon across the chest. He punched out with his shield to the left, staggering the brute on that side, then, with a quick turn of his wrist, brought his sword thrusting ahead, impaling the middle of the group. A second swipe to the right, a bit higher this time, throat level to the sitting, lurching talon, finished the creature, and then a second slam with the shield dropped the last of the three to the floor, dazed.

"What is you fighting 'bout now?" one of the drivers growled, and the talon finished with an even louder roar, one of sheer agony, as Bryan's sword came through the material of the wagon cover, slipped through a crease in the back of the seat, and then deep into the talon's spine.

The wagon lurched as that driver slumped and its companion, whooping in fright, let go the reins and leaped from the seat, stumbling and scrambling in the wet mud and snow.

Bryan was already exiting the back of the wagon by then, moving methodically, casually, leaping to the ground and landing in a trot, stringing his bow as he went. When he came around the corner, he spotted the talon, twenty feet away and running, and foolishly moving in a straight line. An easy shot, one that Bryan gladly took, and the talon lay facedown, the snow turning red about its squirming form.

Bryan didn't bother to go over and finish the task quickly. He went back into the wagon, to the shield-slammed beast, and propped the still-groggy creature up against the sideboard. He slapped it lightly across the face, even splashed it with water, prompting it back to lucidity.

"I seek a friend," the half-elf growled into the talon's face. "Have you seen her?"

The creature looked at him incredulously; impatient, Bryan promptly smacked it across the face. "Have you seen her?" he asked again, more forcefully. A movement to the side caught his attention, and he couldn't have asked for a better chance to accentuate his point, to show the level of his hatred to this ugly, wretched thing. A quick maneuver put him over the squirming talon, the one he had swiped twice in the initial fight, and he promptly shifted his sword tip to the thing's temple, pinning its head.

"Have you seen my friend?" the half-elf asked calmly, slowly, emphasizing each word.

"Duh?"

With a snarl, Bryan drove his sword through the squirming talon's skull.

The last of the bunch breathed hard, in terrified gasps, when the half-elf moved again right in front of it. "I'll not belabor the point," Bryan said evenly. "I seek a friend, a very powerful friend, and if you do not help me, I shall surely make your death slow and painful."

"It go to Corning," the talon blurted suddenly. "The great beast moves to Corning, so travelers say."

"It?"

"Great beast," stammered the talon. "Much fear."

Bryan nodded; it made sense that the dim-witted creatures would view mighty Rhiannon in such a way, and that description was likely to be the best this talon would offer. With a sudden jolt, the half-elf's shield arm came forward again, smashing the talon's face, and when it didn't lose consciousness, Bryan, who showed no mercy to talons, finished the beast with a single sword thrust. He retracted the blade and wiped it on the dying creature's clothing, then moved back outside the wagon. He entertained the thought of using the cart for a moment, but just for a moment, figuring that he would be far too obvious and vulnerable rolling along the open road, and also far from secure with the temperament of the giant and fierce lizard team. He didn't dare go near to the dangerous things, even though they appeared securely harnessed. Rather, he stepped back and drew out his bow and shot each of them through the head until they lay dead upon the ground. Then he retrieved his arrows, finished off the one remaining talon, the one he had shot as it fled, and started his run again, this time with a specific destination in mind, a place that Bryan of Corning knew all too well.

She had been here only once, and on that occasion, Corning had been in desperate preparation for an imminent and overwhelming invasion. Yet even that frenzied scene of screaming folk and frightened children seemed far more pleasant to the young witch than the blasted image of Corning now, for even the grip of winter could not begin to erase the visual memory the place revealed: the wake of Morgan Thalasi's devastating passage. Nearly every building was no more than a burned-out shell, with only its stone walls standing, peaked on two ends, skeletons like the picked bones of the thousands of dead who littered the fields outside of Corning, who littered the streets and the parapets of those few sections of the city wall that had not been flattened. The visual stain of the blood was gone, covered by the snow, but the smell remained, sickly sweet, conjuring images of a massacre.

The predominance of elongated skulls, the sloped foreheads of talons, showed the witch that more talons by far had fallen in the desperate battle for Corning than human—or elven, the witch reminded herself, thinking of Meriwindle—defenders, but if that number had been a hundred to one, a thousand to one, the loss of beautiful Corning would not have been worth it. Corning had once been the second city of Calva, behind only glorious Pallendara itself. It was a place birthed in war and built for the defense of the western fields, but in the centuries of peace the region had known before the return of Thalasi, Corning had grown beyond its pragmatic roots, expanding into something far more wonderful, an expression of artisans and craftsmen, a place of wonderful sprawling gardens and decorated houses.

Now it was only a burned-out skeleton, a collection of walls and bones for the ages. What might someone uncovering those relics in a future age think of Corning, Rhiannon wondered? What riddles would these bones—house, defender, and talon—present? Would the world even remember the scourge of Morgan Thalasi then, and his attempt to invade Calva? Would the world remember Belexus and Andovar, King Benador and Bryan of Corning, and all the others who gave so much to beat back the evil tide of the Black Warlock? Given the recent revelations about the waning of magic, Rhiannon feared that it would not, that all of this would pass into history, to be distorted perhaps, if not altogether forgotten, by those seeking to twist the tales to fit their own personal agendas.

The myriad of thoughts that assailed her as she looked upon the ruins, in themselves, seemed more than a little curious to Rhiannon. She was barely more than twenty years of age, with little experience in the ways of mankind, in the history of mankind. How, then, and more important, why, were such concerns suddenly so paramount to her?

With a deep breath, she shook all the curious thoughts and the questions of them away, and concentrated instead on the task at hand, the grim business that had brought her to Corning. The source of the darkness was close now, she knew, somewhere within the walls of Corning, perhaps, or at least in sight of the wall. Perhaps in sight of her.

She waded through the piles of bones, to the burned and battered eastern gate. That sight also was telling, for the main attack had come not from the east, but from the west. The Black Warlock had apparently sent a sizable number of his monstrous troops around the city to cut off any escape by the defenders. Yet even here, even with the main fighting on the other side of the city, the defenders had obviously held well and killed many of the talons.

With a deep breath, the witch moved through the gate, into the city. There she found the bones of humans mingled with those of talons. Piles and piles of bones: broken skulls, skeletons hanging over the parapets, held together by no more than their frozen, ragged clothing. Rhiannon, so sensitive and perceptive, heard the calls of those dead, the shrieks of agony, the mournful laments. She closed her eyes and remembered her own near-death experience, after her magical battle with Thalasi when she had entered the gateway to the nether realm, when she had watched the solemn procession, the endless line, of those slaughtered in the war.

Hardly conscious that she was gasping for breath, the young witch opened her eyes, and there, all around her, she saw them. The ghosts of the Corning battle, so many wandering spirits, were moving about her, apparently oblivious to her. The ghosts of talons and of men, remnants of those who had died here, their energy emptied into the air by the cut of a sword. The pair of talons she had spied upon on the road the night before had spoken of such specters, advising to a group of their wicked kin who had brought their wagon in to the inviting campfire to avoid Corning at all costs.

Indeed, the place was haunted. And even though Rhiannon's experience with the supernatural was far beyond the norm, it took some time before she could comfortably understand that these spirits were no threat to her, were nothing tangible, were nothing that someone who was not sensitive to, or terrified of, such things would even notice.

A movement to the side, a dark shadow slipping behind the stone of a small cottage, tuned her back to the living world. A talon, she supposed, braving the ghost stories in search of easy loot.

Rhiannon started for the spot, but then hesitated; she had noticed the shadow when her eyes were looking into the realm of the dead, when her eyes were watching the ghost dance. If the moving creature was not of that realm, partially at least, would she have even noticed it?

With that warning in mind, Rhiannon turned about and made her way instead to another nearby cottage. She tried to use her insight, her magical nature, to better sense the presence, and she was not surprised, though surely stunned, when she felt that cold darkness again, the one that had touched her in the Baerendils so many miles away. It was here, so close, feeling her presence as keenly as she perceived its own.

Suddenly the young witch wished that she had not left Bryan, wished that she was still far, far away in the mountains, away from the darkness, this darkness that she feared too profound for the light of Rhiannon. She looked back to the eastern gate, measuring the distance and the time it would take her to cross out of Corning. She considered her magical energy, to transform her into something more agile, more quick, or to attempt to teleport, perhaps, though that was surely a difficult spell to enact, even before the waning of magic.

She thought and thought, seeking an escape, her mind a whirl of possibilities.

She heard the evil laughter, and all those thoughts melted away, false hope indeed.

"Morgan Thalasi, I suppose," the young witch said in a loud voice, as calmly as she could manage. "So ye crawled from the field after me and me friends beat ye down . . ."

That last word stuck in her throat as she turned about to see not Morgan Thalasi, but a creature she did not know. It resembled a large man, and certainly a dead one, though the edges of its features constantly blurred, seeming somehow indistinct, as if the thing was not fully of this realm.

Rhiannon did not know its name, and could not know that this perversion, this stain upon the living world, was indeed the creation of Thalasi. She could not know that this creature was all that remained of one of the ancient ones, that this horrid being had once been a companion of her father, torn from the grasp of Death by the Black Warlock.

What she did know, though she did not understand how she could possibly hold such certainty with the thought, was that this creature, this evil unnatural perversion, was the murderer of Andovar.

"Well, what pleasure has fate sent my way?" the wraith of Hollis Mitchell asked, the timbre of its voice matching its unearthly appearance, a supernatural and evilly charged tone that stung the young witch's sensibilities and set her back on her heels.

Rhiannon trembled with rage, not fear. Her mind focused on Andovar, on the record of his death, which was painted indelibly within the features of this horrid creature. She reached into the earth, felt the life there, dormant beneath the wintry blanket, felt the energy there, the strength, and brought it forth. Strands of grass erupted all about the feet of the wraith, pushing through the snow, climbing higher and thicker.

Mitchell hissed as he felt them brush his half-substantial form, as he felt the sting of earth energy, the burning power of life itself. The wraith growled and lifted one foot, but the grass, moving to Rhiannon's will, was quick to wrap about the other foot and leg, twining about them, tighter and tighter.

Now the pain became intense, as searing as anything Hollis Mitchell had ever known. He worked frantically, first by waving his scepter out at Rhiannon, the black flakes filling the air before her and above her, drifting to attack. Then Mitchell went at the grass, raining the black flakes all about it. The earth energy burned at the wraith, how it burned! But wherever one of the mace's black regurgitations hit, that patch of grass shriveled and died, and gradually, the grip lessened.

Rhiannon worked furiously as well, to dodge the perverted snowstorm that Mitchell had put over her. She waved her hands about in the air, summoned the wind to her grasp, and blew many of the flakes away. A couple did get through, though, and the young witch yelped in sizzling pain, the first real physical battle wound she had ever felt.

When at last the deadly storm was passed, Rhiannon looked up to see Mitchell free of the grassy grasp, his constantly wavering form standing amidst a wide patch of death, an enduring black scar upon the earth itself. Again Rhiannon reacted with anger, at the wraith for what it had done, and at herself for involving the sacred earth in her fight. She grabbed at the wind once more and hurled it sharply at Mitchell, the force knocking him back a step.

But the wraith was laughing now, recognizing that the blow could not truly hurt him and coming to understand that this magic-using creature, whoever she might be, was not so strong, was minor indeed compared to Mitchell's former master, or to that cursed witch of Avalon, or even to the Silver Mage of Lochsilinilume, both of whom had so humiliated and wounded him. He pushed back against the windy assault, but gained no ground. Far from worried, the wraith understood that this small woman would tire first, and then he would fall over her, and then she would cry out for mercy. And so they held, pushing against each other, as many seconds passed.

Mitchell used the momentary standoff to consider his adversary. When the grass had sprouted through the snow, he at first had thought that this was Brielle before him in some disguise. But in looking at Rhiannon now, Mitchell knew that that could not be the case. This woman's features were similar to Brielle's: the same shining eyes, though this woman's were blue where Brielle's were green, and the same flowing hair, though this woman's was dark as night, where Brielle's was golden as sunshine. Most telling of all, though, shone the gemstone, a glittering diamond set in the middle of her forehead, for this was her wizard's mark, and it, the wraith knew, she could not alter—neither in size, nor in shape, nor in color.

Brielle's wizard's mark was green, an emerald.

"Who are you?" the wraith asked aloud, pushing

mightily against the witch's wind, and though he gained no ground, he was certainly not losing any.

Rhiannon fumbled through her thoughts for some smart retort, but only growled and intensified her wind. It transformed into a series of gusts then, rather than a steady blow, showing that the witch was growing magically weary.

"Who are you?" Mitchell asked again. "So much like Brielle, you appear, but with only a fraction of her power."

Rhiannon growled again, more loudly, more stubbornly, and the next mighty gust backed the wraith several steps. The young witch thought to turn and run then, for she feared that she had no tools with which to truly hurt this creature, feared that she had overstepped her bounds in coming to meet this blackness.

On came Mitchell in the lull that followed the wave of wind, his ire rising, his patience gone. He didn't know who this witch might be, but he had his suspicions. Above all others in the world, with the sole exception of Belexus, Mitchell hated Brielle. Brielle, who had stolen his kill of Belexus. Brielle, who had reduced his ghost horse to ashes beneath him, dropping the humiliated wraith on his rump. Brielle, the essence of Nature, the epitome of everything that the undead wraith was not. This creature before him, this young witch, was somehow connected to Brielle, Mitchell understood, had been trained in the same school of magic, at least, and he took great comfort in the confidence that his victory here would surely sting the witch of Avalon.

On he came, roaring, accepting the pounding as Rhiannon's frantic wind caused his form to waver, caused the edges of it to stretch thin.

It would not be enough to stop him now, they both knew, and so as Mitchell neared, Rhiannon abruptly released the wind and raced to the side, the sudden cessation causing Mitchell to overbalance.

But not nearly as far as Rhiannon had hoped, and she was just reaching her arms up to the sky, reaching for the power of thunder, that most violent of natural forces, when Mitchell fell upon her, the flakes of his awful mace drifting over her.

She shrieked and tried to run, but her strength seeped away and she stumbled, falling to the ground, looking up at the towering blackness. Looking up at her doom.

A flying form crossed between the pair, rushing, slashing, and the wraith fell away in surprise.

"Foul beast!" Bryan of Corning cried. "Back to Death's land with you!" And on the young warrior came, unafraid, too concerned with Rhiannon to care for his own safety. His sword flashing brilliantly, wildly, snapping past Mitchell's awkward defenses, scoring hit after hit.

"Bryan," Rhiannon breathed, and she was not relieved, for she knew that the reprieve would be shortlived, knew that the wraith would get her, and get Bryan, too. For even combined, even if Belexus and King Benador stood beside them, they were no match for this one.

Thrust and slash went Bryan's sword, followed by a sudden shield rush that halted abruptly, with the elven sword deftly slipping in from under it, taking the wraith in the belly. But there was no sting to that blade, both Mitchell and Bryan soon enough realized. Like all the others, this sword could do the unearthly creature no harm.

And so Mitchell accepted Bryan's hits, soon didn't even lift his arms to block, and soon after that, wasn't even flinching at the half-elf's cunning thrusts, but rather, was laughing and determinedly stalking in.

Rhiannon reached to the heavens, called out with all

the strength she could muster, with all that she had remaining. She felt the energy gathering there, in the clouds, the tingling sensation, coursing down to her waiting grasp, focusing through her lithe form, and then crackling out from her fingertip, a bolt of white lightning, slamming the wraith, blasting through it and smashing the stone of a skeleton cottage. Mitchell went flying into that pile of rubble, tumbling among the broken stones.

Rhiannon stood panting, trying to hold her balance. She nearly swooned when she saw the wraith pick itself up from the ground, laughing all the while, when she saw Bryan rushing in fearlessly, foolishly, his shining sword leading, and when she saw, worst of all, a flick of that dreaded weapon, only a glancing blow on Bryan, but one that nonetheless hurled the young half-elf through the air, to land hard against the stone. He lay on the ground, jerking spasmodically, groaning between violent gasps.

That would have been the end of Bryan of Corning, except that Rhiannon, rightly judging herself to be the wraith's main target, turned and ran, drawing Mitchell behind her. Through the open graveyard that was Corning she ran, stumbling often, forcing herself to her feet by sheer willpower, by the resolution that she would save Bryan, at least.

Mitchell closed with every stride, his taunting laughter assailing Rhiannon, coming closer and closer.

Then she was a bird—somehow she found the energy—flying away, but not so fast that Mitchell could not keep up. On and on they went, through the gates and across the fields. Seconds became minutes, and those turned to hours, and still Rhiannon flew on, and still Mitchell kept up the pursuit. Before long the river was in sight, and there Rhiannon meant to make her escape, praying that

Bryan had recovered enough to flee and hide. She started to fly more swiftly, started her ascent, out of Mitchell's reach, but the wraith had anticipated such a move, and rushed ahead more furiously right before it began, waving his scepter, hitting the witch-turned-bird with a shower of painful flakes.

Her magic failed her; she came down hard to the ground, skidding in the snow. She was up at once, stumbling, crying, in agony and fear, but then he had her, his gray, dead hand clamped about her shoulder, a grasp so deathly cold! And that awful mace waved near to her head, promising a horrible death.

Rhiannon knew no more.

Chapter 8

A Party of Two . . . er, Three . . . er, Four

As HE HAD suspected when he first set out, on foot, from Avalon, Belexus found that he could not fly on Calamus for long stretches. The wind was simply too cold whenever the pair moved from behind the shelter of a rock wall, and while the shaggy pegasus, winter coat in full and strong muscles working hard to cut that wind, didn't complain in any way, the ranger's fingers and toes grew numb far too quickly. More often than not, each flight ended at the first sighting of a potential campsite.

The stoic Belexus remained undaunted, though, and saw a distinct advantage in having Calamus with him, besides the fine company. The high vantage point on Calamus offered the ranger a better opportunity to plot his walking trails, and to keep a good idea of where, exactly, in the seemingly unending mountains, he was; at times, when the inconsistent weather and mountain walls permitted, he could see for miles, and even when the view was not blocked, the ranger's progress in five minutes of flying time with Calamus was often greater than Belexus could manage in half a day of hiking along the winding and treacherous trails.

It took Belexus nearly two full days simply to sort out the best searching pattern. The Crystals were wide and tall, wider than the ranger had ever imagined, and he came to feel that his journey would surely have been folly had Calamus not come to him. Even with the pegasus, he feared that he had months of searching ahead of him, feared that he might pass over the dragon's lair a hundred times and never notice it. Those possibilities would be greatly enhanced, Belexus knew, if he went at the task in a random manner, and so he began sighting out landmarks, odd-shaped peaks or distinctive valleys. He had to be certain where he had been before he could determine where he next should go.

His progress improved, and so did the weather, over the next few days. "We'll have to go down to the lower valley," he announced to Calamus soon after waking, the sky just beginning to brighten around them. They had camped in a sheltered nook, almost a cave, along the southern face of a rocky mountain. They weren't above the tree line, but on this particular summit, a fire or some other disaster had apparently destroyed the foliage, and the earth had washed away before more trees or any sizable scrub could take hold.

"I'm needing food," he explained, and he didn't feel the least bit foolish in talking to Calamus, whom he was certain could understand his every word. To illustrate his point, the ranger held up his pack, which was much lighter now. "Got to thicken me skin against the cold wind."

The pegasus nickered and stamped the ground.

Belexus threw another log on the fire, taking his time, making sure that he was properly fed and warmed before attempting the move. Impatience would be the death of him in the wintry Crystals, he constantly reminded himself, fighting back his eagerness to be through with this part of the adventure, that he might take his revenge on the wraith, that he might truly put his friend Andovar to rest. But this was a place where preparation was needed before every step. Thus, it was midmorning before he had everything packed neatly in the saddlebags and loops of the saddle. Last, he took up his bow and quiver, keeping it handy, as always, when he was up in the air upon his winged steed.

A movement high above, a black speck flitting through the edges of his vision in the empty air, caught his attention just as he was about to mount. In the blink of an eye, he had an arrow set on the bowstring, the heavy bow pulled back to its limit and leveled. He saw the speck again, and then a larger one behind it, way up high but descending rapidly.

The ranger said a prayer to the Colonnae, and to the spirit of the bird, thanking them for bringing bounty to him, perhaps saving him an entire day of foraging through the low valleys.

Down came the specks, up went the bow. The first of the pair, a raven, swerved fast out of sight, but the second, an eagle, continued its direct descent. Belexus thought it curious that the bird of prey had so given up the chase of the smaller bird, and as the eagle drifted lower and lower, moving into range, he wondered just how great a part the Colonnae might be playing in delivering this meal.

Truly Belexus hated to shoot an eagle, that most majestic of hunters. But he could not ignore the growling of his belly or the importance of his quest, and so he took deadly aim, drew back his string, and let fly.

The ensuing squawk, long before the arrow struck home, was not the sound the ranger had expected, nor was the defensive movement, for the eagle, instead of turning fast on wing, broke its stoop and fluttered wildly, and in frenzied movements, its outline became indistinct, wavering, enlarging, shifting shape and color.

The ranger's fearful cry caught in his throat, for before the arrow had closed half the distance, the creature was no longer an eagle but a man, in blue robes and with a bushy white beard and a tall, pointy hat. The wizard flapped his arms frantically, tried to twist and turn, and cried out, "Oh, I daresay!"

The arrow disappeared into that blue jumble, and Ardaz plummeted down nearly fifty feet, to land with a crunch through the icy snow on the exposed ledge not far from Belexus and Calamus.

"By the Colonnae!" Belexus cried, leaping stone in a desperate charge that sent him skidding down the last slippery expanse to tumble into the snow not far from fallen Ardaz. "Oh, but I'm not for knowing!" he cried, pulling himself upright and reaching to turn the fallen man about.

To his ultimate surprise, the wizard hopped to his feet right before him and began frantically straightening his robes.

"Well, that one hurt, of course it did!" Ardaz scolded. "Too old I am, I say, and I am, I am, to be playing in the snow!"

Belexus gawked at him incredulously, hardly believing that the wizard was apparently uninjured, hardly believing that Ardaz was even alive, and hardly believing that he was here, so many miles from his home in Illuma Vale.

Ardaz continued to fumble with his robes, pulling them around his side. There hung the ranger's arrow, caught in the folds of the voluminous garment right where it covered the wizard's backside. Ardaz tugged the arrow free and handed it to Belexus, a disgruntled smirk on his bearded face. Then he reached back to display the robes, or more particularly, the two holes now showing in the thick material.

"Of course, when the wind blows, it will tickle my fancy, I do daresay," the wizard grumbled. "And oh, but where is my hat?" He looked all around, obviously distressed.

Belexus had noted the descent of the tall and pointed cap as well, and he was not happy to inform Ardaz that it had missed the ledge. Given the strong and swirling wind, that could put it anywhere within a mile or two.

Ardaz was fast to the ledge, leaning over so far to peer down that Belexus cautiously moved up to grasp the back of his flapping robes.

"I can fix the robe, oh yes," Ardaz rambled, turning to face the ranger and slapping Belexus' hand away—and when Belexus did let go, the overbalanced Ardaz nearly tumbled from the ledge. "I'm good at that sort of thing, you know, and have had more than my share of practice, I do daresay! But that hat! There's a loss, and I've had it for so long. So very, very long!

"And where is Des, that silly puss?" he continued, hopping all around the ledge, glancing up and to the side. "Magical hat, you know," he offered to Belexus, and then to the wide wind, he shook his fist, then called out, "Desdemona!"

"I thinked ye were—" the ranger began.

"Oh, yes," Ardaz interrupted, snapping his fingers, and he seemed not even aware that Belexus was trying to speak. "Enchanted hat to keep my head warm. Not much plumage up there when I'm an eagle, after all! But no matter; I'll catch my death of cold and wake every talon in the Crystals with my sneezing, no doubt, and then you shall have to kill every one—every one, I say!—in penance for your foolishness."

"Ye weren't . . . I'm not for . . ." Belexus tried again, futilely.

"Of course, I've got a head full now, now don't I?" Ardaz rambled, grabbing at his thick shock of hair, shining more silver than white in the morning light. "Desdemona!"

Belexus started to speak again, thought the better of it, and clapped his strong hands down hard on the wizard's shoulders, settling Ardaz' dangerous movements, and hopefully the wizard's rambling words, as well. Ardaz looked him right in the eye and blinked repeatedly.

"Take ease, me friend," the ranger calmly prompted.

"Would've, would be, would never have not been, if you hadn't shot me," Ardaz replied dryly.

Belexus couldn't hold back his laughter any longer, erupting in a howl, and drawing a scowl from the old man, but one that fast melted as Ardaz, too, joined in the mirth. "Oh, and a good shot, I do daresay!" the wizard roared, reaching around to the twin holes once more. "Right between the drumsticks!"

His laughter flew away as he thought on that last statement for a moment, his face blanching white. "A bit too good," he muttered under his breath.

"Suren I'm glad to be seeing ye, me friend," Belexus said. "But why're ye here, so far from yer home?"

Ardaz snorted. "Not so far from my home as is Belexus of Avalon," he shot back. "And coming of my own powers, instead of forcing a poor cold pegasus out here with me, I do daresay!"

Belexus conceded the point with a nod, not even trying to explain that Calamus had come of his own volition.

"So what is it, what could it be, that might bring a ranger from the forest in midwinter?" Ardaz asked bluntly. "Especially a one who has so taken a fancy to my sister—and you and I, oh yes, we shall talk about that later!"

Belexus blushed fiercely, but the mere mention of Brielle brought warmth flowing through his veins. "A quest," he admitted.

"A quest?" Ardaz echoed, in a somewhat more sober and controlled tone. "Well, well, so the tale gets more interesting. But what quest?" he pressed. "I'm guessing that a hundred hundred could be found in this time of Thalasi, a hundred thousand, I do daresay! Hunting talons, then?"

"I've but one true enemy," Belexus said seriously.

Ardaz snorted again. "One?" he asked skeptically. "I'll show you a thousand more than one. Fly with me to the Four Bridges . . . er, to where the Four Bridges used to be four bridges, with King Benador, and I'll—"

"One enemy," Belexus said again, his voice so grim that it had a sobering effect even on Ardaz. "And when Mitchell's wraith is put to rest, only then will I be looking for me next."

Ardaz nodded and understood. Of course, Mitchell's wraith, the slayer of Andovar. "I beg your pardon if stupid I prove, but are you not going in the wrong direction?" the wizard said, as politely as he could manage. "The wraith, if it even pulled itself from the river, would be far south of here, and likely to the west. Do you mean to circle the world—and it is round, you know—" he added with a wink, "and catch up with the beastie from behind?"

The absurdity of the question might have drawn anger from serious Belexus, except for the subtle reminder that Ardaz had stood beside him in his last encounter with the wraith, had stood shoulder to shoulder on the northernmost of the Four Bridges and, in fact, had sundered the bridge, thus putting Mitchell in the river.

"I seek a weapon," Belexus admitted. "One Brielle has shown to me, the one in all the world, perhaps, that can truly harm the undead demon the Black Warlock has set upon us."

"No settlements up here," the mage reasoned. "Not a

person to be found. A few talons, perhaps, but hardly any possessing such a weapon, I do daresay!"

"Not a settlement," Belexus clarified. "A lair."

"Oo, but I hate that word!" Ardaz replied, shaking his hands and his head vigorously. "A lair. A lair," he said repeatedly, rolling the words off his tongue in a different manner each time, but shuddering with each pronouncement. "Conjures images of dragons and the like. Oo, a lair."

"So it does," the ranger replied evenly.

Ardaz stopped his babbling and stared long and hard at Belexus. "A dragon?" he managed to ask after a long pause, holding his arms outstretched, his hands waving under the edges of his great sleeves, making them appear as ominous wings.

"So says the witch," Belexus answered without hesitation.

"You are going after a sword that rests in a dragon's lair?"

"I seek the one weapon with which I might be paying back me enemy," Belexus answered resolutely, his tone telling the wizard in no uncertain terms that any obstacles standing between him and the sword were unimportant.

"Whip-dragon?" Ardaz asked hopefully, for Belexus had defeated many of those.

"True dragon," the ranger answered.

"Little dragon?" the wizard asked, again with the hopeful grin and tone.

Belexus crossed his arms over his muscled chest and shook his head slowly, side to side.

"Sleeping dragon?"

The ranger shrugged, again as if that were not important.

"Oh, well, let us hope," Ardaz said suddenly, excitedly.

"Us?"

"You and me, of course," the wizard bellowed. "Us. Though you would probably call us 'weselves' or some other such silly thing, what with that silly accent me—my—sister gave to your father and he to you."

"I canno'—" Belexus began.

"See?" Ardaz accused, pointing a finger at the ranger's mouth. "Canno? Canno what? Canno beans?"

"Stop yer babbling," Belexus scolded, understanding that Ardaz might just be trying to confuse the serious issue—and worrying that the wizard might just be being the wizard! "I canno' think to—"

"Stop me. Right," Ardaz finished. "Of course, you *canno'*. I make my own path, you know. One of the agreements with the Colonnae when they made me a wizard, and quite beyond anything you might say or do."

"I'm not asking—"

"Nor am I, nor am I," Ardaz was quick to reply.

The ranger just gave a great sigh and held up his hands hopelessly.

"I will go, I think, and so I will," Ardaz said with finality. "But, oh, first I must, I must, I must, find my hat. What with the hole in the backside, after all. Oh, the draft does tickle! Where, oh where, might it have gone off to?"

Belexus again started to formulate a more reasonable protest against the wizard's intentions, but seeing Ardaz already hopping about the ledge again, searching frantically for his lost hat, the ranger realized that he might as well scream at the mountain wall. "It flew over the ledge," he explained. "Caught in the wind, is me guess, and long from here."

"Would've had it if you hadn't shot me," Ardaz remarked quietly.

"Would'no've shot ye if ye came in announced, or asked for," Belexus replied in the same dry manner.

Ardaz shrugged and began looking once more.

"Come," Belexus bade him, motioning for the wizard to follow him to Calamus. "I need go to the valleys below in any case. Might be that we'll find it along the way."

Down the pair went on the back of the magnificent steed, Calamus seeming to hardly notice the added burden of skinny Ardaz. The wizard complained continually about the wind whistling through the holes against his backside, but his grumbling fell away soon enough, when they spotted a patch of blue on a ledge halfway down the sheer cliff. It proved a tricky maneuver, but one worth making—or, Belexus realized, he'd have to listen to Ardaz complaining forevermore. The ranger brought the pegasus in as close as possible to the ledge and Ardaz, holding Belexus' bow, leaned out to the side, hooked the brim of the hat, and slipped it free of its perch.

The ensuing shriek startled both wizard and ranger as a curled black cat fell out of the hat, plummeting down the cliff. Desdemona was a quick one, though, fast sprouting wings, fur going to feather, and then drifting down lazily, cawing in protest.

"Oh, silly puss," the wizard muttered, and he said it again when they found Desdemona on the valley floor, comfortably curled yet again in the nook of a pine tree root.

The cat didn't even bother to open an eye.

Their hunting took the better part of the day, but Belexus finally brought down a white-tailed deer, and he and Ardaz had a fine meal as they sat around a blazing fire that evening, Calamus standing stoically nearby, Desdemona curled comfortably on the wizard's warm lap.

"I canno' ask ye to come along," the ranger remarked unexpectedly, in all seriousness. " 'Tis me own fight, I say, one I'll be making for me friend."

"Didn't we already have this argument?" Ardaz asked, seeming somewhat confused. He began reciting the words of their previous debate, but got hung up on "canno' " again, and shifted his line of muttering to the recitation of many other funny-sounding ranger speech patterns.

"We had the fight," Belexus finally interrupted after about fifteen minutes of the rambling. "But by me own thinking, we did'no' finish it."

Ardaz sobered and stared him right in the eye. "That the son of Bellerian could be such a fool," the wizard answered with a derisive snort. "And Andovar was Belexus' friend alone, then?"

"I'm not for saying—"

"But you are!" Ardaz retorted, waggling a long and pointy finger the ranger's way. "You are saying that very thing, I do daresay! And putting the wraith out as your enemy alone, though in truth, all the living world should hate the thing. And you'll not find a dragon—a true dragon and not one of those silly whipping things of the swamp—so easy a foe! But easier the dragon will be, I say, if stubborn Belexus has a friend beside him. And a friend with a trick or two, ha, ha! And one who's good at dodging arrows, to boot!

"Or to butt, I suppose," the wizard ended dryly.

"How can I be asking?"

"Who said you should?" Ardaz replied with a derisive snort. "Oh, I'm going, and don't you think you can stop me." He stared at the fire for a moment, then looked up at the crisp night sky. "A dragon," he muttered, suddenly talking more to himself than to Belexus. "Fancy that! Oh, but I'd dearly love to meet one! Wouldn't we, Des?"

Desdemona yawned and stretched, and then, as if the wizard's words had only then registered, opened wide her mouth in a vicious hiss and smacked the wizard across the face, only his thick beard preventing him from showing three bloody lines from fully extended claws.

"Beastly loyal," Ardaz mumbled.

"I'd not be so loyal, meself, if me friend was leading me to the likes of a dragon's lair," Belexus put in.

"Oh, but you would!" Ardaz countered with hardly a thought. "And you shall, and if you live, you shall thank me for the company, ha, ha!"

The ranger started to reply, but found that he had no sincere argument. Of course, if the situation had been reversed, he would go along with the wizard, and, thus, he had to allow Ardaz a similar show of loyalty. That, above anything else, settled the argument in the ranger's mind, and in his heart. He could not deny Ardaz the opportunity to join him in this quest, whose ultimate implications for the good of all Ynis Aielle went far beyond avenging the death of Andovar. "Yer friendship is truly a blessing of the Colonnae," he said in all seriousness.

Ardaz beamed. "Together then!" he said happily. "A party of two."

Desdemona opened a sleepy eye and looked up at him, as if to ask if she had to hiss and swipe again.

"Er, three," the wizard promptly corrected.

Across the way, Calamus snorted and stamped a hoof.

"Four," both ranger and wizard said together, sharing a laugh.

Belexus slept better that night than on any of the previous since he had left Avalon. Ardaz, though, lay awake a long, long while. There weren't many dragons in Ynis Aielle—fortunately! The few about had been created by evil Morgan Thalasi centuries before, but fortunately, they were not an overly fruitful lot, more concerned with making a meal of each other and stealing treasure than propagating the line. On those rare occasions that a meeting of dragons did produce an offspring—when the female won the inevitable fight after mating—that young dragon would quickly go out into the world in search of its own treasure hoard, and either meet its end at the claws of another dragon, at the end of a wizard's lightning bolt—Brielle was particularly adept at putting an end to the unnatural things—or, in one notable case, at the end of a warrior's sword. Belexus was perhaps the only mortal man alive who had ever seen a dragon and survived; certainly he was the only one who had ever killed a dragon.

But that had been a young one, barely larger than the pegasus the ranger now rode. If Brielle's magic had located the sword in the lair of a dragon deep in the great Crystals, then likely it was an ancient wyrm, one of the originals Thalasi had created as a scourge to the world. And given the weakening of magic, a full-grown dragon might well prove to be the most powerful creature in all of Ynis Aielle.

Ardaz did not sleep so well.

making a meal of each other and stealing treasure rather than propagating the line. On those rare occasions, rare a meeting of dragons (perhaps twice a century)—when the female won the inevitable fight after mating—that young dragon would quickly go out into the world to search its own treasure hoard, and either meet its end at the claws of another dragon, at the end of a wizard's lightning bolt—Belexus was particularly adept at cutting at such the unnatural things—or, in one notable case, at the end of a warrior's sword. Belexus was, perhaps, the only mortal man alive who had ever seen a dragon and survived; certainly he was the only one who had ever killed a dragon.

But that had been a young one, barely larger than the horse the ranger now rode. If Brielle's magic had located the sword in the lair of a dragon deep in the Crescent Isles, then likely it was an ancient wyrm, one of the originals Thalasi had created as a scourge to the world. And given the weakening of others, a full-grown dragon might well prove to be the most powerful creature in all of Ynis Aielle.

And he did not sleep so well.

Chapter 9

What Thief, This?

SHE FINALLY AWOKE, rising up from the depths of a complete, dreamless darkness, an emptiness of thought, an emptiness of hope. The young witch blinked open her eyes and tried to sit up, but found to her horror that her hands were tightly tied behind her, that her whole body was bound, but not by any material strands. Black filaments of swirling vapor wrapped about her, holding her physical form tightly, but even worse for Rhiannon, binding her magic, as well. She tried to reach into that well of power, to bring forth a brilliant light that would burn away these gripping filaments.

But she found no channel, no access at all.

"A small trick I learned," the deep voice of the wretched wraith came. With great difficulty, Rhiannon managed to turn her head enough to regard the ugly creature.

"I find many valuable assets with this form that my old friend gave to me," Mitchell said, and it seemed to the witch as if he was trying to smile, and that only made him seem all the more grotesque.

"No friend'd ever . . ." Rhiannon began, but her words were lost before they ever gained momentum, as the wraith walked, glided, over to stand beside her, his smirk more unnerving than any howl of anger, than any growled threat. For in that misshapen smirk, Rhiannon recognized true confidence. The wraith had taken a full measure of her in their battle, and he knew now, beyond any doubt, that he was the stronger.

He continued to look down upon her, to smirk at her, to belittle her. "Who are you?" he demanded at last.

The young witch mustered up all the defiance she could find, wrenched against the sticky black filaments, and looked away.

Almost immediately those black filaments tightened about her, choking her, crushing her, squeezing every part of her body so tightly that she was sure they were halting the blood flow! Rhiannon looked back at the wraith and saw the monster standing there, eyes closed, fist clenching—and that fist, Rhiannon knew, was clenching the bonds, as if they were some half-substantial extension of the wraith's fury.

No, the witch realized, not half-substantial, for surely they were squeezing the very life out of her.

"Rhiannon," she gasped, and the wraith's hand relaxed, and so did the bonds.

"I have little patience, young fool," Mitchell said in that awful resonant voice. "There are greater foes than you yet to be murdered."

Rhiannon set her jaw firmly and determined to die bravely—she held little doubt that the wraith would kill her, but this evil thing would get no important information from her. She told herself resolutely that it would kill her whatever she did, whatever she said, and so the less she said, the better for those friends she left behind.

"It is obvious that you are of Avalon," Mitchell reasoned. "Your magic, at least, holds the same flavor as that of another I know, though yours is not nearly as powerful." His cackling laughter belittled her even more, though Rhiannon wasn't certain of the truth of that last statement. She could only suppose that this monster had previously battled with her mother, before her duel with Thalasi, before Thalasi had reached too far and weakened the very realm of magic.

"I had thought you Brielle's sister, perhaps," the wraith went on. "A cousin, at the least, for there is indeed a resemblance." He snorted derisively, his black breath seeming a tangible cloud before his ugly, pallid face. "In foul temperament as well as in appearance!

"But you did call out to Brielle, you see," the wraith teased. "In the last moments before I caught you, when you were but a feeble bird. You called out for your mother, and so you are the witch's daughter, Avalon's daughter! Of that I have little doubt, and that, my dear Rhiannon, makes the kill all the sweeter! Wretched offspring of wretched witch."

"And if I be that?" Rhiannon said defiantly, not disagreeing, for she understood that the wraith was not probing for confirmation to its suspicions, but was telling her what it knew to be the truth. The not-stupid creature had figured out her lineage, and she would never find the heart, or the wherewithal, to change its thoughts.

"Brielle's child," the wraith answered, "and in killing you, I am destroying Brielle's heart."

"Might that I am, and might that I'm not," she said coolly, though inside, the young witch was surely terrified.

"Might?" the wraith echoed skeptically, and again came that demeaning chortle. "You are, Rhiannon . . ." Mitchell paused as he uttered that name, for he knew that name, from somewhere.

"Rhiannon," the wraith said again, rolling out the syllables. Yes, Mitchell knew that name, from another time, another place, another world.

Rhiannon . . . an old song about a witch.

"Rhiannon," the wraith said again, eying the bound woman directly. "And do you ring like a bell through the night?"

The young witch returned a perplexed look, and the wraith bellowed hysterically.

"Daughter of Brielle and of what sire?" the cunning wraith asked. "Or do you even know, so likely it is that your mother has bedded half the northern folk."

The insult would have been lost on the innocent young woman had it not been for Mitchell's biting tone. Rhiannon narrowed her eyes and tried again to reach into the realm of magic, but that only caused the smoky bonds to tighten further, squeezing the thoughts from her mind.

"I had a companion when I first came to Ynis Aielle," the wraith went on, clarifying his own reasoning as he spoke. "Another of the ancient ones, for yes," he added quickly, seeing the spark of recognition in Rhiannon's blue eyes, "I was of that select group. My old friend, this companion, Jeffrey DelGiudice by name, was quite fond of your mother, and she of him, I believe."

"No friend o' yers!" Rhiannon blurted, and surely she tried to take back the words as soon as she spat them.

There it was. Mitchell knew without any doubt, from the vehemence of her protest, if nothing else. She appeared to be the right age, since the Battle of Mountaingate had occurred about a score of years before. And she bore a name that came straight out of that other world, that world before Ynis Aielle, the world that Jeffrey DelGiudice knew. Rhiannon was Brielle's daughter, as she was the daughter of Jeffrey DelGiudice! Until that moment, the wraith had thought that its worst enemy in all the world was the ranger Belexus; until that very moment, Hollis Mitchell had almost forgotten about his former companion, the man who had throttled his plans for glory on the field of Mountaingate, the man whom the wraith hated above all others, whom he had hated in life, and so, too, now in death. He almost lashed out then, with his undead touch, with his deadly mace, to utterly destroy this offspring of that man.

But Mitchell calmed, and quickly. There was too much yet to be done, too many enemies yet to face. DelGiudice had not shown himself in the last war; the Black Warlock, as much Martin Reinheiser as Morgan Thalasi, had not mentioned the man at all, yet surely, if DelGiudice were still alive, the Black Warlock would have seen him as a prime threat. Too many questions flitted about the wraith's thoughts, and Mitchell was cunning enough to find a bit of patience. He scooped Rhiannon up under one arm, and how she thrashed! And Mitchell allowed her that, even more, by loosening up the filaments, so that he could enjoy the tangible proof of her complete terror. Of course, her writhing did nothing to weaken the powerful wraith's grip, and baggage in tow, Mitchell started away, thoughts swirling, trying to formulate some plan of action.

Most of all, the wraith understood that he had to move quickly. Rhiannon was Brielle's daughter, and they were too close to Avalon for comfort. And so, with his most valuable prisoner in tow, the wraith made a straight run to the west, toward the Kored-dul Mountains, toward the bastion of blackness known as Talas-dun.

The sharp edge of a broken stone brought him back to his senses. He tried to move away from the stabbing pain, but found instead a hundred hurts along every part of his body. As far as he remembered, he had been hit only once, and that a glancing blow, but apparently he had landed in a bad way. Worse yet, there loomed a coldness within him, colder than the winter, a creeping chill that he suspected was eating away at his very life force. Wicked indeed was the bone mace of the wraith.

Bryan's thoughts shifted quickly away from his own troubles to those he feared Rhiannon was now facing. Finding strength in that foul notion, the young half-elf rolled over and forced himself to all fours, then willed himself up to his knees alone, that he might scan the area. All he saw was the carnage that had been Corning, the rubble that had been his home, with no sign at all of the witch, or of the undead monster. Breathing hard from both exertion and pain, Bryan somehow managed to get to his feet. His first attempt at a step ended in an unbalanced stagger to the side, Bryan crashing hard against the remnants of a wall, that stone being the only thing keeping him upright. Again small explosions of pain erupted throughout his body, and again, that creeping, icy coldness reached a bit deeper, a bit closer to his heart.

But he staggered on, from wall to wall, searching every crevice, every nook in the area. So many bones littered the place, but no fresh kills. No Rhiannon.

He believed that if she had escaped, she would have run off to the east, back toward the river and allies, but he went to the west gate first, for that was the direction the wraith would likely have taken her if it had caught her.

The carnage was even worse, the destruction complete, in that area. The great western gate of Corning, so thick and strong, an image of security—false security!—that had emboldened the folk of Corning for so long, had been hit by some unearthly explosion, had been blasted from its massive iron hinges and blasted apart. In staring at the piles and piles of bones, both talon and human, at the rusting weapons and armor, young Bryan could well imagine the mighty struggle. This had been the main surge, the focal point of Corning's fall, and so the half-elf was not surprised when he happened upon a delicate skeleton, lying amidst a pile of many, many talon bones. In trembling hands, he took the skull, gently, lovingly, and lifted it up before his moistening eyes.

He had known, of course, that Meriwindle, his father, had fallen in the defense of Corning. All logic had told him so; there was no way brave Meriwindle would have left the city while any stood to defend it, and given the massive swarm of talons, no way he could have escaped afterward. But still, Bryan had always held out a little corner of his heart for hope. Perhaps his father had been taken prisoner, he had often silently prayed, or perhaps Meriwindle had run off to the west, to work as his son worked, an independent thorn in the side of the talon army. That was the fantasy that young Bryan held most dear: that his father was alive and fighting in the west, that one day he would meet up with gallant Meriwindle and together they would chase talons all the way back to Mysmal Swamp.

This delicate skull, that of neither a human nor a talon, defeated that fantasy, and all the others, and now young Bryan had to admit in his heart what he had been speaking openly for all these months.

"What thief, Father?" he asked quietly, falling to his knees but keeping the delicate skull steady before his eyes. "What thief has stolen your smooth flesh and drank of your blood? What talon sword or what magic? What carrion bird, what worm? I would strike them down, my father, every one! I would avenge your death, but hollow, I fear, are my words and my efforts."

Bryan paused and rocked back, black despair nearly overwhelming him and allowing that cold chill to sink a bit deeper. Hollow indeed were his efforts, he thought, for no matter how many talons he killed, no matter whether he killed the wraith or the Black Warlock himself, it suddenly seemed to make no difference; the skull was an empty bone, lifeless, fleshless. The brain that had guided Meriwindle had been eaten by the worms. The warmth that had ever come forth from Meriwindle's heart had been plucked by buzzards.

Bryan did not try to fight back the tears. For the first time since he had seen the smoke plume over Corning, the half-elf cried, truly cried, his sobs bending him low over the skeleton of his father. The chill of Mitchell's mace retreated then, considerably, as if the powerful, real emotion gave back to the young half-elf a bit of his life force.

After many minutes, Bryan lifted his head and held the skull aloft before his wet eyes. "Farewell, my father," he said quietly. "Your soul no sword could strike, no bird could peck, no worm could eat. Your soul could not be stolen by Thalasi, as your courage held firm against him.

"Courage," he echoed softly, many times, that single word telling him who his father was, and who he must be. Eyes wide, he looked all around, up at the sky, down at the ground. "Be gentle, Death!" he cried at the top of his lungs. Then, in a lower, somber voice, "Never have you received so worthy a soul."

And with that, Bryan laid the skull back down on the pile. He thought about burying the remains but dismissed the notion, realizing that this cairn of talon bones was more fitting a resting place for his gallant father. He let his hand slide over the smooth skull one more time, then he found his footing and started away. "Courage," he said again.

Bryan, at last, had put his father to rest.

Now his thoughts turned to Rhiannon, and despair washed away, and all thoughts about the futility of his life and his efforts vanished. He could not help Meriwindle, but there were many alive because of his actions, and there were others, one in particular, that he simply would not allow to die.

One word became his litany as he forced one foot in front of the other, as he crossed through Corning's eastern gate. One word, one denial, of all that seemed imminent.

"No."

Chapter 10

By the Colonnae Trained

"OH, THERE IT is, I do daresay!" the wizard proclaimed, hopping up from his bedroll and jumping wildly, his huge sleeves flapping like the wings of a frightened bird. "I knew I would find it, yes I did, and not you, you silly ranger! Me before you, after all! Hah! Old man's eyes aren't so bad, then, eh?"

The ranger sprinted to the spot, dodging trees and skidding at last to the boulder tumble where he had left the sleeping Ardaz, the sheltered place that had served as their campsite the previous night.

"Hah!" Ardaz barked at him, snapping his fingers triumphantly in the air and standing tall indeed, his skinny arms crossed over his puffed-out chest. "An old man's eyes see with the wisdom of ages, I say, I do daresay!"

Belexus looked around skeptically. They had set camp before sunset, and he had personally inspected all the area while Ardaz had unpacked the pegasus. The ranger could hardly believe that he had missed the telltale mountain face, the very focus of this difficult journey. Not quick to doubt the Silver Mage of Lochsilinilume, Belexus looked all around again, scanning slowly through each direction, and truly there loomed a multitude of towering peaks all about them; the shelter afforded by those walls of stone had been a primary consideration in picking this camping spot. So how had he possibly missed the most important view of the entire journey?

Or had he? he wondered after many moments of fruitless scanning. Finally, perplexed, the ranger turned to the wizard for clarification, for he could find nothing remarkable.

"Where?" he asked simply.

Ardaz looked around, his expression growing incredulous. "Well, I saw it. I did!" he protested. "And you know that I see what I said that I saw! Just after I awoke."

"Dreaming the sight?" Belexus remarked, and despite his frustration that they were not, apparently, near the end of their journey, a smile found its way onto his face.

"After I awoke," Ardaz repeated dryly. "Sitting here minding my own business, after all, and then, *poof!* there it was, an old man's profile, not so far away. I am not crazy, you know," he added in low tones.

Belexus glanced up to Desdemona, who was in cat form, lying in the sun across the top of one of the boulders. She regarded him and yawned profoundly, then stretched and rolled over, letting the warm sun—and it was indeed warm for the season—caress her ample belly.

"Oh, she'll be a help," Ardaz said with obvious sarcasm.

"Where, then?" the ranger asked again.

Ardaz hopped in circles, looking all around, eyes darting, arms flapping, scratching his chin repeatedly and muttering "How curious, how very curious" many times. Finally he settled and shrugged his shoulders. "Well, I did see it, after all."

The ranger moved to inspect the wizard's bedroll. "As soon as ye waked?" he reasoned.

"Well, and after a belch," Ardaz replied. "But not too long a delay."

To the wizard's surprise, and confusion, Belexus then lay down atop Ardaz' bedroll, then lifted his head just a bit. The ranger sat up quickly, smiling, then openly laughing, and the tone of his fit was more of resignation than of humor, as if to say, "I give up," and not, "How amusing."

"Are you to let me in on the joke?" Ardaz asked. "I mean, if I am the butt of it, after all, and since there is no one else for you to share it with." As soon as he spoke the words, the wizard snapped a dangerous glare over the apparently oblivious—but Ardaz knew better—Desdemona. "And not a meow from you," he said.

"Ye seen an old man's profile," the ranger explained. "Yer own."

Ardaz snorted a dozen times, but lost his ire as Belexus pointed to a nearby wall of one of the boulders, its side covered by a cascade of ice.

The dumfounded wizard stuttered in protest, trying to refute the claim, but as he bumbled about, crouching to take the ranger's perspective, he came to realize that Belexus had spoken truthfully. "Oh," was all that Ardaz said.

Belexus laughed again, and now lost all of his frustration, allowing himself a bit of true mirth. The situation in all his world remained so very grim—the wraith, Andovar's murderer, walked the world uncontested—but having the always-surprising Ardaz along on this long and perilous journey surely stole more than a bit of the tedium.

"I'll play your fool, then," the wizard said, seeming sullen. That mood lasted but a moment, though, Ardaz' pout vanishing as the corners of his mouth inevitably turned upward. "My own profile," he said suddenly. "Oh how jolly, how very jolly!"

It was a good laugh, a long laugh, followed by a hearty

breakfast, after which Belexus announced that he would do a bit of hunting to try to restock their packs before they took to higher ground.

That left Ardaz alone to pack up the campsite. Desdemona watched the wizard work, the cat comfortably stretched on the warm boulder.

"So much help," Ardaz complained to her.

She just rolled over again, warming the other side.

The cloud was huge, tremendous, beyond comprehension, a swirling mass of matter gradually, gradually contracting, pieces spinning off, the birth of stars.

And he watched it, saw it, the ages compressed into seconds, it seemed, or perhaps the seconds stretched out into ages. For out here, it didn't matter. Out here, time was nonexistent, each instant its own bubble, always there, always recorded.

Immortality.

He knew that he would always be out here, that each moment of this experience would last forever and ever, and yet, he was going back, spinning through the galaxies, the star clusters. He saw the glowing rim, the sudden sunrise, and black turned to blue. So much blue! On and on he went, down and down, and he sensed the wind, though his less-than-corporeal form could not *feel* the wind. At least, not as he suspected he had once felt it.

There were colors below him, shining blue and dark brown, mostly blue, then mostly white and green, then still more white and green until it filled all his vision. White and green and brown and gray, a silver snake, a blue patch. Colors and texture, and familiarity somehow, though in the enormity of what he had seen, of what the angels had shown him, it seemed a distant memory indeed.

Down and down he dropped, and now he understood

that he was indeed dropping, that there was a concept such as *down*. That recollection caused him to flinch, altogether unnecessarily, when he landed, when he did not continue to pass along, his form, somehow and somewhat more substantial than it had been, coming to rest on a hard gray surface.

"Ice," he said, or rather, found himself saying, when he glanced to the side, to the crusted edges of a quick-running stream. The word, the sound, startled him, causing him to look down at himself. He had form again, real form, and not just the light he had been—the light he still was, though now he was encased in a somewhat corporeal coil. Even more curious, that coil was encased in a white material, a robe, he remembered.

"As it used to be," he heard himself saying, and he screwed his unfamiliar face up curiously as he contemplated the notion of *language*, then grew even more curious as he considered the notion of *time*. "Used to be?" he asked, and the different inflection of words when used as a question only confounded him even more. "Always is, always was, always will be," he recited, giving words to what he had learned to be the most pervasive and enduring truth about the universe, about existence itself. A jumble of thoughts came at him all at once, memories mixed with reasoning. He had worn this coil, this body, before, though it had been more substantial then, more attuned to the elements around it. He reached his hand down tentatively to brush the stone, to feel the stone. It seemed too smooth; he recognized that in his previous experience, the stone would have felt more grainy and rough, even painfully sharp-edged at some points.

For the spirit who had witnessed the birth and death of stars, it all seemed too curious. And so he sat, for a long, long while, and the entire concept of time, of the passage of moments, of a continuum, a fluid movement, came back to him. "Ice," he said again, then, "Brook, stream, river . . . water. And snow, yes, of course. Snow." He paused, then, mouthing that last word over and over, the very sound of it conjuring images of wild, playful fights, of rushing breakneck down hills, the wind blowing in his chilled ears. The very sound of it brought images of joy.

"Yes!" he said again suddenly. "Snow . . . and winter." Again came that curious look, the strange-feeling face of this still-uncomfortable coil twisting and contorting. "Winter, cold," he reasoned, and yet he did not feel cold. He looked down at his meager robes, and knew that they should not be able to ward any chill at all.

But as he thought about it, he did indeed come to feel cold—not unpleasantly so, not threateningly so, but rather a cold that he could control, that was there within his grasp only when he wanted to experience it. Already the spirit was beginning to understand that he was not quite the same—no, not at all—as he had once been. He was better now, he supposed, and he left it at that.

Something stirred to the side, moving out from under a tall pine tree.

"Deer," the spirit said at once.

The creature froze in place, sniffed futilely at the air, ears twitching all the while. After some time, it seemed at last to see the form sitting on the stone, and away it leaped, disappearing from view in the wink of an eye.

"Curious," the spirit remarked, and rose to follow. Again the binding form confused him, but he remembered enough to put one of his long lower limbs in front of the other and was soon walking steadily, a crude, but undeniably effective mode of transportation in this tangible, tiny-scale environment. Moving without a whisper of sound, he caught up to the deer in a small clearing not so far away. Once the creature noticed him, it again turned to flee, but this time the spirit reached out to it, imparted unthreatening thoughts to the creature, and it held still. He went to it, then, to examine it. Its fur seemed inviting; he vaguely remembered a pleasant sensation connected with touching it. Slowly, but eagerly, he lifted his arm, reached out his hand.

It passed right through the coat and the skin, slid right into the deer's side.

The animal took flight, leaping wildly, running on and on at the edge of control.

"Oh pooh," the spirit said, and he thought those words the most curious of all.

As if in answer, a bird chattered at him from above.

He answered with a telepathic thought, and the bird seemed less afraid, and would stay and converse with him. So he spent a long time standing there, below the tree branch, and he remembered even more of that past time, of this mortal coil. Soon he sensed hunger in the little creature, and then the bird flew off.

He lifted from the ground, too, thinking to follow, but he changed his mind, and instead went back to his stone by the stream. If the Colonnae had put him here for a purpose, then it was possible the reason would come to him, rather than he going off to try and find it. Because this place, though so infinitesimally tiny next to the star cloud, seemed large indeed when he was trapped within this corporeal coil.

He stood passively on the stone for a long time, then sat down—not because he was tired, but simply because he remembered that he used to sit down. Truly the new position was no more or less comfortable than standing, or than standing on his head for that matter, but he remembered that once it had been. The day brightened around him, then darkened once more, then brightened again and darkened, and again; and all the time he sat there, he recalled more and more of what had been, found more and more the perspectives imposed by this tangible world and these tangible trappings. He had been here once, in this frame of reference, this perspective. He knew that.

"Where, oh where, oh where, oh where?" the wizard mumbled, twiddling his thumbs. "Do go find him, Des. I do not want to waste my magical strength."

The cat atop the boulder purred all the louder and made absolutely no move to leave.

"Beastly loyal," Ardaz grumbled, a chant he felt was becoming all too common concerning Des, and he pulled himself to his feet. Indeed he did not want to delve into the realm of magic this morning; he was still exhausted from the magical flight that had brought him to Belexus, though that transformation had occurred more than a week before. "This is the old-fashioned way," he said, and he started off, walking through the trees of the low valley.

Desdemona didn't bother to follow.

Some time later, Ardaz sensed that he was being watched. At first he thought it to be Desdemona, but when he glanced all around, he came to know the truth. A white-tailed deer stood not so far away, motionless except for a slight trembling.

"Hmmm," the wizard mumbled, rubbing at his thick white beard, for he knew that this was not the ordinary way a deer, a creature born to run, would react to the scent of a man—and obviously the deer had sensed him. *And who could not?* the wizard silently asked, thinking that it had been far too long since last he had bathed. But still the deer did not run, so Ardaz did go into the realm of magic, sent a mental image there, and that image came back to him, multiplied by the power of the realm. The wizard's clothing twisted and changed hue, sprouted many leafy branches and twigs. "Much like a bush, I should say," he quietly congratulated himself, and indeed, he did resemble the area's flora. With that disguise, he moved slowly, very slowly, toward the deer, taking care not to step on any twigs and to keep his usually babbling mouth still.

To his surprise, despite the enchantment, Ardaz soon found himself right beside the creature, and he understood then that its fear was not a fear of him. "What has so terrified you?" he asked softly and, using a trick his sister Brielle had taught him, he attuned his thoughts to those of the deer, let his mind slip into the mind of the animal. A most curious image came over him then, one of a man—or was it a man?—sitting not so far away.

A decisive twang brought Ardaz from his contemplations and sent the deer leaping away. "What?" the wizard babbled repeatedly, looking all around at the brush and at the flicking white tail as the deer disappeared from sight. Then his gaze settled on his own bushy-looking robes, and there he found his answer in the form of an arrow, hanging loosely in the folds of the camouflaged outfit. A moment later, a confused Belexus came running toward him—confused, that is, only until the ranger spied Ardaz.

"Do you mean to keep shooting me then?" the wizard asked, prodding the arrow tip and opening a tiny wound on his finger. "I'm beginning to get the point, so to speak."

"What're ye about?" the exasperated ranger replied. "I telled ye I'd be hunting. I been chasing that deer for all the morn, and now I'll not fill our packs afore the dusk!"

"Skittish deer," Ardaz replied casually. "Says it saw a man not so far from here, sitting by the stream." As he spoke, the wizard pointed to the north.

"A man?" Belexus echoed. The ranger didn't doubt the wizard's words—he had grown up in the shadow of Avalon, where Brielle was known to converse with animals routinely—but how could any man be out this far from the civilized world? "Man or talon?" he asked suspiciously, for indeed talons were known in the Crystals.

"Could be a talon, I suppose," the wizard admitted, for the image the deer had shown to him had not been that detailed. "Don't know that a deer would know the difference, after all. Either way, we should look into it."

Belexus glanced over his shoulder. He had left Calamus in a clearing not so far away. He thought the better of calling the pegasus, though. If it was a talon, or a band of talons, for rarely was one of those wretched creatures ever found alone, then the flying horse and its riders would make too fine targets for arrows or spears. With a nod, Belexus motioned for Ardaz to follow and reached into his quiver for another arrow.

"Take this one," the wizard offered dryly, pulling the arrow through his robe and handing it over. "I really have no need for it, after all, and even should I find a use for one, sure I am that you'll be shooting me again soon enough!"

Belexus surrendered to a chuckle, then turned and led the way down to the one stream crossing this valley. He looked to Ardaz, who pointed north again, and so north they went, picking their careful way, with even the wizard managing to keep his mouth shut after only a few sharp reminders.

The going was easy, and quiet enough with the footfalls hidden beneath the song of the stream, and soon they came in sight of the man, and it was indeed a man, sitting passively on a large stone, wearing only a slight white shift, though the weather was brutally cold. At first, both of them thought that Istaahl must have come, for who but a wizard could have survived in this land in winter in so flimsy a gown, but then the man turned to face them, and recognition only added to the confusion.

Ardaz, mistrusting his eyes, tried to hold the ranger back, but so elated was Belexus that he burst away from the wizard, scrambling over the slippery stones to get near to his long-lost friend. "Jeffrey DelGiudice!" he cried.

"Jeffrey DelGiudice," the spirit echoed, the strange words sounding familiar. "Jeffrey DelGiudice."

"Can it really be?" the ranger asked, skidding to a halt barely five feet from the spirit. "I'd thought ye lost to me and to all the world; the elves been saying that ye jumped from the ledge at Shaithdun O'Illume."

"Stepped, not jumped," the spirit replied before it understood what it was saying, before it could even consider the words. As those words registered, a perplexed look crossed the spirit's features, and indeed, it did remember that moment, long ago—or was it just an instant past?—when it had gone to the call of Calae of the Colonnae.

"Twenty years, it's been," Belexus went on.

That settled the time question, though the spirit wasn't quite sure of how long a year might be. "Thirty-one million, five hundred thirty-six thousand seconds," it replied immediately, and then all it had to do was figure out what a second might be. And of course, it remembered, there was the matter of "leap year" . . .

Now it was Belexus' turn to wear the perplexed expression, but it couldn't hold against his sincere delight. "Twenty years," he said, "and suren ye don't look a day older."

Ardaz skidded to a stop right behind the ranger, seeing

the vision, hearing the words, but unlike with Belexus, they brought little immediate delight to the wizard. His first thought was that this was some trap by Thalasi, and not a very good one, for if the Black Warlock truly wanted Ardaz and Belexus to think this was DelGiudice standing before them, then he should have aged the man, at least.

"What is a day?" the spirit asked. "Truly this concept of time is confusing!"

The exasperation seemed real enough, and Ardaz, himself taken by the Colonnae to be trained among the stars, understood that feeling, understood it all too well. "By the Colonnae," he whispered.

"Indeed," DelGiudice replied.

"They took you in, my boy!" Ardaz reasoned. "The Colonnae took you from that ledge that starry night. Took you and trained you, as they trained myself, and Brielle, and Istaahl, and Thalasi, curse his name!"

"Trained?" the spirit echoed skeptically, and then shrugged its shoulders. "Perhaps. They showed me, is what they did."

"All of it," Ardaz reasoned.

"Not all, but much," DelGiudice replied. "So very much!" He looked to Belexus, and felt a smile—and what a strange and wonderful feeling it was!—cross his face. "Jeffrey DelGiudice?" he asked. "Is that what I am called?"

"That is who you are," Ardaz answered, "and you'll remember it soon enough."

"Me friend," Belexus said, "suren ye've come back to us at a dark time, but one in which ye're needed!" With that, the ranger reached out to clasp hands with DelGiudice, and the spirit returned the motion, but as with the deer, DelGiudice's hand passed right through that of the ranger, a most uncomfortable sight and feeling for poor Belexus, and one that sent Ardaz' bushy eyebrows arching heavenward.

"Oh, there is that," DelGiudice said, and he felt as if he should shrug, though he did not.

Chapter 11

The Warmth of Home

AT FIRST HE ran, tears in his eyes, anger and anguish ripping at his heart, and the awful coldness from the strike of the wraith's bone mace sending dull aches through every muscle in his body, seeming to freeze the very blood within him. But he ran, for Rhiannon he ran, and when he was too tired to run, he walked, and when he was too tired to walk, he crawled. On and on he went, to the river first, and then north along its western bank. He vaguely considered that he was heading for Avalon, but in truth, he wasn't even certain of where the enchanted wood lay, for he had only heard of it in the tales of his father and of Rhiannon, and he had never truly ventured far north of Corning.

The first night proved terrible for poor Bryan, wretched beyond anything the young half-elf, who had seen so much tragedy, could ever have imagined. The wind whipping across the frozen field gnawed at him, all the more for that inner chill that permeated his entire being. When he awoke, shivering, he knew that he was with fever, and when he tried to stand, he found that he could hardly feel his feet at all. Many times he fell hard to the ground, shivering and vomiting. Still, he went on with all the haste he could muster, stumbling often, half blind, half delirious. He would have stopped, would have just dropped down in the snow and let the cold take him, welcoming death, but he could not, he determined, he told himself without argument, for the young witch, the woman he had come to love, would not survive his failure. Bryan had to get to her mother, to someone, before he died.

Later that morning, Bryan spied a black dot, a wagon, creeping slowly through the foot-deep snow, and he staggered toward it, praying that his ordeal was at its end, that he could pass along news of Rhiannon and then die. He fell flat to the ground, though, and huddled in fear, for the creatures mercilessly driving the poor, battered horse team were not humans or elves but talons, ugly croaking brutes, cursing and snarling and beating the animals.

Outrage welled in Bryan and for a moment took away the delirium and the weakness and the cold. He wanted to charge that wagon and destroy the talons, wanted to transmute all of his frustrations and pains into sheer rage, to place all the blame upon those certainly deserving creatures and hack them down, and hack them again and again until their pieces were scattered about in the snow.

Again Bryan thought of Rhiannon and of his responsibility to her. If, as he suspected, the wraith had captured her, then he was her only hope. If he died, then so would she, without hope, and so the half-elf ducked lower behind a snow berm, even covered much of his body with the white powder, and let the wagon pass. Then he was moving again, and soon the pain and the weakness came back to him tenfold, buckling his knees. He had no idea of how far he had to go, hours or days or weeks, and so he denied it all, just kept his mind filled with images of Rhiannon and forced his body to move on, one foot ahead of the other, one knee ahead of the other.

Days blended together, time became irrelevant except

that he felt colder in the darkness of night. Bryan went beyond hunger, beyond any sensation in his hands and feet, and still he scratched along, eating snow, surely no colder than the great dark iciness that filled every corner of his battered body. He saw other talon bands and avoided them, for even if he could have found some way to temporarily dismiss his responsibility to Rhiannon, he was no longer in any condition at all to fight. He would have discarded his sword, his father's sword, his most precious possession, simply to lessen the weight he carried, except that he felt he could not even find the strength to draw it from its scabbard.

Then he was beyond thought, beyond even the images that had for so long sustained him. He crumpled in the snow one night, beyond pain, beyond hope, beyond direction, and then, it was simply over. Bryan could go no farther, not even another inch, even if that inch would have taken him right to Rhiannon, even if that inch would have somehow freed his love from some horrid fate. There was no more strength, nothing, just the cold and the black.

He curled up to die, almost called out for the spirit of Death to come to him and whisk him from the agony.

But it was Brielle who came upon him. She had been restless since Belexus had left, had been looking throughout her forest and then beyond her borders, seeking her daughter, praying for Rhiannon's return. One night she had sensed a presence and had thought it Rhiannon, but it soon blackened, became complete darkness, and she knew it to be the wraith, for she had battled Mitchell before. And she was very afraid then, thinking that her daughter might have encountered the undead fiend. But Brielle could not get out of Avalon that night in time, for she was in the north of the forest, and the sensations proved but fleeting feelings and were gone before she could truly find their focus. Since that night, though, the Emerald Witch had stayed closer to the southwestern edge of the forest, looking mostly south, along the river.

It was more than luck, then, it was the bond of love, that the last word Bryan uttered before he slumped for that final time in the snow was "Rhiannon."

And that word carried on wintry winds, to the anxious ears of the witch of Avalon, and she followed its trail, backtracked its course to find the half-elf lying cold in the snow, Death hovering about him. Only the greatest warmth in all the world could have denied that looming specter, and indeed, Brielle of Avalon was the greatest warmth in all the world. Death did not tread close to the Emerald Witch, and she would not let go of this young hero, not while he held information about her daughter that she so desperately needed to hear. She gathered Bryan up in her arms, used her magic to make herself and the half-elf something less than substantial, and let the wind carry them back across the miles to Avalon.

"You will take all of your soldiers up high," the Black Warlock instructed his talon commander, a muscular brute named Kaggoth. "To the battlements, to the parapets, to every ledge and every window of every tower. The zombies will hold the low ground about the courtyard." Thalasi was agitated, for he knew that Mitchell approached Talas-dun, with more than a few talons scooped up in his black wake, and the Black Warlock knew, too, that the wraith could prove to be his greatest ally, or his deadliest enemy.

Thalasi's trepidation was not lost on Kaggoth, no stupid creature by talon standards. "You fears it?" Kaggoth dared to ask.

All of the Black Warlock's worries came out in a sudden, angry rush. "You dare to question me?" he roared, and Kaggoth shrank back, only then realizing the deadly mistake. The other talons in the throne room scrambled for cover. By the precedents set in Talas-dun, Thalasi should have lashed out magically then and reduced the upstart talon to a pile of unrecognizable gore; the Black Warlock knew that he should do so, as he had on those few occasions when talons had shown less than absolute loyalty in the past. A sudden mighty stroke would obliterate the upstart and thus cement the unquestioning loyalty of the others. He should have done that—every creature in the room, Kaggoth included, fully expected him to—but he could not waste even the slightest of his less-than-considerable magical powers on a mere talon. Not with the likes of the wraith approaching.

"Wretched beast," Thalasi scolded instead, trying to sound ferocious. Out of the corner of his eye, Thalasi noticed that the other talons relaxed just a bit, even dared to come forward, and so, just as a precaution, he willed a handful of zombies, who had been standing impassively behind one of the room's huge tapestries, to move defensively near to him.

"I am considering whether or not to have my pets here dismember you," Thalasi said calmly to the talon commander. He brought a finger up to stroke his chin, to appear thoughtful, to make Kaggoth sweat.

Kaggoth instead glanced around at the other talons, noting the tiny nods of support. Perceptive Thalasi saw those movements, too, and he realized that if he set the zombies into motion, the talons would take up Kaggoth's cause and he would have a major fight right here in the throne room. "Perhaps I will overlook your impudence this one time," he said. "We are all on edge after what has happened. As to your question, no, I do not fear the wraith. Not while I possess this." He held up his black-burnished staff, the Staff of Death. "But I do maintain a healthy respect for a creature as powerful as Hollis Mitchell. Take your soldiers up high, and keep them up high. Too many talons have died already. I see no need to risk any more while I have the command of a zombie army."

Kaggoth eyed him for a long while, confused, suspicious, then nodded and turned to go.

"And," Thalasi called abruptly, stopping the talon in its tracks and turning it about to face him, "if you entertain thoughts of allowing the wraith to do battle with me, in the hopes that perhaps Mitchell will destroy me, then know that your hopes are foolhardy at best and surely misguided. I am Morgan Thalasi; do not forget that! And even if, by some wild chance, your hopes came to fruition and Mitchell proved the stronger, then consider what life you might know under the rule of the wraith. Or your unlife, I should say, for Mitchell will not suffer you, any of you, to live, and will surely tear your spirits from the realm of Death and hold you undead under his power. I could do the same, do not doubt." He flashed that awful staff again. "Yet I am a merciful lord. So go, Kaggoth, and remember your allegiance."

Kaggoth nodded again, slowly, deliberately, then motioned to two nearby talons, his lieutenants, and exited the room.

Thalasi breathed a sigh of relief and leaned forward in his chair, considering the forthcoming scenario. He did well to keep his talons up high on the walls, so he believed. It was possible that Mitchell would be able to exert considerable control over the undead soldiers; perhaps the wraith would even prove strong enough to wrest their blind allegiance away from Thalasi. But Thalasi and his talons would then hold the high defensible positions, and the loyalty of the talons would be unwavering when faced with the choice of Thalasi or horrid Mitchell.

But how confusing it had all become! And how pitiful! Only a few short months ago, the Black Warlock had been on the verge of conquering the world, and now he feared losing even Talas-dun, his last bastion, the heart of his power. Mitchell was coming in with many talons in his wake, so it had been reported, and Thalasi did not know if that was a good thing or a bad. Did the presence of talons, a race aptly nicknamed the children of Thalasi, mean that the wraith was returning as an ally? Or did it portend disaster for Thalasi? For if Mitchell turned against him, not only might he be able to wrest away the zombies, but he would have a considerable talon force of his own.

If that was the case, Thalasi wondered if he could hold out against the wraith. He looked to the Staff of Death again, his most powerful of creations, and hoped that its powers had not too greatly diminished, as had the Black Warlock's own.

Truly she was exhausted after the tremendous expenditure of magical energy, but Brielle would not slow her efforts to breathe warmth back into the cold body of Bryan of Corning. She spent days with him in the heart of Avalon, tending him, warming him, coaxing him back to life, and finally, after nearly a week, the young half-elf opened his weary eyes.

"Rhiannon," he said at once, a clear note of alarm in his voice.

Brielle, despite her fears for her daughter, quieted him, knowing that he was not yet ready. Patience, she told herself. That would be the only way to get the whole story, and get it correctly.

By that night, Bryan was much stronger, and awake

again. And when he told her, her worst nightmares came true. Bryan feared that Mitchell had caught Rhiannon, and had either killed her or taken her captive, and when Brielle considered the sensations that had come to her that night nearly two weeks before, she knew that the young half-elf was correct. Mitchell had not killed Rhiannon, of that the Emerald Witch was certain. If Rhiannon died, Brielle's heart would feel it, no matter how many miles separated them. But he had taken her, or was herding her, chasing her, else she would have surely returned to Avalon.

The Emerald Witch stood silent in a field later on that clear evening, looking up at the starry canopy of Ynis Aielle. She had to regain her strength, after the flight to Bryan and the many hours of magical tending, and then she had to look far and wide, had to call to her animal friends to act as spies, had to search to the ends of the world until her dearest Rhiannon was found.

But in her heart, she already knew.

Brielle understood where the horrid wraith, Thalasi's pawn, would take so valuable a prisoner, and she knew, too, that that place, the black fortress, was beyond her powers.

So she stood quiet under the stars, her heart breaking, her imagination running wild with her fears for her dear daughter, for innocent Rhiannon who did not deserve any of this.

His approach was without fanfare, without announcement. The wraith stalked the last quarter mile to Talasdun in the same manner that it had traveled the hundreds of miles before that. In Mitchell's wake came a thousand talon soldiers, a nervous group indeed, all bloodshot eyes darting to and fro, looking for some signal from the bastion that all was well.

Thalasi watched it all from a tall tower. He first noted the talons' movements, trying to discern if they had come for war or parlay. Then he focused on the wraith, and then, more particularly, on the body the wraith carried.

It was not Brielle, Thalasi knew, for the Emerald Witch had hair the color of gold, not raven black. But what other woman would Mitchell bother to cart across the miles? Certainly the wraith had no lustful intentions, and certainly Mitchell knew Thalasi well enough to understand that such a gift, if it was a gift, would mean little to the Black Warlock. Curious, but ever cautious, the Black Warlock held his ground, high up.

The wraith stalked up to the great iron front gate. "Throw it wide!" he commanded, and when no reaction seemed forthcoming, Mitchell struck the great doors with his mighty mace. The blow echoed about the courtyard, up in the towers, walls and floors shivering. "Throw it wide!" the wraith bellowed again, and this time, to the Black Warlock's horror, some of the zombies moved toward the huge locking bar.

Thalasi reached out to them telepathically, sent his will upon them to stop them. He found that Mitchell's thoughts were already there, and in the struggle that ensued, several of the zombies literally split apart, their rotted forms torn asunder by the war of wills.

At last the wraith backed off, relinquishing control of the zombies, and Thalasi wasn't sure if he had won the battle or if Mitchell was just conserving strength.

"Am I to be shut out, then?" the wraith called.

"Do you enter as friend or foe?" Thalasi retorted, moving into Mitchell's view at one of the tower's narrow and tall windows.

The wraith issued its hideous laugh. "I am a pawn of the Black Warlock," Mitchell replied unconvincingly. "An unthinking tool."

"Never that!" the Black Warlock retorted sharply. He thrust forth the Staff of Death, and took some comfort in the fact that Mitchell recoiled before it. Yes, its power was strong, Thalasi decided, and so he sent his will down to the zombies again, and this time allowed them to open the great door.

In came the wraith and the talons, the living creatures stopping fast when they noted that gruesome undead monsters filled the courtyard.

Thalasi nearly chuckled, despite the tension. A tremendous turnaround might now occur, he realized, with Mitchell taking control of the zombies, and Thalasi similarly stealing away the living talons Mitchell had brought in.

Nothing of the sort happened. To Thalasi's relief, the wraith placed its cargo down on the ground and called up to him. "I have brought a gift," Mitchell explained.

Thalasi started to reply sharply but thought the better of it, and after a moment's hesitation, he swept down the tower stairs and out the door, leaving several talons to guard the portal and hold open his escape should battle begin. Even as he approached the wraith and the body, Thalasi felt the unusual sensation. The wizards of Aielle could feel each other, could recognize each other's aura as a dog could recognize its master's smell. Thalasi did not know this woman, and yet he did, had felt her presence before, on a field so far away . . .

All fear of the wraith flew away, and the intrigued Black Warlock rushed to the woman and turned her over, his hollow eyes going wide indeed to see that she carried a wizard's mark, a diamond set in the middle of her forehead.

"The daughter of Brielle," Mitchell explained.

Thalasi looked up at him.

"Rhiannon by name."

The Black Warlock hardly remembered to draw breath. This was too beautiful, too unexpected. "Why have you returned to me?" he asked bluntly, for, with his hopes suddenly soaring, he needed to have things properly sorted and clarified.

"The war is not yet over," the wraith replied, just the answer Morgan Thalasi had hoped for. "We have been thrown back, but not down; wounded, but not killed."

"And wounded, too, were our enemies," Thalasi was quick to put in. "The wizards will be of little consequence when next the battle ensues."

"Perhaps the time of wizards is past," the wraith dared to say, drawing itself up to its full, imposing height; and there it was, spoken openly and plainly.

A threat if Morgan Thalasi had ever heard one.

Chapter 12

The Benefits of Insubstantiality

"DELGIUDICE?" THE SPIRIT asked repeatedly, pondering the name, its former name, and all the memories the mere sound of the word inspired. "DelGiudice." All through the cold night—though the spirit had no sensation of the wintry mountain chill, unless he willfully experienced it—the spirit had sat vigilant guard over his new companions. Belexus sat propped against a tree, but fast asleep, confident in this new manifestation of Jeffrey DelGiudice as a sentry. Ardaz lay wrapped in many blankets, dangerously close to the fire, snoring contentedly. Calamus stood nearby, wings folded, head down, dark eyes closed. Only Desdemona remained awake, watching DelGiudice. The cat, above all the others, had not taken well to the ghost. She remained apprehensive, and every time Del so much as glanced Desdemona's way, she arched her back and spat at him.

And though he couldn't touch living flesh, Del found cat spittle a bit uncomfortable.

The spirit did not need to sleep, couldn't even comprehend such a notion, and so he agreed to keep the watch, and while he did, he remembered. He kept repeating key words, particularly names, over and over, changing the inflection until the ring became familiar, thus tapping another memory or name, like a growing chain. By the end of the first night, Del had rebuilt his memory to include his time aboard the *Unicorn*, the advanced submarine that had brought Del and some others, including Mitchell and Reinheiser, to this new world. Before the dawn, before the others awoke, he recalled his adventures crossing Ynis Aielle; his first meeting with Calae, prince of the Colonnae; his unexpected rescue by Belexus in Blackemara, the ancient swamp; his meeting with the other rangers, Bellerian and Andovar; and his stay in the most marvelous Emerald Room that served as throne chamber to Bellerian. And of course—and, to his thinking even now, most important of all—Del remembered his first glimpse of, and all his subsequent meetings with, Brielle of Avalon.

Brielle. That name rang most familiar of all, sent a warmth through the spirit, the fondest of memories. How he had loved her, though their time together had been so painfully short. It was, at the end, Brielle's rejection of Del that had caused him to wander to Shaithdun O'Illume, the shelf of the moon, that fateful night, when Calae had come to him and bade him to travel the stars. So had ended Del's life on earth; so had begun his journey with the Colonnae.

He was deep in thought, deep in memory, both sad and glad, when the sun broke the eastern rim and Belexus stirred, rising and stretching, then coming to the spirit quietly.

"A fine watch ye keep," the ranger teased, for Del apparently did not notice his approach. "Or are ye looking out and not in?" he added, nodding to the camp's perimeter.

"Looking in," DelGiudice said, meaning something completely different. "Looking back."

Belexus nodded, then motioned to Desdemona, who was all too happy to go over and wake Ardaz.

"DelGiudice," the spirit announced, the name at

last coming easily to his insubstantial lips. "Jeffrey DelGiudice."

The ranger nodded again. "And Del, ye were called by yer friends," he explained. "Ye're remembering?"

"Much of it," the spirit replied. "The ship that got me here, the journey across Aielle. Our first meeting—you saved me from some altogether nasty creature."

"A whip-dragon," Belexus replied.

"Yes, a whip-dragon."

"And what else might ye be remembering?" the ranger asked. "Arien and the elves?"

"Of course," Del replied, and he smiled at the memory of the fair folk of Lochsilinilume. "And Brielle."

The spirit did not notice the cloud that passed over the ranger's face at that moment.

"Most of all, Brielle," Del went on, and he looked to the south and west, the brightening peaks and the dark, mysterious shadows below them.

The cloud darkened for Belexus, but then a chuckle from the spirit broke the tension. Belexus followed Del's gaze to the sleeping wizard, or more particularly, to the black cat sitting atop the wizard's chest, every so often batting Ardaz across the nose. With a great sneeze that sent Desdemona scrambling and growling in protest, Ardaz popped open his eyes.

"What? What?" the wizard sputtered. "Oh, Des, you silly beast!" He looked all around then, focusing at last on Del and Belexus. "Morning already?" he quipped, so suddenly seeming more wide awake than either of them could ever hope to be. "Off we go, then!"

"Our friend's begun to remember," Belexus announced.

"Splendid!" the wizard roared, coming out of the tangle of blankets, catching his legs in one and falling facedown to the ground but hopping right back up, undaunted, bouncing toward the pair. "All of it?"

"All since the submar— the ship that brought me here," Del replied.

"Submarine," Ardaz corrected. "Went on one once—or *in* one, actually. Wouldn't do to go *on* one, now would it? I do daresay! Beastly tight and cramped in there. Could hardly spread my wings. Of course, that was before I was a wizard, after all, and so I couldn't sprout wings in the first place. Ha ha!"

It took Del a while to sort through that rambling, but as he did, he recalled that Ardaz was from his own world, the world gone twelve centuries, the world before the holocaust, which the elves called *e-Belvin Fehte*. That realization alone brought Del some recollections of that lost time, but they were distant images, far away and unclear. He tried to clarify them for a long moment but gave up, thinking that he had more important business this day.

When he focused on his companions once more, he found Belexus looking up forlornly at the nearest peaks. Or at least, where the nearest peaks should have been, for a low cloud cover was closing in on them, stealing their sharp, rocky outlines in a blur of gray.

"We'll not be finding much this day," the ranger reasoned.

"A bit of, more than a bit of, snow in the air," Ardaz agreed, shaking his head. "Oh bother."

"I thought I'd be finding little trouble in getting to the wyrm's lair," the ranger admitted. "High up on Calamus, and with all the view before me."

"But?" Del prompted, not seeming to comprehend any of it.

"But I can't be keeping up for long in this wind," the ranger explained. "Too cold for me bones, and for Calamus. And the snow's been general, and been slowing me, with a bit of it almost every day."

"The season will change soon," the ever-optimistic Ardaz said hopefully.

"Not soon enough, by me thinking," the ranger said. "The wraith's about, and that one's naught but mischief." Again he looked forlornly at the sky, and already the clouds were lower, gathering thick about the mountain peaks. "I canno' go up in that."

"But I can," Del said suddenly, a smile brightening on his ghost face. To prove his point, he lifted off the ground, floating gently, untouched by the wind.

Belexus and Ardaz exchanged incredulous, and then hopeful, looks.

"What exactly am I looking for?" the spirit asked.

"A mountain peak looking like an old man's profile," the ranger explained, and he illustrated the image by bending low and cutting a likeness of it into the snow. "That's the wyrm's peak, so says Brielle."

"And the dragon is somewhere inside?"

"Ayuh."

DelGiudice stood quiet for a moment, studying the drawing, not so certain that he actually wanted to find this particular mountain. He didn't know much about dragons, for there were no dragons in the world before *e-Belvin Fehte*, none that weren't man-made at least. He vaguely remembered some of the legends—Saint George and Bilbo and Smaug and the like—and in his world there were some generally accepted guidelines of what dragons were like. He didn't remember much of that, but he did understand that dragons were supposedly very, very bad, and not likely to be welcoming his two companions as houseguests.

Whatever business Belexus had with this particular dragon seemed important, though, else why would the ranger have come out into the Crystals in winter? So with an instinctive shrug, which he found most curious, the spirit lifted away from the ground.

"We'll await here for your return," Ardaz called.

Del immediately descended.

"What?" the wizard asked.

"Well, I did not want to keep you waiting," Del explained. "I remember that as being quite rude."

"We'll be looking for yer return after ye've found the mountain," Belexus explained.

"Oh," Del said, and with another shrug, he started into the air once more.

It was quiet up in the clouds, comfortably so, and the floating spirit lost his focus many times, lapsing into thoughts of his previous life, both in Aielle and before Aielle. He thought of Brielle often, of their love, and of his family, the one before the holocaust, of his mother and father and their small house in New England. In his heightened state of being, it was actually more than merely thinking of those times. Through sheer concentration and an understanding of time itself—or rather, an understanding of the *lack* of time—Del put his consciousness back to those moments, relived them as easily as if they were strung out before him, little bubbles that he could enter at will. And each seemed to lead to a dozen more, and so he did very little searching while he floated up above the sheltered vale, but much remembering.

He did not return to his companions all that day, nor that night, nor the next day, which was even more snowy, nor the next night. On the third morning, the weather breaking somewhat, Belexus announced that he would wait no longer, and he began to saddle up Calamus.

"But what of DelGiudice?" Ardaz wanted to know. "Can't be running about separately in the mountains, after all. Too many walls, too many clouds. We'll never find each other again."

Belexus shared his friend's concern, but that did not overrule the urgency of his own quest. "Might that he's gone back to the Colonnae," the ranger said somberly. "We're not for knowing why he was here, or if he really was."

"What could you mean?" Ardaz asked, and then, *pop!*, he figured it out. "Oh, no," he said, wagging his hands in the air before him. "No, no, I do daresay. Couldn't be, no no. No trick of Thalasi, that one."

"Can ye say that ye're sure?"

Ardaz nodded so violently that his great hat fell down over his eyes.

"Well, we're still not knowing what bringed him to us, or for how long," Belexus reasoned. "And every day we're waiting, the wraith's likely bringing pain."

In the face of such simple and indisputable logic, the wizard ran out of arguments, so he went to the campsite, muttering every step of the way, and began packing their provisions. "Cold up there," he mumbled repeatedly, and unhappily, though he didn't disagree with the ranger's decision that they set out again on their way.

Before they ever got the pegasus readied, though, Desdemona gave a long mew, announcing the return of the missing ghost.

"Good that ye've returned!" Belexus beamed, trotting to the spot before the descending spirit. "We were just about to leave."

"Why?"

"Ye been gone a long while, me friend."

Del regarded the ranger curiously, not quite understanding. "I said I would go to find the peak," he replied at length, as if that should explain everything.

"So ye did say, but we were thinking ye'd check back

with us at day's end," the ranger tried to explain, though he was beginning to catch on that he and this ghost were not reasoning along the same lines.

"Why?"

"Oh, never mind," Ardaz interrupted, hopping between the two, impatient for news. Ardaz saw it, if Belexus did not: the spirit's calm demeanor hinted at success. "The peak. The peak. Oh, did you find the peak?"

DelGiudice pointed to the northwest. "Not so far," he explained.

Belexus moved as if to give the spirit a hug, but backed off immediately, remembering their unsettling first encounter.

"But it's hard to see," Del explained. "You have to approach at just the right angle, or all it looks like is rocks. Except from that way," he added quickly, pointing straight north. "From that way, it looks like a shark's fin on an ocean swell."

"Ye're sure it's the peak?" Belexus asked, his excitement ebbing as doubts began to creep in.

"From the south it is," Del replied happily. "An old man, just as you drew. But only from the south. Come along, I will show you; we can get there before the sun goes low if Calamus is swift of wing."

The ranger and the wizard went at their packing with vigor. "Oh, come along, Des," Ardaz called repeatedly to the sleeping feline. "And do hurry, for a grand day it is! It is!"

The wizard stopped in midpirouette and considered the cat carefully. "Grand?" he asked. "I call it a grand day, though I'm about to walk into the lair of a great dragon? Oh, silly me!"

Desdemona spat at him and turned away.

Ardaz shrugged and finished his work.

They were airborne soon after, the wizard and ranger

and the still, sleeping cat, atop mighty Calamus, following Del's speeding spirit through ravines and around great jags of stone. They had to stop several times so that the ranger and wizard could warm their bodies, but, as the spirit had predicted, they came in sight of the mountain—and there was no doubt that it was indeed the mountain—shortly after noon.

They circled it once, then put down on a lower ledge, having found no obvious entrance of any sort.

"Well, if this is the place—and I do not doubt my sister—" Ardaz reasoned, "then the dragon has been inside a while, I daresay, and the snow and the wind have apparently sealed the wyrm away. Not that that's a bad thing!"

"But not a good thing for those meaning to get inside," Belexus replied. "I'm not even for guessing where we might start looking for a door."

"I can get in," Del said suddenly, and both his companions turned on him.

"I thought that nonliving matter presented a barrier even to you," Ardaz reasoned. "Or why haven't you fallen under the ground, after all?"

"Fall?" Del echoed, as if the concept itself seemed foreign to him. "Oh, yes, of course. I cannot fall, for gravity has no hold on me," he explained. "But you are correct in that I can touch stones and the like. They're more dense than your own bodies, you see, and so I cannot pass through them."

"Then how're ye meaning to get in?" Belexus asked.

"Cracks in the wall, of course," Del answered.

The ranger turned to inspect the stone, but saw no obvious cracks.

"You have to look closer," the spirit explained. "They're there, I know, and I can get through them."

"It seems that our meeting was good fortune indeed," the ranger said.

"Lead on," Ardaz bade.

Del did just that, his form becoming two-dimensional, a most disturbing sight, and then slipping into the stone wall easily. He came back soon after, announcing that the particular crack was a dead end, but he tried again, and then again, and over and over, until finally, he did not return so quickly.

He had come to an inner chamber, a tunnel winding through the mountain. To his relief, and surprise, he found that he could see as readily in the dark as in the light. It made sense when he thought about it, for he wasn't actually here, in this physical place, for he wasn't actually corporeal at all. Darkness was an obstacle to physical eyes, but not to the entity that Del had become.

He considered the tunnel before him, its arching ceiling and fairly smooth walls. If he could only find a way for his friends to get in, it would be wide enough for them, he knew. But which way was out, and which deeper in?

On a mere guess, Del went left, floating swiftly along, until he came to a wall, again with cracks through which he could maneuver. He found that the wall was not so thick, only a foot or so, coming out of the mountain under an overhang of rock not so far from where he had left his friends. "Belexus could knock through that," Del reasoned. "Or Ardaz certainly could." The spirit smiled as he remembered the first time he had met the bumbling wizard, the time Ardaz had used a bolt of lightning to remove a huge rock from the meadow at Brisen-ballas. How the wizard had hopped about, his fingers burned by the stroke!

But the spirit reminded himself that Belexus was in rather a bit of a hurry, and he filed the memory away for another time. "Not yet," he decided, and he went back through the crack, back into the tunnel. Before he brought Belexus and Ardaz to the spot and got their hopes up, he thought it wise to make sure that he was leading them correctly. And so he went the other way down the tunnel, past the spot where he had first entered, and farther on into the mountain. Down and down he traveled, the corridor widening and narrowing, sometimes with a low ceiling, and other times covered by long and high shafts, so that there was no ceiling visible. He came to one chamber filled by dark water, which he merely floated over, and was relieved to see that there was enough of a ledge for his friends to get by.

Then came a steep, descending slope, and down Del went. He sensed something different about this area, and in tuning his other senses, found that the air was warmer and that a subtle, rhythmic vibration was all about him.

As he neared the bottom of the slope, he understood the rhythm to be the breathing of a dragon—a huge, sleeping dragon.

Now he moved more cautiously, though he could rationally tell himself that this wyrm, however magnificent, could not hurt him. There was something in the air, beyond the warmth and the snores, some tangible aura, inciting terror. Del tried to tell himself that it was just his expectations of what a dragon might be that were making him tentative, but soon he came to understand that it was indeed something more than that, something very real.

He went through another few passageways, a veritable maze now, though the sound and the heat proved a ready guide. Then he turned a final corner and came into a chamber, and such a chamber as poor Del had never imagined! All those past legends of dragons flooded back to him now, ignited by the incredible scene: the wealth, the jewels, and mostly, the great wyrm itself, fifty feet long though it was curled in a ball. If Del had been a corporeal being, needing to draw breath, he knew that he would not be able to do so. If he had been a corporeal being, if he had made even the slightest sound, the dragon would have awakened and he would have been destroyed. It was that simple, that cut and dried. He would have been destroyed, with no other possibilities plausible.

Those thoughts propelling him, Del was back through the maze, back up the slope, and nearly back to the far end of the tunnel before he even registered that he was running away.

"You do not want to go in there," was the first thing the spirit said to his companions when he rejoined them outside the mountain. "Trust my judgment on this."

Belexus and Ardaz exchanged knowing glances. "So you saw the wyrm, eh?" the wizard asked.

The spirit nodded.

"Big wyrm?"

Again the nod.

"Mighty wyrm?"

Again the nod.

"Scared you?"

And once again, the nod.

"This must be the place," Ardaz said dryly to Belexus.

"Did ye see any o' its treasures?" the ranger asked of Del.

Again the nod.

"The sword I telled ye of?"

The spirit tried to recall the scene. He remembered the mounds of glittering treasures, but nothing in particular stood out to him, nothing except the great dragon.

"It was probably there," he said at length. "But that is not reason enough to go in there!"

"Ye just show me the way," the ranger demanded.

"No."

"I'll not be arguing with ye, ghost o' DelGiudice!" Belexus growled sternly. "I come for one thing alone, and I'm meaning to have it, or meaning to die in trying to get it!"

"You will."

"That big?" Ardaz asked, scratching his beard.

"Bigger," replied Del. "In all my wildest nightmares, I could not have imagined a creature so terrifying."

"Everyone says that when first they see a wyrm, even a little one," Ardaz explained. "A bit of dragon magic to flutter the heart. But no matter. We both have seen the likes of a dragon before, and know the terror and the danger. We came here expecting it, but came here anyway, since that sword which lies in the lair is most important—more important, I daresay, than all three of us put together. So be a good ghost and show us the way in, and let us be on with it."

DelGiudice stared long and hard at Ardaz, and then even longer at Belexus, and seeing the unblinking resolution etched on their faces, he relented. "Get on Calamus," he instructed, and when they were ready, he flew off to the ledge under the jag of rock, a treacherously narrow place where Calamus could not get a solid footing, and so Ardaz and Belexus had to leap off, while the pegasus circled away, a sleeping Desdemona comfortably sprawled across his back.

Ardaz called to the cat repeatedly. Then, with no response forthcoming, the wizard coaxed Calamus into circling close and stooping violently, shaking the cat free. Belexus caught her, and got a good swipe across the face for his efforts. Hoisting Desdemona by the scruff of her neck, he handed her over, none too gently, to Ardaz.

The ranger's mood grew fouler indeed when Del

explained that the passage was behind this wall of stone. "Well, yerself can go through a crack," the ranger remarked.

"But it's not so thick," Del tried to explain.

"We'll be waking the whole mountain, and all the dead things the dragon's eaten, if we go to knocking through the stone!"

Ardaz was already at work on it. He tap-tapped gently with his staff, listening closely to find what was solid stone and what just a thin wall blocking an open passage. Then, the tunnel located, the wizard traced out a rough door with water. He stepped back, tucked his staff under an armpit and rubbed his hands together, then waggled his fingers. "Not so long ago, I could have just made it all go away, you know," he explained. "Blast the fool Thalasi and all that he ruined!"

With a sigh he set back to work, bringing magic into the air about him, sending it in small, focused waves at the wet lines on the stone. He sent the water deeper into the rock, into the very essence of the rock, and soon the line that had been marked with water darkened and sharpened, now seeming more like a smooth crack in the mountain wall.

Ardaz sighed again and slumped, obviously weary. "The door," he explained. "But do be careful not to make a racket when opening it."

"And how are we to do that?" Belexus asked.

Ardaz blinked many times as he considered the perfectly smooth stone. "Oh."

"I'll push it out, you catch it," Del reasoned, and before anyone could question, the spirit slipped through the wizard-made crack. A moment later, the door shivered, and the top portion slipped out just a fraction of an inch, but enough for mighty Belexus to hook his fingers on. The ranger's muscular arms bulged as he tugged and the stone slipped out more and more, so slowly. And then, suddenly, the top came out from under the wall and the slab fell forward, and only quick reflexes and great strength allowed the ranger to hold it steady, get it under control, and then turn it aside and let it fall down the mountainside.

"There. No more noise than the avalanche that likely happens here every week," Ardaz said, and neither Del nor Belexus could tell if he was being sarcastic or not.

"You're sure about this?" Del asked one final time.

Belexus stepped right by him, into the tunnel.

"On we go," Ardaz announced, but he stopped suddenly, snapped his fingers, and brought a small fire to the top of his staff.

"That should properly announce us," Del said, and there could be no mistaking his sarcastic tones.

"We're not for seeing in the dark," the ranger said.

"I do not understand why you are so afraid," Ardaz asked of Del as they started off to follow Belexus. "Can't bite you, after all, and will likely break a nail if it tries to swipe at you. Hmmm, but I wonder about the fire."

Del looked at him and shrugged; then, without hesitation, he moved his ghostly hand near to the fire atop the wizard's staff. Closer and closer Del's hand went, though his eyes and his rational memories of fire screamed in his mind that he should stop. Still, he felt no pain, no heat, none at all. He closed his eyes, then, denied the logic that this semicorporeal form imparted, and moved his hand down and down, finally feeling the knob of the wooden staff against his palm. Del opened his eyes to see that the fire burned about his hand and through his hand, but did not consume the flesh and did not pain him in the least.

"Oh, the dragon will like you!" Ardaz beamed, but he had spoken too loudly, drawing an angry "Sssh!" from

Belexus, and then from himself, the wizard slapping a hand across his own mouth.

They went on quietly then, down and down, through the tunnel, through the maze of chambers and side passages, following the heat and the rhythmic breathing—and that breathing gave them all hope, for if they could catch the wyrm asleep, then perhaps they could find the sword and be away, or perhaps slay the beast before it ever awakened.

Such thoughts were fleeting, though, for both Ardaz and Belexus knew that one did not steal unnoticed from a dragon's hoard, and that slaying an adult dragon quickly was near to impossible; and of course Del, who had seen this one up close, knew better than to believe truly that either task was possible.

They turned the last corner—all but Desdemona, who whacked Ardaz across the face, leaped from his arms, and shot back the way they had come—and there, looming before them, just as Del had described it, lay the great dragon, the huge lizardlike creature, massive wings folded up neatly upon its scaly, spiked back. And such a glitter of treasure was about it to bring great wealth to all of the folk of all of Calva, though, with the spectacle of the great wyrm before them, the others hardly noticed a single coin.

Belexus put a finger to pursed lips, then motioned to the left, but before he could take his first soft step, the monstrous, horned head swung out on a long, serpentine neck, coming to an abrupt halt barely ten feet from the three, and seeming a whole lot closer than that!

"Oh, pooh," Ardaz said.

"WELL, THIEVES," the deafening dragon voice bellowed, and Del feared that the vibrations alone would shatter his semisubstantial form. "HAVE YOU ANY THOUGHTS YOU WISH TO SHARE BEFORE I ENJOY MY FIRST MEAL IN CENTURIES?"

Chapter 13

The Master

LONG AND UNCOMFORTABLE had been the first reunion, the meeting of Thalasi and his former henchman, the wraith of Hollis Mitchell, out in the rainy, mud-slickened courtyard of Talas-dun. That initial discussion had ended without battle, but it had been only a prelude, a testing ground, both of the powerful and evil beings understood, for it was no longer clear which of them was the stronger, which the true master. And both craved that position and that power.

Nor was the pecking order among the castle's troops firmly established. Talons argued and fought with talons: those Mitchell brought in, tribes mostly from the lowland swamps south of Kored-dul, against those of the mountain tribes Thalasi already had stationed in the place; and the zombies, standing perfectly still unless ordered to some action by either the wraith or the Black Warlock, kept every living creature on the edge of its nerves.

That heavy tension had to be alleviated, and soon, Thalasi knew, or their discomfort and confusion would not only destroy any plans of conquest, but would likely spell doom for the mighty fortress itself, an eruption of insanity that would take down the very walls of the place. Thus, Thalasi bade Mitchell to join him in his throne room the next day.

Again the cold rain pelted the castle, the gloomy day nearly as dark as the night, with heavy clouds and drenching downpours and the occasional flash of lightning. Thalasi thought that quite appropriate, and perhaps advantageous. Reaching out for universal power had always been easier in times of thunderstorms, when some of those violent powers were so near and readily available.

Mitchell had to know that, too, and the fact that the wraith came into the throne room without being asked twice was a bit unnerving to the Black Warlock. Why was Mitchell so confident?

"When first I returned to Talas-dun after the battle of Mountaingate, there were two in charge here," the Black Warlock began.

"Talons?" Mitchell said, scoffing, as if to remind his former mentor that no talon could ever prove any real threat.

Thalasi shook his head. "Two within me," he explained. "The dueling spirits of Martin Reinheiser and Morgan Thalasi, each fighting for dominance in this singular mortal shell. It could not be so, not then and not now, not within me and not within Talas-dun. The talons must know without doubt the identity of their true leader, and the zombies cannot be effective if caught in a tug-of-war of wills."

"The talons are yours, the zombies mine," Mitchell decided.

"No!" Thalasi was quick to retort.

"Only the staff gives you any power over them," the wraith went on, not backing down an inch. "Yet I have innate powers to command the undead. With the staff in my hands—"

"With the staff in your hands, you would have no need of me, and no need of any living talons." Thalasi sneered, so easily understanding the true intent behind the wraith's proposal. "Take me for no fool, wraith, and forget not that it was I who created you."

"That alone may mark you as a fool," the confident wraith replied calmly.

Thalasi straightened in his throne, rubbing his hands along the burnished black wood of the Staff of Death, which lay ready across his lap. "The staff is mine; the zombies are mine; the talons are mine."

"And am I also yours?"

"You are my general, as it was before," Thalasi offered.

The wraith's hideous, rasping laughter filled the room and echoed throughout the walls of the fortress. "By whose word? Yours? The time of magic is passed; you admitted that much yourself."

"Not passed, but lessened," the Black Warlock said. "And I have this, always at the ready." He held the mighty staff aloft, level with the wraith's simmering eyes. "And this gives me you, Hollis Mitchell, and all the undead I can spare the time to animate."

"Perhaps you overestimate its power and your own," the wraith replied, confidence still strong in his voice. A peal of thunder aptly accentuated the point.

"Let us see," the Black Warlock said, his voice a hiss, and he thrust forth the staff, reaching his power out through it in a mighty assault on the wraith's sensibilities.

An overwhelming desire to kneel nearly dropped the wraith to his knees, but Mitchell found within him enough independent will to resist, to gradually turn the force back on Thalasi. "Give me the staff!" the wraith demanded, and he came forward, reaching with both hands.

Thalasi growled and redoubled his efforts, waves of energy rolling out to halt the wraith's progress. Mitchell moved forward an inch, then back several, then stubbornly forward again. Soon Thalasi was roaring like some wild animal, and Mitchell was issuing forth a long unbroken hiss.

Thunder boomed outside; waves of energy passed back and forth between them, hammering at them.

"It is mine!" both declared, and then they roared and hissed and fought with all their strength. Mitchell's gray fingers were barely an inch from the staff, and Thalasi knew that if the wraith managed to grasp it at all, his own advantage would be stolen and this creature, many times more powerful than he, would utterly and horribly destroy him, would take Talas-dun and all that he had created.

Sheer desperation caused the Black Warlock to reach out from that room, into the rain and wind, and, as fortune would have it, into the lightning stroke that had just begun. Thalasi's power channeled that stroke into the room, into his body, then down his arms and through the staff, to blast out at Mitchell, hurling him across the room. The wraith slammed against the wall and slumped there, dazed.

Simple luck had won the day, Thalasi realized, but he knew, too, that he could not let the wraith in on that secret. "The time of magic is not fully passed," he said sharply, confidently. "You would do well to remember that, my pawn, for the next time we battle, I assure you that I will decide you are not worth the trouble! Now be gone, before the next lightning, and the one after that, sears the dead skin from your bones!"

The wraith pulled himself to his feet, the red fires of his eyes simmering, simmering, as he looked with the purest hatred upon Morgan Thalasi. Mitchell suspected that the fight had been much closer than the Black Warlock's bravado would indicate, suspected that bad fortune, and not a superior will, had won the day for Thalasi.

But defeated the wraith was, and Mitchell could not rightfully deny Thalasi's words when the Black Warlock proclaimed, "I am the master."

She awoke in a place of near darkness, with only the shadowy light of a single torch burning outside her chamber in a low earthen corridor. Cobwebs hung all about the corners of the small room, about the thick stones of the archways, muting the light, tasting thick in her mouth and nostrils with every breath she took. It took Rhiannon a few seconds even to register that she was not lying down, that she was hanging from the wall, her wrists and ankles tightly chained.

She saw a humanoid form nearby and tried to speak to it through the cobwebs that seemed to be, too, in her throat and mouth. "Please," she begged.

The form turned about, another joined it, and the young witch recoiled in horror, for these were not humans, nor even living talons, but were zombies: horrid, rotting things with skin hanging off in flaps, bones showing in many places. Silently they approached her, and then they beat her, bony fists pounding about her head, until she knew no more.

She awakened nearly an hour later, one eye closed, the taste of warm blood thick on her lips. The zombies remained, standing impassively, seeming more garish statues than animated creatures. Rhiannon thought to speak to them again, but wisely reconsidered and held her tongue. These things, she realized, were mere automatons, incapable of independent thought. Her last words had spurred them to beat her, and so if she spoke again, she would likely get the same brutal treatment. It made sense to the young woman. She was in Talasdun, she knew that beyond doubt, for she had indeed seen the black castle just before the last time she lost consciousness. Yes, she clearly remembered that darkened blur on the edges of her vision, all the darker still for the evil that brooded there. She was in Talas-dun, and these zombies, these guards, were pawns of either Thalasi or Mitchell. Neither of them would want her talking, spellcasting perhaps, and so the orders to the zombies had likely been simple and explicit.

She held silent, just hung against the wall, and soon the realization of her various pains nearly overwhelmed her. Her head hurt, and her face ached with its fresh bruises. Her stomach growled for lack of food—how long had it been since she had taken a decent meal, or any food at all?

But her wrists, her poor wrists, proved the most agonizing of all! She dared to glance up at them, to see lines of dark, dried blood ringing them just under the shackles, and she recognized that if she shifted in the least, those scabs would reopen.

And so she hung there, for hours, until she drifted off to something akin to sleep, but not nearly restful enough to be called so. She hung there, and she fought the delirium and the awful boredom, and the more awful helplessness. Had they put her down in this dungeon to starve? she had to wonder as time passed into irrelevance, just one long aching black pain, a complete emptiness.

And all the while, the zombies simply stood there, rotting, smelling, unblinking, and drawing no breath.

Rhiannon didn't know how long had passed—a few days at least—when at last she heard a commotion outside of her immediate chamber, somewhere along the low corridor. Her relief remained, even when the source of that commotion, Mitchell and Thalasi, walked into the dungeon.

"You live still?" Thalasi asked, his expression showing

that he was amused. "Ah, but that is the curse of the blessed wizards, my dear, for you shall not die, shall hang here in empty torment through all the years, through all eternity."

"I could kill her," Mitchell remarked, for no better reason, Rhiannon supposed, than to boast. She knew that he wouldn't kill her, wouldn't so easily alleviate her suffering.

She tried to reply to them, but could barely move her parched lips.

Thalasi laughed heartily. "Consider this your reward for your actions on the field near to the Four Bridges," he said. "Yes, Rhiannon, daughter of Brielle, I know who you are, and I know what you did. Naughty child."

Now the words did come, the discomfort stolen by the sheer revulsion welling in Rhiannon's throat. "Ye did it yerself," she rasped, ending with a hacking, dry, and dusty cough. "Ye reached too far. Took too much. And so ye breaked it. Ye—" She stopped, gasped, as a cold, invisible hand clamped about her throat. The zombies, too, moved to attack, but Thalasi waved his black staff and stopped them.

Rhiannon felt most keenly the power of that staff, and noted Mitchell's wince as it was presented. She knew then the importance of the item, and the power, for in this time of weakened magic, that staff alone brought the Black Warlock such strength. Her concerns quickly became more immediate, though, as that awful cold hand squeezed tight, cutting off her air, strangling her.

Then it was gone, leaving the young witch gasping. She looked at her two adversaries, and understood that Thalasi, with that staff, had been responsible.

"I had thought to make you comfortable," the Black Warlock said to her. "To pamper you with finery and luxury."

Rhiannon spat at him.

"But there it is," the Black Warlock continued without missing a beat, smiling widely at her disrespect. "That trademark stubbornness, so much like your mother. You would not appreciate my hospitality. No indeed. Not you, the daughter of Brielle. You would do as she would do, act as she would act, and plot against me, every second."

Rhiannon's crystal blue eyes narrowed.

"So you hang here, forever and more," Thalasi said with a laugh. "Know that my pets—" He indicated the zombies. "—are close at hand, and with orders to beat you into unconsciousness every time you move, every time you utter a single sound."

"And know that I will be about, as well," the wraith added, moving so close to Rhiannon that she could feel the deathly cold that clung to the horrid creature's gray body. "And I can do worse things than beat upon you, I promise."

Rhiannon didn't doubt that, not in the least, but while her expression was one of deep despair, her mind worked furiously for some solution. She would not give up, would never give up, no matter the pain, the hunger, the weakness, the cold.

She would find a way to hurt these two, some way, any way, before she left this life.

"The zombies will lead us out of the mountains," Thalasi explained to Mitchell later on, when the two were alone—except for an insignificant talon guard—in the throne room. "Tens of thousands of zombies, and skeletons, too, who have lain in the cold ground for decades, even centuries, but who will rise again to my call. A sea of undead will lead us, to the river and beyond the river, and those who do not flee in terror, who do not yield to the power of Thalasi, will soon enough only add to our ranks."

The wraith said nothing, just stared and wondered at where Hollis Mitchell might fit into these grandiose plans. Mitchell understood the depth of the Staff of Death, its true power, and he did not doubt that Thalasi could raise and control this sea of undead monsters, especially since zombies and skeletons, unlike the wraith, were unthinking and unquestioning animations, mere extensions of the staff and the Black Warlock who held it. But where did that leave Mitchell?

"You will not lead them," Thalasi said suddenly, as if reading the wraith's thoughts—and that, too, seemed a distinct possibility to the wraith, given the staff's connection to him. "For you, I have other plans."

The flames that were Mitchell's eyes simmered.

"You will not disagree," Thalasi promised. "For I offer to you your greatest wishes."

"Then you will kill yourself," Mitchell replied sarcastically.

Thalasi laughed that notion away, taking no offense. "I shall allow you to go out independently, to find Belexus, to find Ardaz, to find Brielle, and to do as you will with them, to torment them, to destroy them, perhaps to kill them—then raise them as undead under our control if we can find a way to facilitate such a thing."

Suddenly the flames in Mitchell's eyes reflected more intrigue than anger.

"You shall be my assassin," Thalasi said with a laugh. "And none in all the world can stand against you."

Mitchell was no fool and understood that Thalasi was deflecting him, distracting him to prevent him from finding some way to gain greater control over the undead soldiers. Mitchell understood, too, that he and Thalasi were bound by an unholy alliance indeed, one that would not hold when their common enemies were no more. But the wraith could accept that for now; there were greater enemies in the wide world yet to be slain, Belexus Backavar principal among them.

It was an offer the wraith could not refuse.

Chapter 14

Salazar

TRULY IT WAS a trying moment for Belexus, a pivotal moment in the life of this man who had been a warrior since his earliest recollections, who had trained for all of his life for battle. He had faced whip-dragons and talons by the score, had run into battle with odds a hundred to one against him, had slain a young true dragon, and had faced the wraith of Mitchell, and had done so willingly—so many times staring down the prospect of near-certain death. And always, even in his very first battle, the ranger had done so without hesitation, with a song—to Avalon, to King Benador, to Andovar—on his lips.

But none of those battles, none of that training, and none of the precepts of his warrior code, could have prepared Belexus for this awful moment. Time seemed to stand still, frozen, as the ranger's thoughts whirled, recollections of every battle replaying in an instant. Everything stopped—the breathing, the heartbeat—and in that awful moment, for the first time, Belexus tasted fear, sheer terror, threatening to hold fast his legs and arms, tangibly weighing down his mighty sword.

Indeed it was a pivotal moment, the truest test of courage. And Belexus found then his warrior's heart. And Belexus stepped through the terror. And Belexus charged.

He heard the wizard's voice, though the words did not

register, saw the dragon's reddish hue, horned head rushing forward, maw gaping, spearlike teeth gleaming. With a growl, the ranger set his feet firmly, legs widespread, took up his sword in both hands, and drove a mighty upswing that connected on the dragon's armored jawline with a screech like metal on metal, white sparks flying from the blade.

The dragon was not biting at Belexus, but at Ardaz: a wizard, obviously, and doubly dangerous to the sensibilities of this creature spawned of Thalasi's magic. The great wyrm would have had Ardaz, too, and that surely would have been the end of the befuddled Silver Mage, but the ranger's tremendous blow deflected the angle of the attack just enough, and the massive maw snapped with the crackle of a huge tree splitting just over the wizard's head.

Belexus' sword rang on and on, vibrating in his hands, and though he knew that its craftsmanship was superb, he feared for the integrity of the blade.

The dragon recoiled its neck past him, head shooting back twenty feet, like a giant snake coiling to strike, and the ranger recognized that he hadn't even hurt the thing! He had hit the dragon harder than he had ever hit anything before, and he hadn't even cracked the outermost scales, hadn't even dug a deep scratch upon them!

A sharp intake of breath, a huge suction that tugged the ranger forward a step, showed that the next attack would neither be slowed nor deflected by any blade.

"My staff! Oh, grab my staff!" the ranger heard Ardaz cry, and he turned and saw the wizard holding the staff out toward him, both it and Ardaz glowing a soft blue.

Belexus dove. He heard the blasting exhale, the fiery gout, as he caught the staff's end and fell facedown to the stone. He felt sticky, gooey, as if he had jumped in a vat of thick cream, and in the instant before the flames engulfed him, he noted that he, too, was suddenly glowing that same bluish color.

Then he felt the heat, and saw only the bright orange glow of the flames rolling over him, engulfing Ardaz, and rolling out toward the spirit of DelGiudice, who was standing off to the side and who was not glowing with the wizard's protective shield. On and on came the searing blast; Belexus could feel the gooey shield thinning, and feared that it would not hold. He heard Ardaz screaming, whether in horror or in pain, he could not tell, and heard, too, DelGiudice's shrieks. Had the ghost, who had not gotten to Ardaz or the staff, been consumed?

Then it was over, as abruptly as it had started, and the ranger pulled himself up from the soft, molten floor. The burn area did not reach to DelGiudice, Belexus noted with relief, seeing the ghost still standing there, terrified and unmoving. Ardaz was making fast through the molten sludge toward the exit, crying for Belexus to hold fast to his staff.

The ranger plodded to keep up, taking care to get his feet up high before the stone could solidify, thus trapping him in place.

They cleared the edge of the burn area, Ardaz tugging Belexus free of the last grasping stone then urging him on, both of them calling for DelGiudice as another line of fire came forth, licking at their backsides, chasing them right out of the room.

"DelGiudice!" Belexus called, his tone frantic, for the ghost was not with them.

"We have to make it into the narrow tunnel!" Ardaz yelled back, pulling fiercely at his staff, offering no room for debate. "Run, oh, run away! I do daresay, that one's breath will melt us both!"

* * *

He heard them running, calling, and initially thought it prudent to chase after them, to get as far away from this horror as possible. But unlike his first visit here—when the wyrm had been asleep, when he had not witnessed the fiery breath—Del found that this time his sensibilities betrayed him. He knew that he should flee, and yet he could not, held firmly in place by a profound, completely illogical, and completely consuming terror. He winced, his will nearly breaking altogether, when the wyrm loosed another searing blast down the corridor after the departing wizard and ranger.

The dragon started after the pair, but skidded to an abrupt halt, its huge claws screeching on the stone, digging deep lines. The reptilian head swiveled down and about, and lizard eyes narrowed, as if the great beast had just noticed the third of the intruder party.

"Greetings," Del heard himself saying, and he wondered why.

The dragon responded with typical impatience, sending forth its fires over poor Del. And the ghost screamed—how he screamed!—as the bright flames washed over him, filtered through him, bubbled the very stone at his feet. On and on it went, on and on Del screamed, but his yells diminished before the dragon fires lessened, as his physical sensibilities broke through the barrier of terror and informed him that he was not burning, was not hot at all, that the dragon fire had no effect whatsoever!

He looked up at the wyrm, could hardly make out its horned head through the flaming deluge, and waited, and waited, until at last the fire stream ended.

"Impressive!" Del congratulated.

The sheer power of the outraged dragon's ensuing roar split stone, and down came the snapping maw. Unsettling indeed was that sight to Del, the rows of spear-like teeth chomping over him, seeming to bite him in half. But again the mouth only closed with a resounding, empty snap, the dragon's maw passing right through the insubstantial ghost, and when the wyrm lifted its head, Del stood impassively in place, looking up at it.

"Again, I must agree that you are quite impressive," Del, growing ever more confident now, mustered the courage to remark. "Ineffective, but impressive."

He nearly swooned at the sheer speed and power of the claw slash, the three-taloned weapon swooshing right through him, screeching off the still-warm stone at his feet, tearing deep jagged grooves.

"YOU ARE NOT REAL!" the wyrm cried, and Del took note of the slightest hint of distress in its godlike voice.

"Yet here I stand," Del started to respond, but the dragon was paying him no heed at all.

"WHAT TRICK IS THIS, WIZARD?" the wyrm roared. "WHAT DISTRACTION? BUT YOU SHALL NOT ESCAPE! YOU WHO DARED TO DISTURB THE SLUMBER OF SALAZAR SHALL NOT LIVE TO SEE THE LIGHT OF DAY!"

"Oh, and it is a bright day," Del remarked, for no better reason than to distract the wyrm again, to indeed distract it that his friends might hustle out of the caverns.

Salazar ignored him though, and moved out of the chamber with awesome grace, seeming more a stalking cat than a bulky lizard.

The ghost thought to follow, perhaps to pester the dragon all the way, or to dance about it in the coming confrontation in an effort to take some of the creature's focus from his friends. Del couldn't help a long glance at the treasure mounds, though, as splendid as anything he could ever imagine—at least in this form, on this world. And when he did glance back that way, a flash of gleaming white light caught and held his eye.

There it was: the sword Belexus had described, stuck into the side of a huge pile of gold and silver coins. There could be no doubt about the identity of this blade, for there could be no other to match it in all the world. Despite his fears for his friends, Del found himself drifting toward the sword. He reached down tentatively and felt its shining hilt: bright, silvery steel woven with threads of the purest gold. Slowly, reverently, Del drew it forth from the pile, marveling at its blade—blue-gray, but edged on both sides with a thin line of roughly triangular diamonds, like little pointy teeth or—the thought suddenly came to Del from some far-off, fleeting memory—like little white-wrapped Hershey's Kisses. He didn't have to run his finger along that blade to recognize its sharpness; in fact, so wicked did it seem that Del was actually afraid to touch it, fearing that this sword would somehow transcend the boundaries of the material plane and his present spectral state and cut his digits clean away.

Del had no idea of how strong he was in this condition, but he understood that this sword was incredibly light and perfectly balanced. He gave it a slow swing, marveling at the diamond light that trailed its swishing cut.

Then he remembered, suddenly he remembered, that his friends remained in dire trouble. Off he went at full speed, and he heard the roar of Salazar, heard the "Oh, bother" of Ardaz, and knew that he had tarried too long.

Belexus went forward in a roll, under the dragon's bobbing chin, between its forelegs. He rose on his feet with a powerful thrust, driving his sword straight up and hoping that the beast would prove less armored underneath.

No such luck, and as the blade jabbed, bent, and

skipped harmlessly to the side, the ranger had to leap and dive again, out from under the dragon, for Salazar, no novice in battle, simply buckled its great legs, dropping its tonnage straight down.

Belexus barely missed that crushing blow, and he came up hard and pivoted abruptly, bringing the sword in a mighty over-the-shoulder chop. Again the screech and the sparks, and this time, the ranger believed that he had actually cracked a scale.

That realization brought little hope, though, for he was working hard, far too hard, for each swing, and the damage, even from this one, proved minimal at best.

Even worse, the last hit only got the dragon angrier, if such a rage was possible, and even more animated. The great claws tore at the stone, bringing the creature in a devastating turn to keep up with running Belexus. The long, serpentine tail whipped about, smashing a rocky outcropping into a pile of broken rubble. And that turning head, trying to catch up to the ranger, held a blast of fire ready to incinerate the man.

"Use yer lightning!" Belexus begged Ardaz, but the wizard, knowing that any offensive spell he might invoke would likely only anger the dragon even more—and even worse, might rebound off the solid scales, doing harm to Belexus or to Ardaz—was busy concentrating on his next defensive shell.

Belexus came running back in a loop, the turning dragon's head right behind, and the ranger dove again for the staff, catching it just as the fiery breath rolled over him. On and on it went, but this time, Ardaz and Belexus, protected by the shell, didn't stand there screaming, but rather used the plumes of fire and smoke to slip away, into the next chamber. Then, when they had put the continuing fires behind them, they broke into a dead run.

The dragon's angry and frustrated roar signaled all too clearly that the beast was again in pursuit.

"Ye keep going," Belexus bade the wizard. "I'll stop and slow the thing, and might that ye'll find yer way out!"

Ardaz grabbed him doubly tightly. "Oh no, no, no!" the wizard cried. "The wyrm will incinerate you, and hardly slow. Or maybe he'll just run you over, flatten you in the corridor, on his way to get to me! You keep running with me, fool hero; I need your speed to help pull me along!"

Indeed, the ranger's stride was much greater than the old wizard's, and Belexus was pulling Ardaz along at a great clip. Not great enough, though, the ranger feared, as Salazar's continuing tirade of wicked threats loomed ever closer.

"We canno' get away like this!" the ranger complained.

"Why did we come in here at all?" Ardaz screamed back at him. "For a sword? A single, stupid sword?"

In reply, Belexus gave a sharp tug that turned Ardaz about ninety degrees. The wizard gave a stifled cry, thinking he was about to slam the wall, but he went into blackness instead, a small side passage.

"Douse yer wizard light," Belexus bade him, squeezing by and pulling the wizard along.

Ardaz looked at his staff curiously for a moment, then, with a word, extinguished the fire burning atop it. On they went. They heard the dragon skid up in the main corridor, near to where they had detoured, and a great sniffing sound told them that the wyrm had not been fooled.

"Run on!" the pair cried together, and Ardaz added, "I do daresay!"

The wizard desperately tried to summon another defensive globe, but he wouldn't be fast enough this time, and only Belexus' pulling saved him, took him far enough down the side passage that Salazar's fiery blast only tickled his backside.

"THIEVES!" the dragon bellowed, and that roar seemed worse by far than the dragon-fire breath. "WHAT TRICK IS THIS?"

"Trick?" Belexus echoed curiously. "Going down a smaller tunnel's no trick. Not a good one, anyway," he added when he turned a slight bend and came against solid stone, the dead end of the passage.

"Something else?" Ardaz asked with a shrug, and his thought was bolstered a moment later when he heard the dragon rush off, back the way it had come.

"Are ye thinking that we should go back out there?" the ranger asked after a long, quiet while.

Ardaz shook his head so fiercely that his lips made smacking sounds.

"Well, put up yer light," the ranger said, and when Ardaz complied, they saw that they had indeed come to a dead end.

"Only one way out," Belexus reasoned.

Again, the wizard's lips smacked wildly, ending when Ardaz pursed them and blew out the fire at the end of his staff.

"Then we'll be sitting here a bit and waiting," the ranger said, and it was obvious from his tone that the notion didn't wear well upon him.

"Just give the wyrm a chance to get farther away," Ardaz begged.

"If DelGiudice coaxes the thing on a merry chase, then might be that we can get back in the treasure room and sniff about for the sword."

The darkness in the tunnel was complete, but the ranger could well imagine the incredulous look Ardaz was offering his way.

"We come for the sword," the ranger announced with more determination than he had been able to muster since first he sighted the terrible dragon.

"We ran away," Ardaz said dryly.

"Only to regroup and go back," Belexus said determinedly.

Ardaz' snort showed that he was far from like mind.

"We can't be letting the wraith—"

"Oh, bother the wraith, and Thalasi, too," the wizard interrupted. "I'd fight them both with my bare hands before I'd go back into the Salazar's room! Have you gone mad, then?"

In response, a grumbling Belexus crawled over Ardaz, none too gently, and started back down the passage. The wizard couldn't make out many of the words the ranger was muttering, but he heard "Andovar" and "vengeance" quite clearly.

"I do daresay," Ardaz mumbled, and with a helpless shrug, he crawled into line behind the ranger, even brought up his staff-torch a moment later—not that his courage had increased, just that he was feeling so ultimately stupid that he figured he might as well take this quest all the way. If they were indeed going back after the wyrm, then they might as well let the wyrm know it. "Might get it over with more quickly," was all the explanation Ardaz offered to Belexus when the ranger turned back to stare incredulously at the light.

They came to the lip of the tunnel and paused there, listening to hear if the dragon was waiting quietly just around the bend. Then Belexus hesitated once more, taking a long while to try to muster the courage to peek out. It mattered little, the ranger told himself, for if the dragon was nearby, waiting to spring, the beast could just as easily go to the mouth of the hole and let loose its fires, for the ranger and Ardaz could never scramble far enough away in time.

Still, thinking about an action and performing it can be two very different things, and Belexus had to wait a moment longer before he found the strength to ease his head and the lit end of the wizard's staff out into that wider tunnel.

All was clear, so the ranger crept out, then motioned Ardaz to follow—then reached back and pulled the trembling and unmoving wizard out. The ranger pointed right, back toward the treasure room, but Ardaz stubbornly pointed left, back toward the exit.

Belexus thrust his finger more forcefully to the right and nodded that way.

Ardaz started left.

Belexus caught him by the beard and turned him about, and then both jumped and yelped, surprised by the approach of the ghost of DelGiudice.

"What're ye about?" the ranger started to complain, but the words were stuck in his throat the moment he noted the precious cargo Del carried.

"There are some advantages to this semiethereal state," the ghost explained, handing the weapon over.

"Ah, but she's beautiful," the ranger said with an awe-stricken gasp, feeling the balance and the clean cut, and witnessing the trailing diamond light.

"Salazar knows I took it," Del explained. "I think he knew the moment I picked it up, though he was out here, chasing you."

"Dragons are like that," Ardaz offered.

"Never have I seen such a blade," the ranger went on, the gleam of the diamonds reflecting off his clear eyes, even in the dim light.

"Knows which way I went, too," Del tried to explain.

The ground shook beneath their feet, then again and

again at even intervals, the heavy footsteps of the approaching wyrm.

"Time to go," Ardaz implored, and when Belexus continued staring at the blade, the wizard popped him on top of the head with the end of his staff. "Time to go!" Ardaz said again, pointing frantically back down the tunnel.

Belexus turned to see the long and empty passage but could hear, quite clearly, the thunderous approach. For an instant, the ranger thought of going back that way, of trying his luck against the wyrm now that he held such a powerful weapon as this.

He decided against that course, only because his duty was to Andovar; and his primary enemy, and the greatest threat to the goodly folk of the world, remained the wraith of Hollis Mitchell.

"Run on and I'll keep the dragon busy for a bit," Del offered.

Ardaz and Belexus exchanged skeptical glances, but it was obvious that Del had already accomplished quite a bit more than they ever could have hoped to, and so they started off, after Belexus tried to pat the ghost on the shoulder and inadvertently slid his hand right through Del's chest.

Del watched them go, managing a supportive smile. In truth, though, the ghost was feeling a bit low, sad that he could not experience that touch, or any touch, from a warm, living creature. He thought of Brielle again, of their lovemaking, and his heart sank.

It was just for a moment, though, as the spirit purposefully recalled his time with the Colonnae—and how distant that memory seemed! It struck Del as more than a bit odd how the trappings of this world and this shape, such as they were, were imposing upon him some very different emotions than any he had experienced in all his time with Calae, as if the form itself were dictating some thought to the intelligence.

That was a question for another day, Del realized, as the dragon came rambling into sight at the end of the corridor. The ghost waited until he was certain the wyrm saw him; then he slipped into the same side tunnel Ardaz and Belexus had recently exited.

Salazar was there quickly, and with predictable, irrational fury, the dragon breathed its fire into the passage, balls of searing flame rolling over calm Del.

"Deeper, deeper!" Del yelled, turning his mouth so that his voice was aimed deeper into the tunnel, as if he were bidding his friends to run for all their lives.

Salazar clawed at the stone and roared repeatedly. "NOWHERE TO RUN!" the wyrm bellowed. "I CAN WAIT A HUNDRED HUNDRED YEARS! HOW LONG CAN YOU STAY IN THERE?"

"Longer than that," Del said, too quietly for Salazar to hear.

The dragon's patience proved the first to go, or perhaps it was just that Salazar was more cunning than Del believed, and would not be so easily fooled. The wyrm began snuffling again, then turning circles in the corridor beyond the side tunnel, finally moving a bit beyond the opening and sniffing again.

Then came such a roar as DelGiudice had never heard, the roar of a dragon robbed, and even worse, the roar of a dragon fooled!

Outside the mountain, both Ardaz and Belexus heard it clearly. So did Calamus, the pegasus shifting nervously as the wizard tried to climb onto its back. So did Desdemona, darting so speedily into the nearest saddlebag that she nearly took the harness from the pegasus' back.

"We should be hurrying," Belexus said dryly.

"Time to run," the ghost concurred, coming fast out

of a crack in the mountain wall, not far to the side. "Or to fly," he corrected, noting the winged horse.

"But the big dragon cannot get down that small passageway," Ardaz reasoned.

"He's not to stay in there, however he comes," Belexus cried, and it seemed true enough, for the mountain itself began violently shaking from the wrath of the great wyrm. The ranger looked back into the tunnel determinedly, his hand clenched tightly about the hilt of the diamond sword, and both Del and Ardaz wondered if Belexus meant to run back in.

Truly it was difficult for the proud ranger to flee at that moment. He had no desire to face the likes of Salazar again, but the sudden notion that his action, his theft, might bring the wyrm out of its hole, and that the dragon, in its unrelenting outrage, might fly off and take vengeance on undeserving souls—perhaps on the elves of Lochsilinilume, perhaps even on Avalon—was heart-wrenching indeed.

"Get on!" Ardaz commanded, grabbing the ranger's shoulder. "Climb on and guide us far, far away! You'll not defeat the wyrm, Belexus Backavar, not if you and all your ranger friends together, and each with blades like that you now hold, caught it curled up in a deep sleep!"

With a frustrated growl that showed he could not disagree, the ranger mounted the pegasus in front of Ardaz and urged Calamus into a short run to the edge of the small ledge and then leaped the horse high into the empty air. The white wings beat furiously, wise Calamus understanding the need for speed. Up they went, and around the side of the mountain, and just a few seconds later, they heard the thunderous rumble of an avalanche, a tremendous explosion of rock and snow bursting out from the mountainside, and they knew that Salazar had come forth.

"Do keep us out of sight," Ardaz cried in Belexus' ear. The wizard turned to look back, but stopped halfway, gawking, seeing DelGiudice floating along easily beside them, hardly working, yet pacing the swift flight of Calamus with ease. Del offered a wink to the wizard and then was gone, reversing his direction so quickly that Ardaz blinked many times before he figured out where the ghost had flown off to.

Around the mountain, Del met up with the dragon. Salazar in flight—wings extended, hardly beating, yet traveling at a speed that mocked the furious rush of the pegasus—seemed even more fearsome than had the dragon in its mountain hole, where the tight stone of ceiling and walls forced it into a tight posture. The dragon spotted Del, who was making no effort to conceal himself at all. Salazar never slowed, never swerved, just came on at tremendous speed, swooshing right through the startled spirit and flying on in pursuit of the real quarry and the stolen treasure.

It took Del more than a few moments to recover from that tremendous shock. He turned and started after the wyrm, but changed his mind and his direction, flying fast instead the other way around the conical mountain.

"He's gaining! Oh, he's gaining!" Ardaz cried, glancing back often and spotting the dragon making its way around the mountain's stone arms.

Belexus did well to guide the pegasus in tight to the mountainside, weaving about the rocks and keeping every jag right behind them to block the dragon's line of sight. This might buy them time, but not much, the ranger knew, for the dragon was obviously the swifter, and was amazingly agile in the air, despite its great bulk. Searching the landscape, Belexus came around the next outcropping, then put Calamus into such a steep dive that Ardaz nearly rolled right over the ranger's shoulder.

A shrieking Desdemona did go over, one swiping claw raking the ranger across the cheek, and then the cat was spinning and falling, spreading wings as she went, becoming a raven and quickly swerving out of harm's way. The wizard, fumbling vainly to right himself, screamed and held on for all his life, but the ranger bent low, and Calamus put his head down, diving straight out. As they dropped behind the rolling wall of a short ravine, the pegasus spread his wings and turned out of the dive, muscles straining to hold straight and steady. Belexus tugged with all his strength in an effort to help lift the steed's head, to help Calamus turn horizontal to the ground.

Somehow they broke out of the dive, and Ardaz stopped screaming long enough to note the shadow of the great dragon as it sped past high overhead. The wizard tried to say as much to the ranger, but found that his lips and all his face were perfectly frozen from the cold, rushing air. To that effect, Ardaz lifted his palm and summoned a small ball of flame, holding it close.

Belexus needed no guidance. He continued to descend among the lower peaks, turning Calamus away from the mountain as soon as he found enough cover, weaving tight turns about the stones. He cared nothing for specific direction, was only determined to get them all as far as possible—and as quickly—from the mountain and the dragon. Still the guilt nagged at the ranger—where would the wyrm go to loose its vengeance? But even that guilt, that longing to finish this properly, did not prepare Belexus for the shock when he came smoothly around one rounded, snow-covered bluff to find Salazar rising up before him.

Fortunately, the dragon was as surprised as the riders and the pegasus, and so they came together too quickly for Salazar to loose its deadly fires. Belexus snapped off a series of sharp blows as they passed right underneath the serpentine neck, the ranger fighting to keep the beast from turning down its terrible maw and biting them all in half. His aim was perfect, it had to be, stinging the wyrm about the chin, and out they came, lifting just over a beating dragon wing, Belexus pulling hard the reins to spin completely over and down, narrowly avoiding a swipe of the tremendous tail.

The ranger thought that the successful maneuver would buy him a few moments, thought that the sheer bulk of the dragon would force it into a long and slow turn, but the wyrm surprised him as it straightened perpendicularly to the ground, thrusting its tail down and forward, outspread wings catching the air and fast stopping the momentum. Then Salazar merely dropped, turning and angling as it went, wings catching the air and propelling it after the thieves.

Down went the pegasus, through another ravine, over one bluff and around another, then climbing rapidly behind a long rocky arm of the higher mountain, the guiding ranger reasoning that height would afford them speed and a wider view.

Again, though, the wyrm proved much smarter and quicker than Belexus believed, and as they continued their steep ascent, Ardaz poked Belexus on the shoulder and pointed in the opposite direction of the shielding outcropping, up *above* them.

Belexus pulled Calamus over and about, a rolling, dropping evasion, nearly dislodging the poor wizard yet again. The pegasus willingly responded, though the maneuver put them into a straight drop. Again, the strength of the ranger and of the flying horse somehow pulled them out of it before too much momentum could be gained, and Calamus tightened his wings and whipped them about the mountain arm, putting the stone between them and the dragon.

Salazar swooped past, talons clipping and gouging the rock. The roaring wyrm pivoted its head as it flew past and loosed its breath, and only dumb luck saved the trio, the fires hitting the stone below them and melting it away to slide, glowing, down the mountainside.

The evasion had cost the friends all their momentum, however, and Belexus desperately tried again to flip the horse right over into yet another swoop. He had to abort that maneuver, though, for the dragon had angled down in its pass and was now below them—and not so far below them!—and in complete control. Up came the huge horned head as the ranger pulled on the reins; the great maw opened wide, barely forty feet away.

Again Ardaz screamed, and Belexus did as well, but the ranger kept his wits about him enough to draw out the diamond sword, readying it for a last desperate strike.

They knew that they were dead, knew that they could not possibly turn fast enough to avoid the snapping bite. At the last possible instant, Ardaz loosed a lightning bolt, albeit a weak one, and Belexus swung wildly.

He hit nothing but air, for as the dragon started to snap its head forward, a black speck zipped across its face, clawed feet raking hard at its eye.

Salazar roared in protest, spun over in the air, and swooped after the newest foe.

"Desdemona!" Ardaz cried, and the wizard's heart caught in his throat when the dragon, so swift and terrible in pursuit, shot a line of flame the raven's way.

The frantic Belexus had no time to worry about Desdemona, turning Calamus again and dropping into a long dive the other way, plummeting, only half in control, past the stones and snow-covered bluffs, then leveling off and gaining speed. Around a corner loomed not the dragon, but the hovering ghost of DelGiudice, and before either the pegasus or the spirit could react, riders and mount sped right through DelGiudice, a most unsettling event for all involved.

Del caught up with the trio soon after. "Give me the sword," he offered determinedly, extending his hand. "And I will go battle the dragon."

Both ranger and wizard stared at him incredulously.

"Salazar cannot hurt me," the ghost said confidently, thinking that he'd found the solution. Indeed, Belexus almost handed the blade over, but then retracted it, clutching it close.

"Ye canno' be hurt by the wyrm," the ranger reasoned. "But suren the wyrm'd tear the sword from yer hands, and then we'd be without the only weapon that might sting the beast."

When he considered his lack of skill with weapons, Del found that he couldn't really argue with that logic. "Give it to me anyway," he said. "Let Salazar chase after me and his stolen treasure. That is what he most wants, after all." He offered a sly wink to his friends. "The dragon won't catch me."

The plan did sound plausible, though Belexus was hesitant about parting with the weapon. Before the ranger could decide whether to agree or argue, though, the diamond sword suddenly appeared in Del's hands. Belexus blinked many times, then looked to his own hand, and the sword he still held.

"A few tricks left in my old bones," Ardaz remarked through his chattering teeth. He, too, would have winked, except that one of his eyelids was frozen closed. "I do daresay!"

Belexus caught on; Del already understood, since the sword in his hands was surely illusionary, a trick against sight, but not against touch. The speeding spirit looked all around, his gaze finally settling on one particular spot, the same ledge beneath the rocky overhang that the friends had first set down upon when they had arrived at the mountain.

"Get up and out of sight and put down on a ledge somewhere to give Calamus a needed rest," Del explained. "If my plan works, we'll be rid of the foul wyrm, and soon enough."

Following the spirit's line of sight and considering the view, Ardaz and Belexus began to figure out what Del might have in mind. In any case, the spirit was right: They, especially weary Calamus, needed a break. And so the ranger lifted his mount up above the outcropping and found a sheltered ledge, tucking them all in tightly behind stone walls. Both of the men belly-crawled out from cover to the lip of the ledge, peeking out and down to see DelGiudice standing on the lower ledge, under the stone, waving the illusionary sword and calling for the wyrm.

"There," Belexus announced soon after, spotting the flying dragon as it sped straight for Del.

The wyrm came in fast, turned upright at the last second, and hovered in the air just before the spirit.

"Looking for this?" Del shouted, holding forth the sword. "A trick, am I? Well, a trick, then, that steals from under a dragon's nose! A trick that now carries the one weapon that the pitiful wyrm fears!"

A low, ominous growl spilled from the dragon's mouth.

"Fire away, then!" Del said with a laugh. "Show me again your pitiful breath, weakling Salazar! No, wait; allow me to find a side of bacon, that I might cook it in the fire, if the fire is hot enough to cook bacon, that is."

On the higher ledge, the wizard's heart leaped into his throat, for he, like anyone who knew anything about dragons, understood that to insult the beast's fiery breath was perhaps the very worst thing that anyone could possibly say.

But Del knew what he was doing, purposely goading forth that breath. Unfortunately, though, the dragon, too, figured out the ruse. The fires would engulf the spirit, true enough, but they would likely also melt out the supporting rock around him, and hovering Salazar was not so far away.

Instead of fire, therefore, the dragon attacked furiously with bite and claw, and with its sheer bulk, rushing to the ledge, barreling right at, and ultimately right through, the surprised spirit.

"Time for leaving," Belexus reasoned, understanding that Del and the illusionary sword would not keep Salazar busy for long. The ranger blew a long breath as he watched the spectacle of dragon rage, as he watched Salazar tear and bite away huge chunks of solid stone. "Time for leaving fast," he added.

But Ardaz had another idea. He pointed his staff out from the ledge, gathered all of his energy, so much so that his white hair and beard began tingling and standing on end. And then he let fly the greatest bolt he could muster, aiming not at the wyrm, for that would have done little more than feed Salazar's anger, but at what he considered to be a critical spot in the overhang. The lightning stroke blasted in, the ensuing crack of thunder rolled and rolled, and so, too, sounded the ominous rumble within the stressed stones.

Salazar thought to leave, wisely so, but the image of that sword, of that prized piece of stolen treasure, held the dragon an instant longer, a clawed foreleg reaching out and grasping for the blade.

And passing right through the blade.

The dragon roared in outrage, and that tremendous sound only intensified the split of the stones. Out from the ledge leaped the wyrm, spinning and diving, but not quick enough, for the falling rock caught the beast by the wing, tangled it and pounded it, taking the dragon on a long and bouncing ride down the side of the mountain.

"Good enough for you, murderous beastie!" Ardaz cried.

Belexus stared at the wizard incredulously, not used to such obvious outrage from the gentle man.

"Oh, Desdemona," Ardaz said softly, and the ranger understood.

For Del, there were moments when the rock was passing him by, followed by moments when one piece hooked him and took him along, followed by a confusing rush of stone that left him wedged into a crack of a dropping boulder. Then all was spinning chaos, the spirit wondering if this slide could harm him or perhaps even destroy him.

It ended three thousand feet below the ledge, the spirit of DelGiudice weaving about the openings in the crushed stone, finally coming to a place of living matter, the buried dragon, that he passed right through. At the very end of one of Salazar's forelegs, Del found an escape, and he came out into the daylight, looking about for his friends. He spotted them at last, circling down slowly on Calamus, and he waved to them and hailed them, then went silent with fright as the rock all about him erupted and flew wildly.

Salazar pulled free of the rubble, roaring madly. Belexus turned Calamus about sharply, the pegasus all too willing to angle away from the dragon. Still, the ranger feared that he and his friends were bagged, for the dragon could out-fly the pegasus and there was no apparent cover anywhere in this area.

But the dragon, as luck would have it, could not outfly Calamus at that time, could not fly at all, for one of its wings had been torn and broken in the tumble. The battered wyrm loosed its breath at the trio, more for show than as a real attack, for they were long out of range. Then, grumbling and growling like a beaten cur, the defeated dragon began climbing through the rubble.

"Farewell, mighty Salazar," DelGiudice, standing near, offered quietly.

The dragon head turned to face him.

"You cannot harm me," the spirit calmly and rationally explained. "Nor should you desire to harm me."

"THIEF!"

"But only of necessity," Del replied. "Trust me when I say to you that my friends and I had no intention of waking you, had no desire to disturb you in any way. What fools would we be if we had come willingly, eagerly, to the lair of the greatest terror in all the world!" The spirit was trying to play up to the legendary ego of dragons, trying to settle Salazar down so that, when the wing finally healed, the dragon might not be so quick to come out of its hole.

"THIEF!" the hardly satisfied wyrm roared, and its breath fell over Del, who gave a motion like a sigh, though no breath was exhaled, and stood calmly, waiting for the conflagration to end.

"Thief indeed," he called again after the wyrm, who had resumed its climb. "And know that if Salazar comes out of his lair, I, DelGiudice, will enter that smelly place and take more than a single sword!"

The dragon's tail snapped down so hard that a wide crack appeared on the ground, but the battered beast did not bother to look back.

It was many hours later, the sun setting over the western horizon, before Belexus and the wizard drifted down to the spot where Del's spirit patiently waited. Calamus dropped lightly to the stone, and Belexus hopped off, helping Ardaz to follow.

"You could have come up to us," the weary wizard reasoned.

"I didn't know where you had gone off to," Del replied. "First rule when you're lost: Stay put."

"Well, stay put no longer," Ardaz said, and Del noted that all the usual cheeriness was gone from his voice. "We're far too near the dragon's hole for my comfort."

"And for me own," Belexus agreed, glancing nervously up the mountainside. The two of them had watched Salazar slink back into the mountain hours before, but that fact brought little easiness, for dragons, particularly when hunting, have the patience of elves, as only creatures who live through the centuries might understand. "We've been too long near this place, and now's not the time for merrymaking," he added, seeing the ghost's widening smile. "Back to Calamus for yerself and me," he said to Ardaz, "and back to the air for yerself," he added, pointing at Del. "And let us be long from this place afore we stop to consider our good fortunes."

The others readily agreed—the others who had accompanied the ranger to this spot, at least, for all about the friends, from behind every conceivable stone, appeared dozens of short, sturdy men, with dark brown skin, and with the knotted muscles that come from years of working stone.

"Dwarves?" DelGiudice asked skeptically.

"What name do ye be puddin' on us den?" one of them replied in a choppy but lyrical accent that sounded somehow familiar to the ghost.

"Hey boss, de Architect Tribe we be," another added, poking Belexus hard as he spoke.

"Well, well," Ardaz remarked. "This does get more interesting by the moment, now doesn't it?"

Chapter 15

The Witch's Gift

HE STOOD UP. It seemed a minor thing to the animals in the forest about him: a man climbing unsteadily to his feet, as one who had been asleep might, or as one who had been sitting too long in an awkward position. But for Bryan of Corning, that movement felt momentous indeed. He remembered the pains and that deathly chill when he had crawled into Avalon more than a week before. He remembered the view of his own feet, black and thick, and he remembered most of all the pain when Brielle had warmed them again, the agony that had so quickly replaced the sheer numbness.

That was all past now. The half-elf wriggled his toes, all ten of them—and how glad Bryan was to see, to *feel*, that he still had all ten of them! And though his legs were surely tingling and prickly, it was a sensation that Bryan savored: the evidence of life.

"I thought ye'd sleep all the winter," came a quiet yet strong voice from the side, from the shadows of the lower branches of an evergreen.

And Bryan saw her then, and surely his heart fluttered, though he had already given that heart to another. If the horrid wraith had been darkness incarnate, then this, before him, was the embodiment of beauty itself, walking softly, a dream creature on a blanket of gentle fog, her golden hair shining, green eyes and the emerald wizard's mark sparkling through the shadows. Bryan understood that the twinkle of those eyes could penetrate the darkest of nights, like the soft gasp or the sharp cry of a lover, like the very stars above.

Bryan's smile widened as Brielle stepped out of the brush, dressed only in her white gossamer gown and her delicate slippers, though the air was not warm and the ground was covered still with snow. "I am truly indebted to you, fair sorceress of Avalon," the half-elf said, bowing low.

"Nay," the witch replied. " 'Tis me place to do the things I do, and nothing more."

Bryan didn't believe a word of it. He knew what Brielle had gone through to save him, knew that she had taken his pains as her own, one at a time, and, with them inside her own seemingly fragile frame, had battled them and overcome them. He knew that she, for the better part of a week, had felt the same agony as he, and he understood, too, from their joining, that Brielle had been near to the brink of death, had come so very close to stepping over that thin line and slipping away forever into the dark realm.

"If Brielle went about the world trying to steal all the pains, as she stole mine, then surely she would have been worn away many centuries ago," Bryan remarked, trying to put a bit of levity in his tone so as not to offend the witch.

"Not to all the world, but to those who come to me door," Brielle replied. "Me magic gives to me the healing power; how wicked I'd be not to share it with those in need."

Bryan nodded, conceding the point, though he still considered Brielle's actions toward him heroic and beyond any call of duty. "Whatever you may call it, you have my thanks and my heart."

"Indeed I could've had it," the witch said with a smile. "I could've plucked it beating right from yer chest, so battered were ye!"

Bryan shared her laugh, but put on his serious expression almost immediately and dipped a low bow.

"Go on, then," Brielle said to him. "For I'm thinking that another's got yer heart."

The half-elf straightened and eyed the witch directly, all traces of any smile fast flown from his serious expression.

"And it's for her that I'm wondering," Brielle went on, a bit tentatively, for she recognized the fear in Bryan's look.

"And was it for her that you healed my wounds?" the young half-elf asked.

"Might be that I tried the harder," Brielle admitted. "But no, for suren I've heard tell o' Bryan o' Corning, and he's not one deserving death at the hands o' Mitchell's foul wraith."

"How do you know about the wraith?" Bryan asked, letting the conversation continue its tangential flow, for he could not seem to muster the courage to tell the fair witch the truth about her daughter. Not yet.

"I know the nature of yer wound," Brielle explained. "And know, too, that the wraith's been about. I'm not so blind and not so much a fool."

"None of neither," Bryan agreed.

"But I'm not knowing of me daughter," Brielle continued. "I'm not feeling her about. And I'm thinking that ye might be."

Brielle didn't miss the cloud that passed over Bryan's face.

"I was with her when Mitchell attacked," the half-elf began quietly, chewing his lips between words. "I could not hurt the wraith, nor could Rhiannon. I do not understand why she went out to find the foul thing! I don't know that it was looking for us, and don't know that we ever would have seen it. But, for some reason, she went out after it."

Brielle nodded; she understood her daughter's purpose, and so would heroic Bryan, she knew, if he just stepped back a bit and considered his own actions across the river.

"I got knocked away, and out of mind for a while," Bryan explained. "And when I awoke, they were gone, the both of them."

Brielle licked her soft lips nervously.

"I do not think that Mitchell killed her," Bryan said suddenly, needing to offer some comfort to this worried mother.

"Me girl's not dead," Brielle responded firmly, with some certainty.

"Agreed," the half-elf said. "I believe that Rhiannon led the wraith away to protect me, and probably that she leads him still on a merry chase across the lands. I started out of Corning on their trail—two separate trails—but discovered that my wounds were too great. And so I made for Avalon to warn you."

"And well ye did," Brielle replied. "Yer wounds should've killed ye long before ye got near to me home."

"But that was so many days ago," Bryan said, his expression puzzled.

"Nine days," Brielle clarified.

"We must out for Rhiannon at once," the half-elf reasoned, looking all about like an animal put in too small a cage.

Brielle's upraised hand calmed him.

"You know of her?" Bryan asked hopefully.

"With what ye telled me, I can find out more," the witch explained. "Take yer breakfast alone." She pointed to the evergreen. "I'll be back to ye afore the sun crests." With that, Brielle was gone, disappearing into the brush so quickly that Bryan blinked many times.

He did as she asked, moving to the spruce tree and finding a most delicious meal set out for him, and though he was too worried for Rhiannon to feel hunger, he ate well, realizing that he would soon need all of his strength. And how he marveled at how much of that strength had already returned! As the morning passed, the half-elf began to feel much more himself. His legs soon steadied, his head cleared, and he felt as if he had spent a year at rest, eating well and training easily.

The only things that tempered the near euphoria were thoughts of and fears for Rhiannon, and Bryan knew that if she did not return to him, his health would fly away.

Brielle came back to him late that morning, her face grim, her gait slow and even awkward. Bryan ran up to meet her, took her by the shoulders, then lifted her chin so that she looked him in the eye.

"No," he breathed.

"She's not dead," the witch whispered, seeming so very old suddenly, the twinkle in her green eyes flown away. "But she's been taken."

"The wraith?"

Brielle nodded. "And Thalasi, I'm fearing, for me divining telled me that Mitchell put out for Talas-dun, and likely he's there already."

Talas-dun. Morgan Thalasi's black fortress. The name hit Bryan like a heavy stone, a name known by every person in all Aielle, a name synonymous with the deepest terrors and the greatest evil.

Brielle straightened and pulled from Bryan's supportive grasp. "I canno' go after her," the witch said bitterly. "Me magic forbids me leaving Avalon at this dark time, yet how am I to abandon me daughter to the clutches of Morgan Thalasi?"

"I can go out," Bryan said with a determined growl.

Brielle nodded, for Bryan's sake not daring to disagree openly, but she understood the futility of it all. The brave young man was no match for Mitchell, let alone Thalasi, and certainly no match for either of them in that dark place, in Talas-dun.

"By all the precepts of me very existence, I canno' go out from me wood," the witch said. "For if I did, then suren Thalasi'd come a'calling, and Avalon'd be taken down, and all the world'd know a deeper pain."

"Deeper than the pain Brielle now feels?"

Her green eyes narrowed as she looked at him, and he understood that, in the witch's estimation, no pain could be deeper than the one that now tore at her heart.

"You said that I am not in your debt, and though I offer you my sincerest gratitude, I accept that premise," Bryan said suddenly, taking on haughty tones that surprised the witch, a demeanor she would have expected from one of King Benador's knightly warders, perhaps, but not from the half-elf.

"And as such, I am not bound here," Bryan went on. "And so I choose to go, at once."

"And yer destination?"

"Is my own to pick," the determined half-elf replied.

"Not so hard to guess," Brielle said.

"Then if you know me so well, dear Brielle, you know, too, that I must go to the west, to Talas-dun, to the court of Thalasi, to hell itself if need be, in pursuit of Rhiannon."

"Ye love her," Brielle stated.

"More than I love my own life," Bryan replied without hesitation, and the words felt so good as he said them, a confirmation of truth, an admission that he knew he'd have to make again, to Rhiannon.

Brielle spent a long while studying the young half-elf, her perceptive gaze reading his body language, reading his heart. After a few moments, she began to nod slowly. "Ye're going after her, though I fear ye'll find the road too dark. I'll not try to slow ye, though I'm thinking that one who might help might be returning to me soon. And I'll not try to stop ye, for I know that I could not, not if I showed to ye the truth o' Talas-dun in all its splendid wickedness."

"Not if you showed me that I would have to wrestle Thalasi and all his minions bare-handed," Bryan replied.

"And if ye die?"

Bryan shrugged, as sincere a reply as Brielle could ever have asked for.

"Ye get yer rest, Bryan o' Corning," Brielle instructed. "I'll gather yer sword and armor—I been mending both—and bring them to ye afore the morrow's cold dawn."

Bryan's expression became tentative, and Brielle read it easily. The half-elf feared any more delays, feared leaving Rhiannon in Thalasi's clutches for a moment longer. "I'm not fighting yer feelings that ye should go off at once," the witch said. "But know that if ye go unprepared, then ye've got no' a chance o' e'er seeing the black castle. Ye give me the one night and I'll help ye, I promise, and I'll get ye a horse that'll run swifter than any ye've known."

That last promise quieted any protests from Bryan. "I fear that I have tarried too long already," he said. "But I trust in your judgment and in your word." Indeed Bryan did, for he, like everyone else, understood that Avalon's horses were the greatest in all the world, both in speed and in heart, and it was common knowledge, too, that none could rope or ride such a beast without the blessings of the forest and the lady who guided and guarded it.

In the morning, true to her word, Brielle returned to Bryan leading a small, well-muscled chestnut mare. Saddlebags bulged with supplies, and Bryan's fine sword was set through a loop on the side of the saddle, his elven-crafted armor and shield strapped atop the seat. When he took down that armor, the young half-elf's eyes widened indeed, for the mail had been interwoven with ribbon, green, laced with gold thread.

Bryan put a quizzical look over Brielle, who only smiled and nodded, all the assurance the half-elf would ever need.

"Ye've got food enough to take ye across the world and back," the witch explained after helping Bryan to don his armor. "And take heart that yer metal shirt'll block most any blow," she added, "excepting, perhaps, the horse-bone mace of the wraith, and I'm not for knowing what terrible weapons Morgan Thalasi will use against ye."

The value of such a gift from the witch of the wood was not lost on Bryan. He started to bow, then changed his mind, stepped forward and kissed Brielle lightly on the cheek. "I will bring her back to you," he promised.

Brielle could not speak past the lump in her throat. She reached into her pouch and produced an amulet: an emerald set in silver and hung on a thread of vine. She looped it around the half-elf's neck, drawing his attention to the green gemstone, turning it up so that it glittered before his eyes.

"Ye know that I'm with ye," she said cryptically, and let the amulet hang low once more. "Don't ye ever be forgetting that."

Bryan nodded and kissed her cheek again, then, without hesitation, he swung up onto the saddle and kicked the mare into a quick canter.

He was out of Avalon soon after, riding hard to the west. That western edge of the forest did not border the rolling green Calvan plains, though, but met with the land of Brogg, the Brown Wastes, the desolation of Thalasi. This was the wildest edge of Avalon's perimeter, a place untamed, and thus, a place always guarded.

The ever-vigilant rangers of Avalon, watching the lone rider gallop out of the forest, were more than a little confused and suspicious of his passage. Lord Bellerian, father of Belexus, leader of the proud warriors, was back into the deep forest soon after, calling out at the top of his lungs for Brielle. He found her after midday, and was surely relieved to see that she was unharmed. He questioned her about the slender rider, garbed in the fine armor of Lochsilinilume.

"A friend o' me daughter," Brielle admitted, taking pains not to lock gazes with the venerable ranger. Bellerian was old and crooked from a long-ago battle wound, but his will remained iron-strong, as great as that of any man alive. "So brave a lad," the witch went on, and the sadness in her voice could not be denied. "Though I'm fearing his days left are not so long."

"He rode an Avalon horse," Bellerian said, a bit of accusation in his tone.

Brielle only shrugged.

"And his armor, too, had been worked by the witch of the wood," the ranger lord pressed. "We saw the green and gold, such as ye've recently put into our own shirts."

"Yer eyes might be a bit too fine, me friend," the witch answered with a dismissive wave.

"Ye helped him."

Again, the shrug. "A fine lad, his blood running near

to elvish," she explained. "His heart's against Thalasi, and so his heart's with me own."

That last line, coupled with the pervasive sadness, hinted at something much deeper to Bellerian. Indeed, he wondered, might the half-elf's heart be akin to Brielle's on the matter of her missing daughter? "I did not know that gifts o' the lady came so easily," he remarked.

"Ye're too old for jealousy," the witch said dryly.

Bellerian caught her by the shoulder and forced her to match his stare. "Ye've never lied to me, Brielle," he said quietly, forcefully.

"And I never telled ye that which I wasn't planning to tell ye," the witch replied calmly, and it was true enough. No man, no elf, no one in all the world held any bond over the witch of Avalon.

"Ye sent him after Rhiannon," Bellerian said.

"Go back to yer kinfolk," she replied, somewhat sternly, and she turned and walked away.

"How dare ye?" Bellerian yelled at her, just as she was about to make one of her trademark disappearances into the brush. Those words stopped the witch short and brought her back to the ranger lord, her eyes narrow. Green flames, they seemed.

"How dare ye?" Bellerian said again, not backing down, though a lesser man would have fallen to the ground and whimpered for mercy in the face of Brielle's terrible wrath. "For two score and more of years, me and me kin've been standing beside ye, helping protect yer forest."

"Me own gifts to yerself and yers have been no less," Brielle answered.

"And all of them to hell, I say, if ye canno' trust me and me kin on this most important ride!" Bellerian yelled right back at her. "If yer girl's in trouble, then know without doubt that 'tis our bound duty, and our heart-bound pleasure, to go and find her. Our duty, I say, and our love, and not the work for a young warrior o' mixed blood!"

"He loves Rhiannon, of that I do not doubt," the witch said quietly, all of the fight suddenly flowing out of her.

Bellerian, too, calmed, recognizing her deep pain. He put his arm about Brielle's shoulders. "He loves her no more than do the rangers," he promised. "For Andovar and for Brielle, and for the beautiful young creature that Rhiannon has become, so much her mother, and yet so different."

Brielle looked up at him, her eyes wet with tears, the hint of bobbing sobs just beginning about her delicate shoulders. "Thalasi's got her."

Bellerian blanched.

"And I'm thinking that Bryan o' Corning might get through where an army could not," she explained.

"But he has to first get near to Talas-dun," Bellerian pointed out. "And the Brown Wastes run thick with talon scum."

"Don't ye be underestimating that one," the witch replied. "Spent all the time since the first battles west o' the river, killing talons."

Bellerian did not disagree, for he, too, had heard the tales of Bryan of Corning, and had been truly impressed. "But 'tis me duty, and the duty o' me kin to go with him," he said firmly. "Out to the west we ride, for Rhiannon, for Avalon."

"I canno'—"

"Stop us," Bellerian interrupted. "Ye canno' stop us," he finished, "for if ye do, then know that ye've ended our covenant. And know that ye've broken our very hearts."

Brielle could not hold her stare against the proud ranger. Truly Bellerian meant his grave threat, and truly,

Brielle came to know that she and her daughter were blessed with some of the finest friends anyone could ever hope for.

"Bring her back to me," she whispered, and then she broke, falling into Bellerian's strong embrace, burying her face in his shoulder, sobbing.

The ranger held her for many minutes, until she found the strength to stand alone once more. And then he looked at her, full of respect and full of love, bowed once, and was gone.

Twenty-two rangers pounded out of Avalon late that afternoon, riding hard to the west on Avalon steeds, in pursuit of Bryan of Corning, in the hunt against Thalasi.

In the quest to find Rhiannon.

Chapter 16

The Architect Tribe

"YOU WAKED DE beast, you stupid bean growers!" the first of the dark-skinned tribesmen protested, and again, his kin poked Belexus hard.

In the blink of an eye, the ranger had the short man by the front of his dusty tunic, lifting him high off the ground.

"Easy, my friend," Ardaz warned, seeing the others bristling, seeing their pickaxes gleaming.

"This man could break de rock," the hoisted tribesman remarked, and he reached over and felt the ranger's bulging biceps. "Could break de rock," he said again with certainty.

"Or the dwarf," Belexus warned.

"Don't you be calling me dat, boss," the tribesman replied.

"No need of this, oh no, no!" Ardaz put in, moving to the center of the group. "Ow!" the wizard added suddenly, a sharp pain sticking him in the butt. He turned about at once but found that none of the short men were anywhere close to him.

"Hey boss, you don't piss her off, eh?" the first man said.

"Piss her off?" the wizard echoed, scratching his head.

"Caribbean," Del said suddenly, his face brightening

with recognition. He looked to Ardaz. "Before the holocaust," he explained. "The dialect, the black skin . . ."

"Lookin' brown to me," one of the tribesmen said dryly.

"Friends o' yer Billy Shank?" Belexus asked, and that gave Del pause, for he had hardly considered Billy Shank since returning to this world, and he remembered now that Billy had once been his dearest friend.

"Ah, yes!" Ardaz roared suddenly. "Caribbean Sea! I do remember, I do daresay!"

"We don't know you, boss," one of the tribesmen said.

"And no Beely Shank," another said.

"Billy Shank," DelGiudice corrected. "A friend of mine, with skin the same color as yours—almost the same, but not quite as dark."

"Hey, you don't be talkin' trash, boss," yet another said and he moved close and poked at Del, and of course, his finger sank right into, right through, the specter. Trembling suddenly, the man backed away, eyes wide.

"Voodoo," Del and his two companions heard someone say, and the respect shown them grew immensely in the next moment.

"Mamagoo not gonna like dat," the first tribesman said.

"Mamagoo?" Ardaz and Del and Belexus asked together.

"Mamagoo de priestess," the man said. "She ain't gonna like that you know the voodoo. It will make it harder for her to kill you, you see. She ain't gonna like no zombies walkin' about her mountain."

"Kill us?" Ardaz echoed. "Whatever for?"

"For waking de big worm," the tribesman said. "You tink we want him out of his hole?"

"Dey tink we be stupid, then," another said.

"Dey be stupid," a third added. "For dey be dead before we be dead!"

"I'm already dead," Del remarked, and that brought a unified "Ooo" from the throng, and indeed it now was a throng, more than sixty strong, all short and woolly haired, with dark skin, dark brown mostly, but some who seemed perfectly black in color.

"Well, the dragon's gone back to its hole, if that is of any comfort," Ardaz said, but again he ended with an "Ow!" as another stabbing pain got him in the rump.

"Oh, yeah. Mamagoo, she like that one," one of the tribesmen laughed.

"She'll be playing wit dat one before she kills him," another said.

"Maybe bring him back in zombie to play some more, eh?" yet another laughed, and all joined in.

"Who are you?" Ardaz demanded, and he hopped and turned, looking suspiciously for anyone who might be trying to stick him with something small and painfully sharp.

"We be de Architect Tribe, boss," the first man said. "Don't you hear so good?"

"Your name, good sir," the wizard insisted.

"Okin Balokey," the man said.

"Unbelievable," Del whispered, more to himself than to anyone else. "Do you realize what this means?" he asked the wizard. "The ancestors of these people must have come to Ynis Aielle right after the holocaust, and they have evolved a bastardized culture . . ."

"Hey, boss!" several yelled at once.

"Don't you be calling names," Okin Balokey said. "And I don't care that you be dead!"

"No names," Del said apologetically. "All I meant is that the culture you have evolved is so intriguing." He looked to Ardaz, who was growing truly agitated, truly excited. The wizard had spent many years trying to prove that others had come to Ynis Aielle, that there had been—perhaps still were—other cultures and other races in the wide world. And now his proof had walked right up to him—and had apparently stuck him in the butt . . . repeatedly!

"They speak with Caribbean dialect," Del went on, "and have the dark skin, of course . . ."

"There he goes again," one remarked.

"He cares too much about de skin," another said.

"And yet, look at them!" Del cried. "They cannot average much over five feet."

"Now he sayin' we too short!" one exasperated tribesman cried.

Okin Balokey put a disgusted gaze over Del, hands on hips and shaking his head slowly.

"Not too short!" the ghost protested. "But you are, and you must admit, shorter than average."

"We below average," one man said with mock sadness.

"No!" Del said. "But I suspect that your ancestors were far taller, probably averaging close to six feet."

"You tink we like bumping our heads on de ceilings of our tunnels, boss?" Okin Balokey asked.

"Exactly my point!" the ghost cried.

"Oh, simply marvelous!" Ardaz yelled, catching on and seeing the beauty of it all. "This is too precious, too grand!"

"Who be dat one?" The unfamiliar voice, a woman's voice, came from behind the gathering. All eyes turned to see a large, older woman dressed in bright colors ambling about the stone, a pair of small dolls in hand, one of which looked remarkably like Ardaz, complete with white hair and blue robes, the other bearing some resemblance to Del, at least in the fact that it was dressed in white. In her other arm, to Ardaz' complete relief, she held a familiar black cat, curled comfortably in the crook of her elbow as if nothing in all the world could possibly be wrong.

"Oh, Des!" the happy wizard cried, rushing forward. The cat merely yawned and buried her face within her paws.

"Mamagoo?" Belexus asked Okin Balokey, who nodded.

"I be stickin' dat one fordy-tree time," Mamagoo complained in her accent, by far the thickest so far, and waving her doll-holding hand Del's way. "And he not be even jumpin'! And my new kitty friend, she be adding a stick or two."

"To both?" Ardaz, taking Des from the woman, asked.

"To yours, mostly," Mamagoo explained.

"Beastly loyal."

"He be a ghost, Mamagoo," Okin Balokey explained, indicating Del.

"Aah!" the large woman sighed in relief. "Priddy ghost he be, too. So very priddy." She replaced the doll in a deep pocket and produced some herbs instead, and began waving them about in the air and singing softly.

Almost immediately Del felt a tug in his thoughts, a mental prodding that it took some effort for him to resist.

"Ardaz," he warned as the wizard came back over to stand beside him.

"Weaving magic," Ardaz reasoned with great surprise. "I do daresay."

Belexus tossed aside the man he was holding and advanced a step toward Mamagoo, and when a host of men jumped in front of him, the determined and deadly ranger drew out his new, brilliant sword.

That set the gathering back on its heels, brought a tumult of gasps, and exclamations of "aah."

"Where you be gettin' dat?" a suddenly very agitated Mamagoo demanded.

The ranger looked to his friends, then all three turned and eyed the dragon's mountain. "It is what we came for," Belexus explained. "All that we came for. We're wanting no trouble from yerselves, but know that we'll not be slowed."

"He talk funny," one of the tribesmen remarked.

"Trouble, boss?" Okin Balokey said incredulously, waving for his companions, who were all tittering about Belexus' strange accent, to be quiet. "You got de sword. De sword!"

"You know it?" Ardaz asked.

"We made it," Okin Balokey replied.

"Ye canno' have it back," Belexus said at once, surprising his friends with his impatience and lack of tact.

"Oh, we don't be wantin' it back," Okin Balokey replied happily, apparently taking no offense. "We just be glad that de worm got it no more!"

Rousing cheers went up all about the companions, then, and the three exchanged confused, relieved glances. Ardaz and Del let their gazes linger together, the pair sharing thoughts of how very strange this group truly was, and both wanting to spend more than a little time with Okin Balokey and Mamagoo.

"I knew it! I knew it!" Ardaz cried repeatedly, pacing across the little warm and comfortable chamber the Architects had prepared for them, far underground—though all three suspected that they had only brushed the highest level of a huge tunnel system. "We could not have been alone, no, no. Makes no sense, after all! The world was a bigger place before *e-Belvin Fehte*, yes, much bigger, with millions of people."

"Billions," Del corrected, and he gave a curious look

after he made the remark, for it, like so many, had come to him from far, far away, from a place he didn't consciously access.

"I knew there were others," Ardaz rambled on. "But I was looking for them in the wrong places—in the east, where the land is more hospitable. And here they were all the time, not so far away at all! I knew other boats made the shores of Ynis Aielle when the new world was young, and oh, the people survived."

"Without the help of the Colonnae," Del remarked.

Ardaz wagged his head, but in truth, he wasn't so certain of that. "They have magic," he reasoned, rubbing his still-sore rump. "Thus the Colonnae must have visited them, or at least have visited Mamagoo or her predecessors. But still, to have survived in the great Crystals! So close to us, and yet, unknown to us!"

"But you not be unknown to us, man," Mamagoo's voice came as she walked into the chamber. "We been watchin' you dese years. You and dem skinny folk with dem pointy ears."

"Then why not come and speak with us?" the wizard asked.

"We tried dat once," Mamagoo said with a visible shudder. "When dem gargoyles come to de mountains. Ooh, but dey whack at us, I tell you boss!"

"Gargoyles?" Del asked.

"Big ugly ones," Mamagoo explained, and she twisted her face in a manner to make it appear all too familiar to the three.

"Talons," Belexus reasoned grimly.

"Dat's why we made de sword, and udder swords," Mamagoo explained. "But dat one, ooh, she be de best o' de bunch!" She eyed the weapon as she spoke, moving right next to Belexus. "You know her name?" she asked solemnly.

The ranger shrugged and shook his head.

"Her name be Pouilla Camby," Mamagoo said.

"A strange name for a sword," Ardaz remarked.

"Pouilla be killed by de gargoyles," Mamagoo explained. "Of course, dis all before I be born, before my mama's mama's mama be born." She finished with a wink at the wizard.

"Of course," Ardaz agreed, and he wasn't sure what the private joke might be. It struck him then that Mamagoo might not be leveling with the others. Perhaps she, like Ardaz and his sister, like Istaahl and Thalasi, had indeed been touched, been blessed with long years, by the Colonnae, and had been alive all those decades, centuries even. More questions, the wizard thought, growing truly impatient. He would have to return here when the messy business with Thalasi was finished. Oh yes he would!

"So we make de sword and call her Pouilla," Mamagoo continued, "and she go and do de bad tings to dem gargoyles!"

Belexus looked from the old woman to the beautiful sword.

"You not likin' de name?" Mamagoo asked, seeing his less-than-bright expression.

Again, Belexus only shrugged.

"Den you just call her by any name dat you be pickin'," Mamagoo offered, patting the huge man's rump.

"Cajun," Del said suddenly, drawing stares from all three.

"Cajun," he repeated, smirking and looking at Ardaz.

"Oh, ho!" the wizard burst out suddenly. "Cajun. Oh jolly, how very jolly!"

Mamagoo and Belexus looked at each other, the large woman running her index finger in a circle about her ear.

"Cajun because it's sharp!" the wizard roared. "Like the food; I remember the food!"

"I will find a name," Belexus said dryly, reverently, to Mamagoo. He offered a glare to Del and Ardaz as he finished. "An appropriate name."

"Dat you do," the woman replied. Then, looking sidelong at the other two and shaking her large head—but smiling as she did—she left the chamber.

Much later that night, Ardaz stirred from a restless sleep. He left his companions snoring contentedly and slipped out of the chamber—to find the "guards" both snoozing comfortably—and picked his way down the dry and smooth tunnel. Voices soon drew him to a side room, and peeking in through the partly opened door, he found Mamagoo, Okin Balokey, and a third person, a younger woman he did not know, sitting in chairs about a blazing hearth, their backs to him.

"I tink dey mean to be fightin' gargoyles," Okin Balokey said.

"Dey good boys," Mamagoo added, and Ardaz realized then that this third woman—a beautiful, slender creature with skin as dark as night and huge eyes—was someone of great importance. He also realized that while the accents remained, the tone of their voices had changed, had become more serious. Ardaz nodded as he considered the tactic. The Architects had seemed almost simple with their speech pattern to the wizard and his friends, jolly and innocent. But there was another side to them, grim and serious and far from simple. There had to be such a side, he understood, for them to have so thrived in such a dangerous environment. Like the elves of Lochsilinilume—to an outsider, at first glance, they would seem joyful to the point of frivolousness. But anger Arien Silverleaf and his kin and one would find as deadly an enemy as existed in all Aielle!

"We should be letting him keep Pouilla Camby," Mamagoo went on.

Okin Balokey started to protest, but the young woman cut him off with a wave of her hand, looking to Mamagoo to elaborate.

"Dey be fighting gargoyles, and dat be a good ting," the old woman reasoned. "Dey waked the dragon, but put de ting back in its hole, and dat be a good ting."

"Unless de ting come back out," Okin Balokey said grimly.

"His wing be pretty broken, man," Mamagoo said. "And if he come out, he not be finding us."

"He be finding dem three that got his treasure!" Okin Balokey reasoned, catching on to her plan.

"And dat put it all back where it be," Mamagoo agreed.

"And if we got de sword, and old Salazar find out, den we be losing many tunnels, I tink," the younger woman said, to which Okin Balokey could only nod his agreement.

"Dey be good boys," Mamagoo said again. "And dat one wit de sword be stronger than any man I be seein'! Metinks dem gargoyles not to be a happy group when Belexus comes calling with Pouilla Camby!"

All three laughed at that.

"You be tinkin' de same, old wizard man?" the younger woman said suddenly, obviously aiming her question at Ardaz.

With a huff and many throat clearings, Ardaz bumbled into the room. "Didn't mean to eavesdrop, no, no," he stammered. "Just walking along and heard you talking."

"And you be liking what you be hearing?" Mamagoo asked.

"Yes, yes!" Ardaz beamed. "And you're right, you know, all of you. None better at chopping gargoyles—we call them talons—than Belexus Backavar, no, no. He's killed a few, he has, ha, ha, a few hundred!"

"He be a good boy," Mamagoo said.

"He needs that sword now," Ardaz tried to explain. "Our enemy, the one who leads the gargoyles, has brought forth a most evil beast, a wraith, you know."

"Dead ting?" Mamagoo asked. Then, when Ardaz nodded, she shivered. "Ooo."

"And that sword, that most beautiful sword, is the only weapon that might hurt it," the wizard explained. "My sister—she's a witch, you know—"

"I'm not liking my sister much eider, boss," Okin Balokey said.

That stopped Ardaz short, until he took a moment to think about it. "Oh, no," he explained. "Not that kind of a witch. A real one, of course. A real one, yes, yes. She found out about the sword, with magic, of course—witch magic, that—and, well, we came to find it."

"And you did," the younger woman said.

"Ah, but my manners be missing!" Mamagoo exclaimed suddenly. "Old Ardaz, dis be Calaireesa, chief of de Architect Tribe."

The wizard bowed low in respect. His expression was one of curiosity as he came out of the bow, though. "Yes, well, I have been meaning to ask, and now seems a good time: Why are you called that? Not a usual name, after all: the Architect Tribe."

"De book say so," Calaireesa answered.

"Book?"

"De Architect Book," the woman explained.

"Oh, de book, she save our lives," Mamagoo added.

"She showed us how to make de tunnels and de rooms, boss," Okin Balokey explained. "We all be children when first we came here."

"Not 'we,' " Calaireesa explained. "But de ancestors. Dey be children, and dey be cold, but de book, she showed dem how to make de tunnels."

Now it began to dawn on Ardaz, yet another marvelous aspect of this unusual culture. With the exception of himself, Brielle, Istaahl, and Thalasi, all of the Calvan survivors of the holocaust had also been mere children. Perhaps the forefathers of the Architects had found a book, or many books, about architecture, a resource that taught them better how to survive in this new world. Might that have prompted them to consider the books as a sort of bible? "Oh how perfectly grand," he beamed aloud, but quieted immediately out of respect.

"I would dearly love to see this book," he said a moment later.

"Sure, man," Mamagoo said, not even bothering to ask Calaireesa for permission.

Ardaz was truly delighted, and impressed. What a wonderful, open society these people had created. Trusting and generous, and always with a smile ready. He would come back here, he vowed silently again. Yes he would, when the situation allowed!

All three then escorted the wizard to a very small, very well hidden chamber, and therein, he found the remains of a dozen texts about architecture, the most prominent one a nearly complete volume titled simply *The Architect*. He found all three Architects quite willing to indulge his endless stream of questions, their answers usually only inciting another hundred questions in the wizard's always-active mind.

Later on, Mamagoo escorted Ardaz back to his chamber. He wanted to ask her many questions, as well, about her magic and about any meetings she might have had with Calae, or with any of the angelic Colonnae.

"Met him once," she answered before he could even really phrase the question clearly, "though I be just a girl den."

"When first your people came to Ynis Aielle?" the wizard asked suspiciously, believing now, beyond any doubt, that Mamagoo had indeed been among those initial settlers, and that Calae had blessed her with the gift of long years.

"Oh, no, man, dat be too many hundred years ago," she said unconvincingly. "I be looking dat old?"

Ardaz laughed and kissed her beautiful cheek. "You be looking simply wonderful!" he said, imitating her accent and drawing a wide smile indeed.

"Now, you be going in de morning, I know," Mamagoo said. "You make sure dat your friend put Pouilla Camby to de good use, man. Too long dat sword be quiet! Too many gargoyles come about in dem years!"

"Do you want it back when he's finished?" the wizard asked, and if Mamagoo had said yes, Ardaz would have certainly honored the request.

"No, no, man," the woman said incredulously. "We don't want no fighting, you know. Dat's why we be living here underground—and don't you be tinking dat any gargoyles might get in here! No, Pouilla will be happy, I know, wit dat big hunter. You tell him to use her good, and den she pass along to de next big hunter. If a gargoyle ever gets her, den we come out maybe, but as long as she be in de hands of de right people, den we be happy."

"Most generous," Ardaz said, starting another bow, but changing his mind and giving another kiss on the cheek instead.

"And we all hoping dat de dragon doesn't come out and eat you all," Mamagoo offered.

"Well, we're hoping the same," Ardaz replied, smiling, a grin that Mamagoo matched and that both held for a long, long while.

"But if he does, den dat be de way of tings," Mamagoo put in, drawing a great laugh from Ardaz.

"You go and sleep," the woman offered. "You got de long road ahead."

"Long and dark," the wizard agreed, but it seemed to Ardaz that the potential ending, if all went well, had just gotten a whole lot brighter.

Chapter 17

Rally Cry

THE AVALON MARE responded with greater ease and greater strength than anything Bryan had ever known, weaving in and out of the towering snow drifts along the twisting ways of lighter snow cover. Not an experienced rider, the half-elf struggled for many miles, soreness settling in across his knotted leg muscles and buttocks. Finally, though, after more than two hours in the saddle, Bryan began to grow at ease, his natural elven affinity for animals helping him to empathize with the mount, to understand the signals he was sending to it, and that allowed him to figure out the proper posture and movements for a smoother and swifter run. His confidence growing, the half-elf loosened his grip on the reins, and the mare bent her head low.

Then the mare was running strong and tireless, the snow-covered land speeding by Bryan as he crouched low, his legs working in a rhythmic and painless posting action.

All the rest of that day, the mare pounded on, with Bryan stopping only when the horse seemed to need a break. Late that afternoon, the half-elf found an appropriate campsite, a patch of frozen brown earth in this mostly white wasteland sea. Though the snow was deep out here, the winds had brought it up in high drifts, and those areas in the shadows of the drifts had little snow cover.

The next day was much the same, and the next after that, but Bryan did notice that the snow cover was gradually lessening the farther he got out from Avalon. The strong winds of the empty plain continued to pile the white stuff up in drifts, but this far out, the winds were more from the west than the north, carrying the warmer air from the sea and turning most winter storms into rainy events. That would prove a mixed blessing, Bryan knew, for though the going would be straighter with less snow obstacles, the concealing cover, too, would be lessened. The brown-and-white streaked plain stretched out far in every direction, a skeletal bush sticking through here and there, and Bryan understood that if he could see that far, then creatures far away might also spot him in his telltale rider's silhouette.

His fears came to fruition later that fourth morning. A fog covered all the region early on, but it lifted rapidly, leaving the half-elf and his mount dangerously exposed on a stretch of flat ground. Sure enough, Bryan soon saw many forms breaking the horizon north and west of his position, and when he veered more to the south, he noted that there, too, were talons. They were not walking or running, but were riding on their lizard mounts, swift creatures that could almost catch a horse.

The half-elf grimaced and considered his course. He knew that his Avalon mount could outrun the lizards, tired as she had to be, but if he split the talon ranks, running straight to the west, it wouldn't be hard for this band to figure out his destination. His only chance of getting into Talas-dun would be through stealth, and this group of obviously organized talons, even if they could not catch him, could certainly jeopardize that, could pass word along secret ways, perhaps with signal fires.

Reluctantly Bryan swung his horse about, turning to the southeast, the general direction of Corning, he figured. He figured that he would allow the talons to close on him, then lead them on a long chase, finally outdistancing them and circling wide in an arc that would bring him around a hundred and eighty degrees.

The talons closed as expected, those north of Bryan gradually catching their closer companions, all the band of about thirty creatures forming together into one whooping mob. They thought they had ambushed a single rider on a tired mount, one they could run down to exhaustion and then easily overwhelm. On they came, hollering and hooting, close enough so that Bryan could make out their every threatening word.

But the talons did not understand the power of an Avalon horse, and the mare easily paced them. Bryan had to rein her in many times to keep the talons hot on the trail. They covered several miles, and the talon hoots grew less and less, and Bryan understood that it was time to fly away. He fast approached a ridgeline, the backside of it conveniently hidden. He would go over the top, he decided, and cut fast to the east, and by the time his pursuers got to the ridge, he would be out of sight. He looked back once, offered a few choice curse words of his own, then turned back and lowered his head, letting the mare run free.

Her thunder had only just begun when Bryan's heart caught in his throat, when the ridgeline verily exploded with rushing forms. For an instant the half-elf thought he was trapped and surely to die, thought that a third talon band had encircled him, thought that those behind him, perhaps, had even herded him in this direction. He winced, even cried aloud as the air about him filled with the buzzing of rushing arrows.

A horn blew, a note so clear that no talon could ever have produced it, and then Bryan understood. "Rangers," he breathed, turning back to take note of the devastation the arrow volley had inflicted on the pursuing talons. When he looked ahead again to the ridgeline, he witnessed the splendor of the thunderous charge, Bellerian and his warrior kin tilting low their long spears, twenty-two Avalon mounts pounding up snow and frozen dirt, hooves ringing on the hard ground.

They passed by Bryan in such a rush that the wind of them nearly tumbled him from his seat, and as he collected his wits, he pulled the mare to a stop, thinking to turn back and join in the fight.

That notion left him as soon as he regarded the scene. The talons, too, had tried to stop and turn, and several had. The others, though . . . Every one that had survived the arrow barrage had been lifted from its saddle by a ranger spear and now lay dead or squirming on the ground. As for those few who had turned in flight, the powerful Avalon horses easily caught up to them, and a ranger sword finished them each with one clean stroke.

Bryan hardly knew what to say as the efficient warriors collected about him, some moving to finish whining talons or to chase off any remaining lizards, others following Bellerian to face the stunned young half-elf.

"Me name's Bellerian," the ranger lord introduced himself.

"Bryan," the half-elf responded, his voice cracking. He steadied himself and took a deep breath. "Bryan of Corning."

"We're knowing yer name, and knowing who sent ye, and knowing, too, where ye're going, lad," Bellerian explained. "Rhiannon's been kin to us since the day o' her birth. Ye'll not be going alone."

Bryan nodded his agreement—what else could he do?—but while he was truly glad to have such fine swordsmen accompany him, he held deep reservations. A group of a score and three would be much more noticeable than a single rider, after all, and Bryan was hoping for stealth, not strength, because he knew that all the strength of all the goodly folk in all the world might not be enough to defeat Talas-dun. He couldn't find it in his heart to argue against awesome Bellerian, though, the legendary ranger lord of Avalon, a man whom Bryan's father, Meriwindle, had oft spoken of, and always in the most reverent of tones. So Bryan would let the rangers accompany him and get him to Talas-dun, however they might, he decided, and then he would go it alone, into the darkness after Rhiannon.

"A dark day," a soldier working on the bridge remarked to his fellows, the lot of them watching the procession as the king inspected the progress. Word had come into camp that morning, dark word, of the suspected fate of Brielle's daughter. Rhiannon was no stranger to these soldiers; during the fierce fighting at the bridges, the young witch had served as healer, and many of the men now working owed their lives to her.

"Work well," King Benador called to the group. "When the bridge is ready, we shall cross the great river; then let Morgan Thalasi tremble."

That brought nods of resolve and a few angry grunts, and the men turned right back to their task, doubling their efforts. The whispers that had carried the rumors out of Benador's tent had also spoken of the king's determination to get across the river, to ride out to the west, all the way to Talas-dun if need be, to rescue Rhiannon or, at least, to punish those responsible for bringing her harm. Every man and woman in the great force gathered on the eastern bank of the river wholeheartedly agreed, and so that same day a secret pact was drawn up among the bridge builders, unbeknownst to Benador or any of the other commanders. All of their work shifts would be lengthened, that the work on the bridge would not cease, all day, and through the long and cold night.

Two days later, when the secretive plan became obvious enough to all around, when word of the double labor reached King Benador's ears, he came out again to the bridge for a conference with the workers, asking for an explanation of the lights burning through the night.

"Two weeks, my king." The grim answer came from the appointed spokesman for the group. "The bridge will be ready within two weeks." All around the man came words of assent.

"It's not safe to work at night," one of the job commanders remarked, to the speaker and to Benador. "Too cold and too dark. One of you might fall into the river, and be swept away."

"A risk we'll gladly take for Rhiannon of Avalon." The reply came from several of the workers, a cry seconded by everyone about.

King Benador spent a long while looking them over, searching their faces to find the truth in their hearts. And that truth, that every one of these men and women agreed and accepted the risks, was indeed heartening to the young king. Unexpectedly, he dropped from his mount and dropped off his kingly robes and moved to a stone. "For Rhiannon of Avalon," he said determinedly, putting his back to the lever, and a great cheer arose.

Benador worked with them those days, and they were able to shorten the shifts once more, less hours and more intense grueling work per shift, but with double the number of shifts, for many others followed the king's lead and came down to the bridge to offer their support. The prediction of two weeks to open the bridge had seemed ludicrous when first proclaimed, but within a couple of days, it seemed as if that prediction might prove far too conservative.

In Lochsilinilume, the city of elves, response to word of the missing witch was instant and universal, and that same day, preparations were made, provisions packed and weapons sharpened, and the very next morning, Arien Silverleaf led his determined forces out of the enchanted valley. The bells on the elvish horses jingled gaily, but the mood was truly grim. This outrage, the abduction of the daughter of Brielle, the daughter of Avalon, the elves could not tolerate.

Not long after the dark news of Rhiannon passed the gathering at the remains of the Four Bridges, it continued south and east, to the gates of Pallendara. Most distressed in all the city was Istaahl the White, a personal friend of Brielle and of her daughter.

"Brielle," the White Wizard called into his crystal ball, sending his thoughts across the miles to Avalon. "Jennifer Glendower, do you hear?" he added, using the witch's ancient name.

Within minutes, Brielle had enchanted her reflecting pool and stood facing the far-distant wizard, and his expression alone told her that he had heard the news of Rhiannon's abduction, and that his heart, too, had broken.

"You believe he took her to Talas-dun?" Istaahl asked.

"Where else might the dark wraith be going?" Brielle replied. "No, he took her there, to Thalasi, to his master."

"Then to Talas-dun I shall go!" Istaahl proclaimed.

"To tear down every wall around the Black Warlock until he surrenders Rhiannon to me!"

Brielle offered a warm smile, though she knew, despite the wizard's good intentions, that there was little Istaahl could truly do. Talas-dun was quite beyond his power, as it was beyond Brielle's, in these times of waning magic. And though Istaahl would remain close to his source of strength, the great ocean, in the region of Talas-dun, he could not begin to match the power of Morgan Thalasi in that evil place.

But Istaahl could not accept that helplessness. For hundreds of years, he had served as advisor to the various kings of Pallendara, had served as wise man and court wizard. For hundreds of years he had been one of the four most powerful persons in all the known world, and now, with this most terrible crisis looming, his impotence did not sit well on his old shoulders. "I will find a way," the White Wizard promised, and he bade the fair witch farewell, promising to speak with her again to allow her to mark his progress.

Istaahl stopped his work at rebuilding the broken white tower that same day, even dismissed the workers assisting him in the task. He considered going out then to King Benador to help in the bridge reconstruction, but no, he decided, by the time he even got out to the river, the work would be nearly completed. He would not go across with Benador's legions, for his power base was the sea, not the inland plains, and by the time he got near to that power again, he would be in the shadows of Kored-dul, in the domain of Morgan Thalasi.

No, Istaahl knew, that was not his place, not his destiny in this great struggle.

Instead, he went into seclusion in the rooms below the ground level of the structure, locking himself in.

No more could he tolerate the impotence, no more

could he, could all the world, tolerate the ugly plague that was Morgan Thalasi. Istaahl fell into a deep trance then, as deep as the one that had sustained him during the score of years he had been a prisoner of the Black Warlock, when Thalasi had stolen his identity to serve in disguise as Istaahl at the side of Ungden the Usurper.

Deeper and deeper the White Mage slipped, far from the world of men and beasts, into the realm of magic—his magic, the power of the sea. He knew the risks, knew the price, and soon enough it became obvious to him that the cost would not be a possibility, but a truth.

And yet he went deeper still, gave himself over heart and soul to this one great task.

This one final task.

Far to the west in the black bastion that was Talasdun, Morgan Thalasi and Hollis Mitchell plotted and schemed, taking heart that they would soon again loose their armies upon the world, their courage bolstered by the fact that they had a most valuable prisoner now, one who would give them tremendous leverage over their enemies—particularly their two greatest enemies, the Emerald Witch and the Silver Mage.

Neither could understand or appreciate the deeper implications of the capture of Rhiannon, the solidarity and sheer determination that heinous act would inspire among their enemies. Neither could appreciate the added hours of back-breaking labor at the broken bridges, nor the ride of Bryan and the rangers, nor the charge of Arien Silverleaf and the elves, nor, most of all, the mounting, desperate efforts of Istaahl the White. That single act of capturing the witch's daughter, who had become so beloved by the soldiers of Calva, by the elves of Lochsilinilume, and by the rangers of Avalon, had straightened the shoulders of war-weary warriors, had forced the grief aside, temporarily, in all of those who had lost so much. Now the expressions were much the same from Pallendara to the Four bridges, to Avalon, to Lochsilinilume; faces locked in grim determination.

This outrage would not stand.

Chapter 18

Tease

THE UNDERGROUND COMPLEX of the Architect Tribe was huge, tremendous, larger than anything Ardaz or Belexus would ever have believed possible. Their tunnels ran on and on, often ending in cavernous chambers, some full of stalagmite mounds, decorated pillars, carved with strange symbols and faces with exaggerated lips or ears or some other such feature. The wizard marveled at the workmanship, the artistry, and remarked repeatedly that he would simply have to return and engross himself in this most wonderful culture. Desdemona, predictably, slept through it all, while Calamus, not used to being underground, remained edgy and anxious, as did Belexus, the ranger wanting only to be on his way now that he had the all-important sword.

He grew quite impatient with Ardaz, for the wizard became distracted by every sculpture, by every ornate pillar lining every side passage. Ardaz babbled and waved his arms and promised Okin Balokey a thousand times that he would return.

On several occasions, the wizard became so distracted that Belexus had to hand over the reins of the pegasus to Del and walk over to pull Ardaz physically from whatever it was he was inspecting. After a couple of hours, with one marvel showing after another, the ranger finally just held Ardaz close at his side, his strong hand resting firmly on the wizard's shoulder, clutching whenever Ardaz seemed about to run off for another inspection.

Despite all the delays and the nervousness of the pegasus, the detour through the tunnels proved worthwhile, when, late that afternoon, Okin Balokey led the way up a sloping corridor, into a wide chamber with only one other exit, one that more resembled a rock than a door. It seemed to the ranger that the door must weigh tons, and when he glanced around, he saw no apparent crank, nor any levers. The craftsmanship proved perfect, though, and a small push by the proudly grinning Okin Balokey had the thing pivoting around, opening the portal to the dazzling daylight beyond.

Belexus stepped out first, squinting and glancing about, looking for familiar landmarks. He did indeed spot one, a peak he knew well, and he realized then that the shortcut through the tunnels had taken them far under the mountains, back to an area that would have taken the pegasus three days of flying, and that in good and warm weather, weaving about the tall peaks and landing often, that Belexus and Ardaz might take a break from the too-cold air.

"Dere you go, boss," Okin remarked. "You should be staying in dem tunnels dis cold night, and be out early in the morning."

It was an invitation that Belexus, to Ardaz' obvious relief, could not refuse, and so the three, and the pegasus and cat, followed Okin back into the complex, to a nearby room that had already been prepared for them.

"We're owing ye much," the ranger remarked to the brown-skinned man before he departed.

"Dat you are," Okin Balokey replied with a chuckle. "So you be using well dat sword!" he insisted. "You make Pouilla Camby sing. Dat be de way you pay back the Architect Tribe."

They shook hands then, and it seemed to DelGiudice that the often-aloof ranger was full of gratitude and warmth toward these mountain folk.

The next morning, after many good-byes·to Okin and several others who had come back with him, the friends were off, Calamus flying hard to the south and west. The day was not especially cold, and the pegasus stayed aloft for many minutes at a time, and that evening, the friends camped in a sheltered lea only three short hours' travel from Lochsilinilume. The ranger was even more eager now, pacing and mumbling, handling often the magnificent sword, the promise of vengeance upon the wraith of Hollis Mitchell.

Del, too, was anxious that night, as memories of the Silver City of the elves flooded back to him, filled him with joy. In his previous existence, the ghost had found his finest moments in Lochsilinilume, except perhaps for those in Avalon, and the prospect of seeing both places again thrilled him—to the bone, he supposed, if he'd had any bones. Ardaz didn't help things much that night, reminding Del of all the joys: the elven dance, the wine, the free-spirited people at play in the snow, and, reminding him, mostly, of the witch of the wood.

Thus, they were out before the dawn, flying though the sun-sparkles that only touched the very tallest peaks of the easternmost mountains. They saw the candles burning as they came over the valley of the elves, and saw, too, many more fires, campfires, down the mountainside from that valley, spread wide on the field of Mountaingate, awaiting the break of day.

"We must investigate," Ardaz reasoned, prodding Belexus to keep the pegasus flying on, right over the Silver City. The wizard looked to DelGiudice then, and bade the spirit to go on ahead, to determine whether those campfires belonged to friend or foe. When Del returned to the other two a few minutes later, he brought curious news.

"Not talons, nor even humans," he explained. "But elves. All of them, unless their numbers have increased greatly in the years of my absence."

"Ye're sure?"

"Arien Silverleaf is among them," the ghost reported.

"Curiouser and curiouser," Ardaz mumbled. "Now why would Arien and his kin come out of the valley? Trouble afoot, I fear." The three went off together then, speeding down the mountainside, and they came upon Arien just as the elves were breaking camp. A series of cries and shouts went up from the low field, and bows did, too, until the approaching flying creature was recognized as Calamus, long a friend to the elves of Illuma.

And then came the cheers, as the elves recognized the riders upon the pegasus: the wizard who had served them for so long and the ranger who had rescued them on the field of Mountaingate in that terrible battle a score of years before.

Down went Ardaz and Belexus, and it wasn't until they landed on the field beside the noble elf lord that they realized that DelGiudice hadn't accompanied them down. At first, the pair exchanged worried looks, but Ardaz broke into a chuckle and nodded knowingly toward nearby Avalon. "Someone else he meant to see first," the wizard remarked.

Somehow that didn't calm the ranger's nerves.

"My greetings, dear friends," Arien said as soon as he determined that he would not be interrupting the private conversation. "You have come at a time when you are most needed, I fear."

"Always seems to be my way, now doesn't it?" the wizard remarked dryly.

"I've come to pay back the wraith of Hollis Mitchell," Belexus answered, and he drew out the wondrous sword.

Arien's eyes shone at the sight; all the nearby elves crowded around, marveling at the sheer beauty of the diamond-edged weapon.

"Use it well, Belexus," Arien said solemnly, "for know that our enemy has struck a mighty blow against our hearts."

"Benador?" Ardaz asked breathlessly.

Arien shook his head. "Rhiannon."

Belexus nearly toppled from Calamus, and did, in fact, slide down from the saddle, barely catching his balance on wobbly knees. Ardaz held his seat, leaning forward when the ranger was out of the way, whimpering softly, and muttering, "Oh, my poor Jenny," over and over.

"We are marching through the forest this day, out the other side, and into the Brown Wastes," Arien explained. "Ride with us for a time, that I might tell you all of the grim tale. But take heart, for it is not a tale without hope."

The elf lord called for another horse then, for Ardaz, that Belexus could ride Calamus alone. The caravan went into the forest as soon as the pair were situated, elvish bells tinkling, and Arien rode beside the ranger and wizard, telling them of the events of the last few weeks.

All the while, Belexus kept his hand tight about the hilt of Pouilla Camby, the wondrous sword he just then decided he would indeed name Cajun, vowing silently that he would get Rhiannon back, and unharmed, or take vengeance upon her enemies.

Brutal vengeance; merciless vengeance.

* * *

The moment he saw her, standing in the middle of a snow-covered field, he knew who she was and recalled vividly all that they had once shared. Brielle, his dear Brielle, whom he had loved more than anything in all the world, and now the mere sight of the Emerald Witch tugged at Del's emotions more than the sight of the birth of stars, more even than anything Calae had shown to him.

The ghost swooped down to the field behind the witch, staring at her lithe form, loving her all over again. And judging from Brielle's expression when she turned about, her eyes wide and mouth drooping open, the effect was no less on her. "By the gods," she mouthed, hardly able to find her breath. "By the gods." And she ran to Del, arms wide to embrace him.

She went right through him, stumbling past, stifling a cry.

"What trick?" she shrieked, spinning back on the ghost. "What torment? What trick? Oh, Thalasi, this is yer evil doin'!"

"No," Del interrupted, the calm in his tone steadying Brielle. "No, it is me. DelGiudice. Jeffrey DelGiudice."

"But it canno'—" Brielle started to reply. "Ye're but a . . ." She took another deep breath and began to sort through the riddle. Brielle was a creature of the first school of magic, the school dedicated to the ways of Nature, and she had great understanding of the spirit world and the connection between the realms of life and death. "DelGiudice," she said more than asked, recognizing now the ghost for what it was.

"My Brielle," he replied, his tone a lament. She was so close, and so beautiful, and yet he could not touch her, could not hold her. Why had Calae done this to him? he wondered. Why hadn't the Colonnae sent him back in corporeal form, as they had returned the other four wizards?

"Then ye're sent to tell me o' me girl!" the terrified witch cried suddenly. "Ye come from the grave to tell me o' Rhiannon!"

"I come from Calae," Del said quickly, not understanding her anxiety, but wanting to dispel it.

"What news, then?" Brielle asked, near hysteria.

The spirit shrugged, obviously not understanding.

"Suren ye know o' me girl," Brielle reasoned.

Again the shrug, and poor Del was truly at a loss.

"O' yer girl?" the witch pressed.

"Who?"

"Rhiannon!" an exasperated Brielle declared. "Yer girl. Yer daughter!"

"I have no daugh—" Then it hit Del like a stroke of lightning; then it was his turn to hear his own words jumble indecipherably, to feel his sensibilities scrambling as Brielle's meaning came clear.

"I have a daughter?"

"Ayuh."

"And you?" Del asked, pointing.

"She's me own," the witch confirmed.

Del's thoughts whirled and whirled, careening back to a night by a small pond, serenaded by the gentle wind and the mournful cry of a single loon, when he and Brielle had made love, had created, so it seemed, a girl child. And such a sensation of warmth, of immortality, of sheer joy overwhelmed the ghost that he nearly floated away on the gentle winds.

"I . . . we . . . have a daughter?" he stammered through a tremendous smile.

Brielle smiled, too, but it was short-lived as she considered the reality of Del returned—returned in spirit only. Brielle, above all others in the world, understood the limitations of such an entity, and suspected that Del would be of little help.

"Tell me," Del implored her, not catching the clue that something was terribly wrong.

Brielle blinked her eyes and snapped out of her terrible worry long enough to register the spirit's understandable curiosity. *Tell him, indeed,* she thought, and she wanted to, wanted him to share in the joy of Rhiannon, wanted him to know his legacy: that beautiful spirited young woman. "Hear me," she whispered, and the breeze carried the words to Del's ears, sent him deeper within himself, to a place where he and Brielle could communicate on a more profound level.

He heard again the cries of a child, of his child, on that fateful night twenty years before, as he dropped from Shaithdun O'Illume, as he fell into the arms of waiting Calae. He followed those distant cries to Avalon now, and saw Brielle with her newborn child, with beautiful Rhiannon, at her breast. Then he saw Rhiannon through the years, saw the child stand on shaky legs and wobble through her first steps, chasing a bunny. He saw her blow a lock of that shining black hair out of her face, blue eye flashing into view for just a second before the stubborn lock plopped right back down. He saw her feeding squirrels from her fingertips, saw a bird alight on her shoulder, saw a bear—a huge and powerful bear—walk right by the child, even allow her to grab onto its hairy flank and get pulled along for a ride.

He saw her dance and sing, and twirl across an open meadow for no better reason than the joy of being alive. He saw her skipping stones on that same pond beside which he and Brielle had conceived her, and saw her hopping on flat rocks across a wide and shallow river, pausing to chase fish that rested in the calm pools.

He saw it all and knew his Rhiannon, so much the

daughter of Brielle. He saw it all, and he understood again the benefits, the highest joys, of the mortal coil that was human life, and for the first time since he had returned to Ynis Aielle, Del was filled with deep regret that he had passed on from this world. For all the glories of the heavens, there were indeed experiences here that could equal the joy.

Brielle, his love, was one of them; Rhiannon, his child, was certainly another.

"Where is she?" the spirit asked, his tone somber, for he suspected now that there was some terrible trouble concerning his daughter.

"The wraith got her, unless I miss me guess," Brielle replied. "The wraith got her, and thus, Morgan Thalasi's got her, and all the world's gone dark."

Del wanted nothing more than to go to her and put his arms around her and hug her close and tell her that she must hold out for hope. That he could not do, though. And he knew then that if anything terrible happened to Rhiannon—if that beautiful life that Brielle had shown to him was cut short—it would pain him evermore. It was not, could not be, Rhiannon's time to pass on—not before she had truly experienced love and life.

But Del feared that he could do no more to help Rhiannon than he could to comfort Brielle, and he considered then the fact that if he went over to hug the witch, his arms would pass right through her physical body.

He almost cursed Calae in that moment, almost called out against this cruel, seeming joke.

daughter of Brielle. He saw it all, and he understood again the benefits, the highest joys, of the mortal coil that was human life, and for the first time since he had returned to Ynis Aielle, Del was filled with deep regret that he had passed on from this world. For all the glories of the heavens, there were indeed experiences here that could equal the joy.

Brielle, his love, was one of them; Rhiannon, his child, was certainly another.

"Where is she?" the spirit asked, his tone somber, for he understood now that there was some terrible trouble concerning his daughter.

"The wraith got her unless I miss me guess," [illegible] said. "The wraith got her, and then Morgan Thalasi's got her, and all the world's gone dark."

Del wanted nothing more than to go to her and put his arms around her and hug her close and tell her that she must hold out for hope. That he could not do, though, and he knew then that if anything terrible happened to Rhiannon—if that beautiful life that Brielle had shown to him was cut short—it would [illegible]. It was not, could not be, Rhiannon's time to pass on—not before she had truly experienced love and life.

But Del feared that he could do no more to help Rhiannon than he could to comfort Brielle, and he considered then the fact that if he went over to hug [illegible], his arms would pass right through her physical body.

He almost cursed Calae in that moment, almost cried out against this cruel, seeming joke.

Chapter 19

Comrades of Convenience

THE LAST SEVERAL blows didn't even register, as the young witch fell far, far away from the brutal beating Thalasi's zombies exacted upon her, escaping from the pain to a place deep within herself. She recalled scenes of Avalon in springtime, of feeding birds and squirrels, of swimming naked and free in the dancing waters of the great River Ne'er Ending. And yet, even here, the Black Warlock found a way to reach her, for each of those calming images were invaded, tainted, by the specters of Thalasi and Mitchell, hovering at the edges of the scene, laughing wickedly, promising doom.

So Rhiannon stopped dreaming altogether, stopped thinking, as she had stopped feeling. She fell so far into herself that she came, at last, to a place beyond Thalasi's reach, and no longer did she hear the taunts or the slaps, and no longer did she feel even the shackles that had her hanging from the wall by her torn wrists.

"I will wake the witch," Mitchell promised, and started for her.

Thalasi held the Staff of Death out in the wraith's path, stopping him short. "You will not reach her," the Black Warlock explained. "She is far from us now, and is strong, so very strong."

"And so very stubborn," the wraith added, drawing a chuckle from Thalasi.

"Like her mother," the Black Warlock remarked.

"Like her father," Mitchell growled, and Thalasi laughed again.

"She cannot hide forever," the Black Warlock calmly explained. "Rhiannon has achieved a state of high meditation, and any tortures we might now exact upon her physical body would be wasted effort."

"How long?" the impatient wraith wanted to know.

Thalasi, who seemed to be enjoying Mitchell's ignorance as much as the discomfort given to the daughter of Brielle, laughed yet again. "Be calm, my dead friend," he said. "Rhiannon will return to consciousness soon enough, and we will be waiting."

His prediction proved accurate, for the next morning, the battered young witch opened her crystal blue eyes to see Thalasi and Mitchell standing right before her, their zombie guards standing behind them, as unmoving and impassive as stone columns.

The wraith growled low and advanced, ready to punish some more, and Rhiannon closed her eyes at once. Again Thalasi stopped Mitchell by presenting the Staff of Death before him. "She will be gone from us in a matter of moments," he explained, and he moved right up to Rhiannon, put his face right before hers.

"They are coming for you," he whispered.

Rhiannon was already moving away from him, slipping fast to that secret inner place. The words caught her, though, and stopped her. She blinked open her eyes.

"They are coming for you," Thalasi said again. He looked back to Mitchell and winked.

"All of them," the Black Warlock said suddenly, sharply. "Coming in a rush to Talas-dun because they know you are mine. Do you understand all the trouble you have caused?"

A slight whimper escaped Rhiannon's lips. She could

take any punishment Thalasi and Mitchell could hand out; she did not fear the pain nor death itself. But the thought that many others—people that she loved and who loved her—were on their way to Talas-dun for her sake assaulted Rhiannon's gentle sensibilities profoundly.

Which was, of course, exactly the effect that the Black Warlock had sought, for adding that anxiety to Rhiannon's fears would confuse her, would jumble her concentration to the point where she might not be able mentally to slip away from him any longer.

Stubbornly, Rhiannon closed her eyes again and began to sing softly, a merry tune that she had often shared with the birds of Avalon.

Thalasi's cackling laughter got through those notes, and so did many of his words as he conversed with Mitchell, as he and the wraith spoke of battle plans to defend against the coming forces. He mentioned Arien Silverleaf and Belexus, and Brielle often. "Out of Avalon, the cursed witch is no match for us," the Black Warlock said pointedly, and before he was finished with that statement, Rhiannon's song was no more. "Brielle knows it, too," he added. "She knows that she cannot stand against me anywhere in all the world save her precious Avalon."

"Then why would she come out?" the wraith asked, cuing on the devious prompt and looking knowingly at Rhiannon all the while.

"Because of her!" the Black Warlock snapped, rushing over so that his skeletal face was right before Rhiannon's eyes, so that she could see his supreme confidence and joy. "At long last, I have lured her from her forest. Brielle comes out because of her poor daughter."

The Black Warlock stood close, examining Rhiannon for a short while. Then, convinced that despair would prevent her mental escape, he motioned for Mitchell to move back in and resume the beating.

Some time later, Rhiannon hanging unconscious in the dungeon, Mitchell and Thalasi walked the parapets of their fortress, surveying their army.

"We must not underestimate our enemy," the Black Warlock cautioned. "Many heroes will come out against us, unless I miss my guess. The rangers of Avalon, surely, and likely Arien Silverleaf and his elven kin."

"And the witch," Mitchell added.

Thalasi wasn't so sure of that. "Brielle would be ultimately foolish to leave Avalon," he explained. "For if she did, then know that I would be quick in the back door, claiming the forest as my own, or at least staining the place evermore. I have never known the Emerald Witch to be a fool."

"But this is her daughter," the wraith retorted. "Could she stand by and let her daughter be tortured?"

"She is grieving, no doubt," Thalasi replied. "And I do not discount her, for it is likely that she will have some surprise to throw our way, as she did with the river at the Four Bridges. But still, she will not leave her forest. Among all the four, she is the most restricted. In coming to Talas-dun, Brielle would leave most of her power behind, and would leave that power vulnerable to my attack.

"But the others will come," the Black Warlock quickly added. "Rudy Glendower—Ardaz—will lead the way, cursing my name every step! And Istaahl will ride beside Benador, and Arien Silverleaf and the cursed rangers beside them. Their powers are no longer great, though certainly considerable, but what they will be counting on is the sword, and not the magic."

"If they all muster, elves and men, their numbers and strength will be formidable," Mitchell asserted.

"They will all muster," Thalasi assured him. "Our greatest weapon against Calvan, elf, and ranger hangs in our dungeon. They will all ride for her."

The wraith appeared pensive.

"And they will all lie dead before my gates," Thalasi was quick to add. "I will bring forth such an army of undead creatures that Benador and Arien Silverleaf will tremble at the mere sight of it. How many thousands shall I need? Ten? Twenty? They are available to me, all of them, lying cold in graves, awaiting my call. Combined with the talon hordes, they will prove such an army that has never been seen before in Aielle, such an army that will sweep away the forces of Pallendara. And you shall lead that army, my friend."

"No friend," the wraith replied bluntly, stewing over Thalasi's exclusion of him as he had recited his plans.

"Comrades of convenience, then," Thalasi readily agreed. "I detest you as much as you do me, I assure you, but I know, as do you, that we are both better off for the other. You wanted Pallendara's throne, and so, with my assistance, you shall have it."

"And if I am to be granted the throne of Pallendara, what reward does Thalasi find for his efforts?" Mitchell asked suspiciously.

"I am rid of the interference of the other wizards," the Black Warlock insisted. "And then alone can I explore the realm of magic more fully. Without their petty concerns and interference, without them constantly tapping into the sources of power that I need for myself, I will bring magic back to what it was, and make it all the greater."

The wraith did not appear convinced, and indeed, Mitchell was not. He suspected that if Thalasi's plan came to fruition, then the Black Warlock would not suffer him to truly act as king of Calva. There was nothing that Mitchell could do about it, though, not while Thalasi held the Staff of Death.

"Comrades of convenience," Thalasi said again, smiling that wicked smile. "We each shall get what we most desire."

"And more," Mitchell said.

Thalasi laughed, but his gaze continued its scan of the wraith as he did, studying Mitchell, recognizing the suspicion. "I have no desire for the petty duties of rulership," Thalasi said to him. "As it was with Ungden, when I was but an advisor. Let the king, be it Ungden or Mitchell, handle the rabble, while I explore the greater mysteries of the universe and exploit the greater powers."

Mitchell did not blink at the hollow words. He remembered well the relationship between Thalasi and Ungden in that time two decades before. Mitchell and Martin Reinheiser had escaped from Illuma and the watchful eyes of the elves and gone to Pallendara to tell Ungden about the secret valley. What they had found in Pallendara had surprised Mitchell, for Ungden, a fop and no warrior, was hardly in control.

No, that control came from behind the throne: from Morgan Thalasi posing as Istaahl the White, the King's "advisor."

The wraith understood too much to find any comfort in the Black Warlock's offers as to how they would sort out the conquered lands. Mitchell understood, too, however, that the Staff of Death gave the Black Warlock all of the trump cards in this game.

Hanging on the dungeon wall, Rhiannon opened a bleary eye. The coldness of the wraith's intrusions remained, a gross chill that stung the young witch to the marrow of her bones.

The zombies remained, too, and as soon as Rhiannon

licked her lips, trying to put some moisture there, they closed on her and beat her.

She fell limp almost immediately and the zombies moved back, and so she hung there, keeping her eyes closed, making no movement at all beyond her shallow breathing. She tried to conjure images of happier days, but they only made her more miserable, for in her ultimate despair, she believed that those days were forever lost to her.

Lost to her, and to her mother, as well, if Thalasi's prediction proved correct. Rhiannon had been no match for Mitchell alone, let alone Thalasi; and so Brielle, if she were really coming out to Talas-dun, would likely be overwhelmed.

The deepest pit of despair opened below the young witch as she hung there motionless, eyes closed, and it took every effort Rhiannon could muster to keep from that fall.

She knew that she could not last, in heart or in body, much longer.

The elven procession passed through Avalon and out the western edge of the wood, following the same trail that Bellerian and the rangers had used, the same trail that Bryan had ridden. Ardaz was with them, on a roan stallion up front beside Arien and Ryell, all grim faced and ready for battle.

Belexus was not among the ranks, but he watched the procession from a grassy knoll north of the troop, with Brielle standing beside him. Despite the dark situation, the overwhelming odds, the loss of Rhiannon, the ranger's heart soared at the sight: two hundred elven warriors riding hard on powerful steeds, bells jingling, armor and weapons gleaming. Belexus had seen Arien's fierce kin in battle before, and he knew that two hundred elves could defeat five times that number of talons. They were a joyous race, more attuned to dancing beneath the stars than wielding a sword or bow, but when battle pressed, none in all the world could fight better. The elves could move and maneuver as a single unit, turning battle into something as choreographed as one of their dances, and their sharp eyes and steady hands made them the finest archers in all Aielle.

But there were only two hundred of them.

"They'll not be catching me father and kin," the ranger remarked as the last of the elves passed out from under the forest boughs.

"Unless Bellerian's found a fight," Brielle replied.

Belexus shook his head. "He'll get around any fight that would slow him down," the ranger reasoned. "Rhiannon's his goal, and nothing more, and horses are faster than lizards."

Brielle didn't openly disagree, though she feared that if Thalasi had spotted Bellerian and Bryan, he would have sent out too great a force for them to circumvent, or might even have gone out personally with his lackey wraith to end the threat once and for all. The witch knew that Belexus understood that possibility as well, but as was his way, Belexus would hold fast to hope.

"Incredible," came a voice behind them, and they turned to see DelGiudice, a part of him anyway, blended into a huge oak tree. Only his face and hands were showing, sticking out from the rough bark.

"It's living matter," the ghost explained. "I can pass through it as easily as . . . well, as easily as I pass through you!" With that, he stepped out of the oak and onto the knoll.

"And it is an incredible experience," he explained. "Every time."

"I've no time for play," Belexus said, rather sternly. He

looked to Brielle. "Arien's not to catch me father, but meself and Calamus suren will. And I'll get to yer girl, don't ye doubt, and pay back that wretched Mitchell in the while."

The ranger started for the witch, then hesitated and looked to the ghost, who was standing quietly before the oak. It was a critical moment for Belexus, with DelGiudice watching him, but he could not deny what was in his heart, no matter if it cost him his friend. He moved to Brielle then and crushed her in his hug, then tilted up her fair face and kissed her.

Both looked to the ghost as soon as the kiss was ended.

"I'm not wanting to pain ye," Belexus explained. "But ye should be knowing that me heart's for Brielle."

The words jolted the spirit from the warmth that he was feeling in watching these two people that he so loved. He turned a curious gaze squarely on the ranger.

"I canno' deny me feelings," Belexus said.

"Why should you?" a truly perplexed DelGiudice asked.

"I know what yerself and Brielle shared," the ranger went on. "And know the beauty o' that; I'm seeing it in Rhiannon's eyes and smile. But . . ."

The ghost lifted a hand to stop the ranger, DelGiudice at last catching on, touched to discover that Belexus was afraid that he would be jealous of the new love that had come into Brielle's life. The spirit smiled as he considered that, for nothing could be further from the truth. To Del—who had seen the mysteries of eternity, who had felt the greater love of the Colonnae—this humanly love was not a thing for jealousy, but a thing for joy. He felt no pangs when looking upon Brielle and Belexus, unless they were from a sense of personal loss, that he could not so hug and kiss the wondrous woman. But in his heart, Del was truly glad that Brielle had found love again, and glad that it was Belexus, a man of pure heart, a man that Del loved as a brother.

"I wish that my own mortal coil was more than illusion," the ghost explained. "I wish that my own arms could so go around Brielle, for in spite of all the greater wonders I have seen, I love her still, and ever shall. But don't fear my reaction to your love." He smiled warmly and winked at the witch. "I always knew that you had good taste."

Brielle returned the smile, then looked back at Belexus, locking stares and then sharing another kiss. "Ye bring her back," the witch said.

Belexus nodded.

"And ye make sure that ye come back to me," Brielle went on.

Again the nod, and with not another word to her, Belexus walked to the other side of the knoll and climbed atop the waiting pegasus. "Will you fly with me?" the ranger asked Del.

The ghost considered the offer for a moment, then answered. "Not yet. I have faith that I can get to the west much more quickly than any of you," he explained, "though of what help I might be, I cannot say. You go on, and fly fast and straight, Belexus Backavar. I will find my place in all of this, I am certain."

"Fare ye well, then," the ranger said. He gave Calamus a kick, and the pegasus went into a short run and then lifted off into the morning sky.

Belexus and Brielle waved, and soon the ranger was no more than a speck in the western sky, easily overtaking Arien's procession.

"And what're ye thinking yer place to be?" Brielle asked Del.

"I don't honestly know," the ghost replied. "I could work as a spy, I suppose."

Something was bothering him, the perceptive witch recognized, and after a moment's thought, she figured it out. "Ye're afraid to go and see yer girl," she reasoned.

"I'm afraid of what I might find," the ghost confirmed. "Suppose that . . ." His voice drifted off to something as insubstantial as his body.

There was nothing more that needed to be said about it, for Brielle certainly understood.

"We'll get her back," Del promised, seeing the fair witch's expression drop. "I know that you must feel helpless, stuck here in the forest," he dared to say, and he wished he hadn't when Brielle looked up sharply. Her expression was not one of helplessness, however, but one of determination.

"Not so stuck," she said. "I gave a piece of meself to Bryan o' Corning, Rhiannon's friend and love, and if he gets to me girl, then I'll be there beside him, don't ye doubt."

Del's thoughts went back to the battle he had fought on the field of Mountaingate, when Brielle had been there, posing as a small horse. The witch had been pivotal in that battle, resisting Thalasi, delivering Del and the one weapon that could defeat the Black Warlock. She had found a way then to be useful, and so she would again, the ghost knew. He took great comfort in that—as he had in the passage of Arien and the elves, as he had in the flight of Belexus—knowing that Rhiannon, his daughter, had so many powerful allies on her side.

For all the days of Benador's march, for all the long nights awaiting word of Rhiannon, Istaahl the White had sat calmly in a private place, gathering his strength, allowing the weakened magic to build strong within his weary bones once more.

He called out to the sea often, and heard its distant

reply, but he came to realize that such a call would not suffice, that to truly find a weapon against the power of Talas-dun, the White Wizard of Pallendara would have to go to the source. As Brielle gathered her power from Avalon, so did Istaahl from the great sea, and so there he went, mind and soul, soaring out and diving down.

He felt the great press of the place as he descended into darkness, more fully engulfed by the watery realm than he had ever before been.

And still his thoughts dove: down, down, to the ocean floor, to the source.

And there, he studied. And there, he called.

And there, he begged.

Morgan Thalasi went out from Talas-dun that very night, his powerful staff in hand. He filtered his senses through that staff as he walked, sensing below him any remains of creatures that had gone before.

And he found them, and everywhere, and with a thought and the tap of his staff, he brought them to clawing animation, struggling, many futilely, for their bones had settled centuries before under tons of solid stone. But many more, garish zombies and white-boned skeletons, did find their way to the surface: lizards and birds, small animals and talons, so many talons.

The procession behind Thalasi grew with every step he took, winding his way through the mountain passes. He found another talon graveyard and promptly emptied it, then entered the remains of a talon village that he remembered, that had been destroyed in an earthquake a hundred years before.

Five hundred animated talon skeletons and nearly half that number of bony lizards followed Thalasi out of that village.

And so it went, through the day and through the

night, and all the next and the next after that, the Black Warlock growing his power out of the very ground, robbing Death yet again. In but a few days, Thalasi's ghoulish army easily dwarfed that of the forces coming to Talas-dun.

And with the Staff of Death in his hands, the Black Warlock found that he could control these unthinking minions as easily as he could clench his own fist.

Hollis Mitchell watched it all, and was not pleased.

Chapter 20

Thalasi's Guest Chambers

"IF ALL THE blackness in all the world had been bunched together, then suren it'd be such an evil sight as this," Bellerian muttered grimly as he and Bryan stared across a wide rocky valley to the black castle perched upon a high plateau overlooking the sea. Patches of fog drifted past their line of sight, obscuring the image—and both were glad for those moments, for the relief offered against the pain of merely looking upon the bastion of Morgan Thalasi.

For Bryan felt no less strongly about the sight than Bellerian, and his heart sank when he considered that Rhiannon was in there.

"We can go no further with the light on the wane," the ranger lord explained. "We'll set the camp about, then be out with the morn. If luck be with us, we'll be into Talas-dun afore the setting of the next sun."

The estimate was obviously optimistic, given the terrain, and truly disheartening to both anxious warriors, but given the trouble the group had already experienced in crossing the Kored-dul range, Bryan knew that Bellerian had to voice a positive opinion if for no other reason than the morale of the frustrated group. They had been in the mountains for several days, winding their way along treacherous trails where even the sure-footed Avalon horses could barely cross. They had followed a path that seemed promising, but that had ended abruptly at a thousand-foot drop on the edge of a long ravine that they had then spent hours and hours circuiting. And always, with every step, the troupe had been aware that danger was never far away. These were Morgan Thalasi's mountains, for centuries infected by his pervasively evil will, serving as a breeding ground for talons and the man-eating lizards the creatures often rode.

Now, at least, Talas-dun was in sight, but there was no clear trail to get to the place, and Bryan feared that they might spend several days simply looking for the correct approach. And each of those days, the young half-elf knew, Rhiannon would remain in the dark one's clutches.

Bellerian kept on speaking of his plans, but Bryan was only half listening—a fact that was not lost on the ranger lord. Thus, when the rangers awoke the next morning, Bellerian was not surprised to find that the young half-elf had stolen away in the night, though his Avalon horse remained tethered beside the others.

"We can find his trail," one of the other rangers said to Bellerian.

The ranger lord thought that over for a minute, then shook his head. "He's gone by ways our horses canno' follow," Bellerian reasoned, and he was not upset—though surely concerned—by the thought. He and his kin had delivered Bryan in sight of Talas-dun, but the rest of the trek was better made by the half-elf alone. The score of rangers could not storm the castle with any hope of success, of course, and a path of stealth was better accomplished by one than by twenty.

"Then what's for us?" the ranger asked.

"Others will be along, unless I miss me guess," Bellerian reasoned. "Benador's sure to come, Arien as well.

And by the time they get near to Kored-dul, we'll have all the region scouted."

The ranger nodded, then ran off to rejoin the rest of the troop, informing them of their new mission.

Bellerian watched them at their hasty, practiced preparations, secure in the knowledge that his rangers were the best scouts in all the world and that when Benador, or Arien, arrived, the rangers would be able to give them a complete report on the enemy's strength and whereabouts, and on the best passes for their approach.

The ranger lord's gaze inevitably shifted back across the misty valley, to the black heart of the mountains. Bryan had done well in slipping off in the night, Bellerian knew; the young half-elf had absolved the rangers of a duty that was better left unserved. If Bryan had announced openly that he planned to go on alone, Bellerian would have had a hard time in convincing some of his more headstrong protégés to agree—might have had a hard time agreeing, himself. And even if they all did come to consensus that Bryan's choice was best, then every one of the proud rangers would carry a heavy heart, beset by the knowledge that they had sent a warrior who was not one of their own to attempt this most dangerous and important mission.

No, Bellerian understood, young Bryan of Corning had done him, and all the rangers, a great service by setting off alone, in the dark of night. No easy path, that, in the dreaded Kored-dul, and such a display of bravery gave the ranger lord hope. Now he held faith in the young warrior. Still, it pained the old ranger that he was not beside Bryan of Corning, and that his son was not there. For forty years, Bellerian had lived in the shadows of Brielle's enchanted forest, and now, when she needed him most, he wanted nothing more than to aid her. But he could not; he was old and he was crooked with a wound from a whip-dragon, and he could not climb steep mountain walls, or castle walls.

"Fare well, young Bryan," he said into the wind. "Bring her back to her home, for Brielle'll not survive losing her daughter dear."

"They are yours," Morgan Thalasi announced to Hollis Mitchell, quite unexpectedly.

The wraith glanced down at the courtyard and the open region surrounding Talas-dun, the whole of the place filled with thousands and thousands of gruesome standing corpses and animated skeletons, mostly talon, but with hundreds of animals in the mix.

"You are my general, the conqueror, and to you I give this army," Thalasi explained.

"To command at your will?" the wraith asked suspiciously.

"To command at your own," the Black Warlock replied, and then, with a wicked grin, he added, "So long as your desires and my own are one and the same."

Mitchell marked well that threat.

"Take them," Thalasi instructed. "Go out from Talas-dun with your army, my general. Meet King Benador and Arien Silverleaf on the field and let them see their folly!"

Mitchell did not immediately respond to the battle cry. "Perhaps our stand would be all the stronger if made here," he reasoned.

"And perhaps our enemies will learn the truth of our power and turn away before they ever reach the place," Thalasi countered. "Perhaps Belexus will not come." He knew that bait would prove too much for Mitchell to ignore.

"Look at your thousands," Thalasi added. "The humans and elves cannot resist us."

Mitchell did look out at the standing throng, so perfectly disciplined, mere weapons for his will, extensions of his very thoughts. Then he looked back to Thalasi and came to share the Black Warlock's confident smile.

And then they went out, a great black wave, and all living things fled before them. And Mitchell had started the march with a mere thought, a telepathic call that the zombies and skeletons could not resist.

After they had gone, flowing like black lava from Talas-dun, Morgan Thalasi gathered his talon commanders and sent them, too, and nearly all of their warriors, out into the field, to flank the army, to watch over Mitchell, and to join in the joy of slaughter.

While the night had been difficult for Bryan, it had gone much better than he ever would have hoped. He had encountered no enemies—none that had seen him, at least—as he nearly blindly picked his way among the boulders and scrub. Instead of traversing the valley, the young warrior had crossed it up high, hugging its western wall, and now he was halfway up its steep northern face, climbing hand over hand, finding holds on juts of barely half an inch, then using his strong muscles to twist his agile body ever higher. When the sun came up—and again, it was a sun dimmed by the perpetual gloom of Kored-dul—Bryan noted that he was nearing the top of the cliff face, fully five hundred feet above the rocky valley floor. The young warrior was no stranger to mountains, having spent many weeks in the Baerendils south of Corning hiking with his father. He knew better than to keep looking down, and focused instead on what lay above him, and soon enough, he was over the lip of the nearly vertical climb.

Talas-dun was not in sight from this vantage, for the ground continued to slope upward, winding among pillars of wind-blasted, gray stone. Anxious, Bryan was off in a slow trot, and he was soon enough berating himself for that eagerness.

He scrambled up a series of narrow and high natural stairs, each about chest height above the previous. The sides were fairly enclosed by rock walls except for a few narrow breaks, almost like the corridors of a castle. Bryan hardly noted them, except to quickly pass them by, until he came alongside one in which a large lizard was resting.

The half-elf cursed himself silently and rushed on, leaping the next stair at a full run, and then the next, and the next. The lizard had seen him, though, and the vicious and ever-hungry creatures could run nearly as swiftly as a horse, and on sure, sticky feet, well-designed for travel in the rocky mountains. Four steps up, Bryan could hear the slapping lizard feet right behind him, gaining on him by the moment, and he had to turn and fight. He scrambled to the back end of the step as he swung about, forcing the lizard to climb before it could attack. Across whipped the elvish blade, the fine sword his father had given to him, scoring hard on the pointy end of the lizard's nose, cleaving through scales, right to the creature's teeth. The stubborn thing came on anyway, putting its hind claws on the lip of stone and propelling itself forward, maw wide, front claws slashing.

Bryan leaped and rolled over backward on the next higher step, landing on his knees and coming ahead once more fiercely, slashing his sword, left and right.

The lizard, surprised by the sudden move, by its own clean miss, lunged off balance, smacking against the riser of stone with only its head and neck going over, with no defense, no chance to do anything except catch Bryan's sword with its face.

The half-elf hit it several times before it managed to get its claws over the stone and come forward once more, and by then, the creature's mouth was hanging open, nose split, jaw shattered. Still, it came on, and Bryan had to be agile indeed, climbing continually backward, up the next step, and several more after that, to avoid the slashing claws. He continued to score hits on the creature's face, tearing out one eye.

But then, as the half-elf backed up yet another step, this one open on his left flank, another lizard came rushing at him. Bryan saw it at the last second and whipped his sword about powerfully. The weapon caught on a foreleg, digging a vicious wound, but the lizard continued forward, its maw rushing for scrambling Bryan. He tried to twist, tried to dart ahead, but the first lizard blocked his way, and the second, coming in like an elvish arrow, clamped its jaws about the half-elf's side.

Bryan beat it again about the head, swinging with all his strength, crying in desperation.

The jaws tightened; the half-elf felt the sharp teeth crunching through his elven-forged chain mail. The enchanted armor held strong—if it had not, Bryan would have been bitten in half—but even still, the lizard's jaws crunched on him so tightly that his hip cracked apart under the sheer pressure.

Bryan screamed out in agony and hit the beast again, but that only sent it into a frenzy, whipping its head back and forth, battering Bryan against the stone riser and putting him in line with the other beast's slashing claws. One got him across the face, digging deep lines, and then, suddenly, Bryan was free, flying through the air to crash hard against the stone. He saw the second lizard amble by him, locking together with the first, all thrashing and biting. Together, they rolled away, bouncing down the steps.

Bryan realized that this would be his only chance for escape, but he could not take advantage of it, could not possibly stand, or even crawl. He tried once, then slumped, clutching at his mortal wounds, and then all was blackness.

He felt the hard stone, but the pressure was gone. The pain remained, however, searing lines of fire across his face and neck. Bryan's hip felt as if a dozen spearmen had embedded their weapons there and were slowly turning them all about. He bit hard on his lower lip so that he would not cry out, and he managed to bring his arm up enough to wipe the blood from his eye.

He saw no sign of the lizard, saw no sign of anything really, for he was surprised to discover that he was no longer on the steps, but lying underneath a mound of twigs and branches set between several huge boulders.

The lizard had dragged him to a secret place, that it might feast upon him later, he knew. With great effort, Bryan turned his head, and saw the glimmer of his sword—that, too, had been collected by the beast. It was out of Bryan's reach, though, and there was no way he could squirm through the pile to get near to it. It rang as the ultimate frustration to the young warrior—his sword in plain sight, yet beyond his grasp—that he could not die fighting.

His thoughts did not stay on his own desperate situation, though, but went back to Rhiannon, always to Rhiannon.

"I have failed," the half-elf whispered. He brought Brielle's amulet up to his lips. "Forgive me, Brielle. I was not strong enough."

And then Bryan kissed the emerald in the amulet's center and passed out once more, settling down under the branch blanket, knowing in his heart that he had indeed failed his love, that the horrible lizard would return and devour him before he ever wakened.

* * *

In Avalon, hundreds of miles away, Bryan's desperate lament rang clear and strong. Brielle rushed to a tree stump, wherein lay a pool of still water. Pouring in some oils, the witch began to sing softly, and soon the pool clouded over, and then cleared again in its middle.

Brielle saw the twigs and branches, saw the half-elf's torn side. She was looking out the amulet, as clearly as if her own eye were set in it. Her heart skipped a few beats as she sent more of herself through the pool to Bryan, to try and discern if he was even still alive.

He was, but wouldn't be for long, she realized.

Brielle saw no options. Bryan was near to Rhiannon—she could tell by the terrain about him that he was somewhere in Kored-dul—and if he could not get to her girl, then Rhiannon's chances diminished by far. Since the last great battle, Brielle had avoided any great usage of magic, but not now. She fell into the amulet, heart and soul, threw her energy into the connection, and gave to Bryan a considerable amount of her own life force.

"Bryan! Bryan!" The call was from far away, but the half-elf heard it. He opened his bleary eyes to find that he was still in the twig pile, still buried. The sun was low in the west, the shadows long and dark. One form came clear to Bryan, though, large and reptilian; the great, hungry lizard.

Bryan was amazed to be alive, to be conscious, and to find such strength as this! Without taking the time to consider his miraculous recovery, he tucked his legs under him and shoved out in the direction of his sword. The lizard was digging furiously at the branch pile by the time he got his hand on its hilt, the snapping, toothy maw barely inches from his leg.

Hope quickly reverted to despair as Bryan considered

that he would soon be right back where he had started. Defiantly, he pulled free his sword and turned it at his foe, just as the lizard cleared enough of a path to bite at him.

"No!" Bryan cried, knowing that he could not possibly kill the armored creature with one strike. His sword flashed by, the blade engulfed by blue arcs of lightning. It hit the lizard squarely in the open mouth, bashing through teeth and bone and scales as easily as if they were a pile of soft snow, driving through the creature's brain.

Arcs of blue lightning flashed about the lizard's head, sizzling and crackling. The lizard fell away, convulsing, scales smoking, and then it tumbled and lay very still.

Bryan fell back against the ground, stunned, confused. He looked at his sword, a normal-looking elvish blade once more, and thanked the Colonnae.

Brielle sat down hard. All the world was spinning. She wondered if she might die from exhaustion at that moment, her energy totally spent. She wondered if she had gone too far in grasping so strongly at the torn realm of magic, in forcing the strength into her body and through her reflecting pool to Bryan, both healing power and lightning magic.

Perhaps she had given him, and his sword, too much of herself.

She rolled to her side and let sleep take her.

He could walk with little pain, just discomfort in the recently crushed hip. As he continued on his way to the north, Bryan replayed the scenes after the lizard attack, searching for some clue. Again and again, his thoughts were drawn to the amulet, and he came to believe that his gratitude, his prayer to the Colonnae, had been misplaced. Bryan understood then that Brielle was with him, that he did not walk alone, and so he was bolstered, striding more boldly as night descended.

Soon after, he came over a stony ridge and lost his breath, for there, right before him, loomed the great castle of Morgan Thalasi. Huge black walls and sky-reaching towers seemed to mock the young half-elf and his desperate mission, and a sense of the deepest hopelessness he had ever known weakened his knees and nearly overwhelmed him. What could he accomplish against the tremendous power standing dark and ageless before him? What could he, a mere mortal, do against the likes of the godlike being who had built this bastion?

Bryan gritted his teeth and determinedly shook the thoughts away. He could do little, he honestly believed, perhaps nothing at all. But he had to try. Above all else, he had to make the attempt, even at the likely price of his life. For Bryan knew the alternative. To walk away when Rhiannon needed him, no matter the odds, would leave him forever in grief and shame, would break him more completely than Morgan Thalasi ever could.

"Better death," he muttered under his breath, and with a look to either side, he started forward. Soon after, he saw the march, the lines and lines of undead, the horrid blackness, and even though he understood that so much power was flowing out of Talas-dun, and that might make his task all the easier, the sight only filled him with dread.

For in his heart, Bryan of Corning understood that all the goodly armies of all the world could not stand against that force, would be swallowed by the blackness as surely as day gave way to night.

With a growl, the half-elf went on, remembering his role, more determined than ever to get Rhiannon out of Talas-dun. He made the base of the castle wall without incident. "Better death," he repeated, for he didn't dare voice his real opinion. For he understood in his heart that if Morgan Thalasi, the Black Warlock, the greatest horror to ever infect Ynis Aielle, ever got him, then death would be the least of his troubles.

But still, his enemy was secure inside that mighty bastion, Bryan knew—secure and unsuspecting. Thalasi was too busy looking for armies to notice the movements of a small and insignificant half-elf. That was Bryan's only chance; that was why he had set out from Avalon alone. He had to tell himself all of those things repeatedly just to continue, just to be able to put one shaking foot in front of the other.

And so he was moving, but where to go? There was one gate evident, a hundred yards east along the wall, set small between two massive guard houses, but from the torches glowing through window slits there, Bryan recognized that it was well guarded.

He looked up instead, thinking of going over the wall. He could only guess at its height—thirty feet? forty? And the surface, unlike the masoned bricks of Pallendara's wall, was perfectly smooth, metallic, without a ridge to be seen.

He went to the west, where the sky was wide, the mountainous land falling away suddenly to the sea. As he neared the southwestern corner of the square castle, Bryan heard the waves far below, crashing endlessly against the unyielding cliff wall. A small strip of land, a curving, uneven walkway open to the west, wound behind the castle, generally descending. It seemed plausible to Bryan that this back side, far too narrow and treacherous a path for any invading army, would be the least defended of all, and so on he went, picking his careful way along the slick stones.

Soon after, moonlight slanting over the castle wall, but

at an angle that left Bryan in shadow, he heard talking, deep and guttural. He fell to his belly and moved to the next ridge, peering over.

A single talon stood below him, bathed in torchlight, the beast grumbling and complaining as it carried a bucket of slop out an open door to dump into the sea.

"Clean the kitchen, Fogump," the talon bitched. "Wipe the blimin' floors, Fogump. Lick me blimin' feet, Fogump!"

The talon moved to the edge of a small landing and tossed the contents of the bucket over, nearly losing the pot in the act. Overbalanced, the talon just managed to keep a hold on the bucket and to keep its own balance, and it was just setting itself firmly in place again when it felt a sudden explosion against the back of its head.

Mercifully, the beast fell from consciousness as it plummeted down the cliff face, and didn't see the ocean ready to swallow its remains.

Bryan moved immediately to the open door; a tiny portal leading into the castle's larders. From his course along the back wall, he realized that he was far below the level of the plateau—indeed the black castle walls began some distance above him, past the natural stones. The half-elf nodded in satisfaction, for it seemed plausible to him that Rhiannon might be in some dungeon below ground level.

Voices from inside the room brought him from his contemplations. He moved to the shadows along the side of the door, clutched his sword tight, and whispered for Brielle, hoping that she would hear.

"Where is you?" a talon barked from just inside the door. "Fogump!"

The talon stepped outside, and then it was dead, in the single swipe of Bryan's sword. The half-elf headed into the room immediately, where two other talons busied themselves cleaning great buckets of slop. He fell over the first before they ever knew he was there and caught the second just before it reached the small chamber's inner door, stabbing it hard in the kidney. He stuck it again and again, rushing up so that he could bring his hand over its mouth to stifle its dying screams.

Even as that one slumped dead to the floor, Bryan rushed back across the room and outside, to drag the dead talon back in.

Footsteps in the hall beyond the inner door alerted him that yet another was approaching. He took up a pot in one hand, his sword in the other, and moved beside the door.

The creature came right in, then stopped, stunned.

Bryan smacked it over the head with the pot, shoulder-blocked it out of the way—closing the door as he moved past it—and pinned the beast up against the wall, his sword tip coming right in under its chin, his other hand, free of the dropped pot, slapping across the talon's mouth.

"If you cry out, I will drive my sword into your puny brain," Bryan promised, and from the look on the brute's face, he knew that it understood.

"The woman?" Bryan asked. "The wraith of Mitchell brought a woman here? Do you know this?"

The talon nodded. Bryan felt its hand move a bit along its belt, and he understood its plan.

"Where is she?" He took his hand from the beast's mouth, but stayed right up against it.

"Down," the talon said, its answer cut short as Bryan slapped his hand back over its mouth.

Again the half-elf felt the movement along the waist, felt the talon grabbing hold of something.

Bryan's sword drove up under the creature's chin, through the roof of its mouth and into its brain. The talon twitched and shuddered and fell limp, upright only because Bryan still had it pinned against the wall. He eased the talon to the floor, taking note of the dagger in its belt.

Then the half-elf set about making the room look as if the talons had engaged in a fight among themselves. He left one dead at the door, but jumbled the other three together, planting the knife of his last kill into one of the wounds of another, then taking the sharp scraper one had been using to clean hardened food from the plates and sliding it into the last talon's garish wound. With one talon missing, it was likely that any guards uncovering this scene would begin a search for the murderous Fogump. That search should keep them from the dungeons, Bryan reasoned, for what fugitive would deliver himself to Thalasi's prison?

"Down," the half-elf muttered. He eased the door open and peeked into the corridor. Torches lined the walls, but they were far-spaced, creating many shadows. Bryan glanced left, then right, looking for some clues.

Nothing.

He went left, moving swiftly and silently, crossing the corridor as he approached every bend to get the best vantage point around it. He took too many turns to keep track, even went through several empty rooms, then slipped into a dark alcove that ended at a door.

He heard the slapping feet of talons beyond and judged from the sound that they were below him, coming up some stairs. Bryan considered the door, then moved to the side of the alcove into which it would open.

He held his breath as the talons—three of them, heavily armed—came through, swinging wide the door then continuing on, the last of the line giving a yank to close the door.

Bryan sucked in his breath even more, for the three stood barely five feet away!

They didn't notice him, though, and just went on their way.

Through the door went the half-elf, and down the stairs. He passed several landings with doors similar to the one he had come through, but he ignored them, thinking it best to start at the bottom.

Finally, the stair ended in a tunnel of natural stone, hardly worked, and with a dirt floor, the only light coming from a partially opened door far down the corridor.

Bryan crept along. He could hear the roar of the fire; it was no mere torch. He also heard a talon chuckle, an evil-sounding laugh, and a low moan, but he was relieved to recognize that the moan was not one of a woman, but of another talon. At the door, he peeked in enough to see a brutish talon wearing heavy leather gloves, studded bracers on its wrists, a leather collar about its thick neck, and a thick black hood rolling a poker about on top of the stone rim of a blazing fire pit. The end of the rod glowed a wicked orange.

The half-elf went down to one knee and dared to peek in a bit more. Hanging on the wall opposite the door was a rotting talon corpse, shackled at the wrists, and next to it, apparently very close to joining its dead companion, hung another talon, trembling and sobbing.

The talon at the fire lifted the glowing poker, turned slowly and deliberately, and headed for its new victim; Bryan slipped into the room, quickly motioning for the hanging talon to be quiet, thinking errantly that this creature would welcome potential salvation, whatever race that savior might be.

"Elf! Elf! Elf!" the hanging talon barked, drawing a blank stare from the torturer.

Three strides brought Bryan past the fire pit, but the

warning had registered enough for the brute to pivot about, bringing the glowing poker up defensively. Bryan batted it aside and thrust his sword straight ahead, but so heavy was the talon torturer's glove that even Bryan's fine blade did not cut deeply. Back came the sword at once, just parrying the swinging poker.

"Yous'll tell the Thalasi?" the talon hanging on the wall said over and over. "I helps! I helps!"

The torturer just grunted and came on ferociously, whipping the poker all about, then stabbing ahead with it. Bryan back-stepped each swing and sidestepped the thrust, snapping a backhand parry that forced the poker across the brute's body and put the talon off balance. Quicker than his bulky opponent, the agile half-elf stepped into the opening and thrust his sword into the heavy shoulder.

The talon yelped and dropped its poker, and Bryan came in hard, silencing the cries with a series of fast stabs about the creature's throat. That finished, the talon squirming and gurgling on the floor, the half-elf looked to the hanging prisoner and again motioned for it to remain silent. This time it seemed as if the creature would comply, but Bryan wasn't about to take the chance. As the talon relaxed, the half-elf rushed in and killed it cleanly with one thrust.

"You should have been quiet the first time," Bryan whispered. Then he went and took the leather collar and hood, and the great gloves to hide slender elvish hands.

There was a second door in this room, leading deeper into the dungeons. As he opened it, Bryan was greeted by a chorus of groaning. He flipped up the hood of his cowl, though he didn't seem very talonlike, and down he slipped, past dozens of cells, their doors solid and with only a high and small barred window. Several desperate, ugly faces peered out at him as he passed, but the light in here was very poor, and they couldn't recognize him for what he was—or if they did, they made no sounds to indicate so. Every few feet he paused to listen, or even to peek into the windows of the few cells that didn't resound with talon groaning.

He was beginning to get discouraged, to think that this area was only for Thalasi's worthless talon prisoners, when he heard another voice, lucid and not filled with pain, utter a short phrase that sent the hairs on the back of Bryan's neck standing on end.

"Pretty lady."

Back in Avalon, Brielle heard it, too.

Chapter 21

The Call of Duty

HE LINGERED ABOVE Avalon for hours, just basking in the beauty of the forest, the purity of the place distracting him despite the urgent need for him to be on his way. Still, Del suspected that his greatest roles would be as scout and as informant, and he knew that he could catch all the others, the swift-marching elves and humans and the flying pegasus, with a mere thought.

But where to go?

And then it came to him: a call, a vision, carried on the wind by Brielle, information about Bryan of Corning and Del's daughter, information about a march greater and more wicked than anything Aielle had ever known, and instructions about what he must do to prevent absolute disaster.

"Find Belexus."

It didn't take Belexus long to understand that he would not catch his father and his kin before they made the black fortress. He had flown past Arien's force soon after leaving Avalon, Calamus rushing at tremendous speed, but as he passed over the Brown Wastes, as he saw talons turning their eyes skyward to regard the strange aerial creature, he recognized the futility of it all. Belexus was confident that he was too high up for the creatures to distinguish his identity, for them to even know that this was mount and rider and not just some huge bird. But they saw him, and marked well his passing.

Up in the empty sky, Belexus could find no hiding. His approach to Kored-dul would be well marked and oft-whispered, and the rumors would inevitably get back to the ears of Morgan Thalasi and Hollis Mitchell. Both had previously seen the ranger airborne upon Calamus—Mitchell had even chased Belexus and the pegasus—and it would not take them long to reason what this strange creature might be.

Belexus wondered if that revelation might prove a good thing. Perhaps he could lure the wraith out and test his new sword . . .

But what of his promise to Brielle? What of Rhiannon? Even if he defeated Mitchell, how would he ever get near to the young witch? Certainly not by alerting Thalasi and his minions of his coming!

The ranger put down on the muddy ground on the edges of a small seasonal marsh and considered his course more carefully. If he meant to go to Talas-dun without alerting Thalasi, he would have to fly in fast to Kored-dul and then ride, or perhaps even walk, Calamus along the rocky trails. He wondered if he might instead fly fast to the south, and then the west, soaring out over the great ocean and then north along the coast until he had gone right past the black castle. Perhaps he could find a less-guarded northern approach.

"We've got a task that's showing me no obvious answers," he said to the great steed. Calamus only looked at him, seeming perfectly unperturbed. The pegasus would go where he commanded, Belexus knew, even if that meant a straightforward assault on Talas-dun and all of Thalasi's thousands.

He took some comfort in that unquestioning loyalty as he settled down that night for some much-needed rest.

Long before he fell asleep, though, the difficult reality of his task came back to him, and he had to admit again that he had no answers to his dilemma.

In the end, he decided that he would fly as fast as possible to the west, trying for stealth, but not to the point where it would slow him greatly. And if any talons came out against him, he would kill them, or fly around them; and if Hollis Mitchell came out against him, he would avenge Andovar and then continue on his way; and if Morgan Thalasi himself came out against him, he would finish the Black Warlock and continue on his way.

He thought that one of those fights had indeed come to him when he was awakened from his sleep sometime later. He didn't immediately move, other than to slip his hand over the hilt of Pouilla Camby. He kept his eyes half closed, shifting his gaze from side to side, and listened intently for any sounds, or any stirring of the alert pegasus.

Nothing was apparent, and Belexus understood that it was his sixth sense, his warrior alertness, that had put him on his guard. That sense railed him now; someone, or something, was in the area.

A snort from Calamus sent him into motion, rolling to his side, then to his knees, sword drawn and ready, eyes scanning the area. He caught some movement to the side, by a large tree, and hopped into a crouch, still glancing all about. Then, satisfied that the other areas of the camp were clear, he focused on that tree, trying to get some measure of his enemy.

"I hope I didn't wake you," a familiar voice came, and the ranger relaxed and lowered his blade. Jeffrey DelGiudice floated into view, drifting right through the tree. "I meant to let you sleep the night," the spirit explained. "And to watch over you." He regarded the ranger's alert stance, the drawn sword. "But I see that you need little watching over," he added with a chuckle.

"Why've ye come?" Belexus asked.

"For Brielle," Del answered immediately.

Belexus quickly fought down the jealous feelings that stirred within him, biting them back fully, determined not to let his pride get in the way of this all-important mission. Rescuing Rhiannon was paramount; however it was accomplished, and by whom, was not really important.

"Together we'll get to Talas-dun, then," the ranger reasoned.

"No," Del replied. "I mean, that's why Brielle bade me to come and get you."

"What news?" the ranger asked urgently. "Is her girl safe then?"

"No," Del answered, and then, seeing the ranger's crestfallen expression, quickly added, "Not yet."

Belexus breathed a sigh of relief.

"But Bryan of Corning is in Talas-dun, so Brielle says," Del explained. "And the witch is with him, in spirit if not in body."

"Then we should be making all haste to join the lad," Belexus reasoned, and started for Calamus.

"No," the spirit replied, stopping the ranger short. "Brielle has foreseen another danger, one more immediate. Arien is marching west."

"I've seen as much."

"And Benador comes from the southeast with a huge force," Del went on.

"Ayuh," the ranger agreed. "And they'll be finding each other in the foothills, so's me guess."

"But before they get there, they'll be fighting," Del explained, "for Thalasi's army is massing in those foothills. And Brielle fears that each force will be hit hard before they can join together, to the sorrow of the not-so-numerous elves, no doubt. She wants us to prevent that."

Belexus didn't know how to take the request. Certainly he understood the valuable role he could play in the forthcoming battle, flying high above the battlefield on Calamus, marking enemy positions and strength, but his heart was for Brielle, and for Rhiannon, and he didn't know how he could leave the young witch in the dungeons of Talas-dun, no matter the callings of duty.

"Brielle has placed her confidence in Bryan," Del said, as if reading his thoughts. "She would not have asked you—asked us—to detour from the course to Talas-dun if she didn't believe honestly that Bryan would get Rhiannon out of there."

Again, the ranger was not so sure of that. For all her love for her daughter, Brielle was an altruistic one, who always, always, placed the greater good first. Belexus understood that her choice in detouring him was based more in her fears for the coming battle than in her hopes for Rhiannon's salvation.

"Yerself can be the scout for the armies," the ranger reasoned.

"What do I know of tactics?" Del asked. "And what do I know of Benador and Arien? How will they—and more important, how will their soldiers—react when a ghost shows up in their midst? A ghost, they might believe, sent by Thalasi to deter them."

The ranger glanced all around, feeling suddenly like his options were running thin. Above the pain in his heart, the mere fact that Brielle had asked him to turn away from Rhiannon revealed how important she thought his role in the coming battle must be. And in considering the scenario, Belexus could not disagree. With the pegasus, and his present position, he could get a fair measure of Thalasi's force and inform both Arien and Benador long before they neared the battlefield. With a bit of luck, any ambush that Thalasi had planned for the coming armies might be turned back on the talons.

"Get yer rest," Belexus said. "We'll be up high in the morning."

"I don't need any," Del replied.

"Then go and play with yer tree," the ranger said, managing a bit of a smile.

He came in wildly, swinging and hacking with apparent abandon. But Bryan was in complete control, his every strike strengthened by rage but tempered by his warrior sensibilities. He saw Rhiannon hanging in shackles, badly beaten, but he did not let the sight truly register, did not let it bring him to despair.

He only let it cause him rage, and in the first few seconds of that charge through the door, Bryan had both the zombie guards hacked down to the floor and had put the talon jailor, the largest and ugliest talon he had ever seen, back on its heels, waving its chain and huge dagger frantically in a desperate defense.

The creature was no match for the outraged warrior, and Bryan's powerful swings kept it backing and scrambling. It tried to retreat in an angle that would give it clear flight out the door, but Bryan would have none of that, dragging his back foot whenever he advanced, so he could change to any direction immediately in perfect balance.

In thrust his sword; the talon leaped back and whipped the chain across, and the metal links wound about Bryan's weapon. Before the talon's smile could ever widen on its ugly face, though, Bryan turned his shoulder and rushed in, slamming the creature hard with his shield, pinning its dagger hand in close to its side.

The talon dropped one foot back, expecting Bryan to continue his press, but the half-elf, recognizing that the talon was the stronger, did not want to play this close in combat. Instead of advancing, the half-elf dropped his sword shoulder and pivoted back across and under his turning shield, twisting the chain free of the talon's grasp. Before the ugly creature could counter the move, before it could slip through the sudden opening for a clear slash at Bryan's side, the half-elf snapped his blade out to the side, launching the chain across the room, then put the sword back in line with the talon.

The creature had only one recourse remaining; it darted to the side and back, nearing Rhiannon. "Yous come on and she gets sticked!" the wretched brute cried.

Hardly thinking of the movement, Bryan tossed his sword in the air, caught it in a reverse grip, and hurled it across the span. He started a rush right behind the flying blade, but no need, for the lightning-spewing weapon had done its work, driving hard through the talon's chest, dropping it to lean against the back wall, where it slid down to the floor, down to death.

Bryan was beside Rhiannon in an instant, not even slowing to retrieve his sword.

"Ye should'no've come," the woman whispered.

In response, the half-elf laughed. Not a mocking laugh, but one of the greatest relief that he had found the woman alive. He considered Rhiannon's chains then, and looked first to the jailor, wondering if he might find keys in its pockets. That didn't seem likely, not for so valuable a prisoner as this. He found another answer, though, and went to gather his sword, the weapon Brielle had so strongly enchanted.

"But I did not come alone," the half-elf explained with confidence, looking from the woman to the sword, and then to the emerald amulet. Almost immediately, the blade came alive with arcs of blue-white power. A single stroke to each chain had Rhiannon free, the weary young woman falling heavily into Bryan's waiting arms.

Holding her, the half-elf felt more warmth and more love than ever he had known, but also trepidation, for now he had to find some way to get the weakened and battered woman out of Talas-dun.

"Me mum," she said suddenly, turning a quizzical gaze upon Bryan. "Ye've bringed her!"

Before Bryan could explain, or ask how Rhiannon knew, he saw the change come over her, saw her face brighten, her bruises lessen. Brielle was reaching out to her through the amulet, was sending her very life force across the leagues to her dear daughter. In mere seconds, Rhiannon stood straight and steady, the look in her eyes transforming from one of a battered prisoner to the familiar, resolute young woman that Bryan had come to know and love.

"We have to get out of here," the half-elf said.

The woman nodded, but the expression upon her fair face was not one of a prisoner looking to take flight. "When we've finished," she replied with deadly calm.

Bryan looked at her curiously.

"Thalasi's got something," Rhiannon explained. "Something powerful, something wicked. We're inside, and not to get a better chance for his evil staff."

"I came to get you out," Bryan protested.

"There'll be no place in all the world that's 'out' if Thalasi keeps his staff," Rhiannon replied with equal determination. "He's bringing up the dead with it, and knowing no limits."

A grunt from the door turned them both that way, to see two talons standing there. One shrieked and charged; the other turned to flee.

Before Bryan could even move to defensive posture, the young witch extended her arms, and from each hand came a line of flames, one enshrouding the closing talon, one reaching out to grab the fleeing beast.

Both fell dead to the floor, mere smoldering husks, a few seconds later.

"I have not used me magics in many a day," Rhiannon explained. "I have hung on Thalasi's wall and gathered me strength, for I knew that it was not me place to be a helpless prisoner. And not me place to run away now, with Thalasi so close, and so off his guard."

Bryan had no arguments in the face of that determination, especially with two charred and curled talon bodies in clear sight.

Perhaps it was the workings of the Colonnae, perhaps simple luck, but the day was clear in the southeastern foothills of the Kored-dul, and unseasonably warm, affording Belexus, high upon Calamus, a spectacular view of the approaching armies. From the south came King Benador and the Warders of the White Walls, surrounded by the thousands of Pallendara's army. From the east came Arien and the elves, no less impressive though their numbers were but a fraction of the Calvan force. From the movements of the two groups, it seemed apparent to Belexus that there had been some communication between them, for their respective courses would bring them in simultaneously to opposite sides of a strategic rocky arm of the mountain range.

The splendor and coordination of the march sent the ranger's spirits soaring, but those hopes were tempered a moment later when he flew his mount in lower over the mountains, when he saw the specter of Thalasi's coming force. They moved along the trails like the inevitable darkness that follows the day, carrying with them, it seemed, a tangible shadow, a visible aura of evil. Belexus noted that there was something awkward about their movements, and noted, too, that several bands skirted the main host, as if afraid to approach. He was about to take a chance and swoop Calamus in even lower when the ghost of DelGiudice came up to him with an explanation.

"They are dead," the ghost said matter-of-factly. "Most of them, anyway. The main host are zombies and skeletons, and are led by a great evil."

"Thalasi," Belexus muttered.

"Mitchell," Del corrected, and the ranger's eyes flared, an eagerness the spirit could not miss. Nor did DelGiudice miss the fact that Belexus had angled the pegasus slightly and was now veering in toward the monstrous horde. "Go to King Benador and warn him what he faces," the ghost firmly instructed. "The men will flee in the face of ghoulish undead if they are not forewarned."

Belexus glared at him.

"I know your desire," DelGiudice said sympathetically. "But right now, you appear to your enemies as no more than a speck in the sky, a great bird, perhaps. That is your advantage."

"Ye find Mitchell," Belexus replied, having no practical arguments against Del's suggestions. "Ye find him and keep him in yer sights. Ye'll be guiding me when I return from King Benador—and from Arien, if the need arises—and know ye that I'm meaning to have Mitchell's ugly head!" With that, the great pegasus turned away in a powerful stoop to the south, and only a few minutes later, Belexus set down before the king of Calva, to the resounding cheers of the soldiers: men who knew the ranger well and who had witnessed, or heard about, his unrivaled valor and skill at the battle for the Four Bridges.

"We had word from Arien that you had gone in search of your father, and he for the witch's daughter," Benador said, obviously pleased to see his dear friend. As he spoke, he rushed over and clasped Belexus' hand warmly.

"I fear that me place is here," the ranger admitted. "For know that Thalasi's lying in wait for ye among the rocks, a great force that will try to keep ye from gaining the mountains."

"We expected no less," the king replied calmly.

"Ah, but such a force as ye'd not expect," the ranger explained. "An army o' the dead, pulled from their cold graves by the magic of the Black Warlock." Belexus looked about, measuring the responses from the many listeners, and was pleased to see that while his words had somewhat unnerved them, their expressions remained stoic and determined.

"Evil tidings," Benador said. "But again, we expected no less."

"And Mitchell's among them so . . ." He paused, wondering how he might explain the reappearance of the spirit of DelGiudice. "So I'm guessing," he finished, deciding that time was too precious now for such matters.

"I have heard of your blood feud with the fiend," King Benador said. "I, too, wish to see Andovar avenged."

Belexus drew out Pouilla Camby, drawing gasps of astonishment from those close enough to view the diamond edge gleaming in the morning light. "Far and wide I went to find such a weapon as could harm the wraith," the ranger explained. "Today I pay back Mitchell for the death of me dearest friend."

"And know that all of Calva stands behind you," the king said.

An explosion ended the conversation abruptly, all eyes turning to the side, to a puff of orange smoke, and to the wizard, a befuddled Ardaz, wisps of smoke rising from the edges of his blue robes, emerging from the cloud.

"Greetings," he said cheerily. "From Arien, I mean,

and from myself, I suppose," he added after a coughing fit.

"Ye should'no be using yer magic," Belexus scolded. "Save it for Thalasi's thousands."

"Had to come, had to come," Ardaz protested, moving to join the ranger, then dipping a curt bow before the king. "Saw you fly down, from the sky of course, and oh, what a sight you make! Had to know what was about," he explained.

"Your eyes are fine then, old wizard," the king said. "For the ranger was naught but a speck to us until he neared."

"Ah, but I knew he was up there!" Ardaz replied, snapping his fingers. "Deductive reasoning does wonders for failing vision, you know."

He looked all around, his eyebrows cocking curiously. "Istaahl has not joined you?" he asked.

Benador shook his head. "He remains in Pallendara, as far as I know."

Ardaz scratched his beard, wondering what his old wizard friend had in mind. He knew Istaahl well enough to understand that the White Mage would certainly find a way to insinuate himself in the battle, but he knew, too, that Istaahl drew his power from the sea, and would be stronger in Pallendara than out here. "No matter," he said to Benador. "Istaahl will be about, or at least, his magic will, ha, ha!"

"I have never doubted the value of the White Mage," Benador replied.

"Nor I," Ardaz agreed. "And he will have something good planned for Thalasi, though not good for Thalasi, if you catch my meaning, I do dare say!" He hopped about as he spoke, and on his shoulder, the shaken Desdemona gave a growl and dug her claws in for support.

Benador instructed his army to rest, then, while he,

Belexus, and Ardaz moved aside to discuss the coming conflict. The ranger gave them the layout of the approaching army and some insights concerning the terrain, and then promised to guide the battle from the sky.

"Oh, Des will assist in that!" Ardaz promised, and he threw the half-sleeping cat into the air. Taken by surprise, she didn't quite enact the transformation fast enough, though, and she hit the ground on cat paws, glowering, spitting, and hissing at the wizard.

"Oh, just do it," Ardaz muttered.

It was a long and lonely wait for the ghost. He wanted to go down and join Belexus, but figured that he'd probably scare away half of Benador's army! He found the wraith easily enough, even from this high vantage point, for Mitchell was a blackness quite beyond the lesser undead, and Del was seeing clearly into both realms.

But was that his only purpose in being here? He had to wonder. Had he come back to the world only to snatch the important sword from the dragon, and now to guide the players in the battle? It was a frustrating possibility for the spirit who had seen the mysteries of the universe and who had returned only to find himself helpless to aid his daughter in her desperate straits.

Del's attention was caught by a group moving high along trails far to the side of the main talon and undead host. Curious, he willed himself to the region, and when he saw Bellerian and the rangers, he knew that he had found another way.

Among the clouds once more, the ranger took note of the movements of the various forces. He saw a flash in the east and knew that Ardaz had returned to Arien's side. He saw Benador's ranks re-form, lines of glittering spear tips, and then begin again their march to the north.

What he didn't find was DelGiudice, a fact that bothered him more than a little. The ghost was undependable, Belexus believed, very unlike DelGiudice had been in life. The ranger believed that he understood the cause: These events that seemed so titanic to Belexus, to all in Aielle, seemed as minor things to the universe-wise spirit.

"Don't ye be running off when we're needing ye," the ranger muttered, looking all about.

He saw a flash, as sunlight might make on a mirror, from the higher foothills of Kored-dul, followed by a second and third in rapid succession, then a pause, and then three more. Belexus knew well that signal, one used by the rangers in their scouting of Avalon's borders, and he could guess easily enough who it was that was signaling. Down he went with all speed, taking a wide route so as not to alert all of Thalasi's forces to the presence of the rangers.

He found Bellerian and the others in a small clearing, their faces brightening at his approach, and their horses, Avalon horses, snorting and stomping when Calamus stepped among them.

"We've met yer friend, the ghost," Bellerian explained, nodding. "And we're knowing the way to Mitchell."

He flew along the mountain trails with ease, taking care to avoid any of Thalasi's marching minions, particularly the undead, for he feared that they would be able to sense and perhaps even do battle with a spirit. Del had seen the black fortress before, when first he and his companions had stepped from their life raft onto the shores of Ynis Aielle, but that previous sight did little to prepare him for the awful spectacle of Thalasi's home: a blackness deeper than anything even he, with his deeper understanding of the universal powers, could begin to imagine. He recognized that Talas-dun was somehow beyond those powers Calae had shown to him, was supernatural, and more than that, was supremely perverted, as if the most beauteous events, places, and things in all the universe had been thrown together and twisted horribly.

Still, the spirit didn't hesitate, couldn't hesitate, with his daughter's life—and more than that, her very existence—at stake, and so he moved to the least-guarded spot along the castle wall and searched for a way in. He knew at once that this was no ordinary construction, was nothing built of the labors of craftsmen, for not a seam could he find, not a crack in the metallic black walls. Finally, his patience running thin, Del floated up over the wall, then down into the courtyard. He was spotted immediately, but before the talon guard could even cry out, he discerned that the interior walls were not like the outside wall, were made of bricks masoned in a more conventional manner, and he was gone, slipping through a crack into the castle's interior. Just inside the thick wall, he paused and listened, but heard no obvious cry, and could only hope that he had been out of sight so quickly that the guard considered him no more than a trick of the morning light.

He moved with caution, but with speed as well, trying not to alert any within—for alerted talons would make escape more difficult for Bryan and Rhiannon, if they were still within the castle—but with the eagerness of a father who knows his child is in peril. He crossed through corridor after corridor, drifted up high in the ceiling shadows of rooms large and small, and gradually, as he collected his wits about him and reasoned out the situation, began to make his way downward.

The place was nearly deserted, most of the talons out on the march to meet Arien and Benador. Del did find a few talon bodies, though, in a scullery room at the back of Talas-dun, and it wasn't hard to figure that Bryan of Corning had come this way. From the placement of the bodies, though, and the fact that the outside door was closed, Del suspected that the half-elf had hit this on his way in, and that he, and Rhiannon, were still inside. He could only hope that Bryan had found her, and that they were together, supporting each other.

And he meant to be there, too, to offer whatever help he might. He set off at once, flying faster now, using less caution.

Chapter 22

Enemies Met

"Can you use it?" Bryan asked, stringing his short bow.

Rhiannon shrugged and eyed the weapon fearfully. "I've not been trained in fighting arts," she explained, and it was obvious from her hesitant, even disgusted, tone that she didn't want to be so trained at that time.

Bryan didn't press the point—in their weeks together as the war had raged down by the Four Bridges, he had come to know Rhiannon's value, and he didn't doubt that she would find some way to be of great help now. Up to this point, the half-elf had preferred his sword to his bow, but now he sheathed the powerful sword and took up the bow, for he didn't want any talons to get anywhere near the young witch.

"Take this, then," he offered, drawing a dagger from his belt.

Rhiannon shook her head vigorously, and again, Bryan could not find the heart to argue with her.

They went up the stairs quietly, Bryan holding his bow ready. He only had half a dozen arrows with him, not wanting to trek to Talas-dun overburdened, and he meant to make every shot count. He glanced back over his shoulder at Rhiannon often, hoping that she had some magic left in her.

On what Bryan figured to be the ground floor of the

castle, the pair exited the stairs. "A large place," Bryan whispered. "Where do you believe we will find Thalasi?"

Rhiannon hardly heard him, for she was silently searching for an answer to that very question. She closed her eyes and let her mind go out, trying to sense the tangible evil aura that surrounded the Black Warlock. "Up," she said at length, recalling the image of the fortress. "Talas-dun's got three tall towers, and he'll be in one o' them."

Bryan didn't doubt her, but that did little to offer any guidance in the maze of corridors and spacious rooms. They moved along with all the speed Bryan dared, figuring that sooner or later, they would find some clue. Around one corner, Bryan came upon a heavy curtain, set, it seemed, in the jamb of a portal. The half-elf edged the tip of his set arrow to the side of the curtain and pushed it back just a bit.

He saw the back of a talon, no more than three paces away. He drew his bow, but too late, for the brute happened to glance back, and came on with a howl. Behind it, in another large chamber, several other talons grabbed up their weapons.

The ugly beast slapped the curtain aside, coming straight in. It doubled over almost immediately, as Bryan's knee came up hard into its groin. "I need you!" the half-elf cried to Rhiannon, and instead of going after the closest talon, he skittered out to the side, dropped his bow in line, and let fly for the group coming in behind.

The arrow had barely left his bow when it split apart, becoming two arrows, and then those split again into four, four into eight, and eight into sixteen before the missile arrow had crossed a quarter of the room. The group of talons, coming in a bunch, halted abruptly, throwing up their arms in pitiful defense as the enchanted swarm overwhelmed them, dropping them to the stone.

Bryan didn't see any of it. As soon as he had fired, he fell back to one knee, hooked the tip of his bow under the shoulder of the stunned talon, then came up in a half-twist, flipping the talon over. The talon, skilled and agile, dipped its shoulder and executed a perfect roll, coming back to its feet and turning about, its heavy axe trailing, going up, up over its head in a wide arc.

Bryan started for his sword, but stopped as the brute charged right in. The half-elf brought his bow out horizontally above his head, hooking it under the blade of the axe as the talon chopped for his head. A twist and thrust of his hands sent the axe flying out to the side, and he punched out—left, right, left—slapping alternate ends of his bow against the talon's face, forcing the creature back, but doing no substantial damage.

The talon shook its head and started right back in, axe whipping across, the brute apparently determined that the half-elf would not get any opportunity to draw out that crafted sword. The ugly creature skidded to a halt, though, as a wall of flames appeared suddenly in front of it.

Rhiannon, still recovering from her trick with the arrow, couldn't hold the magic for more than a split second, but that was long enough, for when the wall came down, and the talon stubbornly came on, it found the half-elf ready, sword in hand.

Across whipped the axe, and Bryan easily hopped back out of its reach, then stepped ahead and poked his sword, nicking the talon. Outraged, the brute roared and came in hard, a second sidelong swipe, this time over-extending its reach to catch up with the retreating half-elf.

Expecting that, Bryan didn't retreat, but came straight ahead instead, sword leading. He accepted the hit of the axe handle against his hip; the enchanted chain mail handled the blow easily enough. The talon's armor was not so fine, though, and did little to stop the progress of Bryan's sword as it burrowed through.

Bryan hooked the arms of the dying beast and held them tight so that the talon, in its last spasms, couldn't begin another attack. They held the pose for a long second, and then the talon slid backward off the blade, dead. Bryan spun about, pulling the curtain aside once more, so that he could see into the chamber; and he nodded with satisfaction, for all seven of the talons lay still in a deepening puddle of blood. The half-elf wasn't as pleased when he retrieved his bow, though, to find that the fine wood had cracked, either in blocking the axe or against the talon's hard head.

Rhiannon took it from him and bade him to lead on with all speed.

"They're knowing about us now," she commented. "Or soon to be, and we've no' the time to fight with Thalasi's minions."

They hadn't gone fifty feet when they heard the howls of discovery behind them, cries of warning that soon echoed throughout Talas-dun, that soon enough fell to the ears of the Black Warlock.

Bellerian pointed to a large rock set about halfway down the rocky arm of Kored-dul. Even from this high vantage point, the rangers could see the forms moving about the area, the armies coming together, the battle about to begin.

"There's the wraith, so said DelGiudice," Bellerian explained. "Guiding his wicked minions. We can get down there."

"No," Belexus replied. "I alone can get down there, and swiftly, on Calamus."

Bellerian wanted to argue, but he knew that Belexus would not be deterred. "Fare well, me son," he mumbled, even as the eager ranger climbed back onto Calamus' back and lifted into the air.

Turning his attention back to the larger conflict, Bellerian and his rangers noted some talon archers moving into position to shower arrows upon King Benador's closing force.

"Our first place to be," Bellerian decided, and they were off, silent as death.

Belexus saw the archers, too, and he wondered if he wasn't overstepping his role in this battle. Wouldn't all the forces be better off if he guided them from the back of Calamus, if he used his high vantage point to all their benefit?

"No," the ranger said aloud. His place was against Mitchell, fulfilling the vow of vengeance he had sworn on the day of Andovar's murder. He had traveled half the world to find a weapon with which to deal with the wraith, and he would not be turned from his course now; his father and kin, and perhaps Ardaz and DelGiudice—wherever the ghost might have gone off to—would see to signaling the forces, and both the elves and the Calvans were commanded by determined and wise leaders. If Belexus could deal with Mitchell quickly and definitively, then the morale of all the men and all the elves would be bolstered.

That thought in mind, the ranger cut a fast, and somewhat risky, course toward the appointed rock. Down lower, he saw the zombies and skeletons trying vainly to shadow his movements, like a dark field of tall, swaying wheat. He saw the talon archers and spearmen rise up from their holes to launch missiles his way.

Calamus was too fast for the initial attacks, but the

excitement was beginning to precede the ranger's flight, and he feared that he would be struck down before he ever got near to the wraith.

But then he saw the hated Mitchell, climbing up onto the rock as if he, too, had awaited this moment all along. The wraith called out to those around him to stand down, to let the ranger in. "Belexus is mine to kill," Mitchell proclaimed, loudly enough so that the ranger heard every word.

And savored every word. Belexus held no illusions—the talons would attack him from every angle if he defeated the wraith, and likely would kill him before he ever got the chance to fly away on Calamus—but he hardly cared. He would willingly give his life in return for destroying the wretched undead monster.

Calamus, as true in heart as the ranger, glided down to land lightly on the wide rock, skipping to a halt some score of feet from the black specter of the horrid wraith.

"Ye're knowing why I've come," Belexus said firmly, sliding from the pegasus' side.

"To die," the wraith replied casually. Mitchell lifted his mace, the strange and awful-looking weapon fashioned of a leg bone and skull of a horse, and started forward, a wild grin stamped upon his gray and bloated face.

Belexus didn't flinch in the least, took any fear within him and slammed it against the memory of Andovar's death, buried it in a cascade of sheer hatred. "Come on then, Mitchell," he growled, drawing Pouilla Camby.

An arrow skipped off the stone behind him, skimming the ground right between Calamus' legs.

"Take flight!" the ranger cried, and the pegasus was already moving, three running strides off the side of the rock, then up into the air amidst a hail of arrows.

"Is all yer life to be treachery?" the ranger asked.

"I never demanded that the pegasus was mine to kill," Mitchell answered. "Just you, ranger. Just you."

A glance back satisfied Belexus that Calamus had risen above the range of the talons without taking any serious hits, so he turned his attention fully back to Mitchell. He was trapped now, with no way out, but that thought, too, ran up against a wall of sheer hatred and was buried.

"All the world will be mine," Mitchell taunted. "All your kin and all the elves, and the witch, too."

"I know not what outcome this dark day will see," the ranger answered calmly, refusing to be caught in the trap of despair. "But whatever's coming, then know that ye'll not be seeing it!" And on Belexus came, Pouilla Camby flashing mightily, trailing white light from her diamond insets.

The two men crept cautiously along the darkened corridor of the partially rebuilt White Tower, sensing that something was very wrong. Istaahl had gone into the dungeons of his crumbled home leaving instructions that he was not to be disturbed, but he had also commanded that these two men, his most trusted aides, could come and "collect" him in a week.

What that cryptic instruction might mean, the two did not dare openly speculate, but they were not overly surprised when, hearing no answer to their knock on the door to the wizard's private chamber, they entered the room to find Istaahl slumped over his desk.

"He dead?" the more timid of the pair asked as his companion went over and bent low, putting his face near the wizard's lips.

"Don't think so," the other answered. He gave Istaahl several shoves, but the mage stirred not at all. "I know not," the man corrected. "Some affliction has come over him."

The two men gathered up the comatose wizard, and he did not stir in the least. They dragged him up the stairs and out of the tower, then through the streets of Pallendara to the house of an old woman known for the art of healing. But she, too, could get no response, could only note that some affliction had come over the wizard.

It was true enough: an affliction that Istaahl had put over himself. The wizard was no longer in his body, had dismissed that limiting form altogether and literally thrown himself out from his mortal coil.

Indeed, the life force, the spiritual entity that was Istaahl the White, was far out at sea, diving to the depths, arousing the power.

Chapter 23

The Last Battle

"I AM NO enemy," the ghost said, trying hard to let his sincerity shine through. But he was distracted—so overwhelmed!—at the sight of the pair standing cautiously in the corridor before him, at the sight of his daughter.

Rhiannon and Bryan held their defensive posture, the half-elf standing with sword drawn, tip tilted toward Del.

"Rhiannon," the spirit said softly, letting the name roll off his tongue like sweet music. "Rhiannon."

She looked at him without understanding.

"Do you not know me?" the ghost asked. "Can you not look into your heart and see the truth?"

"Enough wasted time!" Bryan growled and advanced.

"Hold," Rhiannon bade him, grabbing his shoulder. Then to the ghost, she said, "State it plainly, for me friend speaks the truth. We've not the time for wasting, and're not about to fall for any o' Thalasi's tricks."

"DelGiudice," Del said immediately. "I am . . . I was . . . Jeffrey DelGiudice. I am your father."

"What foolishness is this?" Bryan began, but Rhiannon's gasp and the way she clutched his shoulder made him pause and glance back at her. Her expression, the blood drained from her fair face, told him that she harbored more than a little doubt.

"You know," Del said, "though you cannot admit it,

cannot take such a risk when your friend's safety is also at stake. So hold your thoughts and questions, accept your doubts and let them keep you on your guard, until we are out of this hellish place and somewhere safe."

"We must move along," Bryan said to the young witch.

"The courtyard is guarded by talons," Del offered. "And so are the passages along the way you are headed. Better that, I suppose, than what stalks the chambers that way," he added, pointing down a side passage to the left.

"You know the place well for one who claims to be no friend to Morgan Thalasi," Bryan said suspiciously.

"I have been searching for you," Del explained. "I can move quite fast, and through most walls. I've seen nearly all of this level of the fortress, and most of the next higher level. Except down there and up," he added, pointing again to the left. "Morgan Thalasi is up there, I believe, and so are many of his dead minions."

Bryan and Rhiannon looked to each other anxiously.

"Rhiannon?" the half-elf asked.

"I'm trusting him," she answered. "I'm thinking he's who he's saying he is, or at least, that he's no friend o' Thalasi's. I see no evil upon him, and that's a mark the Black Warlock could'no' hide."

"He said that Thalasi was there," Bryan remarked.

"That's where we're going, then," Rhiannon said flatly.

"I came . . . he came . . . we came . . . to get you out," the spirit of DelGiudice protested, his eyes wide with surprise.

"When I'm done and not before," Rhiannon answered, and started away, down the passage to the ghost's left. She eyed Del curiously as she passed close by him, the first obvious sign that she found the mystery of his identity intriguing. But again, with the determination and stoicism that had marked the last months of her previously carefree life, the young witch would not be deterred in the least, and on she went, boldly.

Bryan scrambled to catch up; the ghost, with a mere thought, zipped in front of both of them. "You cannot do this," Del said determinedly.

Rhiannon moved right to him, thinking to push past, and of course, only slipped right through the insubstantial spirit, drawing a gasp from Bryan. Still, the young witch shook the unsettling experience away and continued on.

And again, the spirit appeared before her. "How can I let you?" Del asked.

"How can ye stop me?" Rhiannon's curt answer came.

And there it was, plain and simple, the truth of it all that only added to Del's frustration. Once again, it seemed to him as if he could do little to protect his daughter, and now, of all the horrors, it seemed as if he had steered her right toward the one above all others he wanted her to avoid!

And she was right, for there was nothing he could do to stop her, even to slow her.

"I will stay ahead of you," Del offered. "And guide your path."

Bryan and Rhiannon didn't know whether or not to trust the spirit; it occurred to both of them yet again that Del might be no more than a manifestation created by Thalasi to lure them into some trap. Still, they could not ignore the benefits of having so mobile and secretive a spy to lead their way. If it came to a pitched battle within this stronghold, the pair, for all Bryan's skill and all Rhiannon's powers, would have little chance of ever finding the Black Warlock. Rhiannon's heart decided the matter, for the young witch, deep inside, found that she believed the tale of the ghost. She remembered the tales her mother had told her of her father; Brielle's description of the man, both physical and in demeanor, seemed to fit the ghost.

On they went, and it didn't take long for Bryan and Rhiannon to realize the benefits of having Del along. They passed by several zombie-filled chambers, slipped through other empty rooms, took a roundabout course through seemingly off-direction corridors, and even crawled through one window in a wall, designed for passing food trays from cook to waiter. The course meandered, but following the ghost's instructions, the pair wound up at a set of wide, decorated stairs without a single fight.

"I can find no other way up," the ghost explained, returning to them as they began their ascent. "These stairs pause at a landing around the bend, and there are a few undead talons standing ready in there, I'm afraid. You'll have to fight them."

That thought didn't seem to bother either of the companions, Bryan even picking up his pace to get a couple of strides ahead of Rhiannon. As the ghost had said, they went around a bend to a landing, wherein stood four animated talon corpses. Following Thalasi's instructions, the zombies moved to block the stairs in a shoulder-to-shoulder line.

Bryan charged ahead, but not before Rhiannon managed to pull a couple of arrows out of the quiver on his back. She lifted one to her lips, kissed it and whispered words of encouragement, then threw it at the zombies.

The arrow, gaining speed with every passing inch, split into two, then into four, and blasted, two bolts each, through the two zombies holding the left of the defensive line. Bryan's sword took out the next in line, a clean slash that severed the creature's head, so by the time the remaining zombie even moved to the attack, it fought all alone.

And the lumbering, unthinking thing proved no match for Bryan of Corning. The half-elf's sword slashed across and back, taking fingers from the zombie's reaching hands, then again, nearly severing one bloated arm at the elbow. In rushed Bryan, sword thrusting at an up angle, catching the monster under the chin and splitting wide its face. Still the zombie fought on, getting one filthy hand on Bryan's shield, but the half-elf pushed that gruesome appendage away and slashed again.

A second zombie head fell to the floor.

"Not much of a defense," the half-elf muttered.

"Slow to react," the ghost of Del agreed. "They are not independent-thinking things, but mere animations, tools for Thalasi."

"Talons would serve as better guards," the half-elf remarked.

"Most people—and most talons—would more likely be frightened off by the zombies," Del explained.

It took Bryan a few seconds to understand that as a compliment.

A few seconds that he didn't have, for he and Rhiannon set off at once, past the landing and up the next set of stairs. The ghost, soaring ahead of them with ease, came back to them before they were halfway up, informing them that these stairs ended at a solid oaken door.

"You'll be fighting again when you go though," Del explained. "Just a pair of zombies this time. And then you'll see a corridor lined on both sides by three doors, and with one door at the end."

"And that's where we'll find Thalasi," Rhiannon reasoned.

"I don't know," the ghost admitted, seeming shaken

for the first time. "He has something, or there is something, warding the place," he stammered. "I cannot approach!"

Rhiannon and Bryan exchanged glances. "Not the time for a mix-up," the witch said to Del.

"On the right," the ghost tried to explain. "There is something through the first door on the right which I cannot approach, nor did I dare even try to pass it by. Something powerful, something wicked."

Bryan's face screwed up with anger and confusion, and he started to berate the ghost, but Rhiannon, who had witnessed the awful specter of the Staff of Death, understood—and understood, too, that Del should not go anywhere near that vile weapon.

"Ye stay here," she instructed the spirit. "Yer job's done now."

"I cannot let you—" the ghost started to protest.

"Ye cannot stop me," Rhiannon interrupted. "Nor can ye help. I seen Thalasi's staff, seen the Black Warlock use it to control Mitchell, a thinking spirit, like yerself. We're not needing ye to turn against us."

"I would never!"

"So ye're saying, but ye've no place in the coming fight, not with the staff in Thalasi's hands," Rhiannon said firmly.

Del couldn't argue, and Rhiannon and Bryan weren't waiting to hear his protests anyway. The ghost watched them go, up the stairs, swift and silent, and again he felt so very impotent. He had been helpful these last weeks, in retrieving the diamond sword, in aiding Belexus' spying, and now, in getting Rhiannon and Bryan through the maze that was Talas-dun, but again, his ability to help was limited, frustratingly so.

He watched the pair go through the door, then heard the fighting beyond—a battle that lasted but half the time of the slaughter on the lower landing—and then he heard them crash through the next door.

He knew that his daughter was in trouble then, and knew that he could do nothing to help her.

Belexus skidded to an abrupt stop, shifted direction, and threw himself to the side as a wall of black flakes filled the air before him. He glanced at Mitchell, then to the spot before the wraith, the stones smoking wherever the deadly flakes had touched.

"How easy your mortal skin shall burn," the wraith taunted.

Belexus' first thought was to rush right in again and score a hit. The time for talking was ended, his rage told him. But his rationale told him otherwise. He saw the eyes upon him—dozens of talons crouched nearby, watching the fight—and understood that even if Pouilla Camby did her work and he was victorious over Mitchell, spears would come at him from every angle.

"Bah, ye're fearing me!" the ranger shot back, and Mitchell laughed all the louder.

"So ye're keeping yer talon dogs about," the ranger went on, managing a laugh of his own. "Ye're needing them in case ye're losing."

With a glare and a word, the supremely confident wraith dismissed those talons nearby, who were all too happy to run away from these two!

Now Belexus was satisfied; now he let his anger take over, fury driving his sword arm. The wraith was still laughing when he charged, and kept laughing, putting up little defense against the ranger's first swing.

Mitchell's smile quickly disappeared. Always before the wraith had counted on its magical nature, an empowerment that prevented weapons from hurting it. But the ranger's slash, a downward cut from shoulder to belly, stung profoundly.

Belexus, hopping back out of range of the wicked mace, stared hopefully at the wound: a line of white across the darkness that was Mitchell, as if the diamond-edged sword had left behind some of its enchanted light. So, the sword was indeed effective, he thought, silently congratulating Brielle, but he had hit Mitchell solidly and apparently done only a bit of damage. How many hits would it take, then?

And how many clean strikes would he get? he wondered, for now Mitchell was on his guard, now outrage replaced the smile on his horrid features. He came on roaring, swinging his mace.

Belexus dove and rolled to the side, came up in a short run, then dove again, changing his angle so that he was going behind the slower-turning Mitchell. He came up gracefully to his feet once more and reversed momentum, hopping in and stabbing hard, then rushing away. He was the strongest man in all Aielle, a warrior who could bash through the defenses of any talon with the sheer power of his strokes, but he needed speed now, and agility, and cunning.

The wraith pursued, and Belexus squared against him. Mitchell's attack came straightforward and predictable, an angled downward chop. Belexus stepped his right foot ahead and swiped across with his sword, hooking the mace under its bulky head before it could gain any momentum, before it could throw forth the deadly flakes.

Powerful Mitchell was quick to improvise, coming forward as well and grabbing the man by the shoulder.

Belexus ignored the coldness of that grip, the permeating iciness that chilled to the bone. He dropped Pouilla Camby, and Mitchell howled, thinking his grip had forced

Chapter 24

The Lure of Power

THEY WATCHED THE old man, the man who had been as their father for all the years, who had taken them in and sheltered them, these children of Pallendara's nobles, when wicked Ungden had stolen the throne. They watched him now, this man who had trained them in the ways of survival and of war, this man who had transformed them into the proud rangers. Now, from a seat on the returned pegasus, Bellerian led them again, soaring out on high and issuing subtle signals concerning the whereabouts and strength of the enemy positions.

So the rangers were not surprised in the least when they came around a bend in the trail to find a rocky dell filled with talon spear throwers and archers—all of whom had their gazes set the other way, out across the long spur of Kored-dul to the approaching armies.

Arrows leading, the rangers charged the surprised talons in a wild rush, and so coordinated and efficient was their attack that not a single man was even injured in the sudden and swift fight. In the span of barely a minute, a score of talons lay dead.

"They've set talons with spears in pockets all about the arm," one ranger remarked, peeking up over the other side of the dell.

"Lord Bellerian will sight them for us," another replied.

"And for the Calvan artillerists," a third remarked, and with grim nods, they were off again, following the signals of their flying leader, in search of new prey.

None could perform such deadly and secretive tactics as well as the rangers of Avalon, but even with such powerful allies, the armies on the field found themselves hard-pressed before they even reached the rocky arm. Arien's elves had approached the foothills expecting to battle for every inch of ground, and when the first talons, even the first of Thalasi's gruesome undead, had risen against them, the elves had maintained their order and their progress, lining their marvelous steeds into a fighting wedge and slicing through the enemy ranks with hardly an effort.

The elf lord fully expected that the talon lizard riders would come next, a more difficult and maneuverable foe, but what he found instead was more undead; thousands and thousands and thousands of zombies and skeletons rising from every shadow, coming out fearlessly though the elves were cutting them down dozens at a time.

"We cannot hope to defeat this many," Ryell said to him. "Weariness will lay our weapons low, if these perversions do not! We should turn to the south and join with Benador."

Arien would have agreed, except that when he and Ryell did look that way, they found that the humans were no better off than they, that the vast zombie army on the southern end of the spur outnumbered the large human army as badly as those on this side outnumbered the elves.

Thalasi, or perhaps the wraith of Mitchell, Arien knew, had marked well the approach of the two forces and had set the monstrous army accordingly.

"May the Colonnae be with us," Arien muttered. "For

foul Morgan Thalasi has called back the corpses of every dead talon in all the world, I fear!"

Around to the south of Arien's position, King Benador did not disagree with the elf lord's estimation, for he had never seen, had never even imagined, that such a force as this could ever be assembled. Tens of thousands of undead streamed out of the mountains, a seemingly endless line, coming on without hesitation, without fear.

No novice to large-scale battle, seasoned in the brutality of the fight at the Four Bridges, the Calvan king had rightly turned his army about, putting some open ground between his soldiers and the now-advancing enemy. He set up a long skirmish line, hundreds of archers shoulder to shoulder, in ranks three deep so that the barrage of arrows flew out in a nearly constant swarm. Even with that, though, the enemy made great progress. Arrows chipped off skeletal ribs, or plowed right through the rotted corpses of zombies, hardly slowing the horrid things.

"Too many," the Calvan king muttered, and he feared that the battle would soon degenerate into a swarming melee, where the sheer press of monstrous numbers would overwhelm his gallant force.

He looked to the north, but not thinking that any help would come from that direction, and his heart sank lower at the sight of Arien and the valiant elves, a force so unified that they seemed as one, a longboat skimming on the very edge of a breaking wave.

But that wave continued to swell behind them.

She came to a hall where two corridors crossed, and glanced both ways, but saw nothing to guide her. Cursing herself for the slight hesitation—for the desperate Black Warlock was right on her heels, closing ground, yelling at her, taunting her—she darted to the left. She had the mighty staff, but had no idea, and certainly no desire, to wield the perverted thing! And, despite the theft, this remained Morgan Thalasi's castle, his bastion of strength, built with his magical power and offering him residual energy from that long-ago construction.

Through a door, Rhiannon nearly ran over a pair of statuelike zombies.

"Kill her!" Thalasi screamed to them from a few yards back.

Rhiannon gave a slight yelp and tried to circumvent them, thinking that her flight had ended. She might destroy the zombies, but not in time to evade Thalasi's pursuit.

But the zombie pair didn't move to attack, didn't move at all to Thalasi's call, and the young witch sensed that they had not even heard him, that he had no connection to them and surely no power over them. She crossed by the pair, then glanced at the staff, and then she understood.

"Kill him," she said quietly, before her good sense could intervene, and the zombies moved immediately, obeying the staff wielder. Thalasi's hollowed eyes widened indeed when he crossed the threshold of the room to find the zombie pair reaching for his throat.

Rhiannon ran on, knowing that the zombies couldn't defeat the Black Warlock, couldn't even hold him at bay for very long. She heard a crackle behind her soon after she had exited the room, and then Thalasi was chasing her once more.

There were more zombies and skeletons up ahead, and these, too, the desperate Rhiannon set to block him.

How easy it was! With a mere thought, she could order them to . . . to do anything, she realized. To kill Thalasi, or to leap from a cliff face. A grander scheme came to the young witch as she moved along, down another corridor, then up a tight spiral staircase. She came to understand the staff and its powers more fully with each step, and she couldn't imagine that she had ever wanted to destroy the precious item. With this power . . .

The thought was intoxicating, overwhelming, and Rhiannon acted immediately, sending her telepathic commands out far and wide. She heard her mother's voice, from a distant place, crying out in protest, but she ignored it, too concerned with changing the tide of war.

With those simple telepathic thoughts, Rhiannon ordered all the thousands of undead Thalasi had raised to shift sides, imparting a mental image of the wretched talons as the new focus of their attacks. She knew that the staff, the brilliant and beautiful staff, had sent the commands out far and wide, knew, somehow, that every undead creature in all the world would take heed.

Kill talons.

Hollis Mitchell heard the command distinctly, a wave of power washing over him, catching him completely off his guard. He closed his flaming eyes, swaying, seeking his own dominating willpower, and Belexus, ever the opportunist, wasted no time in going on the attack, wading in and hammering hard at the wraith.

Mitchell hardly felt the profound stings of Pouilla Camby, so concerned was he with that curious call. Then he understood; it was not the Black Warlock. That meddlesome young witch had gotten her hands on the Staff of Death!

The wraith came out of his trance with a hiss of defiance, the impartation of the staff, which had never really been his master, thrown aside. He had to finish his business here quickly now, he understood, and get back to

Talas-dun to deal properly with Rhiannon. He considered it a promising thing, as he drove the ranger back to a defensive posture. Rhiannon, after all, wouldn't be as skilled or as powerful with the item as Thalasi, and if he could somehow wrest the staff from her, then his control would be absolute. All the dead—including those who would fall on the field of battle this very day—would rise to his command.

But he had to be quick, the wraith realized as he saw battle erupting not so far from the flat rock, yet far from the lines of the humans and elves, as he saw talons scrambling suddenly to get away from their zombie and skeleton allies, the undead reacting immediately to the new commands of the staff wielder.

"They are fleeing!" Ryell cried, and indeed it seemed true. The undead ranks had turned away from the elven wedge, moving back toward the mountains. Elves cried out in victory and joy, for not one of them, brave though they were, had harbored a thought that they could win through this teeming horde.

But to Arien, always calm and thinking, it made no sense at all. And then it made even less sense, as he noted a group of zombies pull down a thrashing talon and fall over the beast.

Something was wrong here, so very out of place. The elf lord looked to Ardaz, who sat atop his horse, scratching at his beard.

"How very curious," the old wizard said, reading and agreeing wholeheartedly with Arien's confusion.

"Might your sister be involved?" Arien asked, for if any in all the world could turn perversion back on Thalasi, it was Brielle.

Ardaz, though, was thinking along slightly different

lines. "Or her daughter," the old wizard replied, and a hopeful smile widened on his wrinkled and hairy face.

Arien's heart soared with hope, too, but he had no more time to sit and ponder. He tightened the elven wedge and drove them hard to the south, ordering them to focus any attacks on talon enemies.

Their first barrage blew great holes in the lines of advancing monsters, but the crews of the great trebuchets feared to launch their pitch balls now, with the undead so close, with melee soon to be joined, Calvan riders sweeping out from the skirmish line in tight formations. The artillerists looked farther back toward the mountains instead, and their attention was grabbed by the sight of Bellerian, high on the winged horse.

Down he swooped, firing his bow, then up again as a wall of arrows rose up against him.

"Oh, fine Bellerian," one Calvan exclaimed.

"Coordinate!" The cry came from King Benador, who had also noticed Bellerian and was riding hard now for the catapult line.

The great arms creaked and heaved their loads, one after another, to the spot below Bellerian.

The ranger moved Calamus far from harm's way, and dipped his wings in salute to the artillerists even as the carnage erupted below him, the splattering pitch bombs scattering and burning the talon entrenchment.

Few of the talons escaped that barrage, and none unscathed. One creature, limping, often crawling, for its legs had been badly burned, managed to get around a rocky wall before the second barrage thundered in. The creature made for that wall, thinking to put its back against it, thinking that it had reached safety.

Head down, belly to the ground, the creature's eyes

widened when it saw the white legs of Calamus. It looked up in time to see Bellerian's sword cutting down.

The ranger lord wiped his sword on the dead talon's tunic, then, satisfied that no others were about, he climbed the pegasus high into the sky once more, thinking to scout out another talon nest.

Something else caught his attention, something he could not ignore.

High atop the tallest tower of Talas-dun, Rhiannon heard the fighting, zombie against talon, raging in the courtyard. She went to the window and saw the carnage—dozens of undead pulling down talons, choking them—and she mused that with a thought she could *increase* her forces—her army—after every battle.

They would need no supplies; any instructions would be imparted immediately to the whole of the force. Their numbers would only multiply, for those slain in combat could be brought back, along with those they killed. This was an army that could not be weakened by battle, an army that fed upon carnage. How beautiful it seemed to the young witch. How logical and efficient.

She looked at the staff then, and was not repulsed, seeing it for the power and basking in that might. This was the promise of strength. This was the promise of victory. This was the instrument that could restore order to all the world, could free the goodly races forever from the horrors of war, even from the drudgery of menial tasks.

Rhiannon looked again to the courtyard, saw another talon get buried under a swarm of zombies.

Saw her army grow.

"Me girl!"

Rhiannon heard the call, heard the lie, coming from a faraway place, a horrid place.

Avalon.

"Me girl!" Now it was more insistent, more demanding. Always demanding. But now . . . Now, holding this staff, no one could make any demands of Rhiannon. She was the staff wielder; she would dictate.

"Me girl!" The plaintive tone of the call this time shook her, and mocked her anger. She pictured the caller, her mother, standing in the forest that had been her home.

That awful, horrid place.

"No," Rhiannon heard herself saying against the tide of images. No, Avalon was not like that, was not horrid, was more fair than any place in all the world.

"Rhiannon," Brielle called from across the miles, and across the greater vastness that now separated Rhiannon from the world, a chasm of consciousness. She was in a place of unreality, of fabrication, and now, suddenly, she understood the source.

Rhiannon opened wide her eyes, saw again the fighting in the courtyard. But now she was not pleased by the brutality. She looked to the staff in her hands, the instrument of power, of perversion, and saw the truth.

Morgan Thalasi stumbled into the room, his hollowed face torn from his fight with the zombies, his black eyes filled with outrage.

But the young witch did not back down in the least.

"Ye're a damned thing, Morgan Thalasi," she said firmly. "To have bringed such a thing as this into the sunlight." With that, she grasped the staff tightly and summoned her power—her own power, and not that of the perverted item. A sheath of shining light encompassed her hand, and suddenly—and Rhiannon did not know how it came about—a globe of greenish light covered her body. Thalasi rushed at her.

She gave a cry and tried to focus on the staff, but thought she was dead as the Black Warlock sprang at her—sprang at her and was repelled, sent flying across the room, by the green globe!

Rhiannon knew then that her mother was with her, that she was not alone. Bolstered, she focused the energy on her hand, shaped it like a blade, and chopped down hard on the staff.

A slight crack appeared along the black wood, and from it poured shadows—not insubstantial things, but living shadows: dark, huddled forms that crawled about the room.

Again Rhiannon gave a cry, but the shadows ignored her altogether, rushing, swarming toward Thalasi, reaching for him with groping fingers.

"Charon!" he cried with understanding. He had played a dangerous game with Death, and now, with the staff weakened and out of his hands, Death had come calling. The Black Warlock fought back furiously, loosed crackling bolts of black lightning that splintered stone and rebounded wildly. But the shadowy forms pressed on, encircling him, tightening the ring, grabbing at him from every angle.

Rhiannon closed her eyes and worked hard to ignore his desperate cries. With her glowing, bladelike hand, she hit the staff again and again, each slice cutting a bit deeper.

"Rhiannon!" an obviously terrified Thalasi begged. "Oh, send them away!"

She couldn't block out that plea, the most desperate tone she had ever heard. She glanced to the side of the room to see the Black Warlock in the clutches of the huddled shadowy horde, his corporeal form shimmering, as if losing its very essence. She knew that she could not help him, knew that the shadowy things were too beyond her control, even with the Staff of Death in hand. They swarmed all over Thalasi now, pulled him screaming and thrashing down, down, right through the floor.

His calls became a distant wail when Rhiannon went back to her work, more furiously now and with tears of terror in her blue eyes. She chopped and chopped; her mother cried out to her repeatedly.

The staff broke apart.

The tower blew apart.

Mitchell felt it keenly, felt as if his connection to the material world was gone, as if he were drifting back, back, to the vast, dark plain that was the realm of Death. Sheer hatred and wretchedness stopped that flight. Mitchell would not leave, would not surrender his lust for power.

He felt that sting again, all about his head and shoulders, Pouilla Camby slashing hard, cutting white lines across the darkness that was the wraith.

But he was back then, fully, growling and rushing fiercely at the ranger, whipping his bone mace to and fro in a frenzy, filling all the air with those burning black flakes.

Belexus retreated desperately, felt the sting and burn as several flakes fell over him. His clothing smoldered; his skin blistered. And Mitchell came on, roaring, swinging, driving the ranger back, accepting the hits from the nasty sword in the hope that he would connect just once. Just once.

Because both knew that one hit from that awful mace would utterly destroy Belexus.

But the ranger was by far the superior fighter, and his sword work as he retreated was nothing short of magnificent. Yet even the beauty of Pouilla Camby could not defeat the momentum of the furious wraith, could not slow the darkness that was Hollis Mitchell, and the wraith rose up above Belexus, the ranger out of running room.

There came a rush of air, the thundering sound of beating wings, as Calamus swooped down and clipped the wraith, not hurting him, but stopping his pursuit and stealing his focus. The bone mace swiped across in futile pursuit of the pegasus' swift flight.

Belexus was quick to reverse the momentum, taking up his sword in both hands and rushing in, hammering away, slashing and beating, knowing that one mistake, one slip, would let Mitchell get that mace in, would surely destroy him. He cried out for Avalon, for all the world. He cried out and he swung with all his strength, over and over, the diamond light spreading, the sword humming through the air. He ignored the pain as the black flakes settled about him, screamed out too loudly, tensed his muscles too tightly. If he had paused and thought about it, he would have realized how heavy his exhausted arms had become.

But he would not pause, would not slow in the least.

Again and again, Pouilla Camby drove through. Again and again.

It ended suddenly, with a great shudder from the wraith that sent Belexus skidding backward. He regarded Mitchell; the curious, stunned look that glared at him through those glowing white lines. Like the flakes of his own mace, Mitchell fell apart, just broke into pieces, the blackness falling to the stone and dissipating there into swirling tendrils of smoke.

And then Belexus, his hunger for vengeance sated, stood alone.

"Come, and be quick," Bellerian called, setting Calamus down on the stone beside his battered son. "The talon devils are all about us!"

Belexus looked at the hollowed corpse that had been Hollis Mitchell, the empty dead thing. He thought of Andovar and felt warmed, felt that his friend could now, finally, rest easy. And now Belexus could rightly turn his thoughts to the more pressing problems, to the larger battle and the good of all Aielle. He bounded over to Bellerian, a talon spear skipping off the stone behind his rush, and leaped atop the pegasus' back, and Calamus, so strong of wing, had no trouble in lifting the two of them high into the air.

His run became a desperate rush, the spirit launching himself at his daughter, seeing her mortal danger, every instinct within him telling him to go and protect her. Fast as thought, DelGiudice careened into the chamber, arrowing for Rhiannon. But that thought had come an instant too late, an instant after the young witch had chopped Thalasi's staff in half. Del reached her as the blast reached her. He dove for her soul, trying somehow to spiritually embrace her, but he found instead a passage; a long and confusing tunnel.

Gone was the blast, the tower, the fortress. Gone was his daughter.

The confused ghost found himself standing in Avalon, beside a shocked and horrified Brielle.

Far out at sea, the swell rolled, mounting and mounting, a giant wall of water. Istaahl threw all of his energy into it, gave to it all his thoughts and hopes, all his memories and all his fantasies.

On it rolled, inevitably for Talas-dun, the last gasp of Istaahl the White, the purest creation of his magic. As he ascended from the pressing depths, he felt himself spreading out in the water, his very life essence thinning, joining with the rising swell.

All of it, all his energy and all his purpose.

He found her atop a pile of blasted and charred rubble, a delicate flower amidst a mountain of scarred black stone. She didn't look the least bit battered, didn't look as if she had been anywhere near that awful explosion, and Bryan watched in pure amazement as the last glow of Brielle's protective enchantment faded to nothingness. Rhiannon's body was intact, completely undamaged, and yet Bryan knew, before he ever drew near to her, that she was dead.

The half-elf, his eyes dripping streams of tears, lifted her gently and bore her out of that dark place. There was no resistance, for all the zombies and skeletons were back to their sleep of death, and those talons who had not been killed in the frenzied moments before the explosion were either fleeing Talas-dun or were simply too confused to pay the half-elf any notice.

But damn the talons, every one, the half-elf thought, and then he dismissed them.

Rhiannon was dead, and Bryan could do nothing to help her.

Chapter 25

Charon's Abode

SHE HAD BEEN here once before, but the experience had seemed far different then, as if she was only a spectator in this eternal ritual, as if she didn't truly belong. On that previous occasion, Rhiannon had been called back from the walk of death. But this time . . .

This time, she belonged.

She saw the poor departed souls wading past her, seemingly floating among the thick fog blanketing the unseen ground. Humans and elves, soldiers of Arien and Benador, walked solemnly along, their ranks insignificant compared to the many, many talons. Even more numerous, though seeming less substantial, came the hosts of those stolen from their sleep of death, Thalasi's undead army, released to rest once more with the destruction of the perverted staff.

Rhiannon understood, and had no choice but to accept. She took her place in the line and began the descent, the crossing of the barrier between the living and the dead. She paused, though, for she found a pair of souls she could not ignore.

Morgan Thalasi and Martin Reinheiser. Joined in life, they were two once more, separate souls moving down, down to their rewards. For them, the walk would not end pleasantly, Rhiannon knew, and she pitied them, despite the horrors they had caused. And then she didn't even care about them anymore. Just like that, she dismissed them, and wandered along.

The thing about the walk that struck the young witch most profoundly was the sense of peace—even the normally brutal talons showed it on their faces—and those returning to the realm of Death showed it most clearly of all. Not Thalasi and Reinheiser, though. Both struggled against the inevitable, tried to turn about and run back the way they had come, back to the living. And they seemed to be making some progress, as if their mighty wills could fight against even this inevitability.

But then Rhiannon spotted the specter, the common image of Death personified, coming for them. The pair tried to scramble away, screaming in futile protest, but Arawn hooked them both with a single swipe of his long sickle and drew them in.

"I have waited for you, John Morgan, who calls himself Morgan Thalasi," the contented specter of Death said. "And for you, Martin Reinheiser. You joined with John Morgan against me. You stole what was mine. You chose badly."

And, with a black flash and a swirl of the fog, they were gone from Rhiannon's view, and soon, she realized, though she did not know how it happened, she was all alone, stranded in a vast, dark plain, the flatness broken by an endless line of barrows.

She kept walking, not knowing what else she might do. There was no sense of time here, so she did not know how long it had been before she came to a tunnel, the flickering light of a fire burning within. Compelled, she entered, and came almost immediately into a wide chamber with a single bier set in its middle. And behind it, holding up a shroud, stood the specter Charon, Arawn, impassive, inevitable.

Understanding flooded through the young witch, the

dead witch. This was her place now, and though she did not want to be here, did not want to be dead, she could not resist. Slowly, regretfully, the young witch moved to take her eternal bed.

"A rout!" a joyous Arien Silverleaf cried to Ardaz. "Never could we have hoped for such a victory!" Indeed, with the undead horde's last attacks against the talons and the ensuing confusion in the enemy ranks, the men of Calva and the elves of Illuma seemed well on their way to the most complete victory ever known in Ynis Aielle. The elf lord surveyed the battle scene before him, saw, far to the south, another ball of pitch soar high and far to scatter a talon position. Then he felt something more profound, a growling rumble beneath his feet, and saw, far to the west, a tremendous plume of black smoke rising. He looked to Ardaz for an explanation, but his question was lost in his throat when he glanced upon the wizard.

Ardaz blanched white. He knew; he felt it. His niece, budding with power, growing into so fine a woman, was gone. Simply gone. Dead and beyond his help. The wizard, feeling very old suddenly, turned about slowly and looked back to the east, toward Avalon. If he knew, then so did Brielle.

Indeed, the horrible sensation, the waves of Rhiannon's last moment, washed over the Emerald Witch, stealing the blood from her face, stealing the rhythm of her heart. Her knees lost all strength and buckled, and she slumped down to the white carpet of snow, kneeling there, unable to speak, to cry out, even to gasp.

All of it was not lost on the father of Rhiannon. He, too, felt the terrible sensation, and at first couldn't decipher it. But seeing Brielle, broken beyond belief, helped him sort it out.

"No!" he cried, and he did not cut the word short, but held it: "Noooooooo!" It was a plaintive wail, a howl almost, torn from his heart and his throat, released into the empty air. He was up on his toes, knees bent forward, back arched and head thrown back, throwing the wail up to the sky, to the ears of the Colonnae.

And surely they were deaf, for they did not respond, did not come to him now, when he most needed them, did not repair the grief, or return Rhiannon.

"Noooooooo!"

She was gone, just gone. Rhiannon, his daughter, was just gone.

But then he knew; suddenly he knew. DelGiudice had wondered why he had been put back in this place, in this time, had wondered if his tasks were no more important than the retrieval of the diamond sword. Now he knew. Rhiannon was gone, but he could get to her, only he: half a ghost, half a man. He had been to Death's dark realm only briefly, an instant of time before Calae had whisked him off to the stars. Only an instant of time, but DelGiudice remembered the way.

The wail continued, so profound, so agonized, that it drew Brielle from her own broken grief to look up at DelGiudice, to wonder what manner of being could offer such an expression of pain. Her expression shifted to one of horror as Del began to thin out, to become more translucent, as if his very life force was escaping this spirit form on the notes of that howl.

"Del, me Del, don't ye be leaving me now!" the witch cried, scrambling to her feet, rushing over to him.

There was nothing to grab onto, and soon, nothing to see.

The wail diminished, spread wide to the winds, and was no more.

* * *

No more was he a separate entity from the giant wave; no more was he Istaahl the mortal man. He sensed the shallows, knew in some primordial way that he was approaching the high cliffs of the shore.

Then he hit, a mountain of water, exploding in ecstasy against the dark stone of Kored-dul, thundering into the stone unabashedly, straight on, throwing all his life into it.

The roar went on and on, reverberating about the stones, and into the stone, the energy of the crashing water reaching every crack like grasping tendrils. And when the water was gone, the wave broken apart and splashed back out toward the sea, the reverberations continued, echoing.

A great slab of the cliff broke apart and slid down, thundering as it bounced off the stone, then hitting the water with a huge splash. The weakened cliff continued to tremble; another piece broke away. And then another; and then another.

And then it fell, all of it, taking the fire-ravaged disaster of Talas-dun with it.

"O Death where is thy sting? O grave where is thy victory?" Del shouted, stealing from an old passage he remembered, from the time before Aielle, from his world and a passage of Corinthians in a book called the Bible. How clear the words of that most ancient tome came to him now. He knew the book so well, though in life he had paid it hardly any heed. It was a book of the angels, the Colonnae, and a work of morality, of life and death, and life after death. He moved along a gray and foggy corridor, a cold place, passing the line of newly disembodied spirits. Their numbers alone told him that the battle was on in full, and also that Thalasi's hold over the undead spirits was no more.

"O Death where is thy sting? O grave where is thy victory?" he shouted again, running now, passing all of them, descending swiftly to a place darker and colder still. He paused and felt within himself, and there, in a deep place, he sensed the passage of his daughter, and was soon fast on her trail. "And where is thy horror, ugly fiend?" he added, his own thoughts, as he came into the passage and then the chamber, in sight of the cloaked lord of the underworld.

"What terrors have thee left? What pains can thee promise, when thou hast taken all?" Del shouted.

"No promise, ghost of Jeffrey DelGiudice," the specter replied in its unearthly, rasping voice.

"Is there no sympathy, no passion, no care for all the pain?"

"None," Charon replied without hesitation. "I take nothing; I give nothing. I am."

DelGiudice hesitated now, digesting the thoughts, the apparent impassivity. It occurred to him that an apathetic Death was, perhaps, more difficult an opponent than a malignant spirit.

"I will bargain," he offered.

"I take nothing," Charon replied. "I give nothing. No barter, no trade."

"You took her!" Del accused, pointing to the bier where lay his daughter dear, so peaceful.

Too peaceful.

"She came to me by her own actions."

Del stared at Rhiannon's spiritual form, mirroring her physical form, lying perfectly still upon the bier, half wrapped by Charon's eternal shroud.

"Give her back, I beg," Del said.

"Back to whom?" Charon replied impassively. "To you? Need I remind you that you, too, are dead, Jeffrey DelGiudice? It is not an evil thing."

"No," Del agreed. "Not evil. But not for her. Not yet. She was just starting to know life."

"That temporary aspect of life," Charon said. "Now she will learn the next."

Del shook his head. "No, no, no," he kept saying, for though he knew that death was not a wicked thing, not an emptiness and certainly not painful, he felt, somehow, that this was not Rhiannon's time, that the manner of her death, the breaking of that perverted staff, did not justify this end to her mortal coil.

But how to tell that to Charon the impassive? How to justify it when so many other young men and women had died, and would continue to die, this very day, long before they had really been given a chance to experience all that the previous life offered?

"I only know," he said quietly, looking up at the specter, "it is not her time."

Arien led them into the foothills, the sure-footed Avalon mounts quick-stepping past rocky jags and over the multitude of corpses. Enemies were not readily apparent, for those talons who had remained near the front lines had been brought down by the zombies and skeletons, and those who had been farther back had run away.

Arien meant to find them, though, every one, and end the scourge of the children of Thalasi once and for all. First, though, he turned his elves to the south, linking them up with Benador's thousands, and he and Ardaz joined with the king.

"The world could not have hoped for a greater rout," the king of Calva stated, his elation apparent. "The evil talons will be many generations recovering, if ever they do."

"Never," a dour Ardaz said, "for Thalasi is defeated, dead and gone forever."

"Your news is wondrous, yet you speak it with heavy heart," Benador noted.

"For my niece, Rhiannon, too, is gone," Ardaz replied. "And so, too, is Istaahl, who has been my friend for centuries!"

The news hit King Benador hard, and he purposefully had to steady himself, else he would have fallen from his mount. "Istaahl gone?" he asked breathlessly, and he seemed a lost child at that moment.

"And Rhiannon," Arien added grimly.

"Istaahl the White," Charon stated. "Would you ask for him, as well?"

The ghost paused, digesting the sad news that the White Wizard of Pallendara was gone. Somehow, though, that seemed all right to him, as if it was meant to be, as if it was Istaahl's time.

"And what of Jayenson Belltower?" Charon went on. "She was killed this hour, taken by a talon spear. Should I release her as well? I can name hundreds more, and thousands of talons, if they, too, are deserving of your misplaced mercy."

"Not her," Del said immediately. "Not any of them. Just Rhiannon. I know this. It was not her time; not like that. Calae put me back here, in this world, to deliver this one message."

Charon did not respond.

"She gave Thalasi to you," Del reasoned. "She broke his staff, that awful staff, that instrument which the Black Warlock crafted and used to steal from you. She gave it all back to you. You owe her this."

"I do not bargain, nor do I ask for anything," Charon said with some determination. "And I cannot be robbed, since nothing here is my possession. I simply am."

"No!" Del cried, thinking he had found his logical

opening. "No, Charon, your actions reveal the truth. How you hungered for Thalasi in that tower room, when the staff was first cracked. How your shadowy minions went after him, pulling him to you!"

The specter of Death did not reply, only, for the first time in all the eons, listened.

Belexus and Bellerian, atop Calamus, moved above the rocky foothills, searching for remnants of the talon army so that they could direct the continuing attacks of their kinsmen and the elves. At Belexus' insistence, the older ranger turned the pegasus inevitably east, toward Talas-dun.

They came in sight of the broken cliff, all trace of the black fortress gone, and any trepidation they held at the sight of disaster disappeared when they spotted, far below, Bryan of Corning, moving along a narrow trail, bearing Rhiannon gently in his arms.

They were with him in a moment, and their fears returned tenfold, for they knew, without doubt, from his tear-streaked face and from the very still manner in which the beautiful witch lay in his arms, that Talas-dun had not been destroyed without a heavy cost.

Bryan lay Rhiannon down on the stone; Belexus moved very close and stroked the young witch's face, beautiful in death as it had been in life.

"She did it," the half-elf said. "She beat Thalasi, and destroyed his staff."

"And all his undead monsters went back to their rest," Bellerian added. "Suren Rhiannon won the day."

Bryan fell to his knees beside her, his emotions pouring out of him.

"We canno' be stayin'," the ranger lord remarked. "The stones are thick with talons."

"Ye take Rhiannon on the pegasus," Belexus said to

his father. "Me and Bryan'll fight our way through, don't ye doubt." He put his hand on the half-elf's shoulder as he spoke, lending some strength, and lending hope in the promise that he would help Bryan find his vengeance upon many talon heads. The half-elf looked the strong ranger in the eye, and Belexus nodded grimly.

"We're all to go," an unexpected reply came, and how the eyes of the three widened! They looked down in unison to see Rhiannon opening her blue eyes, a grin growing on her face. "We're all to go together," she said in a labored voice.

Bryan, after a moment of wavering, nearly fainting, wrapped her in a tight hug, and Belexus was quick to join in, but both backed off reverently when the ghost of DelGiudice appeared suddenly, hovering over them.

The spirit moved close, and Rhiannon reached out to touch him. But of course her hand passed right through the insubstantial body.

"My time here is ended," Del explained, for he had heard clearly the beckoning call of Calae. He considered the angel and the mysteries that awaited him and remembered again that long-lost tome of wisdom, that most holy book from the world that had been, a book inspired by the heavens indeed. How clearly he recognized the truths that lay within that book, how ingrained those truths had been to the man who had scrambled off the sinking *Unicorn* those decades ago! He thought of that now, just briefly, and considered it in the context of those he had come to know and love, and hate, in Ynis Aielle. Honor and courage, tolerance and respect. Truths for the ages, tenets that did not shift with the passing of years, but remained constant and important. How seamlessly Brielle would fit into that tome, though in Del's often-intolerant world, those who followed the Bible unbendingly would have considered the witch an unholy, pagan thing. How grand would be the story of Belexus and Andovar, had it been told in the Bible of his previous existence!

Some things did not change.

"Me father," Rhiannon said softly, her expression thick with love and gratitude. She knew what had transpired in the realm of Death, knew that Jeffrey DelGiudice, her father, had come after her.

Del moved close to her, looked deep into her eyes, then turned his gaze heavenward. "Grant me this, Calae," he begged, and suddenly, Rhiannon's reaching hand brushed against his solid cheek.

Del kissed her forehead and hugged her close, then moved away, to arm's length, until only their fingers were touching, a touch that lessened by the moment as the spirit dissipated.

"Fare well, my daughter," Del said. "Fare well, my love. We will meet again."

And with that promise of hope, Del was gone.

Epilogue

IT WAS SUMMER and it was Avalon, and the threat of the talons, and of Thalasi, was forever ended. But to Belexus and Brielle, Bryan and Rhiannon, Ardaz, Arien, and Bellerian, the edge of joy had been forever dulled, replaced by a distant but undeniable sense of melancholy. An age had ended in Aielle, the Age of Magic, and nowhere was that more evident than in the boughs of Avalon. Still beautiful was the wood, but that preternatural essence of the place had been replaced now. For nearly a millennium Avalon had stood in eternal springtime, but now it was summer in the wood, with autumn fast closing in.

"Suren 'tis time for resting," Bellerian noted, and Ardaz, feeling his great age, was quick to agree.

Also in agreement was Desdemona, the black cat curled about the wizard's neck. She yawned and stretched and dug her claws in a bit too hard.

Yelping, Ardaz pulled her away and tossed her into the air. Unlike those many other times, she didn't transform into a bird, though, for the magic was gone now, simply gone. She landed gracefully on sure cat feet, turned her back to Ardaz, her tail twitching, and moved to Rhiannon, finding a comfortable perch on the young woman's lap.

Ardaz looked to his sister Brielle, their expressions

showing that neither had missed the not-so-subtle reminder that the Age of Magic was lost.

"Thalasi be damned," Jennifer Glendower, no longer the Emerald Witch, cursed softly.

"Indeed," Ardaz said. "Indeed."

Prologue

JILSEPONIE—PONY—sat on the crenellated roof of the one squat tower of St. Precious Abbey in the great city of Palmaris, looking out over the snow-covered rooftops, her gaze drifting inevitably to the dark flowing waters of the Masur Delaval. A bitterly cold wind nipped at her, but Pony, deep in memories, hardly noticed the sting. All the region, the northwestern expanses of the kingdom of Honce-the-Bear, had experienced an early snow only a week before, winter coming on in full force, though the year had not seen the end of the tenth month.

By all estimations, the war against the demon Bestesbulzibar and its goblin, giant, and powrie minions had gone unexpectedly well, had been completed with minimal loss of human life and without a single major city burned to the ground. Now with winter, though, the aftereffects of that war were beginning to show, most notably the food shortages in villages whose supplies had been diverted to towns that had harbored the King's soldiers. Rumors had come to Palmaris of uprisings in some of those villages against King Danube and against the Abellican Church, whose leader had surely acted in the interests of the demon. Other rumors spoke of several mysterious deaths along the coast of the Mantis Arm and of a group of fanatics threatening to break away from the Abellican Church while rejecting outright the notion of any church dedicated to Avelyn Desbris.

So the war had ended here in Palmaris, but it seemed to the grieving Pony as if the turmoil had only begun.

Or was it merely a continuing thing? she wondered. Was such travesty and turmoil, such unrest, merely a reflection of the human condition, an unending procession of one battle after another, of one cause of bitterness replacing another? The notion stung Pony deeply, for if that were the case, then what had they really accomplished? What had been bought by their sacrifice?

Why had Elbryan, her beloved husband, died?

Pony gave a helpless sigh at the futility of it all. She thought back to her early days, up in the wild Timberlands, in Dundalis, when she and Elbryan had grown up together, carefree. She remembered running down the wooded trails beside the boy, running particularly among the white caribou moss in the pine-filled valley north of their village. She remembered climbing the northern slope beside him one chilly night, looking up at the sky to see Corona's Halo, the beautiful multicolored ring that encircled the world, the source, she had later come to learn, of the blessed magical gemstones that served as the power and focus of faith of the Abellican Church.

The next dawn, Pony and Elbryan had witnessed the return of their fathers and the other hunters. How clearly Pony now remembered that, running, full of excitement, full of anticipation, full of—

Horror. For suspended from a shoulder pole had hung a most curious and ugly little creature: a goblin. Never could Pony or Elbryan have foreseen that slain little brute as a harbinger of such doom. But soon after, the goblins had attacked in force, burning Dundalis to the ground, slaughtering everyone except Pony and Elbryan, the two of them somehow managing separately to elude the monsters, each not knowing that the other had survived.

And afterward Pony had wound up here, in Palmaris, bereft of memory and identity, adopted by Graevis and Pettibwa Chilichunk, patrons of the bustling tavern Fellowship Way.

Pony looked out across the quiet city now, in the direction where that establishment had stood. What wild turns fate had placed in her path: married to the favored nephew of the city's Baron Bildeborough; the wedding annulled forthwith and Pony indentured in the King's army; her ascension to the elite Coastpoint Guard and her appointment to Pireth Tulme; the coming of the powries and the fall of that fortress. It had all taken years, but to Pony now it seemed as if it had happened overnight. She could again feel the chill deep in her bones as she had escaped doomed Pireth Tulme, floating in the cold waters of the Gulf of Corona. Perhaps it was fate, perhaps mere chance, that had pulled her from those waters in the vicinity of Avelyn Desbris, the "mad friar" from St.-Mere-Abelle who was being hunted by the Church for the death of a master and the theft of many of the sacred magical gemstones. Avelyn had taken Pony back to Dundalis, and there she had been reunited with Elbryan, who had returned to the region after being trained as a ranger by the mysterious Touel'alfar.

What a dark road the three had walked from there: to Aida and the demon dactyl; back across the kingdom to St.-Mere-Abelle, where Pony's adoptive parents had been imprisoned and had died; and then back again—a road that should have lightened, despite the grief, but that had only darkened more as the evil that was Bestesbulzibar, the dactyl demon, infected Father Abbot Markwart with a singular desire to do battle with Elbryan and Pony.

And so he had, in that same mansion where Pony had spent her wedding night with Connor Bildeborough, the mansion of horrors where Elbryan and Pony had waged the final fight against Markwart, and had won, though at the price of Elbryan's life.

Now Pony wasn't sure what they had won and what it had been worth. She recognized the almost circular nature of her long journey; but instead of drawing comfort from that, she felt restless and trapped.

"It is far too cold for you to be up here, I fear," came a gentle voice behind her, the voice of Brother Braumin Herde, the leader of the band of monks who had followed Master Jojonah away from the Church, believing as they did in Avelyn's goodness, one of the monks who had come to join Elbryan and Pony in their efforts against Markwart.

She turned to regard the handsome man. He was older than Pony by several years—in his early thirties—with black, woolly hair just starting to gray and a dark complexion made even more so by the fact that no matter how often he shaved his face, it was always shadowed by black hair.

"It is too unimportant for me to care," she answered quietly. Pony looked back over the city as he walked up to lean on the wall beside her.

"Thinking of Elbryan?" he asked.

Pony smiled briefly, believing the answer to be obvious.

"Many are saddened," Brother Braumin began—the same hollow words Pony had been hearing from so many for the last three months. She appreciated their efforts—of course she did!—but, in truth, she wished they would all leave her to her thoughts in private.

"The passage of time will heal . . ." Brother Braumin started to say, but when Pony fixed him with a skeptical glance, he let his words die away.

"Your pain is to be expected," he tried again a moment later. "You must take solace and faith in God and in the good that came of your actions."

Now Pony glared sternly at him, and the gentle monk retreated a step.

"Good?" she asked.

Braumin held up his hands as if he did not understand.

"They are fighting again, aren't they?" Pony asked, looking back over the snowy city. "Or should I say that they are fighting *still*?"

"They?"

"The leaders of your Church," Pony clarified, "and King Danube and his advisers. Fighting again, fighting always. It changes not at all."

"If the Church is in turmoil, that is understandable, you must admit," Braumin returned firmly. "We have lost our Father Abbot."

"You lost him long before I killed him," Pony interjected.

"True enough," the monk admitted. "But still it came as a shock to so many who supported Dalebert Markwart to learn the truth: to learn that Bestesbulzibar—curse his name, the ultimate darkness—had so infiltrated our ranks as to pervert the Father Abbot himself."

"And now he is gone and you are better off," Pony remarked.

Brother Braumin didn't immediately respond, and Pony understood that she wasn't being fair to him. He was a friend, after all, who had done nothing but try to help her and Elbryan, and her sarcasm was certainly wounding him. She looked at him directly and started to say something but bit it back immediately. So be it, she decided, for she could not find generosity in her heart. Not yet.

"We are better off by far," Braumin decided, turning the sarcasm back. "And better off we would be by far if Jilseponie would reconsider the offer."

Pony was shaking her head before he completed the all-too-predictable request. Reconsider the offer. Always that. They wanted her to become the mother abbess of the Abellican Church, though nothing of the sort had ever been heard of in the long history of the patriarchal Order. Brother Francis, Markwart's staunchest follower, had suggested it, even while holding the dying Markwart in his arms, the demon burned from the Father Abbot's body by the faith and strength of Pony and Elbryan. Francis had seen the truth during that terrible battle, and the truth of his terrible master. Pony had killed the demon that Markwart had become, and now several very influential monks were hinting that they wanted Pony to replace him.

Some of them were, at least. Pony didn't delude herself into thinking that such a break with tradition as appointing a woman to head the Church—and a woman who had just killed the previous leader!—would be without its vehement opponents. The battles would be endless, and, to Pony's way of thinking, perfectly pointless.

If that wasn't complicated enough, another offer had come to her, one from King Danube himself, offering to name her Baroness of Palmaris, though she obviously had no qualifications for the position either, other than her newfound heroic reputation. Pony wasn't blind to the reality of it: in the aftermath of the war both Church and Crown were jockeying for power. Whichever side could claim Jilseponie, companion of Elbryan the Nightbird, as friend, could claim to have promoted her to a position of power, would gain much in the battle for the hearts and loyalty of the common folk of Palmaris and the surrounding region.

Pony began to laugh quietly as she looked away from Brother Braumin, out over the snow-blanketed city. She loved the snow, especially when it fell deep from blustery skies, draping walls of white over the sides of buildings. Far from a hardship such weather seemed to Pony. Rather, she considered it a reprieve, an excuse to sit quietly by a blazing fire, accountable to no one and without responsibility. Also, because of the unexpectedly early storm, King Danube had been forced to delay his return to Ursal. If the weather did not cooperate, the king might have to wait out the winter in Palmaris, which took some of the pressure off Pony to either accept or reject his offer of the barony.

Though the weather had cooperated, Pony felt little reprieve. Once she had called this city home. But now, with so much pain associated with the place—the ruins of Fellowship Way, the loss of her adoptive family and her beloved Elbryan—no longer could she see any goodness here or recall any warm memories.

"If he retains the barony, Duke Kalas will battle St. Precious in every policy," Brother Braumin remarked, drawing Pony from her thoughts. But only temporarily, for the mere mention of the forceful Duke, the temporary Baron of Palmaris, inevitably led her to consider the man's residence, the very house in which her marriage to Connor Bildeborough had swiftly descended into chaos, the house wherein Markwart had taken Elbryan from her forever.

"How will we win those battles without heroic Jilseponie leading us?" Braumin dared ask. He draped his arm about Pony's shoulders, and that brought, at last, a genuine smile to the woman's beautiful face. "Or perhaps Jilseponie could take the King's offer instead. . . ."

"Am I to be a figurehead, then?" she asked. "For you or for the Crown? A symbol that will allow Braumin and his friends to attain that which they desire?"

"Never that!" the monk replied, feigning horror; for it was obvious that he understood Pony was teasing him.

"I told Bradwarden and Roger Lockless that I would join them up in Dundalis," Pony remarked; and, indeed, as she said it, she was thinking that traveling back to her first home might not be such a bad thing. Elbryan was buried up there, where it was . . . cleaner. Yes, that was a good word to describe it, Pony decided. Cleaner. More removed from the dirt of humankind's endless bickering. Of course, she, too, was trapped here, and likely for the entire winter, for the road north was not an easy one this season.

She glanced over to see a disappointed Brother Braumin. She honestly liked the man and his eager cohorts, idealists all, who believed they would repair the Abellican Church, put it back on a righteous course by following the teachings of Avelyn. That last thought made Pony smile again: laughing inside but holding her mirth there because she did not want to seem to mock this man. Braumin and his friends hadn't even known Avelyn—not the real Avelyn, not the man known as the mad friar. Braumin had joined the Abellican Order the year before Avelyn, God's Year 815. Both Master Francis and Brother Marlboro Viscenti, Braumin's closest friend, had come in with Avelyn's class in the fall of God's Year 816. But Avelyn and three others had been separated from the rest of their class as they had begun their all-important preparations for the journey to the Isle of Pimaninicuit. The only recollection Braumin, Viscenti, or Francis even had of Avelyn was on the day when the four chosen monks had sailed out of All Saints Bay, bound for the island where they would collect the sacred gemstones. Braumin had never seen Avelyn after he had run off from St.-Mere-Abelle, after he had become the mad friar, with his barroom brawling and his too-frequent drinking—and wouldn't the canonization process of rowdy Avelyn Desbris be colorful indeed!

"Too cold up here," Brother Braumin said again, tightening his grip on Pony's shoulders, pulling her closer that she might share his warmth. "Pray come inside and sit by a fire. There is too much sickness spreading in the aftermath of war, and darker would the world be if Jilseponie took ill."

Pony didn't resist as he led her toward the tower door. Yes, she did like Brother Braumin and his cohorts, the group of monks who had risked everything to try to find the truth of the world after the turmoil stirred up by the defection of Avelyn Desbris and his theft of so many magical gemstones. It went deeper than liking, she recognized, watching the true concern on his gentle and youthful face, feeling the strong and eager spring in his energetic step. She envied him, because he was full of youth, much more so than she, though he was the older.

But Brother Braumin, Pony realized within her darkened perception, was possessed of something she could no longer claim.

Hope.